THE
WOUND
OF THE
WORLD

ALSO BY EDWARD W. ROBERTSON

THE CYCLE OF ARAWN

The White Tree
The Great Rift
The Black Star

THE CYCLE OF GALAND

The Red Sea
The Silver Thief
The Wound of the World

THE BREAKERS SERIES

Breakers
Melt Down
Knifepoint
Reapers
Cut Off
Captives
Relapse
Blackout

REBEL STARS

Rebel
Outlaw
Traitor
Ronin

THE
WOUND
OF THE
WORLD

THE CYCLE OF GALAND, BOOK 3

EDWARD W. ROBERTSON

Copyright © 2016 Edward W. Robertson

All rights reserved.

Cover illustration by Miguel Coimbra.
Additional work by Stephanie Mooney.
Maps by Jared Blando.

ISBN: 1539757420
ISBN-13: 978-1539757429

To Robert Howard.

Mallon and Gask.

The Collen Basin and other lands.

1

The half-ruined rear wall of the Reborn Shrine held itself up as best it could. A thousand Colleners kneeled in the hard sunlight, gazes turned down to the ground. Hundreds of Mallish soldiers lay prone on the flagstones, blood staining the geometry of the grout.

And Dante stood alone.

The Keeper had declared him a god. The avatar of Arawn, arrived, as prophesied, to fight back the Mallish and free the Collen Basin from centuries of torment. As the Colleners kneeled before him, he could feel the yearning roiling off them like stink off a dog. They needed him. Not just for his skill. But for what he represented: the hope that he might finally break their cycle of warfare, rebellion, and slavery.

Dante knew two things: first, that he was no avatar. And second, that the Keeper had played him like a reed flute. Jaw clenched so tight he thought his teeth would crease, he turned his gaze on the Keeper. She remained on her knees, but gazed back at him from beneath her white brows. Daring him to undo the moment she had created.

He wanted to throw it back in her face, spit on the Colleners' prophecy, and walk away. A few years ago, he would have done just that. But he had led the city of Narashtovik through war. He knew what a moment like this meant. The morale of a people galvanized to their cause was more valuable than the finest steel.

He closed his eyes. "People of Collen! For ages, your future hasn't been your own. Instead, it's been at the mercy of Mallish warmongers. Today, that changes forever."

He opened his eyes. The crowd had lifted their heads and their eyes shined like lanterns reflected in glass windows.

"They came to your land with soldiers. Priests. Demons. We've thrown them out, but they will come back, just as they always do—unless you unite today. Unless you dedicate your every act to keeping the enemy at bay. Will you do this? Will you fight back? Will you claim your land for good?"

"Are you really him?" Hesitantly, a young woman raised her hand. "Are you really…Arawn?"

The crowd seemed to hold its breath. Dante clenched his fists. "I am just as you see." He drew the nether to him in thin lines, letting it swirl around him like the black streaks of a norren inkpainter lost in manic creation. "And I've had enough."

The woman made a choking sound. Two others beside her burst into tears. Others thrust up their fists and shouted. At first, their words were a babble, but they soon resolved into a single repeated word.

"Dante! Dante! Dante!"

He raised his fist. Their chant doubled in volume. He meant to turn and go, but he stood transfixed, riding their emotion like a boat on the swells. What if Arawn *had* brought him here? Was it that crazy of an idea? The prophecy was an almost perfect match. He was from Mallon; the Reborn Shrine had been destroyed and (again, technically) rebuilt again, completing its cycle; he'd driven not just an army from Collen, but also destroyed an enormous demon. Yes, the prophecy also said that he'd arrive as an incarnation of Arawn, but what if that was figurative? Wasn't his power with the nether more godlike than mortal?

He scanned the crowd, testing out a smile. A man was holding up a young child. Dante's eyes locked on the boy's. He was blonder than Blays, with the pale and piercingly blue eyes common to Colleners. Unlike the rapt faces around him, who were awash with eager and unquestioning devotion, the boy regarded Dante with a calm stare, chin pushed up, mouth slightly puckered: the clear expression of doubt.

Dante laughed dryly. Physically, the boy looked nothing like him, but the emotion on the kid's face was exactly how Dante had so often felt when adults had tried to explain the world to him.

He was no god. He'd come from the same humble place the boy had. To try to convince himself otherwise was to walk down the same path Gladdic was on.

"I can help lift you toward your freedom," Dante said. "But only you can reach up and take it."

He turned his back on the crowd and walked from the square. People murmured questions to each other. Before their uncertainty could fall into fear, the Keeper spoke out, her croaking voice booming through the square.

Dante didn't bother to listen. He picked his way through the rubble of the shrine, joined by Blays, who was as dirty as Dante was bloody.

"Where are you off to, Captain God?" Blays stepped over a severed arm. "Got an afternoon miracle to attend?"

"I'm going to find Naran."

"When were you planning to tell me about the Keeper's plan to add you to the Celeset?"

Dante's face flushed with anger. "You think I knew about that?"

"She pulled that off on her own?"

"It was a stunt. She used me to fulfill the Colleners' prophecy. In the wake of this, she'll be able to bring the entire basin to her banner."

"That's a masterstroke of cunning. You'll have to remember that one for the next time *you're* trying to manipulate someone into war." Blays tilted back his head. "If you didn't know about this, then why did you look so happy about it?"

Dante strode through a thin puddle of blood. "Want to know the real reason I'm getting out of here? Because if I have to listen to one more of the Keeper's lies, I'll kill her myself."

He tracked down a servant from the Reborn Shrine and got directions to where Naran was being treated. Dante was too exhausted to run, so as he walked toward the blacksmith's where they had Naran, he got a good look at the state of the city.

Smoke rose on all sides. Some was from the city burning in the wake of the battle, but other plumes were from cook fires to feed prisoners and refugees starved during the Mallish occupation. The smell of herbed mutton and baking bread mingled with the stink of burning whitewash. The streets were strewn with garbage and debris, most of it so dusty and dingy that it must have been the product of the occupation rather than the day's battle.

All of the corpses, however, were from that morning. An equal mix of Colleners and Mallish. He looked down on the Mallish with the shallow pity of a commander regarding the enemy's dead grunts. He found that he felt little more than that for the dead Colleners. Because the Keeper had alienated him?

Or because he'd seen such scenes so often he was beginning to treat them as part of the landscape?

At the blacksmith's, a pair of Collenese soldiers stood out front, their spear-like wheels planted in the dirt beside them. Recognizing Dante and Blays, the troopers brought them inside. Naran lay on a straw pallet. He appeared to be asleep, but at the sound of footsteps, he popped open a bloodshot eye.

"You're looking pretty good," Dante said. "Considering that the last time I saw you, you were being buried under an avalanche of rubble."

Naran looked him up and down. "And you look as though you just finished butchering a herd of cows. They say you destroyed an Andrac as tall as a steeple."

"He had help," Blays said. "Anyway, don't tell me you've never had to destroy a steeple before. They're not as strong as they look. Mostly because they don't fight back."

"Where is Gladdic?"

Dante sighed. "Gladdic used an illusion to make his assistant look like himself. While we chased after the assistant, Gladdic slipped into the plains. He could have been disguised as anyone."

"He's escaped. Again." Embers of anger flared in Naran's eyes, but they soon faded. Worn out, he leaned back on his pallet. "Perhaps there is no avenging Captain Twill. Better to go on with our lives than to throw them away by running after a man who can't be killed."

"He *is* a man—and that means he's as mortal as the rest of us. Besides, at this point, it isn't just Twill that needs avenging. He slaughtered thousands of innocent Colleners. The only thing that's been saving him is the Andrac. Now that we know how to disperse them, Gladdic's walking out of here in a dead man's boots."

Naran reopened his eyes, turning them on Blays. "Do you agree with this assessment?"

"Oh sure," Blays said. "If there's one thing you can always count on Dante to get right, it's killing people."

Dante kneeled beside the pallet. "He'll have to head back to Bressel to report his failure here. We'll find him, Naran. And when we do, not only will I annihilate his body—but I'll erase the trace of his soul."

With his body on the brink of quitting on him, he spent the rest of the day asleep in the third floor of an empty manor. He didn't think Gladdic would send any assassins for him, demonic or otherwise, but he set undead rats to keep watch on the doors and windows. He dreamed of battling the great Andrac again. This time, as he tried to draw its nether to him, it only grew bigger, its mouth widening, the silver light inside it glaring so brightly it burned out his eyes.

He woke to darkness and singing. He walked out on the front porch. Blays was there already. The people were running through the streets waving burning bundles of wheat stalks which they appeared to be trying to flick against the buttocks of their friends.

Dante frowned. "Are they trying to set each other on fire? This *is* a celebration, right?"

"Looks more like a rebellion against the tyranny of pants." Blays passed him a cup of the local beer.

Dante took a hefty swallow. "Is there anything weirder than foreign traditions?"

"Yes, but I've just handed you a cup of the solution to any strangeness." Blays tipped back his own mug. "The Keeper wants to see us. Before we do that, I consider it my moral duty to make sure you don't want to kill her."

Mention of her name brought Dante's anger thudding into him like a punch. "I'll try to restrain myself. The faster we finish up here, the sooner we can get the hell away."

He expected the Keeper to be lording it up in the ruins of her shrine, but Blays led him to the carved arches of the immense underground well they'd used to swim in and out of the city. There, the shrine's surviving monks tended to the wounded and the sick, the latter of which were being carted in from every corner of the city. Their gaunt faces and sharp collarbones told the story of the treatment they'd received under Mallish captivity.

The Keeper met them, nodding stiffly, though that was more a function of her extreme old age than any disrespect. "You have rested. That is good. There is much work to be done."

Dante laughed humorlessly. "You have no idea. I've been away from my city for months. I'll stay long enough to help heal your people. After that, I'm going to find Gladdic, then return home."

"You intend to leave?"

"Unless you've managed to relocate Narashtovik onto the next butte, I have to leave."

"But you are the chosen one. Prophesied to free the Collen Basin from the shackles of our mutual enemy."

"Are you sure we read the same prophecy? You're supposed to be freed by Arawn. You've seen me bleed way too much to believe I'm a god."

"Are you sure you weren't sent by him?"

"Yes!" Dante threw up his hands. "I came here of my own accord. Do you know what noble intention brought me here? It certainly wasn't to liberate the poor people of the Collen Basin. It was to execute the son of a bitch who killed Mr. Naran's captain."

"Perhaps that was the step needed to lead you to your true cause. When the gods' minds turn, the world turns with them."

"I'm walking away, Keeper. If Arawn wants me to stay, he can ask me himself."

The old woman lifted her head. The rheuminess of her eyes made it hard to see what lurked behind them. "For a man of the gods, you don't have much faith. Yet you put much stock in politics and strife. In that case, don't stay because of a prophecy. Stay because if you go, Collen will fall."

Blays coughed. "Right now, I expect he'd count that as a positive."

"Is that so?"

"You lied to me," Dante said. "Used me as a prop. And now you expect to wear me like a puppet—and for me to smile while your hand's up my ass."

"So she's heard the rumors, then," Blays said.

The Keeper rasped with laughter. "How many times have you done the same? I have heard the stories of the Chainbreakers' War, Galand. You used everyone in reach in service of yourself."

"We fought that war to free the norren!"

"And it was sheer coincidence that Narashtovik was freed as well. I won't argue what we both know to be true. But I will tell you this: if you don't help us, Mallon will return. And for our defiance, we will be destroyed."

Dante lifted an eyebrow. "Is that a promise?"

"Perhaps I should put it in language you understand. Mallon has no love for Narashtovik. There are rumors they intend to repay Samarand's invasion in kind. But they won't dare to make such a move if there is a strong, independent Collen on their doorstop. Especially if our land is indebted to yours, and is happy to threaten their flank if they dispatch an army to the north."

"So your little scheme helps us both. How considerate of you."

"The best plans turn those who are indifferent into happy allies."

"If this was all so reasonable, why didn't you ask me first?"

"I need my people to believe that this time, things will be different. That we will finally be free. If I had asked your permission to invoke the prophecy, and you had denied me, their resolve would have faltered as soon as the Mallish returned." She met his glare without flinching. "I took the route that would make sure to forge them into steel strong enough to turn aside the coming blow. Would you have done any different?"

Dante rubbed his eyes, wishing he'd had a second beer before agreeing to see the Keeper. "I need to speak with Blays."

Without waiting for her permission, he stalked away from the well. Stars twinkled overhead, dazzlingly clear in the cool desert night. Blays strolled along beside him, giving a smile and a nod to everyone he passed.

Dante stopped in the shadow of one of the rune-carved stone posts. The smell of fresh water wafted from the well. "What do you think?"

"I think if you're bothering to ask my opinion, then you've already decided to change your mind about going home."

"What she's saying makes sense. Especially the idea of establishing Collen as a buffer between us and Mallon."

"Yet you don't want to accept it. Because you're so mad at her that you're tempted to set fire to Collen yourself."

"Not only that, but even if I were convinced it was in our interests to help, we've already been here for weeks. It feels like every time we're ready to leave, some new emergency draws us back in. Where does it end?"

Blays shrugged. "When you're out playing a game of thunders, when does *that* end?"

"When you run out of coins. Or everyone else does."

"Pretend for a moment you're not an utter degenerate, and in a much further leap of imagination, that you have a wife. When you're out gambling, how do you avoid running into trouble with her?"

"By setting a limit on how much I can afford to lose," Dante said. "Or on what time I need to be home by."

"So here you are, playing thunders with Collen and Mallon. Back home, your wife—that would be Narashtovik—is starting to get worried. Soon, her worry will become annoyance. How long can you afford to stay out before she uses the window to introduce your belongings to the street?"

"It's just like gambling, isn't it? You lose ten chucks, and in trying to get them back, you chase them with ten more. When those run dry, you throw out ten more. Soon enough, you've lost everything. Unless you set a limit."

Even after reaching this conclusion, his spite was such that he was still tempted to walk away into the darkness, never to set foot in the Collen Basin again. He might have done so if not for the hundreds of sick and injured people crowding around the well. Had the Keeper chosen to meet in this location because she was tending to the casualties?

Or because she knew that, seeing the citizens like this, Dante couldn't help but imagine how much worse it would be if Mallon struck back?

He'd built Narashtovik to be strong. It could last a little longer in his absence. He walked back to the Keeper, hand resting on the hilt of his sword.

"You have decided," she said.

"It's autumn already," he said. "Mallon won't have time to mount more than one attack before winter ends the campaign season. We'll help until the first lasting snow. After that, Collen's on its own."

2

After the Keeper's manipulation, agreeing to continue aiding her tasted as bitter as a fresh-plucked Gallador tea leaf. But the dose of comfort that came with making a decision was even more bracing than the effects of the lakeland's leaves. Consolidating the Collen Basin's resistance against Mallon wasn't only strategically wise, it was morally sound. If Dante could set aside his anger, in a few years, he would look back on this decision with pride.

"I am grateful for your assistance," the Keeper said. "Yet by the time the lasting snows come to Collen, the Dundens will be locked beneath a blizzard. You won't be able to cross into Gask until spring. It would be safer to remain here."

Dante rolled his eyes. "Don't even try it."

"I'm not suggesting you spend the extra time waging war on the Mallish. As you said, after the snows, the campaigning season will be over."

"We've crossed through the Woduns," Blays said. "Compared to that, getting over the Dundens is about as hard as hopping over a turd in the street."

"It was no more than a thought." The Keeper bowed at the waist, pointing the crown of her gray head at Dante. "If we succeed in prying the basin from Mallon's claws, these people will never forget you."

He scowled. She was getting too good at reading him. "We

just handed the Mallish their own asses. Along with a fork and a knife and a tin of pepper. Why are you so sure they'll send a second attack?"

"They can't allow us to defy them. It would signal weakness to their other holdings. Worse, it would embolden their enemies. But mostly, they will return because we are Arawn-worshippers. Our victory defiles the body of their empire. When a wound festers, if you fail to treat it, it will claim the rest of the body as well."

"They might not be able to hit back right away. Especially if I can kill Gladdic, they might have to wait until spring to organize their forces."

"Then that gives my people six months to prepare."

"Is it too late to make demands for our help?" Blays said. "I'm going to require a steady supply of meat pies. And something to wash them down with. In fact, make that three somethings."

Dante turned to take in the darkened city. "That's a good place to get started. To win a war, you have to secure three resources. Your land. Your resources. And your allies. We need scouts in the field and troops ready to respond."

The Keeper lowered herself to a bench, massaging her knees. "Field command is the duty of the despot. And Despot Jodd is dead."

"Then we need a replacement. Cord would make a good choice. We've already proven we can work with her."

"Despots aren't crowned like Mallish kings. They are elected by the people."

"Then fake the election, if it will make you feel better. But remember that you declared me to be a god. As Arawn's avatar, I declare that Cord will be my sword."

The Keeper examined him for signs of mockery, then made a tight line of her mouth. "So be it."

She went to speak to a messenger, who hastened off through the night. Dante's stomach rumbled. To distract himself, and improve his rapidly deteriorating mood, he joined the monks in tending to the casualties, sending the nether to mend the wounds of the suffering. He'd set five people to resting easily by the time the messenger returned with Cord.

Her blond braid was a mess, her eyelids were as puffy as kneaded dough, and she was covered in any number of scratches and bandages. Even so, she walked up to them with the same tireless energy she'd displayed ever since Blays had dueled her on their arrival at Collen.

When Dante explained they were staying to help stabilize the basin, she laughed and clapped her rough hands together.

He couldn't help smiling back at her. "But we aren't here to rule you. Collen needs its own leaders. We'd like you to become the new despot."

Cord crinkled her forehead. "The despot? I can't do that!"

"We won't be here for more than a few months. Someone has to be ready to take the reins. You're one of the best soldiers in Collen. The others will respect you. I know you're up to the challenge."

"The Keeper agrees with this?"

The old woman nodded. "I do."

"Then I will lead the other soldiers. But I can't be despot. I can't run a kingdom any more than I can drink the well dry. To pretend otherwise is to disgrace myself! To let down my people!"

"Then you'll join the proud tradition of every other leader since time began," Blays said. "Present company excluded, of course."

"It doesn't have to be permanent," Dante said. "Right now, the martial side is all that matters. You won't have to bother with policy. Once the war is over, you can step down and be proud of what you've done."

Cord brayed with laughter. "I think you mistake yourself for me. If you need me, I'll command our army. But I won't command our republic."

Blays swigged another beer. Dante hadn't even seen him get it. He was starting to suspect Blays' true talents lay in the hidden art of brewermancy.

"Who cares about tradition?" Blays said. "Just invoke the god clause again. Cord can command the military while someone else handles politics. I nominate the Keeper."

"That can't be." Seated on the bench, the Keeper tugged her robe over her bony shins. "I've spent decades in the shrine. I don't know the ways of our politics. Besides, there are things I must be able to do as the Keeper that I could not do as our leader."

"You know who knows even less about Collenese politics? Me and Dante. The ex-Mallishmen who've spent the last half of our lives freezing to death in Gask. So how about you tell *us* who's a good choice for administrator?"

Cord nodded once. "Ked came with me. He will know. I will get him." She cupped her hands to her mouth. "Ked! *Ked!*"

The man detached from a knot of soldiers and jogged over to them. Dante had first met Ked while saving the man's life from a mortal wound at the hand of Mallish soldiers. This had turned out to be such a horrific insult that Ked had challenged him to a duel on the spot. Still, the man greeted them with a smile, apparently having put all enmity behind him.

"Ked!" Cord motioned to the dark city. "Great things are afoot. These people have named me commander of the military."

Ked's eyebrows swung up his forehead. He took a knee. "Congratulations, Despot."

"Don't be a fool! If I were named despot, my first act would be to imprison those who thought I would be any good at it, as they are clearly a menace to right-thinking people everywhere."

"We need an administrator," the Keeper said. "Someone competent and respected enough to maintain control during the coming troubles."

Ked folded his arms, nodding vaguely. "I would have suggested Yorra, but they executed her. What about Twane?"

Cord shook her head. "Fell in battle. But his son would do just as well, yes?"

"Well, yes, except that they dragged him off to Bressel to be tried for heresy."

They ran through several other names, all of which had either died or gone missing. Cord set her fists on her hips. "Gregg. I saw him just today."

"That's not such a good idea. When the Mallish were here, he showed them to our weapons caches."

"He aided the invaders? But why?"

"There's only two reasons to do a thing like that," Dante said.

"The Mallish offered to make him rich, or make his people dead."

Ked bobbed his head. "Either way, he's out. The people won't trust him."

They lapsed into a second silence. Blays made a thoughtful noise. "What about Boggs?"

"Boggs Twill?" Dante said. "Captain Twill's brother? He didn't exactly strike me as a born politician."

"Which is probably why the Colleners would go for him. Think about it. No one would ever question his loyalty. Not after what the Mallish did to Twill."

"Brother of a fallen hero. From a successful merchant family. Hard to imagine someone who could instantly command that much respect."

"And he already has a relationship with the Parthians, doesn't he? That ought to make it a little easier to get them aboard the victory wagon."

"This is a very cunning piece of politics," Dante said. "Are you sure *you* thought of it?"

"I haven't even finished. He's also got Twill's plans to extend the irrigation canals across the basin and into Parth. If he does that, trade will explode."

"Say no more. I'm ready to declare the Collenese golden age."

"And all we have to do first is thwart the giant empire that's controlled this place since the days when the gods were still learning to wipe themselves."

After getting the enthusiastic agreement of Cord, Ked, and the Keeper, they dispatched a messenger to the Twill residence outside of Dog's Paw. Knowing it would be four days until Boggs or his refusal returned to the city, Dante sat down with Cord and Blays to hash out the initial military strategy.

The first order of business was to establish a scout network along the border, along with sweeps of the interior to ensure that no Mallish forces were hiding out in the vast, empty spaces between the settlements. Lookouts would be established along the king's road from Mallon and across the hills fronting the western border, with instructions to light a signal fire at the first sign of invasion.

Next came the summoning of recruits from the basin's six major towns. Bound by their Code of the Wasp to support each other in times of war, their troops would provide a critical supplement to the city's battered army.

The defense strategy itself was rather straightforward: hole up in Collen. There was only a single road up to the top of the plateau, making it eminently defensible. Starting tomorrow, Dante would open most of a tunnel down to the plains. If the city was in danger of being overrun, he could complete the tunnel with a few minutes' work, providing the Colleners with an escape route.

Unless Mallon's next force was small enough to meet in the open field, they would have to abandon the outlying towns. The Small Senates weren't going to be happy about that. The best Dante could do was suggest they make plans to withdraw their families, livestock, and valuables to the foothills of the eastern mountains, or into the deserts of Parth, with a free-roaming regiment comprised of recruits from the six towns assigned to kill any Mallish scouts who came too close.

A couple of hours before dawn, Dante found himself falling asleep at the table. He excused himself to go to bed. Blays did the same, walking with him toward the manor that was becoming their makeshift command station.

"Still think this is a good idea?" Blays said.

"I think I'd like to be sitting on the roof of the Citadel watching the bay in the company of a large beverage."

"There's nothing keeping us here, you know. This isn't our land. These aren't our people. If you wanted, you could kill a few crows, reanimate them, tie their feet to a harness, and fly us back to Narashtovik."

"You want to walk away? Careful, you're starting to sound like the old you."

Blays shrugged. "Never hurts to remind yourself about your options."

Dante detoured around an overturned wagon. "I think we can do this. But if things turn south, we need a plan to get out of here."

"I'll get some packs of provisions. And map out a route. One that doesn't involve the road into Mallon."

Dante slept heavily, waking to a lake of aches and pains that had swamped his body overnight. He was tempted to sweep them away with a brush of nether, but he didn't like the idea of pretending he wasn't susceptible to pain and exhaustion. That felt like a good way to breed delusions in himself. When an entire city was singing his praises to the sky, the last thing he needed was more grist for his ego.

The Keeper called on him while he was in the middle of a breakfast of toast and honey. "The Mallish emptied the granaries." Her face was stony, her voice harder yet. "There isn't enough left to feed the city for more than a few days."

Dante swore. "What can we expect from the six towns? The farmlands?"

"Most of the crops were burned or pillaged. Gladdic didn't come to occupy. He came to exterminate."

"Send riders out anyway. Bring back anything the towns can spare. In the meantime, get somebody to show me to one of the fields. Potatoes would be best."

She gave him a curious look, then left the manor. Feeling a slight twinge of guilt, Dante wolfed down the rest of his food. The Keeper returned with a dusty youngster dressed in the plain, baggy clothing of Collenese farmers. Under other circumstances, the farmer likely would have appeared of man's age, but as he stared wordlessly at Dante, blinking repeatedly, he came off as about twelve years old.

Dante scowled, catching on: the man believed he was looking at a divine being. "Remember your business."

The young man nodded once, by instinct, then again, understanding. He led Dante to the plaza at the top of the road up the side of the butte. The day before, it had been the site of a pitched battle of ethermancers, infantry, and demons. Today, the bodies and much of the debris had been hauled off, but blood stained the paving setts, the color turning rusty as it aged.

They headed down the switchbacks. Life had returned to the town at the bottom of the plateau. Soldiers sat beneath awnings sharpening their blades, casting occasional glances at the lookouts posted on the road up the side of the butte.

The farmer took a dirt trail out of town, then stopped, looking mortified. "We don't got horses. Should I get some? Lord?"

"By the time you find them, and bring them back here, and we ride out, will we have gotten there sooner than if we'd simply walked?"

Panic flashed in the boy's eyes. "It's less than a mile. But I thought—"

"That I'm too delicate to use my own legs?"

The boy nodded hard and took up a brisk walk. Dante glared at the back of his head. Counterintuitively, it was much harder to get simple things done when the people serving you were terrified of being smote.

It was a beautiful morning, though, making it difficult to stay mad: some warmth in the air, though not unpleasantly so, with the sunlight so plentiful and yellow it felt like you could scoop it up with a knife and spread it on toast. Birds twittered from the sagebrush.

Ten minutes later, the boy brought him to a field next to a small branch of the canal system. The gray soil was so churned up it looked ready to sow, but dying plants lay everywhere, most yanked up by the roots, others trampled. Seeing them, the boy's eyes curdled with a hollow sickness.

"Here they are." His voice wasn't much more than a whisper. "Or what's left of them."

Dante closed his eyes and reached into the soil. Most of the potatoes had been dug up and stolen by the Mallish pillagers, but others remained, along with the broken tendrils of their roots. He got out his favorite knife, the handle made of antler carved by a norren of unsurpassed skill, and cut the back of his left arm.

Nether shot from beneath the flattened leaves. Black motes swirled around his blood with unusual agitation. Stirred up by all the deaths the day before? Or had the presence of the Andrac given them a kick?

He plunged the shadows into the disturbed earth. The technique was still new to him, but it took little effort to convince the nether to soak into the remaining tubers and roots. Unseen, they sprouted and expanded. Within moments, small green shoots broke the surface.

"Ahh!" The boy stumbled back, tripping over his own heels to land in a plume of dust. He swiveled his head between the plants and Dante. "It's you that did that?"

"We have a problem: your people are about to starve. It's a little selfish of them, wanting to eat food and everything, but I thought I would solve their problem by making some."

He drew more and more shadows to him, channeling them into the ground and harvesting the field into an abundance of potatoes. By the time his strength flagged, the ground was carpeted with low green leaves, foretelling enough plants to feed thousands.

Dante closed the flow of nether. "Get some workers out here. Tell them to leave one-tenth of the plants unharvested—and to be ready to pick new ones every morning."

The next day, in addition to potatoes, he grew a patch of wheat, which was the Colleners' main staple. This grew tall and green, stalks wavering in the unsteady wind.

"This is quite a trick, making them bigger like that," Blays said from beside him. "If you could do the same for the male anatomy, you'd be the richest man in the world."

Dante frowned. *Could* the technique be used on animals as well as plants? The Kandeans hadn't seemed to know how to apply it to beasts or people, but the fact a Harvester could grow a seed into a sapling and a sapling into a tree raised the question of whether you could do something similar with flesh. Sometime, he would have to try.

Dante let go of the nether. "The city lost nearly all of its stores and most of its crops. If I do this every day, and the towns have some to spare, that gets us closer. But to get through the winter, we'll rely on hunters bringing in deer, fishermen working the canals and the river, and foragers scooping up anything else that can be chewed by human teeth."

"None of these activities being things we can do in the middle of a Mallish siege."

"Not unless we start building mile-long fishing poles."

"So what's the solution? Start eating each other? May I nominate we start with the old and the weak?"

"We'll have to hope we can buy grain from Parth. Or fish from the Strip."

"The Strip?"

"The coast south of Averoy. Several small cities, all of them independent. They'll sell to us." He grimaced up at the butte. "Although we might have to ask for a loan. The granaries weren't the only thing the Mallish looted."

He trudged uphill. As he entered the plaza at the top of the road, a girl of about fifteen years ran up to him, tugging a younger boy along behind her. He was smiling, but the girl looked like she was staring down from the edge of a cliff she knew she had to jump.

"Mr. Galand. Your lordship." She made a curtsey.

Deciding it would be rude to walk around her, he came to a stop. "Can I help you?"

"Well, that's the thing. My brother Earl, he's slow. In the head. I was hoping that maybe you could fix him."

"He was hurt during the fighting?"

"No, sir. Born like this." She dropped Earl's hand, cheeks reddening. "My parents used to take care of him. But we lost them. I can't do my work and look after him."

Dante grunted. "Why would you think I can change him?"

"I heard about the miracle, sir."

"The miracle."

"You regrew the crops the soldiers destroyed. I thought if you could do that, you could help my brother, too."

His heart sagged in his chest. He wished he'd followed his instinct to walk past her. "If he was born like this, there's probably nothing I can do. But I'll try."

She smiled, a fragile thing, and stepped to the side. Earl was still grinning, meeting Dante's eyes before dropping his gaze to Dante's shoulder. Dante moved his mind into the shadows, following them to the matter within the boy's skull. He'd examined plenty of brains, attached to both the living and the dead, and though he believed they were the seat of consciousness—perhaps where the trace resided, or the ether that comprised the soul—he had learned no more about them than any other organ.

If it were diseased or hurt, he could mend its damage, grow

new blood vessels throughout it, drive away the sickness. But as he moved through Earl's tissue, he saw nothing out of place. At first, he was disappointed, but he quickly grew irritated at his lack of ability to solve the puzzle, pulling himself closer and closer to the nether until each fold of brain filled his vision.

He finished his search. He tried again, forcing himself to go slow. At the end, he withdrew, head aching.

"I'm sorry," he said. "I don't see anything wrong."

The girl lowered her face, voice as soft as washed linens. "Thank you for trying."

She took Earl's hand and walked away. Blays swore under his breath, then called after the girl. "What's your name?"

She glanced over her shoulder. "Nika."

"Well, Nika, the first thing to learn about gods like my friend here is they don't often listen to you. Even when they do, they usually can't *do* anything for you."

Her eyes darted to Dante. "I…"

"Fortunately," Blays continued, "not every problem requires a miracle to solve it. Is your brother otherwise intact? Capable of physical labor?"

"And strong, too. He never gets tired."

"Good news. Because those idiots from Mallon seem to think that buildings are for smashing down rather than for living in. There's rubble everywhere. And all of it needs to be picked up from where it is and set down somewhere else."

He led the siblings away. Dante went to meet with Cord and the Keeper to discuss the food situation. As they went over options for rations, including dire scenarios where there was only enough for soldiers and their vital support, he pictured Earl smiling at the sky as he was marched off into the wastelands. If a siege came, would they have the heart—or lack of it—to do what was necessary to survive?

Four days after the messenger had left Collen, he returned with Boggs Twill. Boggs had the face of a man who spent most of his time outdoors in the low desert. That day, he looked even ruddier than usual. Dante hoped their news of his sister's death hadn't sent him on a drinking binge.

Dante and the Keeper laid out the situation. Boggs listened, face craggily unreadable.

"Administrator of the Collen Basin." He made a noise that might have been a laugh. "Not very fair, is it? I did nothin' to earn this."

"Then you'll fit right in with the Mallish nobility," Blays said.

"There's got to be somebody with more experience."

"You have more than you think," Dante said. "You've run your family's trade for years. Seeing to the basin won't be so much different."

Boggs rubbed his stubbled neck, then shook his head. "Maybe so and maybe not. Either way, I ain't earned this. Someone else deserves it more."

"In a just world, power is handed to those who've earned it, and only when they're ready to wield it. Do you think this is a just world?"

"If it was, would my sister be dead?"

Dante met his stare. "Nothing prepares you for leadership of a people. *None* of us are ready. All you can do is trust yourself to learn your role as you go. To accept that you might not be the perfect choice, but you are the best choice."

"Right," Blays said. "And to understand that if you can't take on the responsibility, someone worse will."

"How about Gladdic? He dead yet?"

Dante grimaced. "He fled the city. But that's because he knew we'd learned how to kill him. As soon as Collen is secured, we're going after him."

"In other words," Blays said, "the sooner you help us get this place sorted out, the sooner we'll be able to present you Gladdic's head as a drinking goblet."

Boggs swore. "You two should have been barristers. Hand over the damn crown and tell me what you need me to do."

Their first move was to dispatch official letters to Parth and the towns of the Strip of Alebolgia. It was likely the other realms had already heard of the Mallish occupation, or would soon, so Collen's newly-forged council of five decided to make mention of that in their request for trade. Revealing that information might weaken their bargaining position, but if it looked like they were trying to hide the fact they were in conflict with Mallon, it might scare off their potential partners altogether.

Once the letters were drafted, Dante leaned back in his chair. "How much can we reasonably expect them to sell us?"

"Parth's always got more wheat and mutton than they need," Boggs said. "And the Strip's got as much fish as you can stomach. Between them, they could have us covered."

"But how much can we afford?"

"Not enough. Until recent events, Mallon's given us more freedom than normal, but they ain't stupid. They've been taxing us into the ground to make sure we can't take advantage of that freedom. What little coin we had left went into keeping our soldiers trained."

A glum silence fell over the table. The Keeper shifted her robes. "What if Narashtovik were to loan us the funds?"

Dante bristled. Funding his lands was his most hated duty. He'd always been able to save more than Narashtovik spent, but the surplus could be wiped out by a single famine or conflict. No matter how reasonable the expense, whenever an advisor or Council member brought him a bill, all he could think about was how much further it put them from financial freedom.

"Not possible," he said. "The Council's already unhappy with how long I've been away. If I tried to convince them to invest in a foreign war, their first order of business would be to build a new tower, and then lock me up in it."

She nodded, but she didn't look convinced. "Then we will have to hope our neighbors are both reasonable and merciful."

When they finished, Dante returned to his private chambers and got out his loon. He'd let Olivander know about the outcome of the battle, but the last time they'd spoken, Dante had been operating under the assumption that he and Blays would be leaving Collen within days.

He clipped the bone earring to his ear and pulsed the connection.

"Dante?" Olivander's baritone voice was halfway out of breath. Around him, hoofbeats thundered. "Is this vital?"

"Decide for yourself. We think Mallon's going to make another attack on Collen. We're going to stay here and stop it."

Olivander sighed heavily. He called out to his men, excusing himself; the hoofbeats diminished. "Can I ask why?"

"Because we don't want to see everyone in the basin put to the sword?"

"The world's a big place. At some point, someone or another is always being put to the sword. What business is it of ours if it's Collen's turn?"

"Collen's on the brink of independence. If they fall, Mallon's going to set their sights on us, both as punishment for intervening, and to get us back for the war that Samarand made on them years ago. You might remember that one, since you were on her Council. But if Collen breaks loose, Mallon won't dare come for us with Collen right there on their flank."

"So you want to battle them in Collen so we don't have to battle them in Narashtovik. That's an interesting idea. But it's built on the assumption that we have to fight them at all."

"This is the end of it," Dante said. "Once the snows come, we're heading home."

Olivander sighed. "I wish I could believe you. But every time you make a promise to return, the next time I hear from you, someone else needs saving."

"What are you, my wife? I give you my word. We'll be back in Narashtovik before the new year."

The next few days were spent rebuilding. In the mornings, Dante used most of his power to grow crops, which were quickly harvested and brought up to the city. Whatever nether he had left, he used to raise ramparts or dig ditches for the defenses Cord was building around the town at the base of the butte.

One morning on his way out to the fields, a messenger ran him down. The Keeper had news. Dante climbed back up the road and found her waiting beneath an awning in the plaza.

"There is trouble at Kaline," she said. "Senator Alder refuses to commit his town to the war."

"So what? Why don't the other senators overrule him?"

"Some won't commit until he does. He owns much of the land around the nearby canals. The senators fear that if they oppose him, he'll raise their rents to intolerable levels."

"Get me a guide and a horse," Dante said. "I'll sort him out."

Within an hour, he and Blays were riding out from Collen in the company of a young woman named Salya, a warrior recommended by Cord. Salya said nothing that wasn't directly related to the way forward. They rode north, trailing dust behind them, the air thick with the scent of sage. Low hills and small buttes interrupted the dry plains.

It took a day and a half to reach Kaline. Along the way, Dante grew a crop of grapes from a wild vine he found, which Salya marked on a map she kept. Kaline was arranged much like Collen, though scaled down in every way: a pint-sized plateau with a village at its base and a town at its top. When they ascended, a canal sparkled in the sunlight. Green fields lined both banks. Presumably, these belonged to Senator Alder.

Most of the buildings on the butte were simple wattle and daub structures with thatched roofs and hides stretched over the doors—wood was always at a premium in the basin—but a few were elegant things of fired clay bricks. Salya took them to one of the largest of these. Inside, she waited in the foyer while Dante and Blays were brought upstairs to a room with a large window overlooking the desert below.

Half an hour later, an older man entered through a side door, giving a glimpse of a cluttered study. The man's silver hair was slicked back from his forehead, a salt and pepper goatee bracketing his mouth. A paunch was visible beneath a blue silk shirt. Silver rings clicked on his knuckles.

"You must be Galand." He gave Dante a faint nod, then turned his attention to Blays. "And he is?"

"My advisor," Dante said. "We've worked together for a decade."

"He will remain outside."

Dante raised an eyebrow, but Blays only shrugged. "You will regret this once you've seen what I've done to your kitchen."

He left, closing the door behind him. Senator Alder strolled toward the window and gazed out at his holdings. "Is your arrival supposed to frighten me?"

"That depends," Dante said. "Have you done something to fear for?"

"*That* depends. Should a man be afraid to stand up for the

well-being of his home?"

"The Code of the Wasp insists you join the fight. I'll assume you heard what the Mallish did to Collen?"

Alder didn't turn from the window. "It sounded like the typical treatment of occupied lands by a hostile army."

"Typical? I've been through several wars. I've never seen someone try to eradicate the population by feeding them to demons."

"Demons. Swords. Starvation. When the outcome's the same, what does the method matter?"

"Why won't you commit to supporting Collen?"

Alder met his eyes, arching a brow. "That's just it, isn't it? Whenever troubles come to the basin, it's Collen that needs aid. So we send soldiers. Food. Coin. It's as much of a tax on the six towns as all the levies of the Mallish."

"If Collen needs aid, I imagine it's because they've taken the brunt of the damage. Would you rather Mallon besieged Kaline?"

"Yet they never do. Always, they strike the city of Collen. Why? I could only speculate. All I know to be true is that the towns give and Collen takes."

Dante's left cheek twitched. "What do you want?"

"You're here because you believe the Mallish will return. When they do, I want Kaline protected."

"You just said that they only go after Collen."

"There are times when they assault a second target as well. Besides, after their loss, they might rethink their strategy."

"Mallon won't deplete their forces on the towns. They'll come straight for Collen. Once it falls, they'll regroup and pick you off one by one."

Alder laughed airily. "If you can scry on King Charles' mind, then we have nothing to fear!"

"The basin's army will be deployed wherever we can stop the enemy. If that means making a stand at Kaline, then we'll make a stand at Kaline."

"And if it means protecting Collen, you'll be happy to sacrifice us. I want a garrison. Two thousand men."

"That's far more than you'll contribute. If every town made

that demand—"

"Then you could deny us. But they didn't think of it. I did. Thus, I get the rewards." He turned back to the window. "Speaking of such, I hear rumors that the canals are to be expanded. Not for crops, but for commerce. I will require a share. Ten percent seems reasonable."

"We're discussing the ruin of the Collen Basin, senator. This isn't the time for negotiation."

"On the contrary, this is the only time Collen is vulnerable to the needs of Kaline. That means now is the only time you'll listen."

"Here is my counter offer," Dante said. "Assist the war effort like the Code of the Wasp insists, and before I leave Collen, I'll spend five days making improvements to Kaline. New canals. Fortifications. Whatever you want."

"Or?"

"Learn the price of betrayal."

The senator examined him for a long moment, then broke into a smile. "No. With ten percent of the new trade revenues, I can buy all the canals and fortifications I please."

"Canny," Dante said. "All right, you have a deal. I presume you'll want a contract guaranteeing your share?"

"Oh, indeed. My study is this way." He opened the door he'd come in through. The room beyond held a desk the size of a door. It supported a number of quills, parchment pages, trimming knives, and documents. "You'll be involved in the expansion of the canals, yes? May I ask what Narashtovik's cut will be?"

"One senator." Dante plunged a knife of nether into the man's heart.

3

As soon as Raxa freed her kids from the Citadel's dungeons, she headed for Herrick's. The walk through the city felt like it took half a day. Every time she passed a guardsman dressed in black and silver, she expected the cry to go out. She drew a few looks, but none more suspicious than would be extended to the average young woman leading a school of six children behind her.

Herrick's yard was quiet. So was his house. Raxa's heart went cold. When Gaits had kidnapped the kids, it would have made sense to kill the parents. None of them were anyone special. None would be missed. Leaving them alive would only make it easier to tie him to the crime.

She told the kids to wait outside, then searched the house. Herrick was tied up under the bed. Blindfolded. Gagged. Was a wonder he hadn't suffocated.

"I'm sorry," he said once she'd cut him loose. Tears brightened his eyes. "I was working in the yard. Splitting wood. Didn't even hear them come up on me. Next thing I knew, I was under the bed and Fedd was screamin' with all his lungs."

"This wasn't your fault." She jerked her head toward the front room. "Fedd's outside. Along with five others like him. I'd keep them at my house, but it's going to be too dangerous."

"I'll take them. 'Cept I don't know how it'll be any safer here."

"It won't be. You're going to take them into the woods. The

only people who'll know where you are will be me and my runner."

Not that she had any idea who that runner would be. After what Gaits had done, she didn't know *who* she could trust. Not with something this important. No matter. If she had to, she'd do it herself.

"Tell me where," Herrick said. "I won't let you down."

The eight of them struck out for the woods. The pine forests were lousy with abandoned cabins and shacks. Most were too ruined to serve as a shelter, and some were occupied by vagabonds, but Herrick spent plenty of time coming out to hunt or cut wood. He led them to a house big enough to fit them all.

"You follow Herrick's orders," Raxa told the children. "I'll let your parents know you're okay. And I'll be back as soon as it's safe."

That much was a lie. She'd be back soon enough. But she wasn't sure that it would ever be safe again.

Once she was back in the city, she called Anya into her office. And explained how Gaits had sold them out.

"He betrayed the entire Order." The wonder and loathing in Anya's voice was the most emotion Raxa had ever heard from her. "I hope you made his death a slow one."

"Faster than he deserved," Raxa said. "But I had to make sure his schemes couldn't do us any more damage."

"What are we going to do about this?"

"Call another meeting with the Little Knives. Gaits might be dead, but that doesn't mean the Citadel's done with us."

She sent a messenger to Vess. The letter was enough of a tease that Vess demanded to talk that same night. As before, they met in the garden courtyard of the temple of Urt. This time, rather than Gaits, Raxa took Gurles with her.

Vess eyed the heavyset bouncer. "Where's your other man? The smirky one?"

"Gaits is dead," Raxa said. "He was working with the Black Star."

"Traitor under your own roof. Nothing hurts worse. You kill him yourself?"

Raxa nodded. "And tracked down the Black Star. A woman named Cee. She works for the Sealed Citadel."

"All the sons of all the bitches. The *Citadel*?"

Raxa explained. As with Anya, she left out all the parts involving her own abilities in the shadows, sticking to Gaits and his betrayal.

"We'll have to work together," Raxa concluded. "Neither of us can fight the Citadel alone."

Vess rocked with laughter. "Whole gods damned Gaskan Empire couldn't fight the Citadel. We can't declare war on them."

"Why not?"

"Same reason the fleas don't declare war on the dog."

"We bite much harder than fleas," Raxa said. "If we do this right, they'll never know it's us."

Vess tipped back her head and stared at the branches hanging above them in the courtyard. Fall was coming and the first of the leaves had started to turn.

"No," she decided. "Ain't doing. Fighting soldiers is one thing. But the Citadel, they got sorcerers. Long as they got the monopoly on magic, they got the monopoly on victory, too."

"I suppose you're right. Then we'll have to back off...after one last heist."

The woman frowned. "Of what?"

"You've heard of the *Cycle of Arawn*?"

"I heard of rain, too. Ignorant me even heard of dirt and fish and wind."

"There's a copy in every temple in the city," Raxa said. "But rumor has it that when Galand came to Narashtovik, he brought the *original* copy with him."

"Think it'll fetch a pretty good price, huh?"

"Think bigger. Rumor has it that, when someone with the talent reads the original copy, it unlocks the nether within you."

Vess thrust out her jaw and beetled her brow. "You believe it?"

"I don't believe it," Raxa said. "I know it."

"You want to put an end to their monopoly. This is how you mean to take revenge, ain't it? And you don't care if it takes ten years."

"As long as they can wield the nether and we can't, we'll always be vulnerable to them." Raxa stared into Vess' eyes. "This is about more than revenge—it's about survival."

The stout woman thought a moment, then chuckled slowly. "I would ask what they'd do to us when they learned we was playing with shadows. But they already tried to kill us all, eh? What we got to lose? Let's steal ourselves a book."

He left Collen behind him like the hive that it was.

For hours, he was incapable of sustaining a thought for more than a few seconds at a time. Walking in the guise of a common soldier, trudging through dust and sagebrush and yellow grass that flung its unwanted seeds at his trousers like a mother delivering her tenth child to the steps of a monastery, he grew worried about his mind's lack of command. He had donned the look of a common man. Had he donned the wits of a common man as well? With sunset coming, and no report of pursuit from the scouts, Gladdic dropped his disguise.

Instantly, he felt better. Of course, much remained wrong. Disaster had unfolded in Collen. One that ran as deep as any of the fears he harbored in the midnight hours. Not only had he lost the city, and the entire basin with it, but he'd lost the only tool he had to recapture these places: the Andrac.

It felt impossible. It *was* impossible. This had to be a fever dream—a test laid upon him by Taim. Yes: he was lost in the throes of a vision. One of utter disaster. If his faith faltered, it would prove that he was not worthy to lead Taim's banners across Collen.

Yet the ground beneath his feet felt real. The night smelled of the desert. The men around him looked weary, their gear clunking in the most mundane rhythms. His defeat was real.

His duties rabbled before him like a legion of devils. There seemed no way past them. His failure ran so deep it was possible the king might see fit to execute him. The thought gave him a horrible thrill. To have it done with!

Yet to end one's life—even to wish for death—was a crime against Taim's law. With a shudder, he imagined a boot. Then, he pictured the boot stamping the thought of suicide to a bloody smear.

He had many tasks, but his first was to ensure his survival.

"Horstad," he said to the stocky young man who moved to attend him. "Prepare to take a letter."

"My name is Liam, Ordon," said the man. His eyes shifted. "Horstad never returned from the city."

Gladdic jolted with discombobulation. Had he known that? "Does it matter *who* records the words I speak? Fetch parchment, man!"

Liam's eyes widened. He retrieved writing implements from his saddlebags, including a board to back the parchment. Gladdic cleared his throat and began a missive to the Eldor.

By the time he concluded his speech, he couldn't remember more than a fraction of what he'd said. It was as if Gladdic's memories belonged to someone else. Panic seared through his veins — and then he remembered that he was a lord, and simply ordered Liam to repeat what he'd just transcribed. Gladdic feared his words would be babbling madness, but they sounded like every other report of a sudden defeat: surprise; dismay; anger at one's foe; but mostly, the conviction that one had only lost the day due to a stroke of poor fate. One that could be overturned by a second effort.

For there would be a second attack. Wouldn't there? Hadn't everyone in the palace doubted his ability to take Collen in the first place? His initial success had been nothing short of a miracle. Undeniable proof that he bore the will of the gods with him.

Yet what could it mean that he had now lost the basin? Did that mean he had lost Taim's favor as well?

They marched on into the darkness. As the night deepened, the soldiers diverted from the road to make camp in the cover to be found between two hills. Gladdic's mind and body were exhausted, but after an hour in his bedroll, even the common victory of sleep still eluded him. His teeth had been clenched for so long his jaw was stiff. He removed himself from his tent, ignoring the glances of the sentries as he walked into the brisk desert night.

Thousands of stars shined down from above. The air was so still he felt sure he could hear a whisper from ten miles away.

There were crickets, yes, and the furtive rustling of mice in the green grass that had sprouted here and there since the rains.

He breathed the cold air through his nose. Sage. Dew. Dust. If the desert was a temple, then these scents were its incense. The constellations were the murals of its ceiling. Gladdic had no love for the voluptuous lushness of the woods. Nor the inconstancy of the sea. The severity of the high mountains carried an austere appeal, but their size and height seemed to embody a form of immodesty.

The desert, however, claimed to be no more than it was. And while it could be every bit as harsh as the mountains, those who devoted themselves to its ways could find revelations beyond mortal knowing.

He walked for some time. With each ridge he crested, he grew angrier that the Colleners, blessed with this landscape, had allowed themselves to grow so twisted and foul. He had thought he'd found the answer to their profanity, yet his efforts had evaporated like all water that fell on the desert.

So many others had found visions in lands such as this. He knew many in Bressel itself who claimed to have heard the voice of Taim, or the other, lesser gods. Gladdic suspected they were lying—he himself had never heard a clear word from those above—but the idea these people were telling the truth gnawed him to the bone. At last, surrounded by nothing, miles from the next living soul, he stopped in a field and tipped back his head to the stars.

"Father Taim," he whispered. A breeze hissed through the thorns of the tumbleweeds. "I am your servant. Your dog. Your hand and your blade. I beg you: put me to use."

For a moment, he felt as though a hand was reaching down from the sky, as if to touch his face. He closed his eyes. Then, for feelings were traitors, the sensation passed, as did they all.

He opened his eyes. Lowered his head. He wept. His tears fell to the greedy dust, absorbed without a trace. So even this was taken from him. Why had the gods let this happen? How could it be just? Was it proof that they weren't? He looked up again. The stars twinkled on, but there was nothing else there. What if there *were* no gods?

The same thrill shot through his spine that he'd felt on thinking about an end to his life. He gazed on the idea with a raptness that was, ironically, almost holy.

Yet just as it had been before, that thrill was a sign of wrongness. A physical pleasure meant to distract his mind from identifying the lies before it. He backed away from the godless thought as if it was a sucking vortex.

There were plain truths: the gods were real, and Taim was just. Therefore, if Gladdic had won Collen because of his own righteousness, his own virtue, his loss of the basin could only be due to the fact that he had stepped off from the path.

"Tell me what I have done wrong!" He thrust his fists to the side. "Help me, Father! *Help me return to your light!*"

His voice died in the desert. The stars gave no answer.

Was he beyond all use? Nothing more than the dried husk of a fruit that had no sweetness left to it? Shakily, he drew his dagger and placed its blade against his neck. If he was of no more use to this world, then let him join the gods.

The knife parted his skin. He gasped at the pain. His eyes stung with tears, then cleared. And so did his mind. Taim *couldn't* give him the answer. To do so would be to strip mortals of all agency. If the gods merely handed you what you needed to correct your errors, then the journey back to the path was over before it began.

He dug his fingers into the dust. He had lost himself. In order to be filled with holiness, one first had to make of oneself a worthy container.

Feeling like a child, he cried again. This time, in joy. For he knew what he must do.

There were greater horrors in the world than what he had seen in the Collen Basin. He would stand against them. He would defeat them. He would save a people who had been damned for centuries.

And he would become pure.

EDWARD W. ROBERTSON

4

Senator Alder gawked at him. The older man staggered back from the desk, arms bowed from his sides. Blood pumped from the hole Dante had cut into his heart. The senator blinked once, then twice, then collapsed on the floor.

Dante moved into the nether within his body, confirming he was dead. He turned to the desk, grabbed one of the ink-stained knives used to trim quills and cut coins of sealing wax from larger cylinders, and jammed the blade into the hole in the senator's chest. Blood washed over the knife.

Dante rifled through the pages on the desk until he found one bearing the senator's signature. The handwriting matched. He seated himself, took up a quill, and unstoppered a bottle of ink.

Years of scholarship had left him with keen penmanship. Additionally, in his early years in Narashtovik, he'd often been assigned the duty of copying manuscripts. In a sign of respect, he'd done his best to match the handwriting of the original author.

Within a few minutes, he had a passable imitation of the senator's hand. He composed a note, matching its rhythms to the man's speech and the writing to the letters on the desk. He signed the man's name, stepped into the brightly lit viewing room, and checked himself for blood. He didn't see so much as a drop, but summoned the nether to him to ensure he hadn't missed any. It floated around him in disinterest.

There were a few blots of ink on his right hand, however,

which he wiped clean on his cloak. After a moment of thought, he entered the study and dabbed ink on the senator's hand.

This done, he flung open the outside door of the viewing room. "Help! The senator's hurt!"

Doors creaked open. Voices and footsteps rang through the stone corridors. Dante returned to the study and knelt over Alder's body, drawing a wash of shadows to him and rendering them starkly visible. As three servants piled into the room, he poured the nether over the man's chest, making it writhe and flow.

A man in a blue vest made a choking noise, circling around the body. "What has happened?"

Dante didn't answer. Instead, he grimaced, summoning a second flock of shadows to join the first. The blood oozing from the wound came to a stop, but Alder remained as motionless as a fallen log. Dante crouched next to the senator, putting his hands on the man's chest. He summoned a third wave of shadows that soon disappeared.

"It's no use." Dante moved away and sat heavily in a chair, cradling his sweaty face in his now-bloody palms. "I'm sorry."

"Sire." The servant's voice was shaky. "Can you tell us what happened here?"

"We were discussing the war. After a while, he excused himself to his study and closed the door. He was in here for close to ten minutes when I heard a thud. When I called the senator's name, he didn't answer. I found him like this. I thought I could revive him."

The servants exchanged looks. One jogged from the room. The man in the blue vest made a search of the room, soon finding the letter. He read it, whispering the words out loud to himself.

"Sire," he said. "Have you read this?"

Dante swung up his head, frowning. "Read what?"

The letter was steeped in regret. The senator, as it turned out, had been bought off by Gladdic, the very man waging war on the basin. Dante's visit implied that the Colleners had discovered his treasonous pledge. Alder's suspicions had been confirmed when Dante made mention of their interrogations of Mallish prisoners of war.

Senator Alder had only seen one way out.

"Do you really think they believed it?"

Dante shrugged. "They let us leave, didn't they?"

Blays snorted. "Because they bought the story? Or because they feared that if they tried to hold you captive, you'd turn them into toads? And then turn their families into flies and make them eat the flies?"

"They don't know what to think, so they let us walk away. Over time, they'll convince themselves he was a traitor, and that I tried to undo his death. That's the only way they'll be able to absolve themselves of their guilt."

Blays considered the dusty horizon. "I think I'd feel better about humanity if it was because of the toads."

A day and a half later, they were back in Collen. Dante washed off the dust, ate a hot meal, then met with the Keeper. He laid out what he'd done, making no attempt to lie, minimize, or rationalize his actions.

Her jaw quivered with anger. "You were sent to convince the senator of his duty. Not to murder him!"

"I wasn't sent," Dante said. "I went. My job was to unite the basin. Now that he can't extort the other senators into withholding their votes, they'll pledge for war."

"He was an elected leader. There were other ways!"

"I know exactly who he was. The other senators wouldn't support us because Alder owned the farmland around the canals. I could have promised them that I'd dredge them canals of their own. That would have allowed them to vote for war, cementing their allegiance to Collen."

"Then why did you kill him?"

"He was trying to extort you while you're in the middle of a war for your survival. He was a snake, Keeper. Did Kaline deserve to be ruled by a man like that?"

The Keeper spoke through gritted teeth. "No. He abused his power. He served himself rather than his people."

"Then I did you a favor."

"They'll suspect it was you."

"Big deal. He *was* the type of person who would sell himself out to Gladdic. When we win the war against Mallon, and your people are delirious with freedom, you'll see how fast they forget their petty old grudges."

Dante believed his words, but he left the briefing feeling uneasy. To himself, he'd admit that he'd brought a barrel of anger into his dealings with Alder. Was that anger providing clarity of action? Or a reckless lack of regard for morals? Had he killed the senator to strengthen the basin? Or to punish the Keeper?

The evening of that same day, a rider arrived from Kaline. The senate had met. They would honor the Code of the Wasp. The towns were united.

The scouts confirmed the defeated Mallish army had crossed the border into their own land. Dante tried to send undead moths and rabbits to confirm their return to Bressel, but much as the loons had broken when they'd been brought too far away from each other, there were limits to how far his spies could roam. At twenty miles, their vision and hearing grew spotty. At forty, his connection to them was lost.

To ensure they weren't in danger of an immediate sneak attack, he spent two days on the border, moths flapping this way and that. He didn't spy any massed Mallish soldiers, but he did get a feel for the hills, plains, and dotty pine forests between the two lands.

The king's road was the simplest path across the space, but an army could take any number of routes. There wasn't much favorable terrain for Colleners to make a strong stand on, either. Seeing it from above, Dante better understood why the basin had had such a hard time defending itself.

There were no armies, but he did find a walled fort a few miles across the border. Hidden in Londren Forest, it was practically big enough to be a castle—presumably, it stood as the first line of defense against Collenese attacks—but at the moment, it was staffed by no more than a few score soldiers. They weren't a threat to anything beyond the local highwaymen.

Needing eyes in Bressel, Naran used the loon to order his crew in the city to make a regular circuit of the pubs, ears sharp for news. At Collen, soldiers from the six towns arrived in droves, training and maneuvering on the plains below the butte. Hunting parties brought back deer and rabbits. Dante grew a new crop each day. They managed to set aside a fraction of the food, but if it came to a siege, they wouldn't last more than a week.

Other than growing food and consulting with Cord, Boggs, and the Keeper, Dante found himself with a good deal of free time. He spent some of it exploring the caverns where Gladdic had been sacrificing Colleners to his demons. Dante found little of physical interest, but it did provide him with plenty of traces, the stains of death left deep inside the nether.

To see them, he first had to get Blays to walk into the shadows and illuminate them with the light of Dante's torchstone. For whatever reason, exposing them to ether from inside the netherworld made them visible in the physical world.

If normal nether flitted around like songbirds, the traces sat about like stones. But they were drawn madly to blood. Dante spent hours watching them move. If you combined enough of them together—for Dante, it had taken as few as six—they would become a tiny Andrac. A demon thirsty for human blood.

What did that imply about the traces? Their nature and origin? Did everyone have a little bit of demon in them? Is that why, when you gathered people into a mob or a tribe where all those little bits came together, they were capable of pushing each other into horrendous acts?

Or was he confusing cause and effect? What if committing an evil act caused the body to produce a drop of tainted nether? It seemed possible to test the theory by killing a few evil men and comparing the size and density of their traces to those left by good-hearted people. The outcome of such a test could answer many questions about human nature.

Yet the test itself would be evil, depending on murder as it did. Dante had to content himself with writing down his theories and observations, along with his questions. If he couldn't answer them in his lifetime, perhaps later generations could build on his writings to reach answers of their own.

He was in the caverns meditating on these matters when he was summoned to the butte to meet with the Hand, the nickname Boggs had bestowed on the five-person governing council of Collen. Their meeting that day was held on the balcony of the shrine where Cord had received her warrior training.

It was another pleasant, sunny day, but Boggs looked ready to punch someone. "Our envoys are back."

Dante grabbed a seat next to Blays. "Both of them?"

"Don't take it for a good omen. Parth and the Strip are both spinnin' the same story: can't help us."

Blays blinked. "Neither one has any extra food? Was there a series of plagues that everyone forgot to tell us about?"

"They know this is about Mallon," Boggs said. "They also know that whenever they've helped us in the past, we've gone on to lose the war. And Mallon's gone on to make them pay."

The Keeper rubbed her bony knuckles. "They are wise to fear. During the Third Scour, when it looked as though we would finally break our chains, Parth sent spearmen to our aid. After Collen fell, Mallish pillagers marched through fifty miles of Parthian towns before they'd had their fill."

Dante leaned his elbows on the table. "I presume our envoys spoke to their official leadership. What about the black market?"

"Our people looked into that. Not worth the cost in coin or in political capital. We try to run an end-around on their decrees by stuffing the purses of their criminal element, and they're apt to shun us completely — or even join the other side."

"Making an enemy is worse than starving to death?"

"That pits us against Mallish swords, Parthian spears, and Alebolgian bows. We wouldn't live long enough to starve."

Blays swore. "Why don't we relocate Collen to the middle of Parth? Then they'd have to feed us *and* protect us."

"Is there anyone else we can go to?" Dante said.

Boggs pulled a face. "It's Mallon to the west, mountains to the east, and assholes to the south."

"That leaves the north!" Cord motioned across the plains. "What about Narashtovik?"

Dante made a series of calculations. "Wagons wouldn't make it. Both the Riverway and Hollus Pass are in Mallish territory."

"What about boats?"

"You want to send boats around the continent during the

winter storms? I thought the idea was to get food to Collen, not the bottom of the sea."

Blays got to his feet, pacing around the balcony. "We can't ship it in from afar. We can't buy it from a-near. We can't grow enough on our own. What else do we do? Send everyone out to dig for beetles? Beseech the gods for a rain of bread?"

"We could send Naran back to the Plagued Islands. If we could convince a few Harvesters to come help us, it could be enough."

"There's an idea. Assuming that the Kandeans are willing to send their sorcerers to a distant land for no reason, and that Naran's crew is willing to pretend the seas aren't full of winter typhoons."

Dante shook his head. "Is that really the best we've got?"

"We could always go to Mallon for help. Maybe they'll be sporting about it." Blays drew back his head. "Wait, why *don't* we do that?"

"Well, first of all, because they'll kill us."

"That fort you saw in Londren Forest. You said it's huge, but there's hardly anyone there. Suppose they've kept it stocked?"

"I don't know," Dante said. "But I know how to find out."

Two days later, the Hand and a small contingent of soldiers and scouts came to a stop in the eastern fringes of the Londren. Technically, they were within Collen's borders, but Dante doubted if Mallon recognized those any longer.

It was already dusk, which suited Dante's purposes. A Collenese soldier lit a lantern to make camp by, drawing several oversized moths to whirl around the flame. Dante killed two of them with pins of nether, then thought about bats and killed all four. A pulse of shadows reanimated them to his command. He sent them flapping up through the canopy, headed west across the forest.

Along the way, one of them winked out, eaten by a bat or an owl. The other three made it to the fort. Torches and lanterns burned within it, illuminating the sentries on the walls. The yard within was quiet.

There, three wooden buildings were elevated on low stilts to discourage the entry of rats, mice, and other vermin. Granaries.

They were windowless, but the door frames were warped enough for the moths to slip through the cracks.

"They're stuffed," Dante said to the camp. "I'm looking at several tons of barley and wheat."

He withdrew the moths and made a circuit of the fort, relaying its fortifications, troops, and civilian count to Cord and Boggs. Getting a good look from above, he sketched out a map.

"A garrison of forty men?" the Keeper croaked. "I'm no tactician, but I'd think we could overrun them with what we've brought here."

Dante made a quick count of their troops. "We could. But we don't have the wagons to get the grain out."

"Should we summon them?"

Dante lifted his eyebrows at Cord. "Your call, General."

"Speaking of wagons," Blays said. "Let's not put them before the horse. Do we know for sure that Mallon is going to make a second attack?"

"The only thing we know for sure is that we won the last battle and Mallon hates to lose."

"But it's possible the war's already over and we just don't know it yet."

"It's possible. And it's also possible that King Charles himself will bake us an apology-cake to make up for his silly little invasion."

"Let me put it another way." He gave Dante a slap in the face. "There, I've slapped you. What's your natural response?"

Dante glared. "To punch you back. Twice."

"Exactly. Mallon might be back either way, but that's no more than a guess. But if we ride into their border fort, slaughter everyone there, and rob all their stuff, we can guarantee their army will be here before the snows are."

"You have a point."

The Keeper stood from her seat on a bench. "If we don't do this, and they come for us, we will starve. Mallon hasn't earned the benefit of the doubt. We know their history too well for that. We must secure our survival even if that means guaranteeing war."

"Cord," Dante said. "You need to think long and hard about

and help me to achieve it."

"Of course, lord." The priest stepped aside, gesturing sweepingly. As the carts rattled into the bailey, Nicols remained at Dante's arm. "May we speak in private, lord?"

Dante made a dismissive gesture. "Now is not the time."

"It will take a great deal of time to fill your wagons, Ordon. I believe the matter will be to your interest. It involves the rebels."

Dante glanced at Blays, who was lingering near the gates disguised in soldier's garb. Blays gave him the smallest of nods, watching from the corner of his eye as Dante crossed the bailey with Nicols. They entered a plain stone building that appeared to serve as the fort's temple. Stray leaves gathered in the corners. Nicols brought him upstairs to a cozy room with a lit fireplace, two shelves of books, and a great deal of maps. Nicols offered him a seat, then tea.

"Galladese?" Dante said.

"I wasn't aware there was another kind."

Dante said nothing—he'd forgotten that before Gallador had split from Gask, tea had been unknown in Mallon. "You said you had news from the basin."

The spalder nodded, rubbing his jaw. His chin was as smooth as the tabletop. Tidy. Kept himself in order. Which meant that the unswept leaves downstairs implied his men disliked him.

"The Collen Basin," Nicols said, as if savoring the flavor of the words. "They call it the riddle that cannot be solved. You believe otherwise, don't you?"

"A riddle cannot be a riddle unless it has an answer."

"At Grayson Fort, we are happy to take in travelers and refugees. It's a way to curry goodwill, but it's also a way to gather news. What I hear from such people makes me believe you've found the solution to the Collenese Riddle. It's like when a blight takes a field, isn't it? The only way to save the field—and the others around it—is to burn it."

Dante let a moment pass. "If a house is built on a rotten foundation, it is doomed to collapse."

"The second campaign—they brought you back to lead it, didn't they?"

"Second campaign?"

Nicols smirked. "The king's already called in new levies. The training grounds are filled from dawn to dusk. Our lord saw how close you came, and he believes you can be the one to finally prise the arrow from Mallon's side."

"You said you had news."

Though it was beyond obvious they had the room to themselves, the spalder glanced left and right, as if afraid of being overheard. He leaned closer. He opened his mouth to speak, then clicked it shut.

A tendril of ether slipped from his hand to probe the nether surrounding Dante. The nether rippled, set aswirl, opening holes in his disguise.

Nicols jerked backward. "Who are you?"

Shadows filled the room.

5

Nether swarmed to Dante's hands. His fury came with it. Before he knew what he was doing, he thrust a blade of shadows straight for the man's heart. Nicols yelled out, voice echoing from the brick walls. Adeptly, he shaped the ether he'd used to probe Dante's disguise into a shining shield. The two forces met with a flash of light, and then a counter-flash of darkness. White sparks twinkled to the floor.

"Galand," Nicols sneered. "You couldn't kill Gladdic. And you won't kill—"

Dante fired another bolt at the man's heart. As before, the spalder blocked it, but Dante had already followed it up with another strike. This one was as thin as a knitting needle. And it was aimed at Nicols' forehead.

The priest was still smirking as he collapsed to the stone floor. His limbs jerked like some awful dance, and then he went still, pooling like spilled oil.

A fist beat against the door. "Spalder? Is everything all right?"

"Indeed."

"I need to come in, sir."

"One moment."

Heart thundering, Dante drew Nicols' features across his own, using a polished silver bowl for his mirror. He thrust a hand at two of the candelabras, snuffing the flames and reducing the room to a soft glow. He flung a blanket over the body.

He moved to the door and flung it open. Outside, a novice in dark gray robes straightened his spine. "Excuse my interruption, Spalder. I heard a shout."

"The ordon and I discuss grave matters. Leave me be before you give me reason to shout more."

The man bowed and left. Dante eased the door's bolt closed. Silently, he cursed himself up and down. He should never have spent so much time in the company of the priest. He'd let his greed for intelligence overshadow his caution. Worst of all, he hadn't even gotten any news. All he'd gotten was another body.

The thought made him smile. But the smile made him pause: What if he'd exposed himself on purpose? Knowing that if he was discovered, it would give him a way to unleash his anger toward the Keeper at the Mallish instead?

Self-recrimination could wait. They were currently inside an enemy fort. If he was found with the body, his people might be hurt. Even if they won the fight, it would all but guarantee the continuation of the war. He pulled the blanket from over the spalder. He wanted to get Blays, who could found a university dedicated to the various methods of disposing of dead bodies, but he didn't want to leave the body alone.

Anyway, he had an idea.

The man was dead, but his tissue wasn't. Dante knitted shut the hole in his forehead, found a cloth, and wetted it with water from a ewer. He wiped the blood from Nicols' brow and hair, then tossed the rag into the fireplace, picked up Nicols, and set him in a chair.

There weren't any moths in the room, but a thorough search turned up a gathering of black beetles hidden in the kindling next to the fireplace. He killed one, then sent it outside to trundle toward the granaries. There, his men were shoveling gobs of grain into chutes angled into the wagon beds.

It was going to be a while. He sat across from Nicols and sighed. "That will teach you to gossip."

It was the middle of the night by the time they finished loading the wagons. Disguised as Gladdic again, Dante rose. So did Nicols. Dante opened the door for him, leading the way downstairs and outside the silent temple.

Along with the wagons, they'd brought a carriage appropriate for a man of Gladdic's stature. Dante walked to it and opened its door. Stiff-legged, Nicols' body followed after him. Somehow, it made it up the running boards and flung itself inside the carriage.

"Er, pardon me, milord," the guard who'd greeted them said, startling Dante. "Is the spalder...going somewhere?"

"Spalder Nicols will be accompanying me back to the capital." Dante swung into the vehicle, closed the door, then popped it open a handspan. "Who is his supporting priest?"

"Why, that would be Horris, sir."

Dante stepped out, dropping his voice to a murmur. "Is Horris a better man than the spalder?"

The guard's mouth quirked. "Everyone is, sir."

"Then for the benefit of the border, I might also take the spalder with me to Tanar Atain. Good night, soldier."

The wagons rolled out, lumbering heavily. Once they were out of sight of Grayson Fort, Blays jogged over to the carriage and jumped inside.

He froze, staring at the spalder, then gave Dante a dark look. "Another body?"

"This was the only way."

"To what? Draw as much attention as possible?"

"He found out I was an impostor," Dante said. "I had no choice."

"Well, I suppose it's easier than negotiating with them. What are you going to do with the body?"

"I had intended to bury it."

"You should at least have a little fun with it. Point it dead east and tell it to start walking. A year later, if it walks out of the west, you'll prove the world really is round."

Dante didn't know what was stranger: that Blays knew the works of the geometrician Acade, or that he didn't seem to be bothered by the reanimated corpse. Such things had always made him skittish, if not outright disgusted. Normally, he would have been happy to see Blays shrug it off, but he couldn't shake the feeling that the only reason Blays wasn't rattled by it was because he'd seen so much madness over the last few months. They needed to get home. Before all the adventure and warring left them permanently unhinged.

"Anyway," Blays continued, "their grain was more than happy to become our grain. You'll never guess what else we found."

"The world's greatest variety of mouse droppings?"

"A barrel full of shaden."

Dante's eyebrows shot up. "Did you take it?"

"The extremely potent enemy weapon? Drat, I knew I was forgetting something."

"That should make the fight a little easier for us." He considered the dead man. "Though I'm starting to wonder if there's going to be a second campaign at all." He nodded to the corpse. "He seemed to think Gladdic was off to somewhere called Tanar Atain."

"Tanar Atain? Why would he go there?"

"You know about this place?"

"I know it's a wretched southern swamp full of unspeakable horrors. So maybe it's his birthplace. Long ways from here, though. If he's down there, there's no way he's leading another attack this year."

The thought should have been comforting. Instead, it only reminded Dante how wide and unknowable the world was—and how easy it was for people to hide themselves in its fringes.

They arrived in Collen three days later. The grain was sorted and stored. If Dante continued harvesting potatoes and wheat from nothing, Boggs and Cord thought they'd wind up with enough to see them through the winter. He used a few shaden to speed the growth of the fields.

The Reborn Shrine had been destroyed by the gigantic demon, but its subterranean layers had largely survived—along with its archives. Dante asked the Keeper to look into Tanar Atain. She seemed happy to have a project. Now that she'd roped Dante into sticking around, most of the business of the war had been turned over to the commanders and logisticians, leaving her with little to do.

She returned the following afternoon with an armload of books and maps. "Tanar Atain lies hundreds of miles to the south. The swamplands are very difficult to navigate without a guide, and little is known about them. However, three hundred years ago, Mallon did a great deal of trade with the area. That is when the neeling came to Bressel."

Dante examined one of her maps, careful not to further damage its tattered edges. "What are Mallon's relations with them like today?"

"Negligible. Tanar Atain has been closed to outsiders for many decades."

"Then why would Gladdic be allowed in?"

She gave him a flat look. "I will saddle my horse to ride south and ask."

"Maybe he's hiding from us. Waiting for us to leave here. Or maybe King Charles booted him out for his failure and this is his exile. I don't suppose you know anyone from the area?"

"I have spent the last ninety years beneath the Reborn Shrine. I don't know anyone from anywhere."

"I don't like this." He stood, chair scraping. "Keep digging. This could be more important than we realize."

Through the loon, Naran's men reported that Mallish troops were drilling outside the capital. Infantry and cavalry, along with a handful of priests. In Bressel's pubs, soldiers complained about being sent off to eat dust and die away from home with the holidays so close. No official announcements had been made, but there was no mistaking the direction the wind was blowing.

The city of Collen threw a festival to celebrate the advance of fall, bowling pumpkins into wooden buckets and drinking cider until they were warned against going too near the edges of the butte. In Narashtovik, the first snows would soon arrive, but Dante had a feeling winter would be in no hurry to come to the desert.

The morning after the holiday, as he came in from growing what felt like his eight thousandth crop of potatoes, Blays intercepted him.

"You're needed on the war balcony." Blays tapped his temple. "I had an idea."

The other three members of the Hand were already there. Boggs looked like he'd enjoyed too much cider the night before.

For that matter, so did the Keeper.

"Here it is," Blays said. "You know that fancy road the king built? We're going to destroy it."

Dante glanced between the others. "Right. With no road to advance on, they'll have no choice but to stop at the border. As long as we steel ourselves against their curses, we'll be sitting pretty."

"Roads aren't built to get the soldiers to do something besides whore and gamble. They make your army faster. This is a tricky leap of logic, so listen closely—but if we destroy the things that makes armies faster, then we make Mallon's army slower."

"Even with the road gone, the basin is mostly open desert. Unless we train the tumbleweeds to throw rods in their axles, it won't slow them down by more than a few days."

"That gives us a few extra days to prepare. Or to harass their every move. Or to throttle each other by the neck and ask why in the hell we thought we could stand against Mallon."

"Their supply lines will pay a tax, too." Cord spat the word "tax" like it was as bitter as lemon pith. "If they leave their wagons behind, we can raid them."

"It does open up some tactics," Dante said. "But if you destroy the roads, you'll shut down trade. You two might not always be at war."

"Trade is the worry of a free people! If our children don't have to spend their days fighting, they'll have plenty of time to rebuild the roads."

"It's their land," Blays said. "If they want us to wreck it, who are we to refuse a good smashing?"

Boggs slid a large parchment map along the table, tapping a spot to their southwest. "They got a second road near the coast. Ain't much used except by smugglers and pilgrims. But they might try to get sneaky."

"We'll take care of that, too," Dante said. "We'll need fast horses. I get the feeling Mallon could march at any time."

On hearing the plan, Naran requested to come along with them. All three were provided with a pair of asties, the mottled, endurance-bred horses favored by messengers and scouts. They rode hard down the pavement, getting some final use out of it.

Dante didn't bother to tear up any of the road that day, opting instead to raise a patch of potatoes beside it. The next day of hard riding, however, they entered lightly wooded hills. Without a road, wagons would be lucky to advance faster than a mile per hour.

They stopped in the shade and dismounted. Dante gazed down the road. "It's funny. I've spent years building these to Narashtovik."

"Great," Blays said. "Then you've earned the right to destroy one."

"They're more valuable than anyone imagines. Like rivers made of stone. Bearing commerce, knowledge, and news. It almost feels wrong to destroy it. Like burning a book."

Naran gave the passage a severe look. "If your enemy can use a book to attack you, then you're right to burn it."

"That sounds reasonable," Dante said. "But that's the same rationale the Mallish use to burn the *Cycle of Arawn*."

Blays tapped his fingernails against the pommel of the sword on his left hip. "I've conducted a thorough examination, and it turns out this road doesn't have any family. We can kill it without worrying about anyone coming after us."

Dante sliced open the back of his arm. Nether zipped to him from the undersides of leaves and stones. He poured it into the earth like black rain. The road's cobbles sunk into the surface, splitting apart at the seams as the soil fell away from beneath them. He let some sections of the earth collapse while raising others several feet, making it impossible for anything with wheels to advance.

He followed the road westward, splitting, burying, and lifting it as he went. After a while, he realized that with the terrain so disrupted, he didn't have to demolish every last inch of road. So long as at least half of the ground was torn up, it would still be faster to cut a trail through the woods than to try to negotiate the craters and steps.

He'd brought several shaden with him, deploying them to augment his strength as they continued onward. Each mile brought them closer to Mallon. Blays and Naran watched the woods, but saw no sign of the enemy.

Another day took them to the border. Dante waited for nightfall before continuing into enemy lands, the road melting away with each step. Two hours before dawn, with his control of the nether growing clumsy, they turned around and led their horses back into Collen.

With the king's road thoroughly smashed, they turned south, making for the smuggler's trail alongside the ocean. According to Boggs, it wasn't cobbled, but by filling in a few narrow spots, or collapsing a cliff or two, it might be possible to render it completely unusable.

As they neared the sea, the air grew denser, cooler in the day and warmer at night. The forest petered out. A few old farmhouses sat in the scrubby land, boards gone gray with age, roofs rotted out, but Dante didn't see any sign of current inhabitation.

They traveled along the western edge of a shallow valley that varied from a few hundred feet across to as much as a mile. Running roughly north-south, portions of it were so straight it looked as though it had been made by a plow dragged by a sky-sized ox. The grass and shrubs in the valley were greener and thicker than on the higher ground to either side.

Once upon a time, Dante would have simply looked at it as a valley and left it at that. Knowing what he did, however, he thought it had once been the bed of a river. One that had been rerouted or destroyed when his ancestors lifted the mountain range to the east.

Cresting a ridge, the sea glittered to the south. Dante stopped to take in the sight. Birds drifted over the distant waves. Here and there, a white sail stood out from the blue-green sea. As the valley neared the waters, it grew shallower and shallower, the floor lifting until the valley disappeared altogether.

Dante's mouth dropped with laughter. "We're wasting our time. We can do more than slow the Mallish down—we can stop them from entering Collen altogether."

Dante traced his finger along the map, sweeping it over many miles of hills and scrubland. Across from him, Boggs, Cord, and the Keeper watched his every move.

"This is your border," Dante said. "Although since there aren't any rivers, mountains, or oceans to form a natural barrier, said border might as well be here, here, or here." He tapped to either side of the meandering line. "And that is Collen's main problem. The border's too wide to defend."

He stuck a pebble on the border. "If you stuck a fort somewhere, Mallon would just march around it. The city of Collen is the only truly defensible spot in the entire country. But when you retreat to your city, that leaves your towns and farmlands wide open. Mallon can pillage whatever they want. Even if you eventually drive them out, you'll have to spend years rebuilding. And just as you're ready to start growing again, here comes another invasion. This process has kept the basin in chains for centuries."

"That is an accurate summary," the Keeper said. "But it isn't news. We are Colleners. To us, this isn't history—it is our lives."

"It doesn't have to be. I can close off your lands."

"How? It's as you said. Our only defense is in this city."

"I'll give you three guesses," Blays said. "It rhymes with 'leather' and it's so dark that the night itself looks at it and says, 'Damn, you're awfully dark.'"

She crinkled her brow. "You mean to use the nether to alter the land. You have the power to change so much by yourself?"

Dante nodded. "With enough time, yes. I don't have to change much. By raising the high places and lowering the low ones, I can form bottlenecks that could be defended by a hundred soldiers. In the right locations, two or three forts could make your lands impregnable."

"I wish to believe this. But I've been disappointed so many times before."

Cord narrowed her eyes at Dante. "What will this cost us? When a god offers to make your wishes real, she never does it for free."

Dante muttered something unpleasant. "Don't tell me you're buying into the Keeper's propaganda. If you're still not convinced of my mortality, you're welcome to inspect my chamber pot."

"But here you are telling us you can reshape the land we live on! If you have the power of a god, then what more do you need to be counted as one?"

"Worshippers," Blays said. "Right now, his follower count sits at one. And that's only if you include himself."

"Setting aside the god issue," Dante said, making an effort to keep his voice level, "the cost is that this can't be undone. Parts of your land will be changed drastically. Rendered completely unusable. As long as you remain hostile toward each other, Mallon will be able to intercept every caravan you try to sneak into their land. Even if relations repair enough to resume official trade, you'll have to expend resources to protect your routes. Otherwise, bandits will eat your merchants for breakfast. Additionally, fortifications can always be used against the people who built them. If Mallon ever took the border from you, they'd command the region until you took it back."

He stopped to think. Blays motioned eastward. "Don't forget the part where forests become deserts, rivers reroute themselves to your neighbors, and cats start sleeping with mice."

The Keeper drew back her head. "Are you planning to raise entire mountains?"

"It would take me years to do that," Dante said. "But even though the changes I'll be making will be relatively small, there's no telling what impact they'll have."

"We already live in a gods damned desert," Boggs said. "Unless you're planning to take away our dirt and make us try to grow wheat from rock, I don't see what we have to lose."

"Take a minute to think about this. Not just as it stands now, but how it will impact your grandchildren, and their grandchildren after that. We're talking about forever."

The three Colleners exchanged meaningful looks. The Keeper was the first to speak. "It may be that there is a time when the cost of freedom is too dear to pay. But that time is not now. Free us, Dante. That is what you are here to do."

He had known that would be their decision. They were so starving for independence they'd lob their firstborns into the volcanoes of the Plagued Islands if that's what it took to win it. His question had been little more than a formality, a way to spare his own conscience in case things turned out for the worse.

Then again, it was their lives. Their land. And their fate. If they'd decided to take the risk, who was he to tell them he knew better?

"I'm not sure what's more appropriate here," Dante said. "Very well? Or so be it?"

The Keeper smiled in pure satisfaction. "How soon will you begin?"

They rode back into the desert, accompanied by a small contingent of guides and scouts. Dante sent moths, dragonflies, and wasps soaring over the contours of the land, following its heights and depressions, discovering the precise course his work would take.

The Green Mountains, a small range far east of the Mallish city of Whetton, would mark the northern end of the border. The ocean would mark it to the south. That left close to 150 miles to cover. At first, it felt like he'd accepted an insurmountable task—even excavating a 150-mile-long ditch could take months—but as he learned the land, he found his prediction was true, and that it would take far fewer modifications than one would guess. Bolstered by the shaden they'd liberated from Grayson Fort, he thought he could finish the job in as little as two weeks.

He returned to Collen to present his plan to the Hand. They examined his maps with two parts wonder and one part horror, seeming, at last, to understand how much things were about to change.

Boggs tapped the southern range of the proposed border. "Could run into trouble there. That's giant territory."

Dante frowned at the map. "I was just there. It's not *that* big."

"The land ain't big, you fool. I mean the people who live there."

"Exactly how big are we talking?" Blays said. "Big enough to stamp you underfoot? Or just tall enough that the tailor's annoyed at how long it takes to make their trousers?"

"Taller than any man you've ever seen. Strong enough to tear you in half. More monster than human."

"You've seen them yourself?"

Boggs nodded. "Only from a distance. Keep to themselves, which is fine by me. They come and go as they please, though, so watch out."

Blays scratched the corner of his jaw. "Nomads? Other than big, what do they look like?"

"Stouter than cows." Boggs spread his hand wide and made a pulling motion down over his face. "Beards from here to eternity. And ears so small you'll wonder where they went."

Dante and Blays looked at each other. At the same time, they said, "Norren."

"You know 'em?"

"Not the ones here," Dante said. "But we know many of them up north. If there's a clan where I need to work, I don't think we'll have any problem getting them to relocate."

Boggs got a quizzical look. "You mean to deal with them? I was only telling you about them so you wouldn't get clubbed and eaten."

They rode out once again, taking the swift-legged asties. As soon as they'd convinced the norren to move, Dante would strike north, altering the land as he went. Unless Mallon marched in a matter of days, he'd seal off the basin before they could breach it.

Boggs had claimed the norren were often seen around the shallow seaside valley, which they used to hem in herds of deer and antelope. As Dante, Blays, and Naran neared it, they slowed, moving from ridge to ridge to take in the surroundings. Tall grass carpeted the valley floor, yellowed from the long summer, though some was starting to regain its green with the autumn rains. A few thorny trees stood in small clusters like gossiping soldiers.

"Well, better get down there," Blays said.

Naran looked puzzled. "We have a much better vantage here along the rim."

"Which means that we'll never see them at all."

The captain blinked at this. "Since they will see us first. You believe they'll try to stay hidden?"

Blays moved his horse toward a game trail down the gentle slope of the valley. "Norren tend to keep away from humans. They have a cultural aversion to being murdered and enslaved."

"How do you know so much about them?"

"Because Dante and I are official clan members. I won a swimming contest, you see. And also we freed their entire people."

The expression on Naran's face said two things: first, that he still didn't understand. And second, that coming to understand would be more trouble than it was worth. Instead, he turned his attention to the wind-tossed prairie. Grasshoppers leaped around them, fat and green. Crickets chirped like they'd forgotten how to do anything else. To left and right, chaotic skeins of spiderwebs matted the grass.

Dante pointed to one messy cluster of threads. "Notice that?"

Blays nodded. "And no spiderwebs across the trail. Either they've been through here in the last couple hours, or we're about to find out how extraordinarily tall deer taste."

The path forked repeatedly. Each time, they took whichever branch was clear of webs. Grass rustled. Dante stopped, listening to the winds.

"If we find them," Naran said, "are you that sure they'll be willing to speak to us?"

"It wouldn't surprise me if they want nothing to do with us." Dante dismounted to take a look around on foot, tying his horse to the branch of a thorn tree. "But they need to hear what we have to say."

Blays dismounted as well. "We're practically family. When we explain that—"

A bow twanged. Something rammed Dante in the shoulder, knocking him to the ground. As he struggled to stand, the bow thrummed again, the arrow coming straight for his throat.

6

In Raxa's experience, there were three kinds of people in the world.

The first kind, and by far the most common, was those who liked to *have done* something. In the Order of the Alley, that was the type who pulled a job, then were happy to spend the next six weeks sitting in pubs, laughing with their friends and drinking away the evenings. Most of these weren't so interested in thieving for thieving's sake, but rather because of all the down time that came with it. If these people stumbled into a big enough sack of silver, they'd never pull another job again.

The second kind of person was those who preferred to think about doing something. The planners and the plotters. The dreamers and the schemers. For them, the kick came from the preparation. Casing the joint. Drawing up maps. Placing an inside man or bribing somebody who was already there. Assigning the right people to the right roles. Anticipating contingencies, and making backup plans to deal with them.

If you ever wanted to pull a job bigger than picking pockets, you needed people like these. Good ones were worth their actual weight in silver. Most, though, they didn't live up to their potential. They'd get so wrapped up in the thinking that they delayed the doing—and sometimes never got around to it at all. For some, following through on it was boring, since they'd already completed the act in their mind.

Then there was the third type: those who wanted to do the doing. Who only felt alive when they were inside the darkened house, listening for sentries, lifting the jewels from the dresser.

Raxa was the third type. As she sat down with Vess to work out how to steal the original *Cycle of Arawn*, it became clear that Vess was a schemer.

"Stop," Raxa said in the middle of a long proposal about tunneling into the Citadel from the outside. "Don't worry about getting in or out. I've got that covered."

Vess gave her a skeptical look. "You sound sure."

"That's a bad thing?"

"Everyone I know who was sure they could crack the Citadel wound up swinging from the hangman's tree."

"I can do this. Besides, there's no point planning to get inside before we know exactly where the book is."

"Don't worry about that," Vess mimicked. "I got it covered."

"You know where they keep it?"

"I know that like I know the color of Galand's underwear. But I got someone inside."

Raxa gave an impressed grunt. "How'd you pull that off? I thought the entire staff was a bunch of fanatics."

"Fanatics with families. Debts. Same troubles as everyone else. You running the Order, you got to get on that, Raxa. Cheaper to buy someone off than to get raided because you don't know what's coming."

She was quiet for a moment. Most likely, the reason the Order didn't already have a set of eyes and ears inside the Citadel was that Gaits had been working for *them*.

"I'll worry about that later," she said. "Find the book, and I'll make it ours."

While waiting to hear back from Vess, Raxa took a number of meetings with Anya, who could rattle off the name of everyone in the Order, along with what they'd earned over the last year. Raxa was glad to have her around. It was easy to tell yourself things would be so much better if only you were in charge. But when you took on the crown, you soon learned that *you* served it.

She didn't think it would be the world's best idea to try to set up a contact in the Citadel at the same time they were conspiring to rob it, but she got Gurles to start laying the groundwork. Other than that, she had to deal with a ton of low-level shit regarding the truce between the Order and the Little Knives.

The part she hated most was coming up with compensation for her people who'd been permanently injured during the war for the streets. You had people who could have earned a fortune stealing jewels and art, but now they couldn't even climb a wall. You were going to console them with two hundred in silver and a job scrubbing dishes?

Everyone who signed up for an outfit like the Order knew damn well what they were getting into. Raxa's sympathy only extended so far. Even so, when she thought about what it'd feel like to be in their shoes—the long years of quiet boredom; fading memories of jumping from rooftop to rooftop; forcing out a smile when some kid came in flushed, sweaty, and hilarious from a successful theft—she knew she'd have to walk away. Find a different life. And try to forget.

As she paid them their due, Anya scribbling amounts in her ledger, Raxa envisioned herself calling down the shadows like the priests did. And using them to make her people whole.

It was three days before a young boy dropped by her tenement with word from Vess. That night, Raxa hoofed it over to the temple of Urt. Its warped exterior made her head hurt. Vess was waiting in the courtyard, sitting on the branch of a tree.

It was a humid night and Raxa wiped sweat from her forehead. "Why do we always have to meet in *your* temple? Do you know how far I have to walk?"

"Didn't know I was invited. Would love to come by and drink whatever you got."

"Speaking of gots, how's the book coming?"

Vess chuckled. "You don't have any love for talk, do you? Every time, it's straight to it. Wonder if the men you're with love that or hate it."

"I haven't had any complaints."

"There is a chapel. Four floors."

"Let me guess," Raxa said. "It's on the top."

"It's on top. And always guarded."

"Inside the chamber? Or at its door?"

"The door. It's in a case. Glass. You know how to cut glass without making it scream?"

"That won't be a problem."

"How will you get in?"

"Ah ah. We haven't worked together nearly long enough for me to tell you that."

Vess smirked. "Can't blame me for trying."

Raxa returned to her offices and pored over maps of the Citadel. She'd have to move fast to get to the chapel and back before she ran out of juice. But it looked doable. The next night, she headed for the hill on the north end of the city where Galand had built the carneterium, the institution of monks who liked to paw through corpses and figure out how they'd died—and, sometimes, who'd killed them.

She slipped into the shadows, the intoxicating world of silver and black, like what it must feel like to live on a star. She walked briskly past the old man sitting inside the cave entrance and hooked down a hallway, reverting back to the real world to save her strength. She reached the side tunnel leading toward the Citadel dungeons. Moving in utter darkness, she shuffled forward until her fingers touched brick.

The last time she'd been through here, she'd used her almighty bone sword to chop her way through the back of a cell. They'd patched it up in a hurry. Not a problem: in the shadows, walking through rock was like walking through an open door.

She moved back into the starry world, stepped through the bricks, and bounced right off a wooden wall.

She flickered back to reality, swearing as she rubbed her forehead. What was going on? Had they slapped up some boards as a temporary cover for the hole, then come in from the other side and walled it over with brick? Strange way to do things. Very strange.

Raxa reentered the shadows. She moved up to the wood, placing her palm against it, then moved to her right; once it ended, she could simply step through the rock and into another cell.

Three steps later, the boards were still going. The coverage was much wider than the door-shaped space she'd sliced open on her way out. Even so, it wasn't until she'd gone another twenty feet and still hadn't found a gap in the wood that she understood something might be seriously wrong.

She retreated to the bricks that marked the original hole and tried walking to the left instead. Same story. Exploring further, she discovered they'd walled up the entire dungeon with wood.

Raxa returned to the tunnel and the normal world. A slow heat moved around her scalp. Wasn't any reason to coat a stone dungeon with wood panels. Check that: there was no mundane reason. But she could think of one pretty crazy reason.

To stop people like her from getting in.

Gaits had told Cee about her little trick. Cee had since taken steps to stop her from getting back in. Raxa did have a sword that seemed capable of chopping through anything, up to and including walls, anvils, and mountains, but there was no way she could whack her way through a brick wall and then a wooden one without drawing the entire castle down on her.

She cocked her head. If Cee knew who she was, and what she could do, then why hadn't she been arrested yet? She'd been careful for the last few days, but not *that* careful. There hadn't been any word on the street or from Vess' inside man that the Citadel was out looking for her.

They didn't really know, did they? In the gloom of the dungeon, Cee hadn't gotten any kind of real look at her. Cee had her name—her first name, anyway—but who else really knew who Raxa was? The others in the Order? The orphans and the families she'd placed them with? The Citadel hadn't come after her because they didn't know who to arrest.

Something stirred in the fun part of her brain. She turned around and jogged back out the way she'd come in.

"Back fast."

"There was a setback getting in," Raxa said. "But I've got another idea."

Vess made a flicking gesture with her fingertips. "Let me guess. I don't get to know it."

"Sorry. A few days ago, we were still trying to kill each other."

"You couldn't get in like you thought. The new idea works, you still sure you can get out?"

"If I can get in, I can get out."

Vess shook her head. "Getting out is always harder than getting in. You got another idea, that's good. Means you still got a few beans between your ears. But if you don't let me come up with a backup exit, I think those beans gone rotten."

"Where do you come up with this stuff?" Raxa said, laughing. "Fine. You got an idea for me? Or do I have to wait for it?"

Vess laid out her idea. Risky, but better than nothing. She thought she'd need two days to prepare.

Back at home base, Raxa woke early and tracked down Anya, who was the annoying kind of person who popped out of bed the instant the sun began to turn the skies pink.

"I'm looking for Lark," Raxa said. "The new fence. Need to move a few pieces."

Anya put on a stern look. "Gaits only hired him a few weeks ago. Gaits was compromised. Lark could be compromised as well."

"That's exactly why I need to test him."

"An alternate choice would be to assume he is tainted and cut him loose. We have other fences."

"Gaits was connected to everybody. If we cut loose everyone he knew, we'll have to start over from scratch. We just have to be careful, that's all."

Anya's expression made it clear what she thought of this idea, but she wasn't the type to buck an order. She gave Raxa Lark's address. Raxa rattled off a note to the effect that she was a collector of jewelry and was looking to sell off a few select items, describing them just well enough for an experienced hand to identify them as coming from the Jerrelec Collection, which she'd nabbed from the Citadel earlier that summer.

She handed the note to Skipper, one of their runners. Skipper jogged off into the city. The girl was back before noon. Lark was interested in the pieces—so interested he'd included an offer. Written in code, of course, but it was a good price. Better than Raxa had been expecting. He said he'd need a couple days to get the funds together.

Raxa sent Skipper back to give him the okay. Lark waited until the next day to send back a time and place for the meet. The night after that, Raxa headed to the place, the back room of a pub inside the Ingate. Not the most imaginative location for a meet, but at least it was a nice location.

As per instructions, she'd worn a green scarf. As she stood in the warm, smoky pub, a tall, slender man approached, dressed in black.

"You're Kala?" he said, giving the name she'd attached to the letter. She nodded. He smiled thinly. "Alone?"

"You think I got a regiment hiding in my blouse?"

His cheek twitched. "This way."

He led her through a cramped hallway and into a windowless room. Boots rumbled behind her. Two Citadel goons in black and silver, swords drawn.

"Hands on your head, scum." One of them stuck the point of his blade against her chest. "Any blades on you?"

She did. Along with two bracelets and a necklace from the Jerrelec. They tied her hands, loaded her onto a wagon, and rolled her straight through the Citadel gates. They marched her through the courtyard and down a staircase. The dungeons smelled like piss and mildew. They flung her in a cell. Before the door closed, locking her in darkness, she saw the cell walls that fronted the hallway were blank stone.

The cell reeked, and they'd roughed her up a little, but she didn't care. Lark had swallowed the bait like a starving cod. Offered too much, and then, despite being that eager to buy, his arrangements had been slow—almost as if he'd had to make arrangements with somebody else first.

She listened to the guards' footsteps fade down the hall. If they took the Jerrelec pieces straight to Cee, who seemed to be head of Citadel's security, the woman seemed smart enough to check in on the culprit for herself. Raxa had two things working in her favor: first, she hadn't told Lark anything that could identify her. And second, the Citadel was a great big gods damn bureaucracy.

Even so, no sense wasting time.

She walked into the shadows and through the wall. Hallway

was clear. She moved back to the dullness of the actual world, sticking tight to the wall as she headed toward the stairs. She ascended. At the top, she moved back into the nether.

From the perspective of the gates, the dungeons were on the left side of the keep. The chapel was all the way on the opposite side. On the outer walls, the guards stood out as silver silhouettes, streamers of shimmering mist following them as they moved. Raxa took off at a trot, cutting straight across the courtyard.

If the Cathedral of Ivars weren't looming across the street like a sentinel of the gods, the word "chapel" would have come across as an eye-rolling piece of false modesty. The building that housed the *Cycle* would have been a cathedral in any other city. Its two spires poked over a hundred feet into the night. Its face was dark granite, swarming with gargoyles, demons, miniature dragons, all that churchly crap they used to humble you. A lantern hung out front, presumably in case anyone couldn't wait until morning to prostrate themselves and beg forgiveness for their latest failure.

For just a moment, Raxa paused, head cocked at the splendid building. By definition, the rich were those who had lots of money. Which made them the best targets. The rich also almost always lived in stone houses. Where her talent was most useful. Was this a sign from Carvahal, the Silver Thief himself? A divine calling? If so, she'd better not ever reject her gift. To do so would risk invoking holy wrath.

She strode through the outer wall, blundering into a tapestry on the other side; the fabric barely rustled, as if she were no more significant than a breeze. The main hall was deserted. She dashed across it, locating a stairwell.

The fourth floor landing opened to an airy foyer with windows overlooking the grounds. The foyer doors were flanked by two grim-looking guards bearing wicked polearms. Within the shadows, nether danced on the blades. They'd tasted blood.

Couple of toughies. But if they wanted to keep their treasures safe, they should have sent a priest.

Raxa skipped through the wall. After ensuring the room beyond was vacant, she relaxed back into reality, letting her eyes adjust from the dazzling glow of the nether. The room had a high, arched ceiling, matched by high arched windows. Desks and shelves held a plethora of objects that looked worthy of her pockets.

But there was no time to indulge in the pleasure of pawing through somebody else's collection. At the back of the room, a glass case stood on a low dais.

The thick rugs swallowed up the sound of her footsteps. The glass was finely crafted—few bubbles, almost completely transparent. Within it, an oversized black book bore the unmistakable White Tree of Barden.

She prodded the glass. It was embedded in the dais, a hinged flap providing access to the interior, but that was locked with a solid loop of iron. Raxa didn't see a keyhole in the lock. Damn priests probably didn't need keys.

Then again, neither did she.

She inhaled, drawing herself back into the world of bright and dark. The White Tree on the cover now extruded a dull light across the room. Raxa reached toward the glass. Years back, on discovering she could pass through it, she'd asked around, discovered glass was made from melted sand. Made sense she could pass through it, then.

But while walking through rock was no tougher than walking through mist, crossing through glass was more like wading through water. She pushed her fingers through, picked up the book, and withdrew it.

She snapped out of the nether. The book was heavy enough to brain someone with. Holding it in her hands, she expected lightning to shoot up her arms, or nether to spill out of her nose, but it seemed intent on doing nothing. Well, that was books for you.

She set it on top of the glass and opened the cover. The smell of old parchment and leather wafted loose. The first few pages were blank, lightly yellowed, speckled with faint, gray-green spots. Then, in elegant script, written with the authority of one who ate kings and shat out priests, the book's title. And beneath that, in smaller letters from a different hand, the name of Dante Galand.

Raxa swore under her breath, chuckling. Just like a high priest to tattoo their own name on an irreplaceable relic that was created centuries before they were messing their diapers. She flipped through a few more pages, ensuring there weren't any demons coiled and waiting to spring from the text, then tucked the tome under her arm.

She hesitated. Maybe it was the book's weight. Maybe her instincts were just that good. Whatever the case, Raxa frowned, head lowered. She couldn't name half the Council priests, and didn't care a bucket of nightsoil about the ones she could, but everyone knew at least a little about Galand, the Mallish boy who'd shown up out of the blue, helped to murder the existing head of the Council, and then roped Narashtovik into an insane war, only to—somehow, unbelievably—win it, and take over the Council for himself.

Ambitious. Ruthless enough, too. But he'd promised to rebuild Narashtovik—and these days, the Dead City was thriving. He'd said the war was going to free the norren—and he'd set them loose, challenging Gask itself in the process. He was a true believer.

And true believers weren't the type to deface the faith's most precious relics.

Keeping the book under her arm, she made a quick pass of the chamber. Dozens of other books, but nothing that looked any different from within the netherworld. Nothing else protected in a chest or a case, either. She moved back to the dais, searching it for hidden compartments, then fixed her eyes on the wall behind it. This was black rock, rough hewn. Except for a patch dead center in the wall, roughly six feet tall and three across, that was nearly as smooth as the glass case.

Raxa shifted into the shadows and walked through the wall. She popped into a closet-sized room on the other side. The silvery glare was so bright she had to shield her face, eyes watering. Nether boiled and churned like a fresh-forged blade quenched in water. The power in the chamber was so dense she could barely breathe.

A wooden end table stood before her, thigh-high. On the table rested a book. On the book, a white tree glowed so powerfully her eyes stung with tears.

As she reached for it, darkness flowed from her hand to its cover. Her arm went as cold as if she'd plunged it into a mountain stream.

The nether was being ripped out of her body. Another moment, and she'd be trapped in the doorless space for good.

7

Blays' swords seemed to leap into his hands. He drove them forward in an X. An arrow bound for Dante's chest scraped into the blades and glanced away.

"I've been shot!" Dante announced.

Blays ignored him, sprinting forward. Naran gave Dante a startled look, but despite his refined ways, the captain was a man of action used to command. He ran after Blays.

Dante sat up, head spinning. A thick wooden shaft jutted from his left shoulder. Just as he suspected, he *had* been shot. It ached dully. Injury seemed to slow everything down, including the sensation of pain. Was the slowness real, or imagined? If a sorcerer broke his own toe with a hammer, only to heal it, break it again, and repeat, could he get time moving so slowly that it stopped altogether?

Steel clanged from somewhere in the grass ahead of him. Dante frowned at himself and called to the darkness. Fortunately, he'd already spilled plenty of blood. The shadows plunged into his shoulder. With a slurp, the arrowhead was expelled from his flesh. He closed the wound and stood.

Black spots filled his vision. He staggered toward the tree, bracing himself against its trunk. He was no longer in any pain, but the site of the wound tingled, and his head was still loopy with after-pain. Fifty yards away, Blays and Naran were holding a conversation with what appeared to be a patch of grass.

Dante picked up the bloody arrow—evidence of the crime—and walked over to them. A giant of a man was sprawled in the grass at Blays' feet, disarmed, bleeding from a pair of shallow cuts. A beard covered the entirety of the lower half of his face. He looked younger than Dante, but he was closer to seven feet tall than to six. His fists looked big enough to knock down a bull.

"You shot me." Dante brandished the telltale arrow. "Why?"

The norren gave him a sullen look. "Because you were standing still enough to be shot."

"Do you normally shoot everyone who stops to smell a flower or take a piss?"

"That sounds needlessly hostile."

"Then why," Dante said slowly, "did you shoot *me*?"

"Well, you were hunting me, weren't you?"

"We weren't hunting you. We were only trying to find you."

The man sat up. "Yes. By hunting me. With weapons."

Blays stepped between them, making a chopping motion. "Mistakes have been made. Arrows have been fired. People have been shot. Now, we can spend all day arguing about who shot who—"

Dante sputtered. "*He* shot *me*!"

"—or we can agree that no lasting harm was done. So we can argue about it, and get mad at each other until we get in another fight. One where someone gets hurt badly, or even killed. Or we can put it behind us and get on with our business."

Dante rubbed his shoulder. "Agreed."

"Agreed," the norren said. "Then again, you've got your sword pointed at my throat. So I'd probably agree to anything. Except the suggestion that I should be stabbed with it."

Blays sheathed his swords. "We need to speak to your chieftain."

"He's not here."

"I'm going to assume by 'here' you mean 'in our immediate presence.' In that case, I request that you go wherever he is and get him for us."

The man stood, brushing off his trousers. "Then I'll go do that."

Dante narrowed his eyes. "No you're not. You're going to run away."

"Are you giving me permission?"

"A great calamity's about to strike your lands. If your people are here when it happens, you'll get calamitized, too. You need to convince your chieftain to see me."

"It sounds like all I need to do is tell him there's a terrible calamity." The norren regarded him for two long moments. "But I'll tell him he should talk to you." He bent to pick up his bow and spear. "Stay here. Or you can choose to leave, I'm not your human king. But if you do leave, we won't know where to find you."

Dante smiled tightly. "We'll be here."

The man gazed at them, then turned and walked away. Dante had half a mind to follow him with a dead grasshopper, but the norren were skittish enough already. If they happened to have a sorcerer capable of detecting the grasshopper, they'd never speak to him again.

Even so, he posted a couple of lookouts in nearby trees in case the clan would rather have a human-hunt than a conversation. Less than an hour later, a lone figure approached through the grass. His height topped seven feet and he looked like he'd have to turn his shoulders to fit through a human door. Their beards, bulk, and features made it harder to peg a norren's age, but Dante had spent enough time among them to guess this man was in his late twenties or early thirties. Feathers and fine silver chains dangled from his spear. His armor was composed of boiled leather and black iron bands, the metal etched with rune-like depictions of wolves, deer, owls, and snakes. His bearing was as proud as his armor.

Wordlessly, he stopped across from the three humans, his gaze settling on Dante. "Alok says he shot you. But you don't look very shot to me."

"I got better," Dante said. "You're the chieftain of this clan?"

"That's who you sent for, isn't it? My name is Ramm. Alok said you think a disaster's coming to the Valley of Northern Spirits."

"It could hit within a matter of days. Before winter at the latest. You need to relocate your people."

"What kind of disaster? And how do you know it's coming?"

"The land will be transformed." Dante paused; he'd been on the brink of saying that he knew it was coming because he was the one bringing it. If he confessed to destroying the clan's land, however, it wouldn't be an illogical response for the chieftain to hoist Dante on the end of his fancy spear. "I'm a...prophet. Of Arawn. He's sent me a vision of this valley being destroyed."

Ramm scratched a bushy eyebrow. "That could mean anything. Gods don't like to show mortals the exact future. What you saw was probably just a metaphor."

"For what?"

"How should I know? Do I look like Arawn?"

"Trust us on this," Blays said. "I know we look like short, scrawny little humans. But my friend and I are members of the Broken Herons Clan from the hills north of Tantonnen."

The chief snorted. "It's impossible that any clan would ever admit a human. So your claim that the Broken Herons took two humans is *double* impossible."

"Our chief's name is Hopp. This happened several years ago, during the Chainbreakers' War. Did you hear of that one?"

"No. And since you're a liar, I can only conclude you're about to tell me more lies. Goodbye, liars." He turned and walked away, broad shoulders swaying.

Blays spun on Dante. "Does Hopp still have one of our loons? Can we get him to talk to this guy?"

"It's worth a shot." Dante jogged after the norren. "Ramm! Do your people speak to Josun Joh?"

The norren stopped in his tracks. "Do they what?"

"In the north, the clans venerate the god Josun Joh. Some speak to him. Do you do that here?"

Ramm's brows bent together. "You mean Dozundo. Wait here."

"For what?"

"For me to get our chieftain."

Dante's mouth fell open. "You said you were the chieftain!"

"No I didn't. If our chieftain would come talk to a trespassing human, that wouldn't make her much of a leader, would it? Now stay here." He jogged away, spear rattling.

Dante clamped his fingers to his temples. "Why did we ever help these people again?"

"We were young and foolish." Blays seated himself under the tree and swigged from a flask of something that probably wasn't water. "Anyway, if these guys are *that* annoying, then we won't feel bad if they're all killed when they don't listen."

Ramm was back in less than half an hour. He was accompanied by two other men with bows and long spears and a woman in a plain brown cloak. Most norren carried an air of calm unflappability around with them, but her bearing was so steady you could have built a house of cards on her.

"I'm Kadda," she said. "I'm chief of the Walking Fish. You're in our valley. What do you want?"

Dante repeated his warning, along with his fabricated credentials as a prophet. "By year's end, this valley will be ripped apart. Please, move your clan before it's too late."

"Do you know why we're here?"

"Because we came to your land, and insisted on seeing you, and showed enough knowledge of norren matters that you relented. Is that a complete enough chain of causality for you?"

Kadda smiled crookedly. "You do know other norren, don't you? It could be that our ancestors knew the ancestors of your friends. Years on top of years ago, we lived in the north, too. Every year, the humans would come for us to take us. Put us to work in their fields and mines. No matter how well we hid, sooner or later, we had to hunt for meat. And they'd find us. And they'd take us.

"One day, the elders gathered. They decided there was only one way out: to leave. So that's what they did. Many died along the way, but at last, our ancestors settled here. For three hundred years, we've been free. The ancestors, they sacrificed their lives, everything they knew, to escape human troubles. Now you're telling me that human troubles have found us again—and again, we need to leave our home because of it."

"That's correct," Dante said.

She burst into laughter. "Do you have any shame at all?"

"Plenty. But my feelings don't matter. Your lives do."

"How do I know this isn't a trick to take the valley for stupid human farms?"

Dante darkened the air around them until their faces were nothing but dark outlines, eyes shining white from within the fog. "If I wanted your land, I wouldn't have to trick you into leaving. I'd just kill you and take it." He dropped his hand, returning the world to its normal brightness. "If I'm right about what's coming, it will happen before year's end. If I'm wrong, you can always come back then."

Kadda exhaled through her large norren nose. "I think you're telling the truth. But we can't go."

"Wrong. You have legs. They will support you in any decision you make."

"When our ancestors came here, they brought a great relic with them. They brought it to that mountain to watch over us." She pointed northwest, where a pair of low peaks rose from the surrounding flatland. "If we leave this valley without it, we'll be cursed."

Blays shifted his eyes between her and the mountain. "Might I suggest you *don't* leave without it?"

"We lost it long ago. We can't find it—but if you can, that will be proof Dozundo knows you're telling the truth, and wants us to go. If you can't find it, then you are liars, and we will stay."

Dante wanted to kick and scream and hit things with other things, such as her head with a large club. But he knew norren. The harder you pressed them, the more stubborn and indifferent they grew. The only way to reach them was to win their trust.

"Tell me more about this lost relic."

"It's called the Face of Dozundo," Kadda said. "It's carved from blue marble by the master Ellin, whose nulla was stonework. And it's the most beautiful statue that you'll ever see."

Blays squinted at the two peaks, neither of which were tall enough to bear snow yet. "Do you remember the last place you saw it?"

"The only place such a sacred item could be: our shrine."

"Interesting. Have you tried checking the shrine?"

"Yes." Kadda gave a lingering look toward the peaks. "But that was lost, too."

"Come now, everyone knows you have to tether your shrines. Otherwise they'll get up and wander away."

"Only our holiest wiseman knew where it was. Then he got eaten by a bear. But we know two things about the shrine: it rests where the moonflowers grow in rings, and that you will know it by the shine of the sea on its grim and stony face."

"First you want us to find the shrine," Dante said. "Then you want us to find the Face of Dozundo. And once we bring it back to you, you'll relocate?"

Kadda nodded. "We haven't been able to find it, but surely a great prophet and sorcerer like yourself can. Perhaps your god will help you, too."

Dante had one of the clan's best artists sketch him a picture of a moonflower, which was a distinctive silver color with petals shaped like crescents. After making arrangements about where they could find the clan in the event that they brought back the statue, Dante, Blays, and Naran took off on horseback, trotting toward the pair of low blue mountains.

"I don't mean to question your wisdom in this matter, but..." Naran wrinkled his forehead. "Actually, I do. I wish to question it most rigorously. We may be days away from invasion, and your plan is to run off to find a lost idol in a lost shrine?"

"The norren are as stubborn as a constipated mule," Dante said. "They'll never leave just because we tell them to. Trying to push them to do something is like trying to push down the surface of a lake. This type of challenge they've given us is very common—if we follow through on it, it's a sign that we're serious, and that we respect their ways."

"Evidently *they* have no respect for our *time*. It could take years to search these mountains!"

"I know. That's why I'm planning to cheat."

By nightfall, they had ridden within ten miles of the foothills. Dante woke before dawn to slay a host of winged insects. He sent these soaring toward the dark mountains. By the time the three of them had eaten a breakfast of flatbread and venison jerky and gotten on their way, his scouts were entering the mountains.

The moonflowers sparkled like steel shavings, impossible to

miss in direct sunlight. They didn't grow on the lower half of the mountains, and quit flowering some ways before the peaks, narrowing the search. On top of that, the only areas with a view of the sea were the southern exposures. At an initial pass, Dante only saw six sites on the closer of the two mountains that might qualify for the shrine's location.

The mountains were weathered and slump-shouldered, no trouble for the horses to ascend, especially when Dante could scout the lay of the ridges from ahead. Early that afternoon, they reached the nearest site: a flat shelf of turf a few hundred feet across, bordered on its north side by a low cliff that looked out on the faraway sea. Most of the ground was covered in grass and weeds, but near the center, a lopsided circle of moonflowers bobbed their heads in the wind.

Dante dismounted and walked around the ring of flowers. The three of them criss-crossed the site, eyes sharp for cairns, norren bones, statues, and so on. Finding nothing but rocks and lichen, they reconvened in the middle of the circle.

Dante folded his arms. "Does anything about this look like a shrine?"

"That depends," Blays said. "Do norren worship empty fields?"

"If so, you'd think they'd choose one closer to home."

They moved on to the next site, a rocky field sporting another ring of flowers. It took nearly two hours to check all the boulders and debris for a blue marble carving or other signs of shrineliness.

"This is absurd," Naran said. "Even if the shrine is here, everything here is so weathered that we might not even know it when we see it. And that itself assumes its design will be obvious to human eyes."

Blays swore. "And if it *was* obvious, you'd be able to see it through the eyes of your bugs, wouldn't you?"

Their logic struck Dante like a hammer swaddled in velvet, leaving him unable to do anything but stand there and stare at them.

"There are only a few more on this mountain," he said lamely. "After that, we'll check the next one."

They moved on to the next ring, an uneven grassy slope. There was nothing there. The sun was already nearing the flatness of the sea. They made it to one more site before the sky grew too dark to see what they were doing. Dante didn't sleep well.

He woke up cold and stiff. They moved out at first light. The next ring of flowers was only a short walk away, but Dante's enthusiasm was waning. Again, they found nothing. They headed on to the final possibility he'd scouted out, a small hilltop rising from the side of the mountain. The view was stunning, but his heart sank to his knees.

"You're right," he said. "This is the Quivering Bow all over again."

Naran swatted at a hectoring fly. "The Quivering Bow?"

Blays chuckled. "That was a fun one. That time, a norren clan tricked us into assaulting one of their worst enemies, hastening the war that was brewing. At least this time they only seem intent on sending us on a wild goose chase."

"I expect that's their game," Dante said darkly. "There's no shrine. There's certainly no Face of Dozundo carved from blue marble. Without my scouts to speed things up, we could have wasted weeks out here."

"Sounds like we should go back and yell at them."

"Agreed," Naran said. "But first, I get to tell you 'I told you so.'"

Dante stalked toward his horse. "And I get to not to listen. It's for your own good, really."

Blays grew thoughtful. "Because otherwise, you would turn him into moonflower chow?"

"Correct."

A frown crept across Blays' face. "Something doesn't feel quite right about this."

"That would be the feeling of humiliation. I'd think you'll recognize it from every time you take your pants off."

"Think about the trick they played with the Quivering Bow. Or just the other day, when they let us assume Ramm was their chieftain. They like to play on ignorance. Sending us on a hunt for something that isn't there isn't very clever. It's much funnier to send us after something we'll never find even when it's right under our nose."

Dante turned away from his mount. "Kadda came up with the relic and shrine business awfully fast. If it's invented from whole cloth, she lies like a Kandean."

"Take us back to the first site. I've got an idea."

Dante led them across the green hills, returning to the flat, grassy shelf backed up by the cliffs. Blays glanced at the grounds, then at the cliffs, then out to sea. He turned back to the cliffs and vanished.

As Blays shadowalked through the netherworld, Dante could feel the barest hint of his presence heading toward the rock wall. And then Blays was gone. A hawk cried out from the heights. Dante had barely glanced back at the cliff face when Blays reappeared.

He grinned, jerking a thumb behind him. "There's a cave back there. Want to open it up?"

Dante opened a cut on his arm. "How did you know?"

"Kadda said it would be at the place where the sea shines on its grim and stony face. I figured she was talking about some big old statue. But she meant a cliff face."

"Stony." Dante shook his head. "Hiding it right under our nose."

He sank the nether into the rock, feeling its shape, then pulled the stone back to either side. A large hollow opened before them. Dante lit his torchstone and walked inside.

They had arranged to meet at the same tree as before, but Dante decided to save time by going right up to the clan. The Walking Fish were arrayed in a thorny grove of trees that had sprung up around an L-shaped pond. Many were working on wooden carvings or birch bark drawings. Others were smoking fish, weaving matting for their yurts, or flaking arrowheads from obsidian.

Noticing the riders, they went still. Kadda strolled forth to meet them. As before, she was flanked by two enormous warriors.

"Back already?" She looked Dante up and down. "Did your

god tell you he's changed his mind?"

"No," Dante said. "But yours told me he missed you."

Blays lowered a battered leather sack to the ground, grunting at its weight. He untied its thong and yanked it open. A blue face stared up at Kadda, its skin and beard marbled with white. Though the coloration was phantasmagoric, the muscles, wrinkles, and hair chiseled into the stone looked so lifelike Dante was certain it was about to blink.

"The Face of Dozudo," Dante said. "Unless you lost some other blue marble relic bust you didn't think to tell us about."

She reached out to touch its face, hesitating at the last moment, as if it might sting her. She composed herself and caressed its brow. "Where did you find it?"

"Behind several tons of rock."

"I'm not sure you can trust that wiseman of yours," Blays said. "We found it in a dirty old cave. If he was telling you all that was a 'shrine,' he needs to raise his standards."

"It was buried in a cave?" She eyed Dante. "Then how did you find it?"

He shrugged. "I told you, I'm a prophet. So you should heed my words when I tell you it's time to leave the valley."

"Our agreement. Yes, I'd like to honor it. But I don't have the authority to make these people leave."

"You're the chieftain. Where you go, they'll follow."

Kadda shook her head sadly. "But I'm not the chief. Not anymore."

"Since when?"

"Since you brought back the Face of Dozundo. That means the clan of the Walking Fish has entered a new era. One I'm not worthy enough to guide us through."

Dante clenched his jaw. "I can't say I disagree with your decision to step down. Who'll be replacing you?"

"Everyone knows it's bad luck to choose a new chieftain before spring. You should probably wait to come back until then."

"You can't be serious."

"It's regretful, but there's nothing any of us can do." She took a long breath through her nose. "Ahh, and yet it feels so freeing."

Heat crept up the back of Dante's neck. "You think you're

putting one over on me. But when I leave here, the disaster doesn't leave with me. You're only hurting your own people."

"We've seen human kingdoms come and go. We're still here. I think we'll be fine."

Blays exhaled raggedly. "I'd try to shame your honor, but it appears you haven't got any. Maybe it's lost in a shrine somewhere."

"We have to leave," Dante said. "Before I start killing them."

Blays snorted, then caught the look on his face and grew sober. "Okay, we *do* have to leave. Keep an eye on the valley, ex-chief Kadda. If it starts to do anything strange, such as rip in half, you might want to run."

Nether flickered around Dante's hands, drawn by the overwhelming urge to lash out at their smug, stupid, stubborn faces. That, however, would defeat the purpose of trying to save their lives, so he strode back to his horse instead. As he mounted up, he was tempted to reach into the blue stone statue and melt it into a hard blue puddle. Kadda hadn't held up her end of the deal. She didn't deserve to profit from it.

But a part of him knew that not all of his anger was caused by the norren—much of what he felt was still the fault of the Keeper. Besides which, if he destroyed the Face, he wouldn't only be taking it from her. He'd be taking it from the clan. And future generations lasting for countless years. Ever since the cracking of Arawn's Mill, people had been mortal. Born in order to die. But art could still be eternal. Whatever talent had carved the Face of Dozundo was immortal. The idea of destroying the statue disturbed him worse than the thought of annihilating the clan.

In most circumstances, Blays would have derided him for getting fooled by the norren yet again. But Blays rode in silence. Naran, too, although he was often so stiff and silent he could be mistaken for the masthead of his own ship.

After several miles, Dante slowed his horse to a walk. "We weren't trying to rob them. We weren't trying to hurt them in any way. All we were trying to do was help—and all *they* did was take advantage of us."

Blays glanced behind them. "How does that make them any different than the Colleners? Or the Kandeans?"

"Is it that hopeless? Trying to make things better? What else are we supposed to do?"

"I suppose we could tend to our own lands. Failing that, there's always rum."

Dante lapsed into silence. Riding along the rim of the valley, his options slowly clarified. He could get lost in his rage, letting it pull him off his path. Or he could forge forward with his work. Do what he could. And pray it was enough.

At the end of the valley, he stopped, gazing northeast. "For now, we'll leave the norren be. There's plenty of other land for me to deal with. Naran, would you mind heading back to Collen?"

The captain smiled. "Am I that useless to you?"

"Just the opposite. We can no longer trust the Keeper. I'd like to have a pair of smart eyes on her."

Naran touched his loon. "I'll let you know if I see anything out of order."

He struck northeast toward the distant city, dust pluming from the hooves of his astie.

"Well," Blays said. "Ready to smash the gods' hard work?"

Dante smiled. "If it offends them, then they shouldn't have left the world unattended for so long."

Having already surveyed his course, he wasted no time riding up the hill to their west. A little past its crown, he dismounted and drew his knife across the back of his arm. Shadows fell on him like rain. He sent them worming into the slope below him.

Rock cracked like thunder. Dust shot into the sky. With a rumble, the western face of the hill slipped loose, shaking the earth as it tumbled downhill.

Dante grinned at the devastation. "Now *that* was satisfying."

Stones broke, smacking against each other as they sought new resting places. When the dust settled, Dante moved to the edge, inspecting the twenty-foot cliff he'd chiseled into the hill. Troops could still climb it, assuming they had ropes, but wagons wouldn't have any hope. And the Colleners could defend it with a handful of soldiers.

He moved north, raising a spine of naked rock, then ripping

open a fault between two massive slabs, creating a ravine as bad as the ones they'd seen in the glacier fields of the Woduns. Though the changes to the landscape were vast, they were slow to deplete his supply of nether. He wasn't building anything. He wasn't doing any fine shaping or meaningful building.

He was destroying. And it was always far easier to destroy than to create.

They slept under the stars. Dante woke angry, but he turned his wrath on the blankness of the land, cracking open cliffs and chasms, lifting ridges and spikes. As soon as Naran was back in Collen, Dante requested a delivery of shaden. A rider delivered the heavy snails to him the following morning. Drawing on the nether collected within the shells, he was able to extend himself five times as far, covering miles per day, leaving a wandering trail of ruin behind him.

He lost himself so deeply in the work that he wouldn't have noticed if a Mallish army had marched up and made camp around him. Blays kept watch, moving from hill to hill as Dante chewed his way north. They didn't talk much and they didn't need to. Sometimes, when Dante paused between assaults on the earth, he'd catch a look on Blays' face that was somewhere between thoughtful and troubled.

Naran reported in via the loon each night. The Keeper didn't seem to be up to any new tricks—either that, or her skullduggery was too subtle for Naran to spot—but a group of Collenese soldiers had run across a party of Mallish scouts investigating the torn-up king's road. They'd skirmished, but the Mallish had escaped.

Naran had word from Bressel, too. According to his crew stationed there, King Charles had announced that the Collen Basin had once again rebelled against its Mallish lords.

And this time, the Colleners had raised demons from the shadows.

It was, the king said, a staggering heresy. But it would not be allowed to stand. A cohort of ethermancers would be sent to purify the realm—along with a second, larger army. Collen would be back in Mallon's hands before the end of the year.

Hearing this, Dante's jaw dropped. "That's disgusting. I can't believe it."

"That a king would lie to his subjects?" Blays said. "If you find that disillusioning, then I have terrible news about the Falmac's Eve fairies."

"Gladdic's behind this lie. I'm sure of it. Knowing his hunger for glory, he'll insist on leading the new army into Collen. He'll deliver himself right to us."

"I thought he was down in Tanar Atain."

"What if that was a ruse to stop us from looking for him in Bressel?"

Blays frowned. "Then it was an awfully cunning ruse, depending as it did on you raiding a fort while disguised as Gladdic, bumping into one of his underlings who happened to have that piece of intelligence, and then being fed that intelligence despite the underling not having any idea who you really were or why you needed to be fed it. If Gladdic's that clever, we should start sewing our white flags right now."

Gladdic's involvement was speculation. But Mallon's intentions were clear. Dante pushed himself to the brink, gouging trenches, tossing up walls of jagged rock. The effort made him stand tall. The catharsis of devastation had him eager to rise each morning. Hard and clear, the desert sunlight seemed to be trying to show him something. But all it shined on was more wasteland.

Somehow, the wasteland seemed to be enough. Everything fell away except the brightness of the sky, the crispness of the nights, the flaming wall of orange and pink that erupted at the end of each day when the sunset struck the dust in the air.

The land was as empty as a bowl that had never been used. And that seemed to be the point: Dante had nothing except himself, a trusted friend to watch his back, and the job. All of his other troubles were petty nothings. Soon, he would walk away, and his work here would remain in testament to what he had done.

Mile by mile and day by day, they forged north. The Green Mountains sharped on the horizon. Blays stopped to stare, then turned around, taking in the trail they'd left behind them. Parts of it looked like a god had stabbed at the earth. In others, it looked like a dragon was burrowing beneath the soil, with only its horns and spine breaking the surface.

"Know what's funny?" Blays said. "No one's here to see this being created. But the Colleners will see the results. They'll come up with stories to explain it. Some will be true, or close to it, but others will be exaggerated, or just plain made-up."

"Let me guess. You're going to spread stories of your own. Like this was all your work, and while you were slaving to save the realm, I was busy wandering around eating berries and crapping my pants."

"That wasn't my idea. But it might be now." Blays's smile faded. "People who didn't see it happen will tell other people all about it. Kids will grow up with the stories, and they'll only remember the craziest parts, which they'll tell to *their* kids, who will only remember the craziest parts of *that*, and so on. A few hundred years from now, the Colleners will all swear to the story of Don Tay the Stone-Shaper, who waved a hand and summoned a thousand-foot wall between Collen and Mallon, booting out the oppressors for all time."

"I really must learn how to live for another few hundred years."

"What if it's always been like that? What if our holy books are just stories of powerful people who did something great long ago? People who got turned into gods by the passage of time — and by us wishing that there was something more for us to follow?"

Dante blinked. "It's a good thing we're in the middle of nowhere, because that might be the most heretical thing I've ever heard."

Blays squinted at the sky. "I suppose we'll never know. So we might as well believe so we don't accidentally piss any of them off."

The next day brought them within five miles of the Green Mountains. The day after that, Dante's loon twinged in the middle of the morning. It was Naran.

Mallon's army was on the march. It would arrive in Collen within three days.

8

Dante ran his hand down his face. "Three days until the Mallish are here? Why couldn't they have waited just one more day?"

"I don't know," Blays said. "But it's probably best to spend our remaining time complaining about it."

"You're right. We've got work to do." He jogged north toward the Green Mountains, leading his horse beside him.

Blays matched pace. "Do you realize you're going the wrong way? Or are we deserting?"

"If we leave this route open, they can use it to strike straight at Collen. We'll be trapped in a siege. It could be months before we're able to make it out."

"*We'll* be fine. I can shadowalk away at any time. And you can do your little mole act. It's just the entire Collen Basin that'll be trapped."

"At least my nightmares would have plenty of screaming faces to choose from. I'm finishing the barrier. If we ride back as fast as we can, using the nether's help, we'll beat the Mallish to the fort."

"Assuming the Mallish don't pull any forced marches. They probably won't, though. After all, the first thing they taught me in warring school was that it's always safe to make assumptions about the enemy's capabilities."

Dante knew it was a gamble. If the Mallish beat him to the

fort he'd set up near the king's road, the Colleners would only have a single sorcerer to their name: the Keeper. The Mallish ethermancers would rip straight through their lines.

But it would be just as much of a gamble to leave a gaping hole in their line of defense. A hole for which they had no back-up plan.

All in all, finishing the barrier took nearly a day and a half, along with all the remaining shaden in his possession. As he turned around to gallop south, he reached for the nether, but it was sluggish, reluctant. Of course. He'd been counting on being able to use it to refresh the horses' muscles, allowing them to make as much haste as possible, but somehow, it hadn't occurred to him that he'd use most of it up reshaping the earth.

They pushed their mounts as hard as they dared. By nightfall, they were within a day's ride of the fort where the Colleners intended to make their stand, but the Mallish had advanced within twelve miles. They could be upon the site by the next afternoon.

Cord's scouts had placed the enemy's numbers at five thousand men, including eight hundred cavalry. In sheer numbers, the Colleners were their equal. But the priests alone could tip a battle in favor of the Mallish. If Gladdic was among them, and he summoned his Andrac, it would turn into a slaughter.

Dante made himself awaken by four in the morning. Lighting the way with his torchstone, and then a small ball of ether, he galloped onwards, Blays right beside him. Their haste was for nothing. After sunrise, Naran informed him the Mallish were turning south. Bypassing the fortifications and making for the road along the coast—the road that remained open.

"Is Cord ready?" Dante said.

"She's preparing to march as we speak," Naran said. "Though it remains to be seen whether this is a ruse."

"After last time, the Mallish won't want to rush into another pitched battle. They'll try to slip past our guard and capture Collen while it's undefended."

"And we're sure we can stop them?"

"I think we've traveled together long enough for you to know we're never sure of anything."

Naran made a sound that was almost but not quite a chuckle.

"In that case, I look forward to finding out what we're about to do."

Dante hunched behind the pale green sagebrush, certain that one pair of eyes among the five thousand passing below would be sharp enough to spot him. He was perched on a hill on the west end of the Valley of Northern Spirits. Behind and to his right, gray seas churned under slate skies.

A Mallish cavalry vanguard had already claimed the eastern rim of the valley, holding it against the several hundred Colleners who had made a desperate march to cut the enemy off before they could penetrate deep into the basin. The remainder of the Mallish army was on the verge of catching up. Thousands of men in blue shirts gathered on the western rim.

A strip of land directly along the coast was raised thirty feet above the ocean, as well as the valley it sloped down to on the other side. It was here that the coastal road ran. No more than a hundred feet wide, the rise would have made a natural chokepoint, but the Mallish had beaten them there. Already, the infantry was starting to cross, forming two well-ordered columns.

Blays shifted beside him. "Any sign of Gladdic?"

"A few priests. But none that look like a shambling corpse."

"Is that a good thing or a bad thing?"

Dante hesitated. "I don't know. But it's what we've got."

The blueshirts marched onward, the stamp of their boots carrying on the damp, cool air. The smell of rotting kelp drifted up from rocky, crab-pocked beaches. Dante waited until the army was strung out along the entire length of the elevated road, then drew his knife and slipped it along his arm.

Blood trickled down his wrist. He dived into the dirt, rushing forward along the strip of land the road lay on. The earth there wasn't a solid mass of rock; rather, it was a mixed jumble of boulders and hard-packed silt and sand. Like the mouth of a river gone dry, then disguised by the deposits left by a few hundred years of oceanic waves.

He found a soft spot near the western bank and shook it loose. The outer wall collapsed into the ocean. Gray-green water rushed forward, sluicing inward. Dante softened the soil in front of it and the water surged on, churning and brown, pummeling all the way through the dirt and into the valley on the other side.

The ocean roared through the gap, ripping it wider. Men were screaming, running for the eastern edge of the strip. Dante opened a second channel there, cutting them off.

The water flooding through the two channels would have done away with the plug of boulders and silt by itself, but Dante had no intention of giving the Mallish priests the time to figure out an escape. He continued to jostle and weaken the soil, letting the titanic strength of the ocean take care of the rest. The strip of land shrank on all sides, opening a third gap through it, then a fourth.

Soldiers ran from the crumbling embankments. As the land dwindled beneath their feet, spilling them into the tide like grain poured into a boiling pot, a few flung themselves over the northern banks. The foamy eddies swallowed them up. Dante watched with a perspective that didn't feel entirely human.

On the eastern shore of the flooded valley, the Colleners unleashed a battle cry that could barely be heard over the torrential wash of the sea. They charged the Mallish vanguard, which had scattered from their formation, trying to get away before the flood claimed them next.

Dante watched from afar as the most organized of the enemy commanders redrew their lines. Most didn't. The Colleners punched through their slipshod ranks like a spear through untanned leather.

In a matter of minutes, five thousand men had been reduced to five hundred.

On the west bank, less than two hundred yards from where Dante crouched in the sagebrush, Mallish officers yelled commands to their men. Dante killed each officer with a bolt of black nether. The enlisted men cried out and danced back, covering their heads.

Dante reached out with his right hand. Black mist congealed over the fallen bodies, sinking into their skin. The dead staggered to their feet, launching themselves at the men they'd once commanded, biting ragged hunks of flesh from faces and necks.

Blays grunted. "I almost feel bad for them."

"If they'd taken the basin, they would have murdered every last person in it."

"I said 'almost.'"

Dante brought ten more undead to their feet. They grappled with the soldiers and made clumsy hacks with their swords. After a brief skirmish, the surviving soldiers broke, streaming west through the yellow grass.

"Why are you letting them go?" Blays said.

"So that they'll be able to tell King Charles the story of what happened here."

The entire valley had flooded for miles inland, running all the way to where Dante had started his barricade of ridges and ravines. He and Blays rode north along the new arm of the sea. The water was as brown as tilled earth, sloshing chaotically as it made sense of its new shape.

The waterway was at least a quarter of a mile across at its narrowest, widening to a mile or more at others. Conceivably, the Mallish could sail a fleet up it and debark on the eastern bank, but with a few watchmen along the coast, the Colleners would have no troubles defending it. The rocky cliffs bordering the shore would prevent a landing elsewhere.

The barrier was complete.

They swung around the northern tip of the inlet and struck south along the eastern shore. Blays scanned the horizons. "Suppose the Walking Fish made it out?"

"No idea," Dante said. "And I'm not sure if I want them to have."

Blays laughed. "You're in a dark mood these days."

"That's the natural reaction to getting jerked around." He was quiet for a moment. "The norren are stubborn. But they aren't stupid. After we found the Face of Dozundo, Kadda knew we weren't just lunatics. She would have people watching for any signs of trouble."

"Then I'm sure they had a great time watching the giant, inescapable flood."

"We warned them. We did everything they asked of us. If they chose to stay, then that's on them."

Riders appeared ahead. Cord galloped at the front of the Colleners who'd crushed the Mallish vanguard, grinning like she'd gone mad. She reined her mount to a stop, dust blossoming from its hooves.

"Friends!" She carried her wheel in one hand. Both the point of its spear and the iron ball on its butt were coated in blood. "Do you know what we've done?"

"Won a war?" Blays said. "Or are you referring to this brand new beach you've acquired?"

"We did more than win. As I killed the Mallish, I felt the calling of the gods. This was where they always meant for us to triumph. We've fulfilled our destiny!"

Around her, the other soldiers thrust up blades, spears, and fists and screamed at the sky.

"Collen is free!" Cord bellowed. "Today and forever, Collen is *free!*"

The atmosphere among the other soldiers was equally ecstatic. Almost religious in its fervor. When Dante and Blays returned to the city of Collen, they were greeted with such overwhelming gratitude Dante was afraid his ass would fall off from all the kissing.

Men rolled kegs of beer into the street, pouring cups for any and all. People danced in the squares while women strung strips of red cloth between the upper windows of the buildings. Boggs had arranged a great feast for them, peppered asparagus and quail eggs, venison with gravy, squares of almond paste served at the end. The volume of beer tapped for the occasion was enough to flood the Valley of Northern Spirits all over again.

"Have you ever seen people this happy?" Blays said between bites of red venison. At a nearby table, two men were in the process of falling out of their seats from laughter. Others were dancing with their plates in hand, asparagus spilling to the tile floor.

"No," Dante said. "But then again, I've never seen people celebrating the end of nine hundred years of armed occupation."

Until that moment, he'd felt removed from the outrageous good cheer of the Colleners. But when he put their achievement into words, he was brightened. No matter how much awful shit had come attached to the victory, they had nonetheless done some good for the world.

He was kept up late by the well wishes of a steady stream of farmers, who in Collen were granted the esteem of minor lords. At last, he was allowed to sleep. He dreamed of walking a world free from people, questing in perfect solitude. As he moved on, the landscape shifted around him with each step, and he was supposed to find a silver doorway, with the other side holding the answers to all his questions. Yet every time he glimpsed it and tried to walk toward it, the world shifted again, and the doorway disappeared.

When he woke, he summoned a meeting of the Hand at their customary balcony. To his lack of surprise, no one was in a state to convene until well into the afternoon. Even the Keeper had the glassy eyes and flushed skin of someone who'd struggled valiantly to empty a keg all by herself.

"I'd congratulate you on your victory," Dante said. "But from the look of your face, you probably don't remember it."

Boggs laughed raspily. "And as soon as we're done at this table, I'll be getting back to the one with venison and ale on it."

"We would never be here without you," the Keeper croaked. "Thank you for your aid. And for playing the part given you."

Dante raised his eyebrows. "The part was 'given' to me? More like 'thrust upon.'"

"Clobbered by, as if with a giant mallet," Blays said.

"Ground up and fed to, like corn to a fatted calf."

"You have made your point," the Keeper said. "Regardless, you will always have friends—and a home—in Collen. Will you require horses for your journey back to Narashtovik?"

"You think we're leaving?" Dante frowned out at the sunny fields below the butte. "I don't see any snows yet."

"Mallon is defeated. They won't have time for a third attack before winter. I doubt that they have the will to continue the war at all."

"I expect you're right. But this isn't the first time the Collen Basin's booted them out, is it? They've always come back. It might take years, but the king's army will return."

"Let them!" Cord pounded her fist on the table. "You've built a barrier from one end of our nation to the other. If they want to shed their blood against it, we'll use it to water our wheat."

"It isn't the barrier I'm concerned about. Not when they have a much easier route into Collen."

He unfolded a map he'd copied from one of their own. Setting his finger over Bressel, he moved out to sea, tracing his way along the coast.

"Our coasts are sheer cliffs," Boggs said. "But they can make landfall in the Strip. Come straight up through our guts."

Dante tapped the coastline. "That's what I'd do. If you want this victory to last, you're going to need allies. Starting with the Strip of Alebolgia."

"They will have no desire to ally with us," the Keeper said. "They wouldn't even sell us grain."

Blays twirled a knife in the air, catching it by the blade. "That was before you kicked King Charles' ass clean off his hips. Go to them now, while the afterglow of your victory's still blinding everyone, and they might switch sides."

"Even if they don't, you can't leave the matter there," Dante said. "The cities of the Strip are ruled by individual families, right?"

"Dynastic houses," Boggs said.

"Families with fancy titles. Go straight to the top and see if they'll support you."

"I been running the Twill business for years now. I know that nobody does nothin' out of the goodness of their hearts."

"It's one thing to run a business. It's another to run a kingdom. There are always houses who aren't happy with the current order. If the ruling house isn't willing to help you, we might have to replace it with one that is."

They prepped for the trip that same day. Dante was fairly sure the news of the battle would reach the coastal cities on its own, but just in case rumor was sleepier than normal, he had Boggs dispatch a rider to the south. It would be best if the houses had a few days to gossip and scheme amongst each other before the Collenese delegation arrived.

They left the next morning: Boggs, Dante, Blays, and the Keeper, who seemed hellbent to take every opportunity she could to violate her oath not to leave the Reborn Shrine. Then again, considering the Reborn Shrine was in the midst of being rebuilt from the ground up, remaining in it would be something of a health hazard.

They took a small retinue of servants and soldiers as well. Dante thought about using the time to ask the Keeper to show him more of the ether, but the thought of spending so much time talking with her was exhausting. Maintaining his temper while he traveled with her was hard enough.

After two days of riding, the landscape shifted to rolling hills of tall grass and stunted trees. Small farms scattered the slopes, trellises of vines growing in orderly rows. Most had already been harvested, but a few sections sagged with bunches of red grapes hanging from the vine.

"What do they think they're doing?" Blays said. "Aren't the frosts due any day?"

"Yes, forget the Strip." Dante tightened his reins. "We must save the wine!"

"Laugh all you like. When dinner comes, and you have nothing to drink but water, you'll have no one to blame but yourself."

"Freezing them's the whole point," Boggs said. "Makes the sweetest wine you ever drank. The price they pull is even sweeter."

According to Boggs, whose trade had left him well-informed with regards to Collen's neighbors, the land they were currently crossing was under the control of a hilltop city called Poloa. Originally, it had been a colony of Cavana, the port city they were headed toward, but over the last several decades, its burgeoning wine trade had swelled its wealth and influence to the point where it had broken loose.

Poloa, Cavana, and as many as a dozen other small cities composed the Strip of Alebolgia. This was a geographical title, not a political one: the cities were regularly at war with each other. At the moment, however, Alebolgia was trying out a radical new notion known as "peace." By presenting a unified front, it was hoping to leverage more favorable deals from Mallon, Parth, and various trade partners to the south and out to sea.

The group that had forged this alliance was House Itiego. Cavanese spice merchants, they'd amassed a gigantic fortune which they were currently employing to make their home city the jewel of the Strip. With most of the coast being rugged cliffs or jagged reefs, the city was the only deepwater port in the area large enough to accommodate a Mallish fleet. If the Colleners could convince the Itiegos to deny Mallon the right to make landing, the basin would be all but closed to attack.

Their delegation arrived on a blustery afternoon. Cavana was dug into a steep hill overlooking the ocean, its levels descending in concentric rings down to its heart, the bustling piers where it did business. Arms of rock embraced the bay, protecting it from rough seas. Ships jammed the waterway.

The grander houses were built with their backs against the hillside, pale stone with long, slanted roofs to keep the rain off the verandas. The people of Alebolgia had the same olive-toned skin as in Mallon and Collen, but the streets jostled with sailors and merchants from all corners of the known world. It was far smaller than Bressel or Narashtovik, home to no more than thirty thousand residents, yet it felt no less vibrant.

House Itiego occupied a small hill of its own. Its sandstone central tower climbed to nearly three hundred feet, overlooking a sprawling compound of high walls and lush courtyards. The wrought iron gates were decorated with the albatrosses of the Itiego family crest.

Boggs had sent a messenger ahead to announce their arrival. The gates were opened by pikemen wearing purple tabards bearing the white albatross. The Colleners were greeted by a man with thigh-high boots and a collar so big that a good gust of wind might blow him halfway to the Plagued Islands.

"Welcome to House Itiego." The man bowed over one knee. "I am Gareno. Master Itiego awaits you in the Hall of Soaring Sails."

Grooms materialized to lead their horses away. Several of the Colleners' servants went with them. Gareno took the rest of the expedition to the central keep, a round and massive sandstone fortress with two shorter rectangular wings of the house extending in a V from the center.

Inside, sunlight spilled through high windows, splashing the black marble floor. The hall was an immense cylinder, the walls rising for thirty feet before bending inward to meet in a dome. A walkway encircled the wall just below where the ceiling began to curve, protected by a railing of thin copper bars. Great sheets of dirty canvas hung from the walls, completely at odds with the dark bleakwood furniture and copper fixtures.

Gareno's assurance that Itiego was awaiting them turned out to be highly optimistic. While they waited for his arrival, Gareno, who was either a high-ranking servant or a low-ranking noble, told them the history of the canvas sheets, which turned out to be from some of the House's most famous ships.

He'd gotten halfway around the room when hard steps echoed from the front doors. Gareno smiled and bowed over his knee. "My friends! Give welcome to Tanelo Itiego, Lord of House Itiego, Prime Navigator of Cavana, and first Speaker of the Confederated Cities of Alebolgia."

The Colleners made their bows. Dante winced. Mallish nobles had trained them to bow as inferiors rather than as foreign equals, but though Lord Itiego surely noticed this lack of worldliness, no sign of it touched his expression. Like Gareno, he wore an enormous upthrust collar, which enfolded his head like a palm cupping an egg. He had hard, narrow features like carved wood and a long black mustache that drooped below his chin. His boots were turned down above the knee. He wore a dark coat fitted at the waist that was crossed with multiple belts.

As Gareno introduced them, Itiego gave them each a respectful nod. His gaze lingered for an extra moment or two on Blays, who could have passed for a Collener, and then Dante, whose features were a picture of the basin's mortal enemies.

"In Cavana," Itiego said in staccato-voweled, accented Mallish, "we have a saying: what separates us from the fish is that, among people, sometimes it is the smaller who wins. Congratulations, then, to the victory of the smaller fish."

Cord grinned, rolling her shoulders. "Are you calling me short?"

"Only your odds, General."

"Ah! Then I won't have to give you a display of *how* we sent the Mallish running."

Itiego's eyebrows flickered, as if he couldn't decide how to feel, then he laughed. "The only red I tolerate being spilled on these floors is wine. Be seated, and let's have some."

They took their places around a bleakwood table. Servants arrived with pewter cups of wine; Itiego toasted the Collen Basin's victory. Dante was no expert on vintages, but every sip of the deep red seemed to taste like a different.

"I am happy to hear the war concluded so swiftly," Itiego said. "Given the nature of my last contact with Collen, I was afraid a siege might prove very costly."

Blays gave Dante a flat look. Dante blinked twice, the equivalent of a nod. Itiego was making a gambit to get them to boast about how exactly they'd ruined a superior Mallish army in the open field—he'd heard rumors, no doubt, but was now trying to determine how much truth was in them.

And thus how much, if any, he needed to fear the people in front of him.

"We took a risk," Cord said. "And our victory was so large Gashen must treasure us like his own children."

"Gashen?" Itiego raised a thin dark brow. "Or Phannon?"

Boggs chuckled. "Got to wonder what the Mallish did to piss off the lords of war *and* the sea."

"I'm sure their priests will be scurrying to divine the same thing. In any event, I'm glad events turned out as they have."

"That so? Last time we sent people your way, you seemed happy to send 'em back empty-handed."

"There was nothing happy in that decision."

"In hindsight, I'm sure there wasn't. But only because you gambled on the wrong horse."

Itiego stared Boggs down. Dante wasn't sure if it was a rebuke, or if he was just taking the man in. Boggs' face was chapped and weatherbeaten. His speech was as plain as yesterday's bread. He was a good fit to lead the farmers and soldiers of Collen. It was an open question as to what kind of fit he would make with the lords and merchants of Alebolgia.

"Publicly, I said many things to many people," Itiego said. "In the interior of my heart, however, I hoped that Collen would win. Not because I admire you so much, mind you. Nor because of any especial dislike for the Mallish. Rather because your survival—and, one hopes, your growth—is better for balance. Just as you must prefer that the cities of the Strip remain independent and not proxies of the empire on your doorstep."

"That is so." In the echoing hall, the Keeper's deep voice sounded like a godly command. "And that is what brings us here. For the first time in years, Collen is free. For the first time in ages, we will keep it that way. We have secured our borders with Mallon. We request that Cavana closes its port to their army."

"Why would we do such a thing?"

"It's as you just said. If you let them land their troops, and they steal our lands from us once more, then they also steal the balance of the region."

Itiego leaned back. Without breaking eye contact with the Keeper, he accepted a glass of wine from a nearby servant. "Do you understand why the cities of Alebolgia fare so well?"

"An abundance of wise leadership?" Blays said.

"Which includes an immunity to flattery. Are any of you familiar with *The Gold Road*?"

Dante nodded. "I've read it."

Itiego smiled strangely. "I would have thought you'd consider it heresy."

"Do you think that makes it *less* interesting?"

"In Cavana—indeed, across the entire Strip of Alebolgia—you might say our only heresy is the concept of heresy itself. This is taught in *The Gold Road*. In it, Carvahal shows that everything must flow. Oceans and rivers. People and currency. And ideas, too. Just as still water goes stagnant, so does a still mind. It must be fed with a constant flux of ideas."

"That sounds good enough," Blays said. "But flowing water is the kind with all the monsters in it."

"To dam the waters is to damn your self," Itiego continued as if Blays had never spoken. "That is why we call nothing heretical; to do so would be to place a dam on ideas. It is just as important not to place a dam on trade, for currency is the water that nourishes civilization." He paused, thin eyebrows raised, letting that sink in. "This is why I can make no agreement to cease business with Mallon."

"You could still sell them whatever you like," Boggs said. "All we're askin' is you don't let them march an army in through our back door."

"You fail to understand. They pay for the right. To sell them this right costs us nothing. To take it away is to take prosperity from my people. And to threaten *my* people with war. For picture this scene."

Itiego stood, pacing around the table, gazing up at the sails strung from the walls. "You are Charles IV, upon your throne. Your province of Collen has thrown out your military. Repulsed a second attack. Now, when you approach Cavana—long a friend, open to all offers—Cavana shuts you out of its ports.

"Very curious. This act violates Cavana's deepest principles. Why would it do such a thing? Has Collen paid them to close their port? So you make an offer of your own to reopen it. It is a good offer, but sadly, Cavana turns it down. So you make a second offer. One that Collen can't possibly have matched."

He clicked his heels together and swiveled toward Boggs. "What happens now? If Cavana accepts Mallon's offer, then the agreement with Collen is null. If Cavana rejects the offer, it exposes an alliance between itself and Collen. This means that Cavana is now an enemy of Mallon. Isn't it thus within Mallon's rights to pursue war against Cavana? To pluck the jewel of Alebolgia and add it to its own crown?"

Itiego stopped, face titled forward, hands clasped behind his back. Silence fell over the room, as heavy as wet canvas.

Cord stood. "Have faith in your strength! You can defeat them as we did!"

"But General, that is not the point. Win or lose, war destroys *both* sides. I will have no part of it—not today, and not ever."

9

Raxa stood in the doorless room behind the chapel wall, feeling the nether drain from her body. Another two seconds, maybe three, and it would be gone.

She'd come too far to lose the loot. She snatched up the second *Cycle of Arawn* and stumbled toward the wall she'd walked in through. She was already falling out of the shadows, the light and smoke fading to plain darkness. Her right heel caught in something firm. She spilled onto the floor of the room beyond, the boot ripping from her foot.

She spun about. The boot jutted from the wall, its heel embedded in the rock. In dumb disbelief, she set down the book, grabbed her boot, and pulled. It was like trying to uproot an oak with your bare hands. She fell on her back, breathing hard.

She was on the fourth floor of the chapel, with two guards outside the doors, in the middle of the Sealed Citadel.

And she didn't have a drop of juice left.

Squeezing her eyes tight, she gave herself a moment to scream — internally, mentally — and to pound her fists against the lush rug.

With that task completed, Raxa took inventory. She had the book. And judging from the way it had stolen the shadows from her, as well as the blinding, terrifying light it had cast when she'd seen it within the netherworld, it was the true copy. The *first* copy. The one that, according to rumor, could turn you into a sorcerer.

She also had a way out. Vess' exit. What she didn't have was a way to get to the exit without being riddled with arrows, spears, and bolts of shadow.

Would have to do it the old-fashioned way.

On her arrest, the guards had confiscated everything but her clothes. Searching the room, she found a small knife, if you could call it that—designed for trimming quills and such, you'd have to put it in the exact right spot to kill someone with it. Still, better than nothing.

No matter how hard she tried, she couldn't pull her boot loose from the wall. Instead, she took off her other shoe and hid it under a chair, then draped a table cover over the stuck boot. She put the book she'd taken from the case back on top of the glass. Somebody might wonder what idiot had left it out of its case, but at least it wouldn't look like anything was stolen.

Long black curtains hung beside the windows. She took one down. Using the knife to start the tear, she ripped off a length of cloth and wrapped it around her head, leaving a slit for her eyes. She wrapped the remainder of the curtain around her torso, tucking her book underneath it snug against her back.

She climbed into a window and took a peek out. Forty feet down to a cobbled surface. Not the sort of thing you wanted to fall from. At the same time, she didn't want to leave a makeshift rope dangling forty feet to the ground. Someone would spot that before she'd made it over the walls. She pulled down a second curtain, cut it into four wide strips, and knotted them together. She tied one end around her left wrist.

She went back to the window and checked the stars. Closing in on one o'clock. At three o'clock, the guards were scheduled to make a change. One of the sentries had been paid very well by Vess to leave a door unlocked in the outer walls. Raxa would enter the door, climb the stairs to the top of the wall, then jump down into a hay wagon Vess had parked outside.

Raxa was tempted to kill time reading the book, but you never played with your loot before you had it home. Good thing she waited. Not five minutes later, a key scrabbled in the lock to the door.

She popped to her feet and into the window. As she dropped out, the door's hinges squeaked open. Raxa gritted her teeth, stomach flopping as she began to fall. With the rope of curtains tied around her left wrist, she grabbed hold of the loose end with her right hand, forming a loop. She snared this around the body of a gargoyle. The rope snapped taut, slamming her against the outer wall of the chapel.

She dangled, heart racing like it was ready to gallop out of her throat. Above her, men's voices murmured from inside the room she'd just vacated.

She was secure, but if they glanced out the window, she was done. Holding tight to the loose end of the curtain, she let out some slack, lowering herself until her foot touched another gargoyle. She crouched atop it, holding on with her left hand, then let go of the curtain with her right, gathering it in.

Looping the curtain around the gargoyle she was standing on now, she lowered herself to the third floor window. This looked into a dark room. She stuffed herself into the window and waited.

Two hours later, the bells of the Cathedral of Ivars rang, the clapper muffled so as not to wake the entire city. Raxa bided another five minutes, then used the loop of curtains to descend the face of the chapel. The feel of her bare toes against solid ground had never felt so good.

She untied the rope from her wrist, watching the night. She'd spent the last two hours watching the patrol routes of the sentries. She waited for a gap in the coverage, then crossed the courtyard at a brisk walk, coming to the tall outer wall. She counted down doors to the one Vess had bribed the guard to keep unlocked. She tried it. Stuck fast. Heart back to doing its best impression of a stallion, she tried again. It jerked open.

Whispering a dozen curses, she moved into the gloomy stairwell. Smelled like sweaty men. She jogged up it, bare feet silent on the stone treads, and barged right into a guard on his way down.

He swore, slapping a palm against the wall for support. "What the hell—?"

Raxa swept the rope of curtains around his throat and pulled it as tight as she could, entangling the fabric around her elbows for extra leverage. The man gave a single strangled gasp, then whacked at her head with his fists, but they were so close he couldn't put any strength behind the blows. Within seconds, he sagged. She kept the pressure on until his eyes bulged from his purple face. His weight dragged down against her makeshift rope.

Shit. *Shit.* Nowhere to put the body. Would have to get over the wall before someone found him. She left it and hurried up the stairs, poking her head from the trapdoor-style entrance to the top of the wall. And caught her first break: no guards in sight in either direction.

The wagon was supposed to be ten paces ahead. Raxa hurried along the merlons, counting steps. At ten, she stopped and leaned over the wall. The wagon wasn't there.

Her chest froze. Had Vess betrayed her? Gotten arrested? It was a thirty foot fall to the ground. The walls were smooth rock, deliberately unclimbable. The ground below was dirt rather than pavement, but that wouldn't help much. Looking closer, she spotted a small pile of something directly below her, but it was too dark to say what.

A silhouette moved along the wall. Coming her way. She grabbed both ends of her makeshift rope, slung it around a merlin, and swung over the side. She jerked to a stop after falling six feet, the rope sliding from her right hand. Between the length of the rope and her arms, she'd cut nearly ten feet from the descent, but there was still a hell of a lot of space between her and the ground.

The rope slipped out from her fingers.

She flattened herself against the wall, slowing herself, but this pushed her away after a fall of a few feet. Empty air whisked past her, the rope of curtains fluttering behind her. The pile rushed to meet her. She got in position, landing with a crunch of straw. As she tucked into a roll, pain speared through her right ankle. She popped to her feet, ankle giving out beneath her.

Broken. No doubt. But hurried steps were smacking along the top of the wall. Already sweating cold drops, Raxa hobbled into the city as fast as she could.

~

"You're hurt."

"It's nothing." Raxa took a step toward the bench, limping hard. "That's not true. Hurts like Gashen whacked it with an axe handle."

"Let me see." Vess kneeled beside her, undoing the cloth Raxa had wrapped tight around her bare foot and lower leg, revealing an ankle so swollen you couldn't tell where the calf ended. "Broke good. Or else you need to start eating less frybread and more fish. What happened out there?"

Raxa stared through the darkness of the sweet-smelling courtyard. She'd considered stashing the book on her way there, claiming she hadn't been able to find it. If she had what she thought it was, it was worth killing for.

But if she was going to pay back the Citadel for what they'd done to the Order—and what they'd tried to do to her adoptees—she was going to need help. If Vess had inclinations to betray her, she'd had plenty of opportunities already.

Raxa gave Vess the rundown, altering everything that had to do with shadowalking. At the end, she shot Vess a dark look. "What happened to *your* end of the deal? Not a great time to cheap out on the wagon."

Vess shook her head. "We put the wagon where I said the wagon would be put. The guards, they ran us off. I dumped out some straw for you. Best I could do."

Vess offered her a drop of whiteweed to help with the pain. Raxa swallowed it, working her tongue around to be rid of the bitterness.

"Guess a broken ankle is a great excuse to get some reading done," she said. "Want to take a look?" She removed the book from the makeshift sling she'd wrapped around her back.

Seeing the white tree on the cover, Vess' face went as sober as a Mallish priest. "Sure this is safe?"

"It's a book that can supposedly turn ordinary people into sorcerers. It's about as safe as swinging a sword by the wrong end."

"Well, we got it. Waste of good taking not to check it out."

Raxa propped the heavy tome on her knees and opened the

front cover. There were no signatures in this copy. She flipped through a few freakish illustrations to the first page of text.

She frowned. "What the hell is this?"

Vess leaned over, neck extended as she examined the page. "Mallish."

Raxa paged forward. "Why would the holiest book of the Gaskan region be written in Mallish?"

"Don't know. Want to complain? Or to hear me tell you what it is that it says?"

Raxa examined her for signs she was joking—Vess couldn't even speak Gaskan right. With nothing to lose, she handed the heavy book to the other woman. "By all means."

Vess ran her finger over the first few sentences, muttering under her breath. She cleared her throat. In slow and sometimes backtracking words, she began to read. Within the first minute, Raxa knew what she was hearing: the story of how Arawn came for and eventually spared the life of a man named Janth.

Vess stumbled here and there, complaining that she hadn't seen several of the words before and doubted if they were Mallish. Despite this, Raxa got the gist of nearly everything, helped by how often she'd heard the story before.

After they talked briefly, concluding that there was nothing that stood out to them, Vess read onward, telling tales of kings, heroes, sorcerers, and gods. After the better part of an hour, Raxa stopped her.

Vass raised an eyebrow. "Feel anything?"

"From what?" Raxa pinched her upper lip. "These are just... stories."

"In the church every week, what do they do? Tell stories."

"How is any of this going to teach us to throw the nether around?

"Don't know. How do stories teach you how to live? Act? Be?"

Raxa quashed a sigh. Vess read on, but it was more of the same. As dawn neared, Raxa was having a hard time keeping her eyes open despite the steady throb of pain in her ankle.

Noticing this, Vess tucked a ribbon into the book to mark her place and closed the covers. "Think we done for tonight, yeah?"

"Yeah." Raxa rubbed her eyes. "Question. When we go our

separate ways for the day, who gets the book?"

"I do. You can't even read it."

"But I'm the one who snagged it. At great personal risk."

Vess shrugged. "Don't have a head full of dumb. You're the master thief in this city. I take it from you, and you just take it right back."

"Ha," Raxa said. "We'll split it."

"Cut it in half? Good thinking." Vess reached for a knife.

Raxa slapped at Vess' hand. "Are you crazy? If this is what we think it is, we can't *desecrate* it. Arawn would burn us to a cinder, then send a plague of locusts to eat the ashes. We'll alternate nights with it. You can have it first."

"You got more trust than most of us."

"Maybe. Or maybe I'm just that sure that if you run off, I *will* find you."

Vess grinned and helped Raxa to her feet. The other woman whistled softly to one of her goons, ordering him to send for a horse. He came back with a donkey. Raxa didn't care. At that point, her ankle hurt so bad she would have ridden home on a flatulent goat.

Before sleeping, she had the Order's physician set her ankle. Wasn't fun. A hefty swallow of rum and whiteweed helped.

When she woke up, she grabbed a mug of tea, spiked it with more whiteweed to take the teeth from her pain, and tore through the day's business. As soon as she was done, she sent a runner to Vess, who showed up an hour later.

Raxa smiled. "You didn't run off with it."

"Decided it wouldn't be fair." Vess nodded at her splinted leg. "With that, you'd never catch me."

They retired to Raxa's office. Vess opened the book and began to read. As she narrated stories of Jack Hand and Stathus the Wise, a weight mounted in Raxa's gut. Even when the *Cycle* was talking about the feats of the greatest nethermancers in the history of the shadows, there was no mention of *how* they did what they did. What if the rumors she'd heard about its power to train you were as wildly off the mark as most rumors were? What if they reached the end of the book—a process that could waste weeks, given how long it was—and found they were no different from when they started?

"That's that." Vess closed the book, standing and stretching her arms about her head.

Raxa glanced at the window. It had gone dark, which was a surprise, but it couldn't have been that late. "Come on. There's way more night than this."

"Got a thing needs doing that needs me to do it. Keep the book. Maybe you can't read it, but it's thick enough you can use it to prop your foot on."

Raxa grinned. "See you tomorrow, asshole."

Once Vess was gone, Raxa hobbled to her door, locked it, and sat down across from the book. Sitting in front of her, the *Cycle* didn't look like anything special. Old, yeah. But nothing like the nethereal hellstorm that had nearly gotten her trapped inside a doorless room that was hardly big enough to sit down in. Had that been the book itself? Or a boobytrap set to protect the book?

Grimacing, wary, she eased into the shadows.

As before, light spewed from the book like a lord expelling his fourth bottle of wine. Tendrils of darkness lashed from her to the pages. The shadows poured from her like blood. Her instincts were to jump out of the darkworld as fast as she could, but the book didn't seem to be hurting her. And this time, there was no danger of getting trapped.

Specks of darkness floated in the air, like mist churned up by the torrent of nether. She looked closer. The specks were tumbling toward her. Landing on her skin and sinking in. The book was draining her, yes.

This time, though, it was also giving something back.

Within moments, the book had sucked her dry, booting her out of the nether. Compared to the shining silver of the other world, the room around her was as dark as a cave. The weight on her stomach eased up. There *was* something potent about the book. All she had to do was find out how to unlock it.

They fell into a comfortable if frustrating routine: handle their responsibilities each morning, meet up by early afternoon, read the *Cycle* together until well after the sun had set. Day by day, Raxa's ankle hurt less and less. In the normal world, she still couldn't walk without a crutch, but in the netherworld, she was so light on her feet she felt no pain at all. If anything, visiting the other realm seemed to hasten her healing.

"Feel any power?" Vess asked a few nights into their efforts. "Any feel like you could clench your fist and make the walls fall down?"

Raxa shook her head. "The only thing I feel is the urge to go ask a priest why all their old heroes were so murderous. How about you?"

"Feel like I need to get one of my lowlings to write a book about *me*. Maybe we call it *The Cycle of Vess*."

It was like being dumped overboard far from sight of land. No way to tell which direction to head in. No way to tell if they were even getting close to something. It didn't take long before she was frustrated. Angry. Ready to toss the book in the bay and forget it.

But she had to press on. Until the nether was hers, she'd never be able to protect her people from the Citadel—or to take her revenge.

Whenever Vess hit a point where a nethermancer was doing his or her thing, Raxa took notes, quoting anything that might point to their methods. At the end of each session, she and Vess went back over everything Raxa had jotted down, phrases like "When Eyosa's breathing matched the nether, at last she felt it on her fingers" or "and so Kamrates spilled his blood, and the darkness flocked, and his foes fell before it."

Each night she had the book to herself, she stood before it in the shadows, watching it pull the nether from her body and into its pages, the black dust rising from it and settling into her skin. The first time she'd encountered the book, the process had been almost instant. After having four nights with it, though, it was taking twenty seconds before the *Cycle* drained her to nothing. And each time took a little longer than the last.

Because she was making progress? Or was the opposite true, and the book was slowing down because it was petering out, like an unbunged barrel getting down to its last few drops?

Midway through the night's reading session with Vess, Raxa stood, stretching her back. "Gonna hit the privy."

She walked into her office's front room, opening and shutting the door to the hallway. She shifted into the nether and moved back into her main office, where Vess was hunched over the book. Dark tendrils stretched between Vess and the *Cycle*, but they were much thinner than Raxa was used to, more like threads than yarn. There were hardly any dark specks in the air, either. Though the specks were sinking into Vess' skin, they seemed less excited about it. Like snow landing on cobbles and taking a long time to melt.

Whatever was happening to the two of them, it was happening at different rates. In hindsight, not that surprising. Everyone had the nether in them. According to some people, everyone could learn to use it, but in practice, the talent varied widely. Most could train for years and never learn to summon more than a drop.

That thought exposed a hundred others. Like ruins unearthed by a sudden flood. Funny how much you could forget if you tried. You didn't have one life, you had many, as separate from each other as towns strung out along a road. People liked to think their lives were a progression, a building-upon, as cohesive as a song, complete with crescendo. But it was more like a bard who'd gotten so drunk he couldn't remember which story he was telling. Every ten minutes he'd switch to a new one, leaving his audience annoyed and confused.

Vess turned a page. Raxa blinked. Still in the shadows. She returned to the foyer, dropped back into the plain world, and rejoined Vess at the table.

Vess glanced up. "Ready to go on?"

"Where else am I going to hear about how Jack Hand killed another rat?"

Vess smirked. She launched into a new story about one of the nethermancers who'd been imprisoned in a tower or a dungeon and was fiddling around with the rats in it. Raxa tried to listen, but it felt like her mind was ready to vomit. And her whole dinner was on its way up.

She closed her eyes and let it come.

~

Her mom had died giving birth to her. Her dad was a woodsman and they lived in a log shack in the pine forests outside the city. She remembered being happy. She remembered little else except for the way the sunlight pierced through the pine needles. The feeling of a blizzard outside while you had a fire and blankets inside. The spicy smell on her father's breath that she would recognize, years later, as rum.

When she was five, he cut himself while felling a tree—he'd probably been drunk—and the wound became infected. She told him to see a priest. He said they didn't have the money. He lay in bed with his rum, which he said would drive the infection out.

Within five days, he was too weak to get out of bed. He was pale and had dark streaks on the arm where he'd been hurt. He asked her to go get their neighbor, a young farmer named Garren who always talked about finding a wife. She did so. She brought Garren in and her father sent her outside. After a few minutes, Garren exited, gave her a tight smile, and headed to the city.

It was hours before Garren came back. Raxa's dad sent her outside again. When Garren walked out, he told her that her father wanted to see her.

The inside of the cabin smelled funny. Her dad gripped her hand tight. "Your aunt and uncle will be here tomorrow morning. They'll care for you."

"What about you?"

"I'll come for you when I'm better." He smiled. "It won't be long."

By morning, he was dead. Raxa waited all day, and then the next. Then she went through the forest to Garren's and told him what had happened. He said he was sorry to hear that.

"I can take care of you," he said. "And when you're older, we can take care of each other. After all, time turns stems into flowers."

He smiled. It was a selfish smile. When he went out to tend to his fields, Raxa ran into the city.

She looked for her aunt and uncle every day. As she searched, she learned the city was a place where if you wanted to eat, you had to steal. She got used to the taste of hard bread and soft cucumbers. There were other children there too, filthy and quick-footed. Most would steal from her if they saw she had something, but some became her friends. They helped her look for her aunt and uncle, warned each other when the city watch was coming, shared crusts and cheese when they'd nicked more than they could eat.

The streets had a fleetingness to them. People came and went. Sometimes they came back after a few days, but sometimes she saw them months later, servants in the retinue of the rich. Often, she never saw them again.

Often, she was cold. Always, she was hungry. In winter, which in Narashtovik lasted nearly five months, she was both. She still wasn't sure how she'd made it through the first winter. By the time the air began to warm, the points of her hips and shoulders could pierce leather. Before the snow melted, her shoes rotted off. She tried to eat them, but her jaw got sore before they were soft enough to swallow.

The snows still hadn't thawed. Ice cut the soles of her feet, leaving bloody tracks behind her. Every day, the pain got worse; soon, she might not be able to walk at all. In the streets, your feet were your life. Couldn't walk, and you couldn't steal. Couldn't run, and someone would catch you.

And the kids and the crazies weren't the only ones out there. Men walked through the crowds, faces as cold as a blizzard. Hunting those like Raxa. The children of none that no one would miss. If your feet hurt too bad to run, they'd take you. You'd be one of the street people who disappeared and never came back.

She tried to hole up, giving herself the chance to heal, but if she hid out for more than a day, her stomach hurt worse than her feet. She limped from block to block, trailing blood through the snows that fell every afternoon. Raxa prayed to Arawn to melt the ice, but it only got worse.

One day, on her way to the alley where Waldon the baker sometimes took pity and gave them his old bread, the hurt got worse than it had ever been. Like nails were being pounded up through the bottom of her feet. Her vision speckled over from pain. She dropped to her knees, palm braced on the freezing ground.

She could get up. Maybe she could get home. But that would be it. The only question from there was whether she froze or starved.

She hung her head. Footsteps crunched in front of her. Raxa opened her eyes, expecting a beating from a city watchman sick of yet another of Narashtovik's fleas falling in the middle of a public street. Instead, she saw another girl, a year or two older, too dirty to be from anywhere but the streets.

"Take these." The girl held out a pair of shoes.

Raxa frowned. Trap? But it didn't matter anymore, did it? She reached out, took the shoes. They were worn and cracked, but they were only a little bit loose. She smiled and tried not to cry.

The girl's name was Alna. She helped Raxa until Raxa's feet healed up. Like that, they were best friends. For a year, they roamed the city together, fishing coins from pockets, nabbing broccoli and apples and squash from stalls, ducking the older kids. Alna was keen-eyed, fast to make a decision. She could read the mood of the street like a farmer read the weather.

The day it happened was sunny, warm, a day and a season after Alna had saved Raxa's life. Raxa had only been away for a minute—running back to one of their stashes to pick up their fishing hook to try in the bay—but when she jogged back to the alley where Alna was waiting, it was empty.

She ran into the street. Her eyes leaped at once to a tall man striding down the street, a young girl held limply in his arms. Raxa sprinted after them. She hadn't gotten three steps before another man turned. His face was as cold as all the other takers. He strode toward her, hands open by his sides.

Raxa turned down a side street. Empty except for a few vacant stalls merchants had parked out of the way. The man was almost on her. He lunged for her. His sleeve pulled back, revealing a tattoo of a spider on his wrist. She dived behind a stall.

Footsteps moved around the side of the stall. A shudder racked Raxa. A shadow and a shimmer seemed to pass over the world, dimming it. The man swung around the side of the stall. He seemed to look right through Raxa, then swore and ran further down the alley. As the world brightened around Raxa, the man's steps faded to nothing.

She edged back to the way she'd come in. Alna was gone.

Raxa never saw her again.

Alone, she grew reckless. Stealing coin purses, whole meat pies, packets of spice. She knew the city well enough to get away—most times. Other times, she caught a beating, but it almost felt good. And now and then when she was running or hiding, the dimness came over her, and it was like they couldn't see her at all.

She was jogging away from one such escape when she bumped right into a pair of legs. A woman stood over her, tall and tanned, looking as calm and strong as one of the statues outside the big cathedral where the monks shooed her away with brooms.

"Do you like this life?" the woman said.

Raxa turned to run. The woman made a subtle gesture. Invisible hands seemed to grab hold of the bottoms of her shoes—the shoes Alna had given her—locking her in place.

The tall woman gazed down at her. "I can give you a different one."

Raxa thought about spitting at her. "Different what?"

"A different life. No more hunger. No more stealing. No more being hunted."

"And what do I have to do for you?"

"The hardest thing of all: you have to learn."

Raxa should have been afraid, but she'd come to hate the city. If she tried to leave it, and something happened to her, then maybe that was okay. Maybe that was what was supposed to happen after what she let happen to Alna.

The tall woman's name was Yona. She had a horse. They rode out of the city through fields, pine forests, and hills full of huge, watchful men. Next came mountains, a valley of lakes and another city; past this, a grassy plain. Then black cliffs like storm clouds strung across the end of the world.

Yona called it Pocket Cove. There was no city, just the cliffs, the beach, and the ocean beyond. A few dozen women and girls lived in the cliffs. For the first time since her dad had died, she was given proper food: crab soup in salty broth; mussels mixed with crispy, brackish reeds; chunks of whitefish on beds of seaweed mixed with tiny orange eggs that popped between her teeth in salty little snaps.

If the food was the best thing, the second best was that she no longer had to look over her shoulder every second she was awake. There was no town watch. No bigger kids looking to rob her. No frozen-faced men with spiders tattooed on their wrists.

"Why did you bring me here?" she asked after a few days.

"Because I think you can do something special." Yona softened her face in what was almost a smile. "You're starting to look healthy enough. It's time to begin."

And then she taught Raxa to shadowalk.

Raxa had already been touching the fringes of the other world. But only enough to hide herself from view, and only if she didn't move. Under Yona's tutelage, Raxa learned to enter the netherworld itself. To walk in a land of blazing silver and deepest shadow. Finding it was like finding home.

"That was almost too easy," Yona said after a few months of honing her skill. "But that's only a small fraction of what I think you can do. The nether you follow into the darkness—you're going to learn to wield it."

It was nearing the end of the year, the waves lashed by wind and rain. Even so, Yona took Raxa out on the beach and told her things about the shadows. Raxa already knew how to see them, so Yona tried to show her how to touch them. Lesson after lesson, Raxa tried, and she failed.

The rains turned to snow. One morning, with the wind biting Raxa's ears, Yona told her to strip down to her skin and swim out into the waves until Yona told her it was okay to come back.

"But it's so cold," Raxa said.

"That will bring you closer to the nether."

"Why?"

"Because it will help you to understand death."

Raxa didn't understand any of that. "But I don't want to."

"When you agreed to come with me, you made a vow." Yona stood over her. "Now strip. And swim."

Raxa looked up and down the beach. There was no one to go

to. The cliffs hemmed them in; there was nowhere to run. Hating Yona, trying not to cry at the unfairness of it, she took off her clothes.

The water was so cold her muscles locked up like rocks. Yona yelled her onward. She paddled into the waves, the breakers smashing down on her head. Salt water flooded her lungs. She turned back for shore, fighting to keep her head above water. Another wave swept her into the icy, swirling madness. Just as she was ready to let out her breath and inhale the cold water, sand scraped underfoot. She heaved herself ashore, bedraggled with kelp.

"I didn't tell you it was time to come back." Yona's voice was low, the warning of a growling dog. "Go inside."

She was left alone in the darkness of her room. After three days of solitude, Yona brought her back to the beach. Again, she tried to show Raxa how to touch the shadows. Further down the beach, a young girl swam in the swells, vanishing under walloping walls of gray water. She was watched by a grown woman standing among the kelp stranded above the tideline.

In time, the woman waved her in. The girl crawled in on hands and knees. She was nude. Her sodden black hair was stuck to her face, but Raxa identified her as Luru, who'd been brought to the Cove a few weeks before her. At the woman's orders, Luru stood naked to the wind. She shuddered so hard she fell to her side. The older woman made no effort to help her up.

Day after day, Raxa got no closer to being able to touch the nether. Yona, once so optimistic about Raxa's potential, grew puzzled, then short. She sent Raxa out on another swim, then a third. Raxa tried her best to do as Yona said, but the shadows always seemed to be just out of her reach.

Two months later, with the worst of the storms behind them and hints of spring in the air, Yona told her she was to go up to the Fingers, the black cliffs above the bay. She would be there alone for three days. It would be tough, and it would be painful, but it was that same fear and pain that would help her understand the shadows.

Raxa thrust out her lower jaw. "It's going to be cold and wet, isn't it? How come you make me do these things?"

"Our ancestors were hunted for years before they came to Pocket Cove. Since then, they've fought off half a dozen Gaskan invasions with no more than a hundred people. We have to be tough, Raxa. Tougher than everyone who might want to kill us."

Raxa lowered her head. They took her shoes, but at least they let her keep her clothes. The Fingers were named like that because the of the rocky spires that stuck up into the air, slick with moss and mist. Between the mist and the spires, you couldn't see more than sixty feet around you, which was terrible, because the banks of moss were full of centipedes as big as rats.

Going back to old habits, the first thing she did was try to find food. When her feet started to hurt—scraped by rocks, numbed by cold—she found a place in the lee of one of the spires where the wind-driven mist wasn't so bad and sat down.

It wasn't that much different from winters in Narashtovik, but it was still awful. On the second night, she broke down in tears. Why were they so mean? Were they bad people? Was *she*? Was that why her aunt and uncle hadn't come for her? Was this meant to punish her? For not saving her dad? For not stopping the man with the spider tattoo from taking Alna away?

When the time came, starving and half frozen, she limped down the staircase to the beach.

"Well?" Yona asked. "Did you find any answers?"

"Yeah." Raxa accepted a blanket from her. "Maybe all I can do is shadowalk. Maybe I won't ever be able to use the nether."

"Careful, Raxa. This world isn't as firm as you think. Sometimes, believing something is enough to make it true."

Raxa nodded, but she didn't believe that. Adults weren't always right. Especially the ones here. They were weird. And cruel. She thought they *liked* hurting kids. She hoped a giant wave came and washed them all away.

A few days later, while she was outside hanging wet laundry, Luru stole up beside her. Luru's eyes were all lit up like when people had a fever.

"Raxa." She reached for Raxa's arm. "They're sending me to the Fingers."

Raxa clipped another dress to the line. "It's not that bad."

"Not that *bad*? I already been up there once. I got stung so many times." She lifted her shirt, revealing a dark crater in the skin below her ribs. "It still hurts. When I tried to drink the water, it made me so sick I saw things. I thought I was going to die."

"But you didn't. You won't die this time, either."

"You don't know that! It isn't just the Fingers, Raxa. It's making us swim in the cold without any clothes. It's making us work all morning and practice until night comes. I hate it. We have to leave. We can run away together."

"How? There's no way out from here, you dummy."

"We can find a way down the other side of the cliffs. Or try to swim around them. We have to try!"

"We can't," Raxa said. "We agreed to this. We vowed it. 'Sides, if we try to run away and they catch us, don't you think they'll hurt us even worse?"

Luru stared at her, eyes awash with some inner fire. She turned and ran away.

They sent Luru to the Fingers the next day. The day after that, as Raxa and Yona stood on the beach practicing the same old things for the two hundredth time, something fell from the cliffs to the north. It hit the rocks with a hard smack.

Yona's face went as gray as the waves. She took off at a sprint. Raxa followed. And saw Luru's body, bent and bleeding, draped over the rocks.

Yona bent over her, nether swirling to her hands and flowing into Luru. As she worked, the redheaded woman who bossed everyone around ran toward them from the caves. Face twisted in a grimace, she drew a knife and cut open her arm, showering the body with blood. Raxa yelled out in horror:

Clouds of nether surrounded her. Far more than Raxa had ever seen. But when they went away, Luru was still dead.

They sent Raxa back to the Fingers the next week. She walked to the far end where the cliffs overlooked the prairies below, then walked north until she found a staircase carved into the rock.

And then she ran away.

~

"Raxa. Hey, *Raxa!*" Vess snapped her fingers under Raxa's nose. "You listening, girl?"

Raxa glanced at the book spread across the desk. "Sure."

"Then repeat to me the words I just said?"

"Some boring stuff about some boring guy."

Vess scowled at her, then chuckled. "Not wrong. But if I have to suffer through this, so do you."

Vess cleared her throat and continued reading. Raxa quit listening almost immediately. It had been sixteen years since she'd left Pocket Cove; she'd only been a child. They'd taught her to enter the world of light and dark. She gave them credit for that much.

She'd tried, and mostly succeeded, to forget everything else they'd done to her.

As Vess droned on, Raxa frowned. When the redheaded woman had cut herself, shedding her blood over the body, Raxa had thought it was some perverse ritual, a way to prepare the body for death. Or maybe to profane it. She'd never been sure.

But a line from the *Cycle* echoed in her mind: "Kamrates spilled his blood, and the darkness flocked, and his foes fell before it."

Raxa rubbed her jaw, then got out one of her knives—at that moment, she was carrying four—and pressed its point to the back of her arm, same as she'd seen the redheaded woman do. The steel bit through her skin, cold as a winter dip at Pocket Cove. Blood welled from the wound.

Vess looked up from the book. "What's that?"

"It's a red fluid known as blood. Don't want to alarm you, but your body's full of it."

"Why get out your blood?"

"Got a hunch," Raxa said. "Either that, or listening to this book all day has scrambled my brains."

The blood slid down her arm, gathered, and fell, hitting the wooden floor with a sound like a finger tapping at a door. Tap. Tap. Tap.

After returning to Narashtovik, it hadn't taken her long to realize how useful her Pocket-honed talents were. Moving in and out of the shadows, she could steal as much bread and vegetables as she liked. When she got a little older, and tired of the simple food they sold at the markets, she started to sneak into homes and churches to steal pastries and fresh-cooked slices of venison and beef.

One day, coming out of a cobbler's with a new pair of moccasins—ones she'd paid for, not stolen, though if you wanted to get technical, the money *had* come from stolen goods—she bumped into a tall man with a grim face, his hair tied back behind his head. Casually, wordlessly, he cuffed her, knocking her down.

The blow gave her a good look at his wrist. And the spider tattooed there in black.

She waited for him to go on his way, then followed, heart beating hard. There was fear in it, but there was something else, too. The man had a club on his hip. People got out of his way without seeming to know they were doing it. He headed for the Sharps, one of the neighborhoods Raxa tried to stay away from. He took long strides and sometimes she had to run to keep up.

In a square that smelled like pee, he stopped to watch the people come and go. After a while, his eyes set on a young girl. Dirty-faced and stringy-haired, she couldn't have been more than five, and was trying to use that to pry loose a few iron coins from the people going about their business.

After scoring a handout, she smiled and ran into an alley. The man with the spider tattoo followed. Raxa trotted after him, entering a tight space carved between two tenement buildings. She'd only meant to watch him, but as the man drew the club from his belt and closed on the little girl, anger clapped through Raxa like thunder.

She speared into the nether and broke into a run, silver motes winking past her face. The man was almost upon the girl. As he reached out and grabbed her blouse, she broke back toward the mouth of the alley, spinning him around.

Raxa leaped into the air and back into the plain old world. She had a knife in her hand. Iron. Nothing special. It punched through his chest all the same, sticking in his heart.

He gawked at her. Tried to say something. The knife twitched once, twice, a third time. With a rattle of lumber, the man collapsed onto a pile of scrap. Blood leaked from his chest, hitting the boards beneath him.

Tap, tap, tap.

"Girl," Vess said.

Raxa heard her, but it didn't register. She was still in the alley, watching the man's blood drip from his chest and onto the boards. It was scary and it made her want to faint.

But it also made her feel like maybe she could be scary, too.

"Girl!"

Raxa nodded vaguely at Vess.

The man with the ponytail had been the first. He hadn't been the last. She followed the next one she saw back to an old building deep in the Sharps. Everyone there had the spider tattoos. Later that week, in the middle of the night when they were too drunk to wake up, she burned the place down. That got rid of most of them.

The survivors went to ground. It was a couple months before they turned up again. Raxa hunted them down one by one. After five deaths, they left the city. It had been twelve years since then. She hadn't seen a spider tattoo since.

"*Raxa!*"

Vess shoved her so hard Raxa staggered to the side. The other woman was on her feet, jaw dropped. The room was so dark that, for a moment, Raxa was afraid she'd walked into the shadows without meaning to, exposing her secret to Vess.

Nope. Wasn't the netherworld. The nether was in *their* world, flocking around her blood like bees on honey or flies on shit, climbing up her arm to reach the blood still trickling from her vein.

"Look at that." She smiled at Vess. "The Citadel's got a problem on their hands."

10

Itiego's words hung in the air, as final as the turning off of a hanged man.

Boggs rose, eyes as hard as flint. "You can't take it with you, Itiego. All that money won't do you no good on Arawn's grassy hill beneath the stars."

"Arawn takes us all," Itiego said. "But Carvahal finds those who spent their lives to spread the light."

The members of the Hand filed out of the room. Dante gave Blays a small nod, stopping at the door.

Alone, he turned on Itiego. "I get why you're not interested. For all the times that Collen's rebelled, it's never held onto its independence for more than a few years. Why would this time be any different? And when Mallon brings them back into the fold, and sees you gave them a hand, why wouldn't you be next?"

The Prime Navigator of Cavana gave a small shrug. "There are many reasons I have declined your deal. That is among them."

"A good leader protects his people. Always. But what's happening now *will* be different. Just as it was for Gallador. The Norren Territories. And for Narashtovik."

"I know your record, Galand."

"Then you know what happens to those who cross swords with me."

Itiego's gray eyes stared into his. "They say you summoned

the sea against the Mallish. Drowned them all. I wonder the terror they felt. The pain of it. Crushed under so much water. Helpless to swim back to the sunlight. If Despot Boggs truly cared for my soul, he would not have brought you into my home."

The merchant-prince bowed over his knee, drawing his right hand to the side. Dante walked away.

"Well?" Blays said once Dante caught up in the courtyard. "Any luck?"

"I might as well have asked him if he wanted to gargle into each other's mouths."

Gareno angled toward them, smiling broadly. He expressed disappointment their business was over so soon, but informed them that Itiego would be happy to house them on the grounds until they were ready to depart Cavana. As soon as they were shown to their lodgings, they convened on the balcony outside Dante's room, where afternoon sunlight dazzled yellow from the blue sea.

"So," Blays said. "That was a disaster."

"He is a coward." Cord glared at the dome rising above the rooftops of the compound of House Itiego. "Money's made of metal, but it's so fragile it should be spun from gossamer. That's why men like Itiego love it. Even the *threat* of war can smash it like crystal thrown on a stone floor—and the fear of its loss gives them the excuse to throw away their principles the instant they get too dangerous to follow."

"To him, his money is his faith," the Keeper said. "What principle can be stronger than faith?"

"Honor. Duty. The righteousness of planting your spear against the giant and shouting 'No more!'"

Dante folded his hands on top of the table. "Going into this, were any of you aware that Cavana follows *The Gold Road*? Or are you that ignorant of your neighbors?"

The Keeper looked appropriately sheepish. "I was unaware that they were so strict. This is a bad sign. If his reticence stems from his faith, then his resolve will be unbreakable."

Dante broke into laughter. "You really didn't get out of your shrine much, did you? People betray their faith like it's a sport. If you want to be charitable to them, you can argue that they fail because the gods make too many demands of us for anyone to follow."

"And if I'm not prone to charity?"

"Then we fail because we're corrupt. And every last one of us has our price."

"That is a sad thing to think."

"Oh sure, so our souls might be damned forever," Blays said. "But right now, we should be thrilled. Because it means Itiego's got a price, too."

Dante nodded. "He said no. But that doesn't mean he hates the idea so much that he'd rather eat his own children with applesauce than to strike a deal with us. It only means our initial offer wasn't good enough. How do we make it more appealing?"

"Bribery?"

"Collen's broke."

"And you're so cheap that when your old boots start to fall off your feet, you'd rather give up walking than by new ones. I bet the thought of coughing up enough cash to bribe a merchant-prince makes you break out in hives."

"Itiego would never risk being funded by Narashtovik. If Mallon found out, they'd stomp him into a well-dressed paste."

Blays grew thoughtful. "Blackmail? He probably has mistresses. Then again, hearing a noble's having an affair is about as shocking as hearing a fish has wet skin."

Boggs sniffed. "How 'bout threats? 'Do like we say, or we'll annex your borders.'"

"Threats are counterproductive," Dante said. "You might strongarm Itiego into doing what you want for a while. But it'll only make him resent you. As soon as you turn your back, he'll find out how many knives he can stick in it."

"We should shame his honor," Cord said. "And if that fails, we should show him the color of his own blood."

"I just told you, threats won't buy his loyalty."

"Who says it's to buy his loyalty? I just want to hurt him!"

Blays gestured to the high towers, the view of the ocean. "Itiego's already got so much money he got bored with it. We won't be able to buy him off. Not with silver."

"Of course," Dante said. "This is the man who united all of

Alebolgia underneath him. The only way to reach him is by offering him more power."

Boggs smirked. "What've you got in mind?"

"It's your land. What can you afford to give up?"

"Could do like we were thinking and expand the canals. Not just to Parth. To the Strip, too. Sign him access to both the basin and Parth."

"Make it clear he can divvy up his rights to the canals, too. No better way to buy influence with the other houses and cities than to give them special trade rights. He'll realize he can use that to play the other cities against each other, too."

Blays kicked his feet up on the table. "*Now* you're thinking like a manipulative bastard."

They drew up plans for the new canals, then a proposal for the division of their rights-of-way. In the morning, they asked Gareno to speak with Itiego again. Gareno returned to tell them Itiego would grant a second audience, but only to the despot.

After Gareno left, Boggs grunted. "I get the impression he don't trust you all."

"Could be," Blays said. "Either that, or he thinks you're particularly stupid."

Boggs grinned. The following morning, he went off to make his case. He returned within forty minutes looking rather less amused.

"He heard me out." The despot dropped into a chair, expelling a hard sigh. "But he didn't ask more than three questions. Doubt if he'll bite."

Boggs' skepticism proved right on the mark. After lunch, Gareno returned with word that their proposal didn't suit Itiego's current needs.

"Lord Itiego wishes to know how much longer you intend to stay?" Gareno smiled, the model of politeness. "So that he can continue to make proper arrangements, of course."

"Of course," Dante said. "We won't trouble you more than another three days."

The servant smiled again, bowed, and left.

Cord swore. "I told you we needed to insult his honor. When you tell a man he has no balls, he'll act so fast to prove you wrong he'll drop his breeches in the middle of town square."

The Keeper shifted her legs, rubbing one knee. "What now?"

Dante met her eyes. "Unless you're willing to offer Itiego the entire basin, he'll never work with us. If he won't, we'll have to find someone who will."

She leaned forward, dropping her voice. "You mean to depose him."

"I mean to explore our options. A man like Itiego will have enemies. They might be able to pressure him in ways we can't."

To provide lodging for their retinue, they made arrangements to hire out an entire inn down near the docks. The marine air smelled like kelp and salt. Sea lions barked from the rocks. As soon as they settled in, they went over a list of the city's other major Houses, deciding on seven that had the strength and wealth to make a legitimate challenge to Itiego. Boggs' messengers dispersed throughout the city.

One response came back that same day. Regretfully, the House's master was indisposed. It wasn't known when he would be available again, but it was implied that it could take weeks. Two others replied the following day, stating they had no interest in such a meeting. The other Houses gave no response at all.

"Itiego's gotten to them," Dante said. "He's poisoned the entire city against us."

"That's a bit of an extreme move," Blays said. "Your reputation must have preceded you."

"Cavana ain't the only city in the Strip." Boggs fetched a map from his trunk and spread it over the table, standing over it. "Could try Hemalio. Word is they had to be dragged kicking and screaming into the confederation."

"It's as good a start as any." Dante stared glumly at the map. "But whatever promises and threats Itiego made to the Houses of Cavana, he'll do the same in Hemalio."

Boggs set to penning another slew of letters. While the servants went to the work of settling their debts and restocking their provisions, Dante went for a walk around the town, hiking up its steep streets, grateful for the coolness of the sea. He'd badly hoped that sealing off the Strip would be quick and clean, requiring no killings or fracturing of political schisms.

What if protecting Collen required sparking a war in Alebolgia? Did he have it in him to fight another battle for a land that wasn't his? Did he even have the time for that? The snows would be falling in Collen any day. This time, if he stayed longer than he'd promised, he couldn't blame the Colleners. The fault would be no one's but his own.

He returned to the inn without any answers. As he opened the door, he nearly slammed into a trim young man dressed in subtly expensive knee-high boots. The young man bowed and stepped aside.

Upstairs, Blays stuck his head out a doorway. "There you are. You're going to want to see this."

Dante entered, shutting the door behind him. The other four members of the Hand were arrayed around the room's only table.

"Note came in," Boggs said. "Somebody wants a meet."

"Really? Which House?"

"It don't say. Don't even know for sure it *is* a House."

Brow creased, Dante read the note. It was a request for the delegates from Collen to show up at one in the morning at a place called Doche's Point. The opportunity would only be offered once.

Dante shrugged. "So we go meet the mysterious stranger. We're leaving tomorrow anyway."

"Not if the mysterious stranger is a Mallish ambush," Blays said.

"Would be a fine opportunity to behead Collen and Narashtovik in one blow."

Cord stood, the tallest one of them. "Then I will go."

"We'll all go," Dante said. "But we'll do it in a way that minimizes the chances of us all falling victim to a predictably sudden death."

Doche's Point was a spar of rock a short way south of town. Accessible only via a shepherd's trail, and with the steady boom of surf and hoots of sea lions drowning out any other sound, it would be a fine place to murder some of your enemies without drawing attention.

They struck out for the point at midnight. Cord and Blays

walked out onto the damp rocks, black crabs scattering away. The Keeper and Boggs were stationed on the cliffs above. Dante killed a pair of crabs and sent them scuttling down both sides of the trail, then climbed up to join the Keeper.

The air was frigid. Mist streamed inland, dampening Dante's cloak until it hung on him like an anchor. As one o'clock neared, three silhouettes appeared on the southern trail. They carried swords, but seeing no army backing them up, Dante deemed it safe to join Blays and Cord on the rocks.

There, he bit the inside of his cheek, keeping the nether close. The trio of strangers moved out onto the rocky arm and stopped in front of the members of the Hand. Two of the figures were bulky, clearly soldiers, but the figure between them was as slender as the saber she carried at her hip.

"You came," the woman said. "Brave? Stupid? Or just desperate?"

"It's quite obviously brave," Blays said. "If we'd been stupid, we wouldn't have thought to rig the rock you're standing on with bear traps."

The woman looked down sharply, jerking her right foot from the ground. As her bodyguards went for their swords, she relaxed and chuckled, lifting her hooded head. "You would be Blays Buckler. The necromancer's pet clown."

"I prefer to think of myself as his wrangler."

"Who are you?" Dante said.

"Me?" Her rapid, staccato accent was a match for Tanelo Itiego's, making Dante feel like he needed to lean forward to keep up with her. "I am the only person in this rotten city with the guts to stand up to the Itiegos. Do you have the blood to do the same?"

"Yes," Dante said hurriedly, cutting off Cord, who'd thrust her fist in the air in preparation to launch into a declaration of their unyielding courage. "But you still haven't told us who you are."

The woman flipped back her hood. The face she revealed was as smooth as glass. Her dark hair was swept behind her head, held in place by a silver pin. Her high cheekbones were an artist's dream. She looked no older than twenty, but her dark eyes bore the authority of an executioner's axe.

"I am Vita Osedo, House Osedo. The Houses of Cavana turned away your requests to speak because Tanelo owns them as firmly as he owns the spices within his ships. But he does not own me."

"And you speak for your father?" Dante said. "Or mother?"

"If I'm too young for you to trust, I will be happy to find someone closer to your age for you to do business with. Shall we head to the cemetery to find a proper candidate?"

A tall wave disemboweled itself on the rocks, spattering Dante with cold spray. "That won't be necessary. How can we help each other?"

Her expression warmed, however slightly. "Itiego can buy the other houses because he has the fortune to do so. Do you know how the Itiegos made this fortune?"

Boggs shrugged. "No secret about it. Spice trade."

"Every House trades spice. So how is it Itiego can buy so many other Houses? Because his family is the only one that trades this." She tossed a tiny glass jar at Boggs, who fumbled it, dropping to a crouch to catch it before it shattered on the rocks.

He unstoppered it, sniffed, then cocked his head. "Tallas?"

Dante blinked. Tallas was the most expensive spice in Narashtovik. And, as far as he knew, everywhere else. A pale blue powder that tasted like something between pepper and cinnamon, it was worth more than its weight in gold.

"The Itiegos are the only ones who know where it comes from," Vita said. "With the wealth it brought them, Tanelo's grandmother bought Cavana House by House. Fifty years later, Tanelo swept all of Alebolgia under his cloak."

Dante nodded. "You want to end his stranglehold on your city."

"I *want* to know where to find the tallas."

Blays folded his arms. "Crazy idea, but have you tried following his ships?"

Vita gave him a brief glance. "Theirs are the fastest on the seas. And they have the wealth to hire their own sorcerers. They destroy anyone who tries to get close."

"Ask one of their sailors, then. If they won't talk, apply rum and repeat as necessary."

"The sailors of the Tallas Route are chosen as children. Once they join their ship, they're never allowed on these shores again. When they finish their term, they're retired to a southern island." She took on a wry look. "Or that is what they're told. I assume it's easier—and safer—to kill them."

"Well, that sounds like the strongest retirement you can give them."

Dante was looking out to sea. He turned to find Vita staring at him. "We can get you the route," he said.

She lifted the outer corner of one brow. "How?"

"Leave that to us. Do you know what we wanted from Itiego?"

"You come in the company of Colleners. So you want one of two things: either for Cavana to turn away any Mallish warships that come to port. Or to learn everything we know about how to remove dust from one's clothes."

This drew a snort from Boggs, a bray from Cord, and a low chuckle from the Keeper.

"Correct," Dante said. "Itiego won't agree to stop the Mallish from landing here. We have to change his mind, or break his power. You think finding the source of the tallas will be enough to make that happen?"

Vita gestured to herself. "If I am the only woman in town, every man will fall to his knees if I so much as wink, utterly beholden to the rarity of my presence. But if the town holds as many women as men, who in his right mind will devote themselves to me like he is a slave? No one."

Dante wasn't sure that was strictly true, but he had the impression that if he said so out loud, she might push him into the waves. "We'll give you the Tallas Route. And you'll dethrone the Itiegos."

"In exchange, I close the port to Mallon?"

"Just their soldiers. Call it a threat to the sovereignty of your new and fragile confederacy. If you tried to shut their ships out completely, you might find yourself bludgeoned to death by copies of *The Gold Road*."

Vita smiled. The light it brought to her face didn't seem fair.

"We have a deal."

"I wasn't done. One more thing: I want a cut of the tallas for Narashtovik. Three percent of whatever you bring back, sold to us at the cost of its acquisition. And another three for Collen."

She looked him up and down. "You speak like a Mallisher. But you bargain like an Alebolgian. I will offer you two percent each. And in coming years, you will marvel I was so generous."

He looked into her eyes and judged them unyielding. "Agreed."

They hashed out the details of how to stay in contact with one another, then went their separate ways. Dante sent his undead crabs up the trail to make sure no one was spying on or awaiting them, but the way was clear.

As they neared the city, a dense fog rolled in from the sea, smothering the town's lanterns and making everything feel vague and unreal. For half a moment, Dante's mind was certain there'd been an ambush after all — that he'd taken an arrow in the brain and died before he knew what was happening — and he was now in the Mists, the gentle afterlife where you made your peace before continuing on into the forever expanse of the Worldsea.

Except if that were true, he'd skipped right past the Pastlands. Meaning these weren't the Mists, but just an everyday (if pleasantly mysterious) fog.

Dante stopped, turning to the Colleners. "Did you agree with all of that horse-trading back there?"

Boggs shrugged. "If I'd have had a problem with it, you would have heard about it."

"I heard nothing but politics." Cord grinned. "Your responsibility, not mine. Wake me the next time there's a war to declare!"

"Thought I'd better check," Dante said. "You guys didn't talk much."

The Keeper made a noise that might have been a laugh. "That is because you seem to like to speak for us."

"Vita seemed most comfortable negotiating with me. Besides, this is a good thing. If word gets out that you're meddling in Alebolgian affairs, you can blame it on Narashtovik."

"This is so. But the leaders of the newly free Collen will need to learn to handle their politics on their own."

This seemed so self-evident Dante didn't bother to respond. The streets of Cavana were damp with mist. Water condensed on the bare branches of trees and fell to the cobbles in a heavy and irregular rain.

By morning, the fog remained, slipping between houses and tumbling over roofs in little streams. Dante was going to eat in the inn's common room, but Blays had chatted up the locals and been bewitched by rumors of a legendary bakery and coffee house down by the piers.

The two of them ventured down the steep, slick streets. They could have found the shop by smell alone: the rich, almost scorched scent of coffee was even thicker than the fogs. Most of Alebolgia was built in pale stone, but the coffee house was constructed with dark brown bricks. Its roof was shaped into three thick cones.

The interior was an unusual mix of raggedy sailors, local merchants in respectable but unspectacular trousers and jackets, and nobles in their high boots and higher collars. Blays approached the bar and ordered two of their strongest brews spiked with a dollop of cream. The coffeewright turned to the stove and removed a pot that resembled a chunky copper hourglass. He poured two cups that were irritatingly small for the price Blays paid.

They took their cups out to the patio. It was nearly freezing, and the fog spoiled the view of the ocean, but that meant they were alone.

Blays took a seat and then a sip. He immediately slapped his hand to his mouth.

"Too hot?" Dante said.

"Stopping myself from drinking it all at once. This is the best thing I've ever tasted. We have to buy this."

"Are you drunk? We just did."

"Not the coffee." Blays motioned toward the building. "The house!" For a minute, the mist thinned enough to see the ships bobbing in the harbor. Blays nodded to them. "Speaking of consumables so delicious they'll drive men mad, how were you intending to find the Tallas Route?"

"How the hell should I know?"

"My mistake. When I heard you telling Vita you knew a way, I assumed that meant you knew a way."

"I had confidence in our ability to come up with one," Dante said. "So let's not tarnish our reputations by screwing it up."

"I figured you'd follow them with one of your moths or something."

"Won't work. If I tail it with a moth, and we fall more than fifty miles behind them, I'll lose my connection to the bug. If we stick close enough to maintain the connection, they'll be able to see us. Although it sounds like their ships will be too fast for us to keep up with anyway."

Blays took a contemplative sip, slurping much more loudly than was necessary. "Bugs are out, then. So do what you did to find me. Get some blood from one of the sailors, and you can follow him all the way to the end of the route."

"Got a suggestion for how to acquire that blood?"

"Sure. Go up to a bar and punch one of their crew in the nose."

"Vita said they never let their sailors off the ship."

"Gods damn it, I'm getting tired of all my brilliant ideas getting slain by these peasantish facts. Vita said these sailors are trained as youths, right? Right, so here's what you do: collect the blood of every child in Alebolgia. Eventually, one of them will be chosen to crew on the route. You'll already have his blood, hence you'll be able to follow him."

Dante swirled his cup. "What a wonderful plan. It will take a minimum of ten years to unfold *and* it will give me the reputation of someone who sucks the blood from little children."

"Like that's any worse than the stories they tell about you now?"

"What stories?"

"Don't worry about it." Blays stood, brandishing his empty cup. "I require another."

"You just got that one!"

"And I depleted it in the service of our work. If you want more ideas, I need more coffee."

He went back inside the building, returning a minute later

with a refilled cup. This time, he sipped like a reasonable person.

"You're okay with this?" Dante glanced at the patio door to make sure they were still alone. "Overthrowing the Itiegos?"

"Yep."

"You're sure?"

"If I wasn't, rather than saying 'Yep,' I might say something like 'No,' or 'Your idea is so dishonorable I demand satisfaction in the form of a duel.' Are *you* okay with it?"

"Why wouldn't I be?"

Blays eyed him. "We're supporting the Colleners in order to win their freedom, right? Particularly the religious freedom that Mallon's always denied them. And in support of that cause, you'll happily subvert the religious freedom of the Alebolgians, whose holy scriptures insist on keeping the port open."

"Yes. And?"

"And some people who aren't you would consider that hypocritical."

"Gladdic wants to exterminate everyone in Collen for believing in something that Mallon doesn't like. If we can stop him from doing that by twisting one small tenet of Alebolgian belief, it would be cruel *not* to intervene here."

"I'm starting to think the most important skill a leader can have is the ability to rationalize anything." Blays took a drink of coffee. "Here's a different tack. We cut out the middlemen altogether. If we can find some tallas seeds, you can harvest them into a full crop."

"That's not totally crazy. But I don't think I've ever seen a tallas seed. Even if we could find some, Vita wants a regular supply. They won't grow here on their own. That means I'd have to keep harvesting them for her—but the whole point of all this scheming is to untangle us from this region for good."

"There's no way they can keep the entire crew confined to the ship when they come to port. The sailors might tolerate that, but what about the captains? Or young Itiego nobles assigned to sail off and check on the family investment? Should be able to nab a bit of *their* blood."

Dante tapped the rim of his mug. "Could put the House under observation. I'll slip a moth or three into their villa. Though

Vita made it sound like the Itiegos have their own sorcerers, so maybe I'll try something sneakier."

Blays' eyebrows lifted like canoes on a swell. "Mosquitos."

"People hate mosquitos. They'd only draw more attention."

"Not to spy on the House. When the next tallas ship comes in, you send over the mosquitos."

"To bite the crew. And bring back their blood to me." Dante laughed. "Time to ask Vita if she knows when the next ship's coming in."

They returned to the inn to send a messenger to their contact in House Osedo. The messenger returned stating that while the arrival of the tallas ships wasn't known with precision, the first ones always arrived early in spring. Dante thanked the messenger, feeling disappointed they hadn't had another chance to speak to Vita in person.

He was right about to summon the Hand and explain the situation when his loon pulsed in his ear. He expected it would be Naran updating them on the situation in Collen, but it turned out it was Nak, contacting him all the way from Narashtovik.

"No need to berate me," Dante said. "We've been delayed a little longer than I intended, but we're almost through here. We'll be back in Narashtovik before the summer."

"I have a feeling we'll see you well before then." Nak's usually cheerful voice was tight with stress. "The first copy of the *Cycle*—it's been stolen."

11

Dante touched his loon, uncertain he'd heard right. "The first copy of the *Cycle*."

"Correct," Nak said.

"Not the false copy?"

"Indeed."

"But the original was hidden. Inside a stone wall. How could they have found it?"

"We are as perplexed as you are, mighty commander. One of the guards noticed that the chapel study looked like it had been disturbed. When I investigated, it didn't look like anything was missing besides a few curtains. However, you will be pleased to hear that I am as thorough as I am insightful, and withdrew to reflect on my suspicions—"

"Get on with it, Nak."

"—which in turn led me to mount a more thorough search of the chambers. At which point I discovered a boot lodged in the wall."

"A boot?"

"Yes, sir."

"In the wall?"

"I was as confused as you are, sir."

"There was a boot. Lodged in the wall. And you didn't notice this the first time?"

"Well, it was hidden under a cloth, you see. May I move on?"

Dante grasped his temples. "I'd like nothing more."

"This curious boot was stuck in the wall concealing the original *Cycle*. Being a man of great reason, I deduced that I should look behind the wall. Short of a sledgehammer, I had no ability to check on the original myself. However, I knew that Minn was in the Citadel—she's waiting on Blays, incidentally, and is growing rather annoyed—and inquired if she would open the wall for me. She obliged. And I found that the book was gone."

Dante's head spun. The original copy of the *Cycle of Arawn* held an immense and largely mysterious power. He knew firsthand that if someone with latent skill in the nether read its pages, the book could somehow unlock their abilities. Before Samarand had been sent off to Arawn's starry hill, she'd claimed the book could be used to open a portal that the god himself could step through.

Dante doubted that strongly, and wasn't entirely sure that it was a good idea to find out if it was true, but there was no denying the potency of the book, which he'd intended to spend more time studying at a time in his life that was less interesting. Aside from whatever magical properties it possessed, its value as a cultural and religious artifact was second to nothing in the Arawnite faith.

Which was why he'd sealed it up behind a stone wall for safekeeping.

"Other than the boot, the wall was intact?" Dante said. "No sign of entry?"

"None."

"Its floor and ceiling were undisturbed?"

"I checked it as thoroughly as an empty closet can be checked, which is to say with extreme thoroughness. I found no evidence of the burglar—excepting, of course, that perplexing boot."

Dante's mind spun in circles. "I'm coming back. We'll leave today."

"Er, you are? Aren't you in the middle of terribly important business?"

"That business can be left on hold until the spring. In the wrong hands, the original *Cycle* could be a lot of trouble—and anyone capable of stealing it definitely counts as the wrong hands."

"I regret the circumstances of your return," Nak said. "But it will be good to see you home again."

Dante shut down the connection, then gathered the Hand, explaining the change in circumstances. "My goal will be to recover the book and deal with the perpetrator as quickly as I can. Even accounting for travel time, I expect we can be back here before the first ship arrives from the Tallas Route."

"'We'?" Blays said. "You're volunteering me for all this travel?"

"You're free to go back to Pocket Cove if they need you. They've probably been overrun by crabs without you there to eat them all."

"But you will return?" the Keeper said.

Dante ran his hand down his mouth. "I don't like to make promises I'm not certain I can keep. But as soon as I've dealt with this, I'll be back here to complete our deal with Vita. Maybe this is for the best. I can clean up a few messes in Narashtovik without compromising matters down here."

"Then let us depart. The sooner you leave, the sooner you can see to your affairs."

They set about packing their things and gathering up the caravan. Some of their retinue was out in the city, running errands, trolling for gossip, or simply enjoying themselves. While servants went out to gather them up, Dante headed for their contact in House Osedo. The man was perturbed that Dante had come in person—quite understandably, Lady Vita didn't want to be seen working with the Colleners—but agreed to go see her. As soon as he left, Dante slew a nearby bee and sent it after the man to make certain he wasn't being followed by any Cavanese spies.

The contact returned in half an hour, providing Dante with a set of directions. Dante followed them to the rear of a small church. It was a cold day and the scent of wood smoke mingled with the fog.

After waiting long enough that Dante was starting to wonder if he had the right place, an old woman shuffled up to a statue of a pious-looking man, supporting herself with a cane. A heavy wool shawl warmed her against the chill. She kneeled before the statue.

Without looking up, Vita said, "What is so important that we have to meet in such a reckless way?"

"We're leaving," Dante said. "We'll be gone by day's end."

"Is your word that worthless? We had a deal!"

"We still do. And we know exactly how we're going to fulfill our end of it. Something's come up in my homeland that I have to see to myself. I mean to be back by spring."

"This news couldn't have been brought to me by a messenger?"

"I thought telling you in person would make it clear that I'm serious about honoring our arrangement."

"Mm." Vita touched the statue's feet. "Then I will see you in the spring."

That afternoon, they headed up the road to the top of the cliffs overlooking Cavana. Dante was hoping for a last look at the scenic coastal city, but the fog blurred everything to gray shapes. They rode forward. As they crested a line of hills a few miles north of the city, the temperature dropped abruptly, along with the coastal humidity. Ahead, the fields were dusted with snow.

In the basin, fields of snow glittered under a distant sun. Buttes thrust from the whiteness like unfinished blocks left behind by a forgetful sculptor. They'd made good time, and with a rider ranging ahead to the city to make preparations, everything was set for Dante and Blays to continue to Narashtovik at once.

Collen provided them with four horses. Asties weren't suited for the brutality of northern winters, so they went with raggies instead, shaggy and hardy beasts like oversized ponies.

"Stay on your toes," Dante told the Hand as the provisions were being loaded onto the raggies. "Mallon won't be able to launch another invasion until spring, but snows won't stop saboteurs."

Boggs smirked. "You think you're tellin' us something we don't already know?"

"I have to say *something* before I leave. It might as well masquerade as wise advice."

The three Colleners dispersed to go about their own business.

Naran replaced them, crunching up through the thin snow. "Did you intend to depart without saying goodbye?"

Blays tightened a strap on his saddlebag. "Maybe we're smart enough to know that you would come to us."

"You asked me to stay in Collen while you're away. I've decided to leave as well."

Dante looked up. "But we need a set of eyes here."

"Why? If something happens, will you snap your fingers and teleport to the Reborn Shrine? While you're in Narashtovik, you can't do anything about what transpires here. So what does it matter if you know every detail?"

"It would still be much more helpful than if you're in Narashtovik."

Naran gave him a dubious look. "I don't have any desire to freeze my unmentionables in your blizzard-racked wasteland. I want to go to Tanar Atain."

"To hunt Gladdic?"

"That would be my main motivation."

Blays put his hand on Naran's shoulder. "Captain, is your mind that troubled? Suicide is never the answer, my friend."

Naran snorted, shrugging off Blays' hand. "Did I say anything about looking to assault him? My intention is to *find* him. I'll leave the matter of dying against his wicked sorcery to you two."

Dante tapped his chin with his thumb. "There's no guarantee he's down there. That's only the rumor."

"I appreciate that. However, my crew's growing restless—and light in the pocket. If the *Sword of the South* doesn't start earning money, my tenure as captain will be short-lived indeed."

"Fair enough. But take a loon with you. And leave someone you trust in Collen to act as a relay between us. If you and I try to share a loon when you're heading that far south, I'm afraid the connection will be stretched until it breaks."

They decided to leave two loons with Naran's trusted crewman Jona, who wasn't happy to be stuck in Collen while the *Sword of the South* would be out making cash and visiting fun new ports, but he was mollified when Naran doubled his regular earnings.

With this and everything else settled, or at least as settled as it could be, Dante and Blays rode out from the city. The first few days were spent traveling overland through the desert of Collen and into the Mallish woods on the other side of the hills. The snow and lack of roads made it slower than Dante would have liked, but with two horses apiece, they still managed to keep a fair pace.

Once they'd bypassed Bressel, they intercepted the Chanset River and struck north. Under the overcast skies, the mile-wide river was the gray of hammered iron.

Though they were traveling through enemy lands, within a few days, Dante felt more carefree than at any time since they'd first left for the Plagued Islands. Some of that was the act of travel itself, which he always enjoyed, but putting physical distance between himself and the Collen Basin allowed him to get some mental distance from it as well.

His anger at the Keeper's betrayal wasn't only about the act of manipulation. He'd done similar things in the past, and expected to do more of them in the future. At least when you were manipulating someone, that meant you weren't killing them.

Instead, he was angry because he'd thought they were friends. Untrue: to her, he was a game piece. This was disappointing, but it simplified his relationship with both her and Collen. Once his objectives were achieved there, he could walk away and wash his hands. He'd have no further reason to ever get involved there again.

"The Keeper played us good, didn't she?" Blays said. He smiled wryly. "Just like the Kandeans."

"Funny, I was just thinking about that."

"Oh no. Please tell me your thoughts aren't a communicable disease."

"Is being taken advantage of just the natural risk of trying to do good?"

"We could test that theory by doing evil instead."

"Have you ever been tempted to walk away?"

"I'm tempted right now," Blays said. "If we never went back to Collen, *I* wouldn't blame us."

"What's stopping you?

"For one thing, the thought of leaving all those innocents in the lurch isn't my favorite idea of all time. For another, what if this sort of thing is like our calling?"

Dante twisted in the saddle. "I thought you'd been getting cranky about getting dragged into everyone else's business."

"I am. In large part because other people's business never seems to end. But when I saw what Gladdic had done—those people in the cave..."

Dante nodded, gazing blankly through the leafless forest. Finding Gladdic's stash of bodies had troubled him, too. It wasn't so much the quantity of the dead—he'd seen many more during the war with Gask—but rather the methodicalness of it. Gladdic had stacked the corpses like the proverbial firewood. Like salmon packed in salt.

"The deaths on a battlefield make a certain sort of sense," Dante said. "War is a storm. When a storm hits, people die without reason. But what Gladdic did was different. It was deliberate. Precise. The murder was the entire point."

Blays grunted. "It's like he was a farmer of lives. How many people out there do you think could have stopped him?"

"How many people could have destroyed the Andrac? Not many. The Council together might have been able to. Moddegan's sorcerer school could. And there are more than enough ethermancers in Bressel to take them on."

"In other words, if we hadn't been there, the entire city of Collen would have been slaughtered. There are horrors out there. People who act like monsters, and monsters that *are* monsters with big sharp claws and fangs that could rip a pig in half. Maybe we were put here to smite them."

"I don't think we were put here to kill the wicked. Arawn doesn't care about saving lives—he knows we're all his sooner or later. Wherever we are, we brought ourselves here."

"That makes it all the more important." Blays ducked under a reaching bough. "If the gods aren't putting anyone here to kill the monsters, then there's no guarantee that anyone will fight them at all."

As they neared Whetton, they left the road to ride around it; they were still telling stories about Blays in the city. Miles later, Dante considered detouring to Shay to check in on the norren monk Gabe, but it wouldn't be more than a pointless social nicety. Anyway, according to Nak, they still hadn't found any trace of the true *Cycle* in Narashtovik. Every day they lingered was another day for it to get more lost.

The towns gave out, and the farms too, and there was nothing but wilderness: forests, hills, blue mountains beyond. The only sound was the thump of the horses and the snow sifting through the branches.

They entered the mountains. The pass was ugly. It took Dante two days to alter the rock enough to where the horses could make it through. When he'd first seen the blue glaciers and searing green lakes in the heart of the Dundens, he'd thought they were the starkest, most beautiful things he'd ever seen. But after their crossing of the Woduns—a range that had been designed to be impassible—the mountains of his childhood homeland felt rather tame.

The raggies handled the heights well, delivering them to the endless hills of what had once been southern Gask. The grass was buried under two feet of snow. Boulders and haggard trees poked from the white blanket.

"Look." Blays nodded.

Dante followed his gaze across the hills to where a pair of towering figures stood underneath a copse of trees, spears in hand. Norren. The two figures watched them for a minute, then turned and vanished over the hill.

Dante didn't expect any trouble from the norren—after all, Narashtovik had helped liberate them—but norren were nothing if not unpredictable. Fractious, too. It wasn't out of the question that a clan would assault them simply because they were enemies of another clan that was friendly with Narashtovik.

Unfortunately, winter had killed all the bugs, leaving Dante nothing obvious to scout with. As they entered a small forest, leading the horses by the reins, he kept his eyes open for field mice, getting so absorbed in the hunt that he nearly walked right into the waist of a norren warrior.

The man gazed down at him from a height of seven feet. He wore a long cloak over weatherbeaten buckskins and carried a spear with an oval-shaped point the size of a human man's hand.

Behind him, a score of others emerged from behind the trees. Dante pulled the nether close.

The norren looked disappointed. "You got older."

Blays laughed. "Mourn? What are you doing out here?"

"Speaking to you. And wondering why you didn't recognize me."

"Come on, man. Between the hood and the beard, I wouldn't be the wiser if you were a talking dog."

Blays strode through the snow and wrapped Mourn in a hug. Mourn appeared to tolerate this. At any rate, he didn't look any more perturbed than he usually did.

"How long have you known we were here?" Dante said.

"Since we saw you." Mourn glanced up at the snowflakes trickling through the branches. "This wasn't a very good time to choose to go through the mountains."

"It wasn't much of a choice."

"Then I'll have to have my scouts beaten. They must have missed the hostile army marching you through the Dundens in the dead of winter."

"Ah, how I've missed you," Blays said.

Mourn invited them to the Nine Pines' wintering grounds, which it turned out were only a few miles northeast. The clan had set up its yurts in a stand of pine trees on the south face of a hill.

"You look at least a hundred strong," Dante said. "The clan's recovered nicely. No wonder they won't let you step down as chief."

"I know," Mourn muttered. "I need to trick a few of them into walking off a cliff. Or hunting kappers. See how long they tolerate *that*."

Blays waved to a few of their old friends. "Is it really that bad? Leading these people?"

"It's awful. The only thing worse would be if one of *them* was leading *me*."

They found seating on a line of logs encircling the camp's central fire. Around them, many of the norren were casually working away at their nulla, the life-craft they dedicated years to perfecting. Some were carving wood or bone; two were dabbing black lines on a canvas, arguing after every stroke; some were carefully stretching hides into bossen, the seamless clothing that remained popular with humans across Gask.

There was nothing hurried about their efforts. Presumably, the clan had already done the bulk of the work needed to see itself through the winter. They didn't depend on selling their work, either, although that did allow them to purchase weapons-grade steel, which was still rare in the Norren Territories. Yet bit by bit and day by day, they all became skilled enough that the least of them could turn their talent into a trade. Meanwhile, the best of them created art and artifacts that looked like they'd been handed down from another age, or burgled from the houses of the heavens.

Warmed by the fire, enjoying the smell of the smoke, they caught up with Mourn. The Nine Pines had been rather quiet for the last few years. The occasional skirmish with another clan, but otherwise, the most exciting thing to have happened to them was the discovery of an ancient norren cave system loaded with stone statues of such quality the Nine Pines' masons were still trying to reproduce their techniques.

Behind the curtain of clouds, the sun moved toward the horizon. As the light began to dim, most of the norren who'd been at work on their nulla packed away their projects and set to work preparing dinner or tightening up the yurts for the night.

As they set to their chores, others who'd been laboring earlier — chopping wood, cleaning a deer — cleaned themselves up and got out flutes and small drums. As they began to play, practicing *their* nulla, those working smiled, humming along with their favorite bits. The rhythm of the clan's actions felt as cyclical as the comings and goings of the tide from day to day and season to season. It was as if they were all players in some great symphony, yet they moved without a conductor, or any orders at all.

They ate, talked more, fell asleep in the warm comfort of the yurt. In the morning, after a leisurely breakfast, Dante went to prepare the horses to continue their journey.

Mourn crunched up behind him through the snow. "What are you doing?"

"Preparing our dragons for the flight to Narashtovik."

"You're leaving already?"

"Trust me, if I could spare the time, I'd stay here for a month. It would be a thousand times more pleasant than what I'm off to do."

"You should stay for another day. It will improve your mood. When you lighten your heart, you lighten your responsibilities."

Dante gave Mourn a sidelong glance. "Don't tell me you've missed us that bad."

Mourn sighed, breath steaming from his mouth. "Go on, then. I'll just tell Sonn he won't be able to play Nulladoon with a human after all."

"You have a Nulladoon set?"

"Would I lie to you?"

"Have you forgotten how we met?"

Behind his beard, Mourn might have blushed. "The hunt for the Quivering Bow led to every norren in Gask throwing off their chains. If every lie could accomplish that much, only sadists would tell the truth."

"One more day," Dante said. "But Sonn better be good."

Sonn turned out to be a fifteen-year-old girl—though, being norren, she was still taller and heavier than he was. Seeing how young she was, Dante felt mild disappointment in his prospects for a challenging match, but as long as she wasn't a complete pushover, he still expected to have fun.

As they laid out the board and selected their pieces, half the clan dropped what they were doing to come watch. Bets of nulla flew fast and furious. The action was mostly on Dante, but the bets on Sonn were large enough to make him suspect the game would be better than he'd thought.

They began. Through the first few rounds, both Dante and Sonn played cautiously, until a minor skirmish of slingers turned into a wholesale slaughter of drakes, swordsmen, and sorcerers.

Both sides withdrew in tatters. Dante consolidated his forces on favorable terrain, then advanced with methodical precision. Sonn arranged her defenses with impeccable strategy until Dante played a run of three cards that allowed his cavalry to ford a river and rush her flank. The attack should have been crushing, yet Sonn fought back so hard that Dante wasn't certain he'd win until six rounds later, when he claimed her last pieces.

Sonn pressed her lips tight, face going red. "You got lucky. You should have lost the first battle."

"Strange, considering I didn't," Dante said. "Then again, 'you got lucky' is about the level of analysis I'd expect from someone who thinks you need to keep your sorcerers hidden in the rear." Suddenly aware he was taunting a teenager, he stuck out his hand. "Thanks for playing me. It's been too long."

She shook his hand. After a moment, she returned his smile, too. She'd said her nulla was sculpture, but it took a form he'd never seen before: the skeletons of mice glued together and equipped with tiny spears, bows, armor, and little tiny bossen, all of which she'd also made. Sonn presented his figurine with her eyes downcast, blinking rapidly.

"Are you embarrassed?" He lifted it for a closer inspection. "The craftsmanship is great."

"Yeah, but it's..." She risked a look up. "Silly."

"You're right. It's a mouse with a spear."

Her voice fell to a whisper. "I'm sorry."

"But that's part of what makes it great," he said. "Life is serious enough. We need songs and stories and armored little mice to remind us it can be silly, too."

Sonn lifted her eyes to his, blushing harder than ever. She made a small noise that might have been gratitude, then bobbed her head and walked away.

Blays ambled up beside him, watching her go. "You do realize you essentially just stole from a child?"

"It's not stealing if you earned it." He leaned closer to Blays, sniffing. "How much beer have you had?"

"Lots! They've got a guy whose nulla is brewing!"

This was interesting enough to occupy them through the afternoon. It likely would have held their interest throughout the night, too, but they were interrupted late in the day by the arrival of another clan. In most cases, this would involve the hoisting of weapons and the preparation of threats, but the Nine Pines looked completely unconcerned.

As the other clan neared, Dante found Mourn hanging

around at the fringe of the camp. He stood beside the norren. "Expecting guests?"

"Bet you'll recognize *them*."

As the other clan grew nearer, Dante thought he recognized the gait of the man in their front. Seeing him, the man gave a cheery wave.

"The Broken Herons?" Dante's jaw fell open, then lifted in a grin. "Was this why you wanted us to wait another day? Why didn't you just tell me Hopp was coming?"

Mourn gave him an affronted look. "If you had a *good* reason to stay, then what would it prove if you did so?"

The two clans met, exchanging handshakes and hugs. Once Hopp had done some chatting, he made his way to Dante and Blays. He was starting to sport some silver around his temples and in his beard, which he'd finally allowed to grow long enough to cover the R branded on his right cheek—once, he'd kept it shaved to remind the world he'd once been a Gaskan slave. It seemed he no longer felt the need.

"Are the rumors true?" Hopp said.

Blays tilted his head. "You'll have to be a lot more specific than that."

"That you were going to go straight to Narashtovik without so much as saying hello to your own clan. What have we done to earn such disgrace?"

"You made the mistake of not causing a disaster worthy of Dante's attention."

"Sorry about that," Dante said, meaning it. "There's trouble in Narashtovik. It could be bad."

Hopp studied him. "Have you ever noticed that there seems to be trouble everywhere you go?"

"So just imagine how much more there would be if I didn't show up to deal with it."

Hopp went to greet a few of the other Nine Pines, who'd remained on relatively terrific terms with the Broken Pines ever since the war. In time, Hopp joined them outside Mourn's yurt, where they were continuing to appreciate the craftsmanship of the Pines' brewer.

Hopp took a tankard and then a seat. For close to an hour, he rambled on about the particular coldness of that winter, his recent squabbles with nearby clans, and an expedition into the Woduns he was planning to make during the coming summer. After asking several dozen questions about the kappers that infested the mountains, he fell silent. Blays and Mourn excused themselves to find more beer.

Once they left, Hopp's eyebrow perked up. "Did I tell you why we're here? No, of course I haven't. Or why wouldn't I remember it?"

He twisted in his chair and rooted around in his pack. With a noise of satisfaction, he turned back around and extended his hand.

An empty shaden shell rested on his broad palm. "Do you know what this is?"

Dante blinked. "Do *you*?"

"Is it the former home of a snail?"

"And this is remarkable to you?"

"It's a large, fine shell, isn't it?" Hopp ran an oversized finger over the shell's black swirls. "Very pretty."

"Why don't you tell me what you know?"

"Why don't *you* ask the right questions?"

Dante pressed his lips together. "Where did you find it?"

Hopp waved a hand at the low hills. "Oh, somewhere out there."

"Which is strange, right? I know I've been gone for a while, but I don't think it's been long enough for a new ocean to form in the Norren Territories."

The older norren smiled, fox-like. "That's what led me to ask our clan about it. And when they didn't know what it was, to start asking other clans."

"You were that interested in an empty shell?"

"I should see a strange thing, say 'How strange,' and think nothing more of it? If you found something unusual in your house—someone else's shoe, say—you wouldn't wonder how it came to be there?"

"At this moment, the only thing I'm wondering is if this conversation could be any more baffling."

Hopp gave him a crooked look. "What do you think matters

more? The point? Or how you come to reach it? No matter how widely I asked, no one knew much about the shells. But I did hear that you'd know about them."

Dante blinked. "How did you hear *that*?"

"With my ears."

"You norren gossip worse than fishwives."

"Do you humans think you're so clever that no one else will notice what you're up to? Don't answer that question. Answer this one: should I be concerned to find the shell inside the Norren Territories?"

Dante took the shell, turning it over in his hand. "They're called shaden. They come from an island far to the south. The meat is like a warehouse of nether. Exceedingly useful to people like me. Until very recently, the Mallish priesthood was gathering them in great numbers."

"Am I to infer this practice stopped when you arrived?"

"More of that 'trouble' you were referring to earlier."

Hopp's face had been sobering rapidly. "Why would Mallish priests be using the nether inside the Norren Territories?"

"I have no idea. Could be they were just passing through on their way to Narashtovik. If so, these people might be the same ones I'm on my way to deal with. But we can't assume it'll be that easy to settle. It could also be an arm of something far more sinister. Will you and the Herons keep watch on the pass?"

"What are we to watch for?"

"The aforementioned Mallish priests, for a start. And anyone else who looks suspicious."

"What if all humans look suspicious to me?"

"Then only tell me about the ones *I'd* think were suspicious."

Hopp nodded, satisfied. "What brought you to this island of nether-snails in the first place?"

Dante took a deep breath and began to explain. He hadn't meant to say more than a few vague sentences, but before he knew it, he was relating a detailed account of the last half year since being called away from the tunnel he'd built for Gallador. The note from his "father," the business with the Kandeans, the pursuit of Gladdic, the warring in Collen. It took some time.

When he finished, Hopp was frowning. "That sounds dreadful. Why take on so many worries for people you'd never met before?"

"It seemed more polite than letting them get slaughtered."

"And it sounds like you're sick and tired of it." Hopp snapped his fingers. "You know what you should do? Join the Broken Herons."

"In case you've forgotten, we already did that. Blays nearly drowned himself in the effort."

"I'm suggesting you join us and stay with us. Don't you want to walk the prairies? Explore the mountains? See the sun touch a new hill every morning? Set down your concerns, pick up your bow, and hunt the deer with us?"

Dante was about to reject this out of hand. Instead, he found himself gazing across the trampled snow of the camp, envisioning himself out in the wilds in the company of a hundred brothers and sisters, with no worries beyond what they'd catch for the night's meal. He could still practice the nether—clearly, it would be his nulla—but from then on out, his pursuit would be purely for himself. If he wanted, he could even resume leading, to whatever extend Hopp would welcome. It would be far easier to take care of a clan of a hundred than a city of a hundred thousand.

"It's tempting," he said. "Genuinely. But I can't."

"Why not? If you leave, will the walls of Narashtovik come crashing down? Will the townsfolk fling themselves from the bridges in despair? Will Arawn get so angry he'll smash his fist down on the city, leaving nothing behind but a crater?"

"If *I* left? No. But what if everyone tossed aside their responsibilities?"

"Do you always worry about things that aren't happening? Do you know why norren don't build towns?"

"What are you talking about? Plenty of you do."

"Do you think I'm talking about them?"

"Why don't norren build towns?"

Hopp opened his hand as if releasing a trapped bird. "So we can always walk away."

It would have sounded self-congratulatory if not for the fact it was true. The norren looked after themselves and their clan.

Other than the occasional scuffle with a foe-clan, their lives were more or less open to do whatever they wanted, which they took full advantage of. If the norren acted like this, and were perfectly fine people, why couldn't humans do the same? Why couldn't he?

Abruptly, he realized that he hadn't had someone like Hopp to talk to in a long time. Cally (and, briefly, Larrimore) had served that role in Dante's earlier years, and Olivander sort of had for a few years after that, when Dante had been easing into his role of leader of the Council.

But he was Olivander's superior, and over time, any type of mentorship had ceased. Anyway, Olivander wasn't exactly sage material—competent, yes, and as dependable as a sunrise, but he lacked the mischief of a truly effective sage.

Dante missed having such a figure in his life. He would probably never have one again: getting too old, and definitely too high up the hierarchy. If anything, people would look to *him* to be the mentor, the sage.

Now there was a scary thought.

He gave himself permission to quit worrying for one night. Instead, he ate, drank, and bullshat with the norren. In the morning, mounting his horse to leave took far more willpower than he expected. A handful of norren had gathered to see him and Blays off, but most were busy with the slow rhythm of their lives, little currents within the tide.

Narashtovik grew ahead, a great sprawl of buildings on the low hills before the bay, its outskirts hazed with wood smoke, its center defined by the spear of the cathedral and the upthrust fist of the Citadel. He had been to many places, and would admit that some of them were more beautiful. Even so, the city was his, and the sight of it made him sit taller in the saddle, shoulders pulled back with pride.

He didn't announce their arrival, but the word of their return beat them to the Citadel. The gates creaked, opening before them; among the battlements, soldiers in black and silver saluted. Dante and Blays clopped into the courtyard. A legion of grooms assembled to tend to their horses.

Gant resolved from the scramble of activity. The majordomo was approaching old age, but remained as hard and thin as a nail. He was normally cheerful, and lightly, almost formally mocking of them, but that day, there was no humor in his eyes.

He gave them a deep nod. "Sir Galand. Sir Buckler. The air always seems clearer when the lords have returned to their home."

"You sure you're happy to see us?" Blays said. "You look like Gashen got a little too drunk and mistook your house for his chamber pot."

"Olivander wishes to speak to you. He is currently within the Council chambers. He will explain."

Dante and Blays exchanged a look. They hustled upstairs to the chambers near the top of the keep. There, Olivander stood alone next to the round, sprawling table. Olivander was a lifelong military man, and Dante expected his stiff posture was so thoroughly ingrained in him that they'd be able to use his corpse as a cloak rack. Yet on that day he looked shorter, somehow smaller.

"It's Cee," he said without preamble. "She's been looking into the theft of the book—and last night, she was attacked."

12

She lay in bed, wan and deflated, like a butterfly that's just left its cocoon. As far as Dante could tell, she was fine. They'd healed her whole, her throat didn't show a scratch or a scar—but she'd been in a deep sleep since the attack. There was no telling when—or if—she'd wake up.

Dante sent the nether within her, questing for damage the others hadn't noticed, but found nothing substantial. He withdrew from Cee's chambers and summoned the one who'd been with her during the attempted murder, an acolyte named Sorrowen.

Dante didn't know Sorrowen personally, but Olivander had already briefed him. Growing up in Farning, a village in the Mallish earldom of Wicks, Sorrowen had shown a knack for the ether when he was just six years old. He'd quickly been inducted into the priesthood at Wicks, with expectations he'd be sent to Bressel's Primacy School by the time he was ten. For years, he remained in Wicks, making little progress with the ether, his promising start stalling to a standstill.

As it turned out, this was because he just wasn't very good at it. His true talent lay in the nether. Initially, he'd refused to practice it at all—smart, considering that in Mallon, the practice was punishable by death—but over the years, his curiosity with the shadows and his frustration with the light had eroded his resolve.

So he'd begun to practice in secret. Realizing that if he stayed in Mallon, he would at best never progress beyond an amateur, and at worst be executed by the ethereal rite of the Piercing of a Hundred Stars, he'd snuck out of his temple and made the long pilgrimage to Narashtovik.

There, he'd been allowed to become an acolyte at one of the lesser cathedrals. He'd made progress with the nether. Changed his name from the obviously Mallish Sorley to the upstandingly Gaskan Sorrowen. Following some testing of his skill, and an investigation into his background to make sure he wasn't a spy, he'd been elevated to the monastery within the Citadel.

At that point, he'd been fourteen. Now, four years later, Sorrowen was skilled enough to become a proper monk, but was being prevented from doing so by some kind of bureaucratic logjam that Dante couldn't solve without alienating one half of his monks. So he'd left them to solve the dispute for themselves. Needless to say, the logjam wasn't being received well by the acolytes being held back.

Nak, who still thought of himself as a simple monk mistakenly promoted to the heights of the Council, continued to take an interest in the monastery's affairs. It had been his suggestion to assign Sorrowen to Cee as she investigated the theft of the book. Paired up, Sorrowen would provide magical muscle for Cee. Meanwhile, as Sorrowen waited for his official promotion, the task would give him something to do and provide him real experience out in the field.

Dante awaited the acolyte in the Council chambers. Sorrowen arrived looking perfectly anxious. Ten years the boy's senior, Dante thought Sorrowen looked absurdly young.

"Sit down," Dante said.

The boy's eyes darted from chair to chair as he attempted to decipher which one he was meant to occupy. He glanced at Dante for a sign, found nothing, then shot a look at Blays, who was leaning against a wall, arms folded. Looking as though he might spontaneously shatter, Sorrowen simply chose the chair closest to him.

"Tell me what happened last night," Dante said.

Sorrowen frowned. "I've already told Olivander. But you're

not Olivander," he added quickly. "And you're giving me an order. So I should probably shut up and talk."

Dante hadn't bothered to light a fire and the room was cold, but sweat dewed Sorrowen's forehead. He spoke with a moderate Mallish accent. "I was out with Cee. Obviously. She was supposed to meet someone named Waller. This was after midnight, I remember because the bells had made me jump—"

"Who's Waller?"

"I don't know. There was a lot Cee didn't tell me. Sometimes I felt like she didn't like having me around."

"Hard to believe. Where was the meet to be held?"

"A rooftop on Flinders Street. Next to the Green Beetle. Cee had me get up onto the roof across the street and hide behind the water barrels. Everything looked fine to me—I mean, there were a lot of dirty-looking people around, but that's Flinders Street for you—so I signaled Cee the okay.

"Well, she started to climb up to her roof. I remembered I didn't have any blood on hand, so I poked myself in case I needed to call the nether—"

"Where?"

Sorrowen furrowed his brow. "To my hands?"

"Where do you cut yourself?"

"Right here." He tapped the left side of his chest. "I know they recommend the back of the arm, but sometimes it leaves a bit of a scar. I got to thinking, what if I ever go back to Mallon and one of the priests sees me with a bunch of cut-up arms and thinks, 'Hmm, that fellow looks like a nethermancer'?"

Dante nodded, mildly impressed, and made a note to mention the idea to the monks who trained the acolytes. "Did Cee make it to the roof?"

"Yep. There was some moonlight, so I had a clear view of her. She was all alone on this flat part of the roof—and then this guy in a cloak seemed to step out from nowhere."

"You mean it was hard to tell where he came from?"

Sorrowen shook his head. "I mean that one second, Cee was the only person on that roof. And then it was like someone walked out of an invisible door."

Dante twisted to raise his eyebrows at Blays, who nodded.

"And then he just *stabbed* her!" Sorrowen's eyes were wide. "He drew back a knife and was going to stab her again, but I threw a shadowbolt at him. Right before it hit him, he vanished as fast as he'd shown up."

"You reacted that fast? From across the street?"

"I was supposed to be looking out for her, wasn't I?"

"Then what?"

"Cee was bleeding. Bad. So I closed her up as best I could, yelled for help, and stood watch. Nothing else happened until Nak and the monks showed up and got her down from the roof."

Dante leaned forward at the table, pinching the bridge of his nose. "Anything strange leading up to the attack? Or during it?"

"That's all I can remember."

"Question," Blays said. "Are you sure the attacker was a man?"

Sorrowen shrugged his shoulders tight. "I guess not. He—they—were wearing a cloak. And I couldn't see their face."

"Thank you," Dante said. "Close the doors behind you."

The boy stood, bowed to Dante, then seemed to think he should bow to Blays too, which apparently required a second bow to Dante. He walked quickly from the room, clicking the door shut behind him. Dante waited for the boy's footsteps to fade down the hall.

He turned to Blays. "Shadowalker?"

"Absolutely."

"Does that disturb you as much as it does me?"

"Because the next question is whether this was one of the People of the Pocket?"

Dante nodded. "Is there any chance we've done something to offend them?"

"Well, we *have* kept one of them away from her husband, who the rumors hold is as dashing as he is brave. Such an offense is truly worthy of death."

"But the real answer is no, right? They don't get involved in outside affairs. They're not even supposed to leave Pocket Cove. And we haven't done anything to them in the first place."

"I'll check with Minn." Blays folded his arms. "But if they are involved, they might hide it from her so she wouldn't tell me."

"If she did know, are you sure she'd tell you?"

"I'd like to think so." Blays headed for the door. "But I'd like for a lot of things to be true."

While he went to find Minn, Dante headed for the chapel where the theft had taken place. At his request, they hadn't changed anything since then, not even to replace the drapes or sweep the floors. The only major thing they'd done before Nak had contacted him was to remove the boot from the wall.

As such, after weeks of intentional neglect, the place was a colossal mess, full of grit, dried leaves, cobwebs, and mouse droppings. Dante went over it bit by bit. Nothing stood out as suspicious.

He picked his way across the dingy floor to stand in front of the sealed rock wall. As far as he could tell, the stone was undisturbed except for the small triangular divot where the boot's heel had been captured. More evidence they were dealing with a shadowalker rather than someone capable of moving the earth. Although most of the People of the Pocket were both.

Just in case someone was playing a bizarre trick on him and hiding the book right under his nose, he moved his mind through the rock, feeling for empty pockets or hidden compartments. Nothing there. He hadn't expected to find anything—it had been over a month since the theft, and Somburr, Nak, and Cee had already been over the room multiple times—yet his failure was still disappointing. Every failure took them one step closer to running out of options.

Lastly, Dante inspected the boot. It seemed worn and ordinary. If the wearer had left some blood in it, or even a stray hair, Dante could have tracked them down with a quickness, but the only hairs he found on the boot belonged to the people who'd handled it. He severely doubted any of them was a secret shadowalker, but he had them try it on anyway. It was too small for all of them.

All of this took Dante close to three hours. Even so, he still had to wait for Blays to return from his "conversation" with Minn.

When Blays finally arrived, he sprawled in a chair, putting his feet up. "Minn says she doesn't know of any schemes from Pocket Cove."

"Hmm."

"Come on, why would they steal the *Cycle*? Think they got bored of staring at the ocean and decided they needed some new bedtime stories?"

"Maybe they want to use it to identify new recruits. Same way Samarand did."

Blays considered this, then shook his head. "The People of the Pocket don't have any interest in growing their numbers. The only thing they care about expanding is the freshness of their fish."

"Even if it wasn't them as an institution, that doesn't mean it wasn't one of their number acting on her own. Ask Minn if she knows whether anyone's left recently."

Minn didn't, but she promised to ask. With the People of the Pocket lacking loons—unless they were deceiving Dante about that, too—that meant dispatching a messenger, meaning any answer was weeks away. Still, that was all the more reason to set it in motion at once.

The rest of the day was eaten up by Council business. By the time Dante finally got to his own room, he was so tired that he almost didn't notice that his sword was missing, too.

He sat on his bed and thought about screaming. The theft of the sword was somehow far more personally humiliating than the stealing of the *Cycle*. To the point where he was almost tempted not to say anything about it to anyone else.

That, however, was stupid, and completely at odds with his overall goal of getting it back. Somburr was off spying in Setteven and Cee remained unconscious, meaning the active head of security was...well, he didn't know; he'd been gone too long. He decided to burden Olivander with the information, trusting his second would deliver it to the appropriate parties. After that conversation was over, Dante was so tired he was starting to regret turning down Hopp's offer to wander away with the Broken Herons.

Still, in the morning, it felt good to wake up in his own room in his own city. To be surrounded by familiar faces in a familiar building. He ate breakfast, then returned upstairs to head a formal meeting of the Council. Dante gave them a full account of Collen's rebellion against Mallon, including the particulars of his and Blays' involvement in it.

There were questions. Lots of them. Dante answered without flinching, satisfying them by making it clear that Narashtovik's involvement would end as soon as they'd secured the agreement between Alebolgia and Collen.

Dante glanced around the table. "Anything else?"

"One small matter." This came from Tarkon, the oldest member of the Council, and one of the few remaining from Samarand's time. Like many old men, he no longer cared about being polite—or, maybe, had forgotten how. "Why in the shrieking hell do you think this is a good idea?"

Dante laughed. "If you'd told me from the beginning where this was going to lead, I might not have gotten involved. But if you knew what was going to happen before it did, I'd do whatever you say, because you must be a god. As for me, I'm still a human—"

"Despite your best efforts to join the Celeset."

"—and as a human, I didn't know what was to come. I had to make my decisions as things played out. It got messy. But if I'd walked away, it would have gotten even messier. That made it hard for me to pretend I had no responsibility to the people in need."

Tarkon stroked his beardless chin. "There are troubles here, too. If we cleaned up every mess that happened a thousand miles away, we'd never have any time to deal with our own."

Dante didn't try to argue with that. He wrapped up the meeting. As soon as he entered the hallway, he was intercepted by Gant, who looked much sunnier than the day before. With good reason: Cee was awake.

Blays accompanied him to the mending chamber at the monastery. Cee was sitting up in bed arguing with a bald old monk. Seeing Dante, the monk bowed and left the room.

Dante moved to the side of the bed. "How are you feeling?"

She rubbed the faintly visible line on her throat. "Better than most who take a knife to the windpipe. How did I make it out of there?"

"Sorrowen drove off the assassin before they could finish their task. Then healed you enough to hold on until the monks arrived."

Cee grunted. "Sorrowen did all that?"

"Talking to him, he comes off like he couldn't talk to a girl without breaking into full-fledged retreat. But he's quick on his feet. Hard to teach that."

"What about the assassin? Did you catch her?"

Dante nearly smiled. Cee always got straight to business, tossing all of the social niceties aside like the froth they usually were. "She got away. But we're going to find her. You know it was a woman? Did you get a good look at her, then?"

"Couldn't see. It was too dark. And then I was too stabbed."

"Nothing at all? The color of her hair, whether she was younger or older?"

"Nothing." Cee smiled weakly. "But I could tell you her name."

Blays cocked her head. "You know her name? What, did she write you a signed apology?"

"I've been hunting her for weeks. Ran into her once before, but it was down in the dungeons. Too dark then, too. Her name's Raxa Dosse. She works with an outfit called the Order of the Alley. Typical thieves' guild. The word on the street is that Dosse comes and goes as quietly as a shadow. What they don't understand is that she *is* one."

Dante added the name to his notes. "Is this related to all the thefts from last summer?"

"Right. Seemed like they were robbing a different noble every week. Hit us, too. Took the Jerrelec Collection."

"And my sword."

Cee swung up her head. "They took that, too? I'm sorry, sir. I swear to you I'll get it back."

"Wrong. You're staying here."

"Don't trust your healers' own work? Finding things is my job. That's why I'm here."

"I don't remember hiring you to fight sorcerers and volunteer for impromptu throat surgery. This woman is insanely dangerous. It was your job to find her. You did that. Now it's our job to take care of her."

Cee gave him a hard look, then relaxed into her pillows. "Isn't fair to be born like this."

"Like what?"

"Normal. Trying to compete against people like you. Who can tear me apart with a thought."

Dante made a thinking noise. "Am I supposed to feel guilt for that? It's the way I was born."

"I know that." Cee smiled grimly. "Nothing's fair. And that's why I work as hard as I do to keep up."

"Why was Dosse trying to kill you?" Blays said. "Because she knew you were coming after her for the book? Or did you forget to invite her to the last cotillion?"

"After the Order robbed the Citadel, I turned one of them traitor. Guy named Gaits. With his help, we set up an attack on the Order. Pinned it on their rivals. The idea was they'd wipe each other out and we'd mop up whatever was left."

"Nice plan," Dante said.

"Thought you'd like it. At first, it went great. Thieves, thugs, and killers were cutting each other down every day. Meanwhile, the citizens were safe. So were our troops. But Dosse bit her teeth into investigating the attack and wouldn't let go. When it looked like she was closing in on the truth, Gaits came up with a plan."

Cee paused, lowering her gaze, then made herself look up at Dante. "It wasn't pretty. Dosse has these kids. Gaits wanted to put them somewhere she couldn't get to them, then use the threat of hurting them to make sure she wouldn't try to hurt *him*."

Blays bit his lip. "You helped him to kidnap her children?"

"If it matters, I don't think they were hers by blood. Gaits made it sound like they were street urchins. She was looking after them or something. I didn't like it, but Gaits thought she was too dangerous to go after unless he had a trump card. He was more right than he knew. He never came back. And she headed straight for the kids. She must have tortured the answer out of him, then killed him."

"If she hadn't rescued the urchins, would you have hurt them?"

"What would that have accomplished?"

Blays shrugged. "People do all sorts of unpleasant things that don't accomplish anything besides satisfying their spite."

Cee stared him down. "Do you think I'm one of those people?"

"Oh, we *all* are. But I'm glad you weren't in this case. Even so, it's no wonder this woman's hot for our blood."

Dante pressed a knuckle against his temple. "Do you know where we can find her?"

"That's been tough," Cee said. "A lot of her people went underground during the fighting. Isn't easy to get the people who know about them to talk. They're afraid of getting knifed. Or they just hate us. Most of the info we get turns out to be a wild goose chase."

"We can't let this woman go. If the streets are too afraid of her, we might have to teach them to be more afraid of us."

"We do know some of the Order's buildings. I can get you the addresses."

"One of your people can do that. I want you to rest for another day. We'll have work for you tomorrow."

"Doubt it. Now that you're here, she'll be dead by dawn."

Dante and Blays walked out. The bald monk walked in and resumed his argument with Cee right where they'd left off.

Blays closed the door. "What's our move? Deploy the moths and wait for one of her people to lead us to her?"

"We'll try that," Dante said. "But if she's at all smart, she'll be insulating herself. I think we need to hit the streets."

"Just stroll up to the den of villainy, knock on the door, and let them know the high lord of the land would like a chat?"

"I'm not going to send anyone else out there. Not after what happened to Cee."

It was the dead of winter and bugs of any kind were in short supply, especially the flying kind best suited for reconnaissance. Fortunately, Somburr had foreseen this eventuality long ago, and had tasked one of the monks with setting up a creche of darkling beetles.

This was a small wooden structure attached to the stables. The air inside it was warm and smelled a little foul and a little sweet. Dante slew a dozen beetles, reanimated them, and sent them buzzing over the walls toward the addresses in Cee's logs.

He was still dressed in the formal garb of the High Priest overseeing his Council. He changed into dark trousers and a long wool coat. The coat's hem hung past his knees, but that was the only thing about it that adhered to proper Narashtovik style. Otherwise, it was as plain and shabby as the mugs in a public house in the Sharps.

Similarly attired, Blays joined him and they struck out for the city's livelier neighborhoods. It was near noon, but the sun was blocked from sight by a thick tarp of clouds. Snowflakes skirled from above. The temperature likely hadn't been above freezing in weeks and the streets were bedeviled with hard-packed patches of ice. An icy wind gusted from the bay on the north end of the city.

But people still required food and homes and so forth, which meant they required the money to buy them with, which meant they required forms of employment. And so, for all nature's efforts to convince people to stay indoors until the outdoors wasn't actively trying to kill them, the streets bustled with people going on about their business.

Though the city continued to grow with each year, Dante still knew most of it. He headed for a public house near the inner wall of the Pridegate. Years back, with Narashtovik's coffers growing fat following the surge of trade from their allies following the war, Dante had funded a project to invest in those who wanted to start businesses but lacked the coin for the initial costs.

With the aid of a pair of monks who'd been trained as interrogators by Samarand, the project's choice of partners had hit the mark often enough to make the program self-funding. For a while, at least; recently, it had been struck with increasingly cunning forms of fraud. During the salad days, though, when Dante had been personally involved in the selections, he'd approved the city's investment in a public house called the Stagger Home, run by one Lanina Ock.

The Stagger's emblem was a man leaning so heavily that it looked like he was about to tumble off of the sign. Icicles the size of a man's arm hung from the eaves. Inside, the main room was welcomingly warm, dense with the scents of beer, damp wool and leather, and the beef stew that seemed to exist in every land that had a proper winter.

Several of the patrons stared at the two of them, trailing off mid-sentence. For a moment, the only sounds were the crackle of the fire and the clink of crockery on a serving boy's tray. As Dante headed for the bar, conversation resumed, though more softly than before.

The man behind the counter hustled to the back, then returned to tell Dante that Lanina would be happy to see them. They walked to her office. Seeing them, Lanina rose from her chair, grinning.

She ran her eyes up and down Dante's frame. "Where've you been off to this time? The ass end of the world and back? You look ten years older!"

"You're one to talk," he said. "You're grayer than Blays' face the morning after you tell him drinks are on the house."

"That's what happens to you when all your customers are drunks. Did you want something? Or did you just come here to insult me?"

"We're looking for someone. Raxa Dosse of the Order of the Alley. Do you know her?"

"Do I know about the woman who pulled a heist on the Sealed Citadel itself? They're probably singing songs about her out front as we speak."

"Know where we can find her?"

Lanina knitted her brows. "I don't. And I'm glad I don't."

Blays folded his arms. "Bit of a terror, is she?"

"I've never heard so many rumors about one person. Some say she's a vampire—turns into a bat and flits into the place she wants to rob. Others say she can fly by flapping her arms. Or that she's got a blade that can cut through solid rock. I believe about one word in a hundred, but what I do believe is that she's got more bodies on her than that carneterium of yours."

"That's exactly why we need to find her," Dante said. "Do you know anyone who might know more?"

Lanina rolled her lips together. "There's a person named

Thumbs that comes in here most nights. Around his fifth cup, he likes to brag about how he used to run with the Order. Normally, I'd say it was no more than drunk talk. A way to puff himself up for his fellow souses. But Thumbs seems to know just enough that I might believe him."

"Then we'll find out tonight."

"I'll consider myself warned. But if you plan to beat it out of him, do me a favor and do it outside."

"Think we'd need to? I thought he was a braggart."

"A most annoying one." Lanina met his gaze, but there was something guarded in her eyes. "Just don't be surprised if he suddenly acts like he'd rather swallow his own tongue."

She promised to send a runner to the Citadel if Thumbs arrived that evening. Dante and Blays moved on to their next potential source, a pawnbroker Blays sometimes went out drinking with. While Blays spoke with his man, Dante cycled through the eyes of the beetles that had arrived at the Order's known haunts. With no idea what Raxa looked like, he had to listen to each conversation carefully. Her name cropped up now and then, but always in the context of speculation or gossip, and never as though they were sitting there in the room with her.

The pawnbroker gave them nothing of note. Neither did their next three sources. Snow continued to fall. The night joined it. Nak looned Dante to let him know that Thumbs had arrived at the Stagger Home, "whatever any of that meant." Dante and Blays beelined for the pub.

Inside, Lanina commanded the bar. Seeing Dante, she shifted her eyes to the right end of the counter, where a man in a disintegrating fur hat jabbed his index finger in all directions, punctuating his loud speech. Soon enough, the man in the hat stood and walked outside to use the latrine.

Blays moved behind him, smiling. "Mr. Thumbs?"

Thumbs spun, jaw tight and head tipped back. Seeing the two armed men across from him, he eased back. "What do you want? To watch a grown man take a piss?"

"Better take care of that first. Otherwise, when you hear what I have to say, you'll wind up wearing it."

Thumbs scowled. There was a latrine around the rear of the

building, but he turned his back on them and urinated into a snowbank. Dante knew that countless people did it every day—in moments of desperation or over-inebriation, he'd done so himself—but the sight of someone pissing on his city made him want to drag the man off to the dungeons.

Thumbs finished and walked back toward them, keeping his right hand in the pocket of his long coat. "Get on with it before someone steals my drink."

"The other night I heard you say you used to belong to the Order." Blays tipped his head to the side. "Is that true?"

"Damn right. One of their top men. Raked in so much silver I could retire by an age when most men are still learning their trade."

"Did you ever know...*her*? The shadow who calls the shots?"

"'Course I did. A man like me knows everyone." Thumbs smirked. "But if you're angling for an introduction, well, that means you don't got what it takes to deserve one."

"I think you'll tell me how to get in touch with her. You see, my name is Blays Buckler. I work in the employ of the Citadel. Or maybe it'd be more accurate to say that I've agreed to lend my talents to the Citadel because I'm fond of it and the people in it. In either event, I need to speak with Raxa Dosse. You can help me find her. Or I can give your friends reason to call you The Man with Two Weird Little Nubs Where His Thumbs Used to Be, and *then* you can help me find her."

Over the course of Blays' speech, Thumbs' face had frozen as fast as the ice in the streets. His right hand twitched in his pocket. Dante drew on the shadows.

Thumbs went perfectly still. "It was lies. All of it. I was never in the Order. Damn sure never knew Raxa Dosse."

"Then why pretend to be part of a vicious gang?" Blays said. "To avoid the horror of ever being hired again?"

"Why else? Make myself look important. Be the one everybody else looks up to."

"I think it's time to see about those thumbs."

The man edged back an inch. "You're mad at me because I *don't* associate with known criminals?"

"I've got nothing against criminals. Used to be one myself.

Would probably still be considered one, except I became one of the people who gets to decide who the criminals are." Blays took a step forward, gazing down at the shorter man. "I'm getting mad at you because I think you're lying to me."

Thumbs whipped his hand from his pocket. A knife slashed past the falling snowflakes. Blays stepped to Thumbs' left, grabbing the collar of the man's coat and pulling it over his head. Thumbs yelled out, slashing blindly. Blays turned with him, yanking the coat inside-out over Thumbs' arms, ensnaring him. Blays grabbed his wrist, located an elbow within the fabric, and bore down with his forearm. The knife fell into the snow.

Blays made a few more maneuvers Dante probably wouldn't have been able to follow even in full daylight. He came to a stop standing over Thumbs, locked onto an arm that was in imminent danger of snapping.

"Right," Blays said. "Talk."

"I *was* in the Order." Thumbs sneered up at Blays, snot smeared across his upper lip. "But I left almost two years ago. I never knew Raxa. Don't know where to find her."

Blays cranked the man's arm another fraction of an inch. Thumbs gasped, then retched.

Blays shifted his grip. "You're sure about that?"

"Then take my arm, you jackbooted priest-lover. Even if I did know, telling you would write my name on a grave."

Blays looked up at Dante. "What do you think?"

"Can't hurt to try it." Dante nodded at the man's arm. "Except, obviously, for him."

"I just have this nasty suspicion he's telling the truth."

"Your call."

Blays tipped back his head to the falling flakes, swore, and let go of Thumbs' arm. The man plopped into the snow and sat up, rubbing his arm.

"Let this be a lesson about the dangers of vanity," Blays said.

Thumbs got to his feet. Blays picked up the knife from the snow and underhanded it to Thumbs without any spin. Thumbs tracked it and caught it with a cradling motion. He returned it to his pocket and crunched through the snow toward the pub.

Halfway to the corner of the building, he turned and glared at them, eyes icy-bright. "You call *us* thugs. Then you beat me. Threaten me. Every day, your soldiers do the same thing to people like me across the whole damn city. That's why we need someone like her. Who else is going to protect us?"

He turned and stamped around the corner. Empty-handed in a grungy alley that stank of urine, Dante headed back toward the distant lump of the Citadel.

"This is a bad idea," Blays said.

"To call it a night? We've been running down sources all day with nothing to show for it. I need a break."

"That's exactly what I mean. Everyone we've talked to has stonewalled us, lied to us, or passed us off to someone else. If we were anywhere else, we'd be able to make some progress. But we're trying to infiltrate the same underground that we're constantly arresting, imprisoning, and executing. Worst of all, we're trying to find the only one of them who can stand up to us. You really think they're going to turn in Raxa Dosse, their folk hero? You might as well ask the slice of beef on your plate where to find its brother."

"Then we put our power to use. Raid all of the Order's hangouts. Imprison every one of their people until someone talks."

"Giving Raxa the motive and opportunity to light out with the book and your sword."

"What else are we supposed to do? Continue spying on the Order's minions who will probably never step foot in the same neighborhood that she's hiding in?"

Blays was quiet for a time, the snow squeaking underfoot as he hiked toward the Ingate. "We're overthinking this. Put out a reward."

"Think that'll be enough?"

"Even if everyone loves her, there's always someone desperate or selfish enough to betray what they believe in."

Dante tugged his hood forward to cover his freezing ears. "But that's what we're searching for right now. And you're claiming we won't find it. That they won't turn her in to the same authorities who rule them."

"We can't squeeze the answers out of them. That only makes them want to kick back."

"But we can coax them into doing what we want. Plant the seed of the idea and let *them* grow it."

"Precisely." Blays smiled suddenly. "Best if we're not even involved. Have whoever comes in to claim the reward speak to a monk, or someone outside the higher echelons of authority. If the squealer doesn't have to say it right to our faces, they can tell themselves they're not a snitch."

"You're getting more cynical as you get older."

"Hardly. I'm just better at understanding what I'm seeing."

As always, the forging of a new plan bolstered Dante's spirits. Yet something chewed at him. Were they missing a key detail? Some flaw in the plan? He glanced at Blays, about to voice his unease. Blays was staring down the street with a look of such blankness Dante could have believed his soul had departed for the Pastlands.

With that image in his mind, he knew the source of his own troubled thinking. Blays' plot, while cunning, didn't feel like Blays. At this point in life, Blays had seen too much to be naive, but through it all, he'd always maintained a certain optimism. That by and large, people were good, and worth sparing.

This felt colder. The careless knife of truth that cuts as deep as the sea. Blays seemed to be expressing the belief that everyone was as cracked and broken as Arawn's Mill. Inherently flawed. And his solution to their problem carried the implied belief that these flaws weren't necessarily a bad thing: because if you accepted the basic meanness of humans, then that granted you the power to exploit them.

Dante stepped over a long lump in the snow. The lump was covered in fabric; it was the arm of a beggar who'd frozen to death and been buried in the drifts. What had brought this change on Blays? The genocide in Collen? The Keeper betraying their faith in her? Or were they simply getting old?

Whatever the case, Dante had always suspected these darker truths himself. Lighthearted even when he was being cynical, Blays had always held him back from stepping into that drop of unknown distance.

A bitter wind howled from the north, driving powdery snow before it. It was snowing harder now, in slanted, irregular gusts that made the buildings look as though they were fading away into another world. Like the turning of a page, or the clicking of a gear, Dante's mind shifted, too.

And he didn't think he liked what he saw.

In the end, it took just two days for someone to collect the reward.

The someone in question was a young and angry-looking man who refused to give his name. They'd had any number of false reports from drunks and saboteurs, but there was a spiteful intensity in the young man's words that made Dante all but certain he was telling the truth about Dosse.

According to him, Raxa Dosse was operating out of the upper floor of a tenement deep inside a part of the city where a respectable person would in fact be caught dead, but only because someone there had killed them and used their body as a bridge over the nearest puddle.

The monk handling the conversation thanked the young man and made arrangements to pay him if his information led to anything useful. The tenement was only two blocks away from a pub where one of Dante's darkling beetles was currently crawling around on the ceiling spying on the overly loud blather of the crooks beneath it. He guided the beetle outside and directed it toward the tenement. On the way, the fierce winds knocked it down half a dozen times.

They had the shutters closed against the storm. Dante landed the beetle on a windowsill and directed it to search for a crack. This process took several minutes—apparently they'd weatherproofed the upper floor for their princess of thieves—but he finally wiggled his way inside.

He was in a dim room with four pallets on the floor. He crawled to the ceiling and out the door into a common room. There, two men sat at a table playing dice. They'd put a cloth over the table so their rolls wouldn't rattle. They had scarred arms and faces and the unnaturally calm look of enforcers. A third man stood beside the door to the hallway, hand resting on the hilt of his sheathed dagger.

Other than the beeswax candles burning on counters and

shelves, there was nothing in the way of luxury. Just places to sit and places to sleep. It could be abandoned as quickly as they could get out the door.

In a back room, a severe-looking woman sat at a writing desk reading a book. Her gray-streaked hair was bunned behind her head and she was frowning vaguely. She looked to be about forty; for some reason, Dante had thought she'd be younger.

The woman was probably Raxa, but he needed confirmation before he did anything crazy. While he waited for her to talk to someone, he brought two more beetles in from elsewhere in the city, using them to explore the apartments. They found no sign of the book or the sword.

Wonderful. They were going to have to take her alive, then.

As he was angling for a closer look at the book the woman was reading, curious about whatever she was so interested in, someone knocked on the door in a complicated code. The guard standing inside the door knocked back and was answered with another code. Satisfied, the guard opened the door, allowing in a burly man with a dense beard and a young woman with wide-spaced eyes and shiny black hair that hung to her shoulders.

They hung up their long coats and headed for the back room. The big man leaned his head through the doorway. "Raxa? Ready to report in."

The severe-looking woman continued to read for another few seconds, then marked her place and closed the book. "Enter."

He obliged, followed by the other woman. He clasped his hands in front of his waist. "They're ready to meet. Practically starving for it. They want to see you this same night."

Raxa nearly smiled. "Where?"

"There's a stable on Alloden Street. Next to the old temple, the one that got smashed up in the war."

"They want to meet at a stable? Why?"

The man's bearded cheek twitched. "They didn't say. Guessing they own the place. One o'clock."

She thought for a moment, then nodded. "Tell them I agree."

The burly man bobbed his head and left, accompanied by the younger woman.

Dante watched for a few minutes more, then withdrew his attention to his room in the Citadel. "Got her. Right where the source said she'd be."

"About time," Blays said. "What's the plan, then? You tear off the roof in a god-like surge of power while I rappel in and snatch her up? Or would you prefer something more subtle—a nethermancer on every rooftop backed up by a full cavalry charge down the street?"

"She's on her way to a meet in less than an hour. There's no need to complicate this. We ambush her in the streets and take her back here."

"And if she takes her guards along with her?"

Dante shrugged. "I won't cry if the dawn shines on a city with four fewer cutthroats in it. Going to have to hoof it if we want to catch her before the meet."

They were still dressed in their common garb. They grabbed their knee-length coats and headed outside, pulling their hoods tight over their heads. Gant intercepted them at the gates, looking perturbed. Dante told him they were on their way to secure the book and they'd be back before the four o'clock bells. Gant nodded and made for the keep.

Jogging through the gates, Dante glanced back at the Citadel. "This was a lot simpler before I had to tell everyone who I'm off to kill."

"Time to implement a new rule," Blays said. "If anyone asks, you'll kill *them*."

In this weather, horses would be more trouble than they were worth, leaving them to jog toward Alloden Street. Dante knew it couldn't be so, but their choice to meet next to the damaged temple felt like a personal affront—he'd been meaning to patch the place up for years, but there had been so many other projects to attend to that it had slipped through the cracks.

"So," Dante said. "Ideas for how to take down a shadowalker?"

"Don't tell me you've never thought about how you'd fight *me*."

"I'd keep twenty feet away from you at all times, force you out of the shadows whenever you try to dive into them, then blast you into a pile of pulp topped by floppy blond hair. Unfortunately for that plan, we can't kill her. Not until we've got the book."

"She'll try to bolt." Blays wiped half-melted snow from his cheeks. "Don't think I've ever fought anyone in the shadows before. Think you'll be able to keep track of where she is?"

"Not sure." Dante grinned. "But I won't have to. You can follow her in the shadows. Wherever she goes, you point her out to me and I'll force her back out. We can keep that up until she runs out of strength."

"Assuming I can spend longer in the shadows than she can."

"Hopefully, I'll be able to lock her down tight and we can just carry her back to the Citadel."

"In this snow? New plan: you do the carrying while I scout ahead."

The larger avenues had pathways tunneled through the snow, but in many of the smaller streets, the drifts ranged up to their waists. Annoying. Then again, it would limit the routes Raxa could take to the meet.

Movement in the tenement. Dante switched to the beetle's vision. "They're leaving. Just her and the big guy."

They broke into a run, slipping in the loose snow and the packed ice beneath it. Dante watched with half an eye as Raxa and her underling went downstairs and trudged toward the distant stables. Once it was clear he and Blays would beat her there, they got several blocks ahead and parked themselves at the corner of a major intersection, huddling down like a couple of drunks with nowhere to go.

Raxa left the main street, opting for a smaller one that would take her right behind the stables. Her enforcer stayed on the main road.

Dante stood. "The big guy's peeled off."

"Is she trying to make this easy for us?"

"Probably scouting their escape routes. Let's take her down."

They ran down the cross street. Nearing the intersection of her route, they slowed. There were no lanterns out and the only light was what little spilled from shuttered windows, but most of these were dark as well. The streets looked as vacant as the snowfields of the Woduns.

Dante hooked around the corner, squinting into the gloom. A lone figure stood out from the whiteness of the snow. He moved toward her, making himself sway and breathe hard, like he'd been out drinking. Beside him, Blays belched.

They neared. Raxa had both hands in her pockets. It was cold, but Dante was sure there was a knife in there, too. He bit the inside of his cheek and called to the nether. Black flakes swept between the white ones. Blays stumbled to the right, putting space between them to create a second angle on Raxa.

Dante came to a stop twenty feet away from her. "Raxa Dosse. You can try to run, if you like. But the only thing that will accomplish is getting more snow in our boots."

The woman had halted as soon as he'd spoken Raxa's name. He couldn't place the expression on her face, but he knew one thing: it wasn't fear.

He felt something in the darkness to his right. As light as a mosquito landing on his arm. And as unmistakable as their whine.

He whirled, going for his sword. "Blays!"

But the dark figure was already materializing in front of Blays, her dagger plunging for his heart.

13

Raxa lunged out of the shadows and into the cold darkness of the street.

The man who'd done the talking—Galand, had to be, a realization that turned her veins to ice—yelled, "Blays!"

Her long dagger dived toward the blond man's heart. He was already turning, reaching for his swords, but it was too late. Yet he was smiling.

As abruptly as a man clapping his hands, Blays disappeared.

Raxa's blade speared through empty air. Her mind seemed to lock up. Galand's sorcery? An illusion?

Down the street, Anya had already turned and was running away as fast as the snow allowed, just like Raxa had told her to do. Nether bloomed in the priest's hand. He condensed it into a black dart and sent it streaking toward her head. Heart booming, she grabbed up a lump of shadows and whipped it toward his dart. The two forces met and dashed apart in black twinkles. Galand looked gobsmacked.

She waved at him and leaped into the nether.

She shouted out. Blays was right behind her—he'd probably been right about to shift back into reality and jab both of his swords through her back.

Seeing her, he grinned. "Ready to find out if we can die in here?"

The words sounded dreamlike, almost like they were coming

from inside her own head. He should have been driving one blade at her throat and the other at her gut, but he seemed to be waiting on something. Giving her a sporting chance to speak her mind?

Okay then. She sucked nether to her hand and flung a dark blade at his throat, its edges shining silver.

His eyes flew wider than Galand's had gone. He skipped back, flicking instinctively at the bolt with his right-hand sword. The bolt should have passed right through the steel and into his flesh. Instead, the two objects met with a whopping sound not unlike slapping a wet pair of trousers against a flat rock. The nether dashed into a thousand little sparkles and poofed away.

He looked as surprised as she felt. Before she could make sense of what had just happened, something rammed into her side. Felt like a bag of sand wrapped in a down blanket. She staggered hard, flickering between worlds. Not good. If she had to stay in reality for longer than a few seconds, the priest would smear her across the snow.

She plunged back into the land of black and silver and took off at a dead sprint, putting distance between herself and Galand. Blays shouted out and gave chase. The two of them skimmed over the snow, the soles of their boots barely sinking in. Galand slogged through thigh-deep piles, quickly falling behind.

As she neared the end of the block, she slowed. Blays closed on her. Without warning, she stopped, skidding over the snow, and whirled on him, jabbing for the base of his neck. Blays was sliding straight toward her blade, trying futilely to slow his momentum. Seeing it was hopeless, he threw his feet out from under himself, smacking down on his back. The knife passed over his head.

Lying on top of the snow, he lashed at her ankle. Raxa hopped over the horizontal strike and dropped to a knee, stabbing down at his ribs. He rolled to the side, long coat flapping, and popped to his feet.

He was good. Faster than anyone she'd ever fought. Had the reach advantage on her, too. Raxa fell back a step, tossed her dagger to her left hand, and drew a small knife with her right.

She hurled it at his chest. He spun to the side and swept out his coat, catching the knife in its folds.

She felt something nudge into her side. Galand was getting closer. She took off again. Blays swore and followed, dropping out of the nether for a moment to yell directions at Galand. Rada slipped another small knife into her hand. She saw another way for her to win: see if she could outlast him, and then when Blays was forced back into reality, gut them both.

Thing was, she had a deep-down feel like he had more juice than she did. Even if she had more, every time Galand tried to bump her out of the nether, it took serious energy to stay put.

The Order had been around for years. Enough time to assemble its own codes and lore. Like Urt's commandments, none of these were written down. You had to be initiated. Ironically, it was Gaits who'd taught her the four rules of surviving an encounter.

First, don't get in one.

Second, if you absolutely have to fight someone, hit them before they know what's happening.

Third, think ahead so you can recognize when the fight isn't going your way.

And fourth? Always have a route out.

As they danced over the snow, Galand was falling further behind, but Blays was making gains. Raxa adjusted her grip on the knife. With Blays closing on her, she spun and feinted a throw. As he sidestepped a knife that wasn't there, she threw it for real. He twisted his shoulders, but the blade punched through his sleeve and into his forearm.

Raxa had never fought anyone inside the darkness before. Hadn't even been sure they could hurt each other. That question was answered definitively as blood leaked from his arm, as bright as molten fire, bright silver flecks of nether racing toward it as thickly as a swarm of locusts. The light from his arm was dazzling, hypnotic in a way that made her want to drift to a stop and gaze deeply into the full glory of the gods.

She wrested her mind away from the awe of the blood, turned her back on Blays, and broke into a sprint. She raced around a corner and pressed herself to the face of a stone building. Inside the netherworld, living bodies gleamed like moving moons. It was all the nether in them. Your average slab of stone or chunk of dirt had a little bit in it, too, but compared to something alive, they were as dull as...well, dirt.

She reached inside herself, gathering up great handfuls of nether. When her body was as plain as the rock behind her, she flung the shadows into the night air, sending them whirling away.

Blays veered around the corner, boots whispering over the snow. A tight spiral of glowing shadows trailed from his wounded arm. He passed by without so much as glancing her way. After continuing for a hundred feet, he came to a stop, staring down the street. Chips of snow spun in the breeze. Galand came around the corner, scowling as hard as he was breathing. His trousers were crusted with snow past the knee.

He came to a stop just up the street from Raxa. "Blays? Is that you up there?"

Blays popped out of the shadows, going hazier, the glare around his arm dimming to the glow of a candle. "Don't suppose you've seen an invisible crimelord come through here?"

"You *lost* her?"

"Wrong. *We* lost her. Now help me search."

Blays sharpened as he reentered the darkness, light blooming once more from his arm. He jogged down the street. Galand wandered a few steps further away from her. Pressed against the wall, Raxa could feel his mind questing through the shadows, rustling them like a dog crawling beneath a blanket. She had the feeling that if she tried to move, his attention would snap to her in an instant.

His focus wiggled from one side of the street to the other. When it reached the end of the block, Galand turned around, frowning at the way they'd come in. His mind reappeared. Coming toward her.

Raxa clenched her teeth. He was forty feet away. Too far to try charging at him; he'd strike her down before she was halfway there. Think. Think, or in another thirty seconds, he'd find her, eject her into the real world, and cut her into a thousand pieces.

As his focus moved to the other side of the street, Raxa delved into the nether in the building at the far end of the block. Her hold was shaky. Threatening to collapse at any moment. She clamped down with everything she had, pulling the shadows out into the open and shaping them into a loose oval the height of a person.

Galand spun, snow crunching beneath his heels. His attention flew down the street. Raxa sent the oval of nether darting around a corner. Galand headed for it in a dead run. Keeping herself tight to the building, Raxa headed the opposite way down the street, hooking right at the intersection.

She ran as fast as she could. She didn't let go of the shadows until they were on the brink of spitting her out like a bite of bad fish.

Vess rose from the low stone wall she'd been seated on. In the darkness of the snowy courtyard, her teeth shined white, but Raxa wasn't sure it was a grin.

"Made it back," Vess said. "That mean you got them?"

Fresh anger pulsed up Raxa's spine, spilling into her head. "It started off exactly like I planned. They thought Anya was me. Tried to jump her. Instead, I jumped them. But they had powers I wasn't expecting. Spotted me before I hit either one. I barely made it out with my skin still attached to my body."

"Shit." Vess made the oath sound like a sigh. She sat back down on the stone wall. "They make you?"

"There's no doubt."

"Shit again."

"That's my assessment."

"How you know where to jump them in the first place?"

Raxa kept her gaze steady. Vess knew she'd made a breakthrough with the book, but didn't know about Raxa's ability to blink on and off. Unless Vess *did* know, and was hiding that knowledge from Raxa for the same reason Raxa was hiding her ability from Vess: because you always kept a final knife hidden up your sleeve.

"Galand sent beetles to the safehouse," Raxa said. "They were full of nether. I could feel them trying to get inside the shutters. At the time, I didn't know exactly what they were, but I had a hunch. I had Anya pretend to be me. Fed them a false story about how she was headed to some meet. When they showed up to take her down, that confirmed the beetles were spies."

"Quick thinking you got."

"I'd heard Galand was looking for me in person. That's the only reason I put things together so fast. And all for nothing. Now that they know what I can do, ambushing them's going to be ten times as hard."

"Third shits." Vess flicked snow from the top of the wall. "They're hunting you. They know who you are. And they got powers to hurt you before you can hurt them."

"Is this going somewhere? Or are you just rubbing it in?"

"If I look at a fight with those odds, I drop it like I picked up a turd."

"That's disgusting."

"And so is the splatter they are going to make with your pretty little face." Vess narrowed her eyes. "Leave town. Soon, they'll go back to their stupid little war. That's when you come back, and we continue our war on them."

Raxa paced across the courtyard. Snow was sifting from above, but at least they were out of the wind. "Can't. I've only been in charge of the Order for a few months. If I leave now, somebody who thinks they got screwed at the election will take over."

"You come back, you kill them too. Good chance to take out the trash."

"Not if they resume the war with you in the meantime."

"Citadel won't stop hunting you. They kill you, someone else takes over the Order anyway. Only there's no you around to take it back and set things straight."

Raxa tipped back her head, blinking at the snowflakes sticking in her lashes. Maybe she *should* go. Or turn herself in. They'd kill her, but if she confessed, and told the others to lie low, maybe she could avert a war between the Order and the Citadel. Running away wasn't going to cut it. The Citadel wasn't going to be happy until they had a body.

Then again, who said it had to be hers?

"You're smiling," Vess said. "Why?"

"How would you like to go back to war?"
"With the Citadel? Right now? That's *your* funeral."
"Not with the Citadel," Raxa said. "With me."

Finding a body would have been a snap. Finding a body that resembled Raxa closely enough to fool somebody who'd only seen her from within the eerie glow of the shadows would have only been slightly trickier: as a commercial and religious hub, Narashtovik had drawn a non-trivial population of foreign merchants, pilgrims, and refugees, but most of the population was as pale and dark-haired as Raxa.

Even so, killing an innocent young woman to take the blame for Raxa's crimes felt like the kind of sleaze that would bring down the wrath of the gods. Not just on her head, but upon her entire house. Rather than taking the easy route of finding a lookalike and killing her, they had to wait for one to drop dead.

Then again, their plan was going to need a few days to unfold anyway. Raxa relocated to an old cabin the Order kept in the pine forest outside the city. There, she spent every waking moment focused on the nether. Partly to try to learn more than the couple of minor tricks she'd put together, but mostly to watch out for any more nether-bearing bugs.

While she was away, Vess reopened the war between her Little Knives and the Order. It would be a thin bridge to walk down —they could only trust their inner circles with the knowledge the war was a fake—but after two falsified skirmishes, the two groups ordered their people into hiding. Meanwhile, agents on both "sides" fed a steady stream of gossip to the pubs.

Within days, the entire city knew about the resumption of the war. In the meantime, the agents they'd installed in the bodywagons that picked up the dead for the carneterium found their mark: young woman, dark hair long enough to be tied behind her head, bit of muscle to her.

Raxa was called in from the cabin to take a look. Disguised under a bundle of scarves and coats, she walked into the city with a heavy limp, coming to a rickety old house on the outskirts.

Vess' two guards let her inside the front door. Vess sat at a long table drinking something steamy. The body rested on the table. Its throat was cut wide open.

Raxa frowned. "I thought you said she died of greencough."

Vess gave her an irritated look. "We have to make it look real, don't we? The Citadel's going to believe you happened to drop dead of greencough?"

"She doesn't look anything like me."

"She not as pretty as you think you are?" Vess reached out and patted the dead woman's leg. "She'll fool 'em. You wait and you see."

Using the various oils and powders that were typically used to hide facial flaws, but which outfits like the Order and the Knives used to disguise themselves, Vess made a few small adjustments to the woman's face, then dispatched a messenger to the Citadel and Raxa back to the pine forest.

A day and a half later, the crunch of snow woke Raxa from her pallet. Someone knocked on the door. Good sign. A murderous High Priest wouldn't knock. Raxa opened the door. Vess strode inside, smirking. She went straight to the stove, stoking it and placing a metal cup of spiced rum on top of it to warm up.

Raxa moved behind her. "Well?"

"Well what? Never seen a woman celebrate selling a corpse before?"

"They believed you?"

Vess removed a heavy pouch from inside her coat, jingling the coins inside. "Paid me for it, see? Either they believe it, or they want me to think they believe it."

"How did they seem? Happy? Reserved?"

"Pale one was smug. Cute blond one was happy. Or maybe just drunk."

"What about the war between us? Think they bought it?"

Vess gave her an exasperated look, then sighed and got out a cloth to pick her cup up from the stove. "I told them all that I was supposed to tell. You broke the peace, I took out your throat. The Citadel's reward was just a happy bonus. I don't know what they bought and what they sold."

Raxa found a second cup and poured herself a slug of what Vess was having. When the drinks were properly heated, they bonked their cups together and drank to Raxa's freedom. Could it be as simple as that? Feed them a plausible body, then keep her head down until they dropped their guard? If she was smart, even when it was safe to move against them again, she wouldn't come in flashy and violent. No, she'd poison them slowly. Arrange accidents. Make it look like it wasn't her that hated the Citadel, but the gods.

To be on the safe side, she stayed in the cabin for another week. Before returning to the city, she cut her hair short and choppy, and got Gurles to bring her one of the heavy hooded dresses worn by the women who pushed sledges of firewood through the winter streets, delivering their goods to houses and manors, or simply selling them to passers-by. When she actually tried the dress on, with its heavy folds weighing down her arms so badly she could hardly swing her blade, let alone throw one, she immediately sent Gurles back to a tailor to rush-order the same cut in a lighter fabric.

By the time that returned, and was deemed satisfactory by herself, she'd been away from Narashtovik longer than any time since her aborted apprenticeship at Pocket Cove. Returning to the city—the smell of horses and wood smoke; the trampled gray snow; the spires and walls and all the excellent things locked inside them—Raxa's heart lifted like the coming of a southern heartwind after weeks of freeze.

As nightfall neared, which she loved best of all, especially in winter when the air was so hushed and clear it was like the whole world was made of nether, Gurles rushed through the door of the pub, veered toward her table, and grabbed her arm. Raxa drew back her hand to give him a stiff-fingered jab in the armpit, but the look on his face dashed her anger. She skittered out the back door with him.

After a couple of minutes of rabbiting through a warren of alleys, Gurles came to a stop, glancing behind them. "Blays Buckler was right up the block. And he's asking about you."

"But they think I'm dead. If they *don't* think that, they wouldn't be dumb enough to make their disbelief so obvious."

"Oh, he wasn't looking for you. He was sniffing around for places you used to live."

She stared blankly, steam curling from her mouth. Then it hit her: he *wasn't* looking for her. Just the places she'd inhabited. The places she might have stashed the book and the sword. Blays and his master would never give up the hunt until they had them back.

She turned and crunched through the snow.

Gurles hustled up beside her. "Where are you off to?"

"Away. I'm endangering all of you by being here."

"So you're runnin' back to the woods? How long you mean to stay there? Until we're all so old the only thing we're fit to steal are glances at pretty young girls?"

That had been her plan, more or less. Remove herself from the city until it was safe to come back. But there was more than scorn in Gurles' voice. There was anguish, too. She suspected it wasn't so much for her as for the Order she was supposed to be leading.

She stopped and looked up into his dark eyes. "I'm not going off to hide like a sick cat. I'm going there to come up with a new plan. Until then, I need you to keep a steady hand on the Order. For just a little longer. Can you do that?"

He nodded. Raxa smiled. She turned and ran away, disappearing into the darkness and the snow.

The remains of the old wall reached up into the night like the arm of a heretic repenting to the heavens as he died—and getting denied.

Most of the ruins were much lower, no more than uneven piles of rubble. In two places, great stone blocks stood like dumb sentinels. Their sides were carved with what had once been runes or pictures, but time had worn their meaning away into dust.

Raxa had found the place a few days into her exile during one of her walks, which she told herself were about learning the surrounding terrain, but were mostly about staving off the boredom before it grew lethal. She'd asked Gurles to find out what the ruins were, and after looking into it, he reported they'd once been a fort. The big upright blocks had been part of a temple inside that fort. The fort itself had been built to protect Narashtovik, or at least to get some of the fighting outside the city itself, which in days of yore had been ransacked more often than the Order's liquor stocks.

She'd found it a good place to think. Especially on nights like this, when you could pretend that the entire world was empty ruins, every bit as barren and decrepit. A little morbid, but it also lent her a sense of distance she found helpful.

That night, though, she was distracted. *Had* it been time that had ruined the fort? Or had it been destroyed during one of the many, many wars? Looking for answers, she walked through the snow, which had only been disturbed by herself and a few birds that had left trident-shaped tracks in the white. Many of the walls had fallen into shattered piles. The result of sorcery in a heated battle? Or the work of an old thing falling and busting into bits?

She leaned in for a closer look at a slab of black rock, wiping away the snow with a gloved hand. The edges looked broken but worn. Its surface was patchy with pale green lichen. Too old to tell. All of it. Even if it had fallen down yesterday, she wouldn't have known what she was looking at.

She stood and pulled back her hood, unmuffling her ears and expanding her field of vision. What was she doing? Distracting herself from her real problems? Then again, her *problem* was that she'd gotten into a war with one of the most powerful orders of sorcerers on the continent. And she wasn't anything more than a trumped-up thief dabbling with the nether. So why not spend her time contemplating what had brought down this ancient old fort? At least that was a problem she had a chance in hell of solving.

Something about the place was bothering her, though. Setting aside the matter of what had destroyed the fort, if Narashtovik really had been getting attacked that much—and supposedly, it had been sacked more times than a field of potatoes—why hadn't it ever occurred to its people to go somewhere else? Had it really been that much easier for them to build the Citadel, then the walls of the Ingate, then the Pridegate, then these forts out here in the middle of nowhere? Even if their mighty defenses had prevented them from utter annihilation, how many lives had they lost clinging to this particular scrap of dirt?

The thought hit her so hard she stood up straighter: if she tried to hang around and duke it out with the Citadel, she'd be committing the exact same idiocy the city once had.

She hustled back to Narashtovik. The gates were closed, but the walls weren't; she shadowalked through them. She sent a messenger to Vess, then headed for the temple of Urt. Vess showed up an hour later. Her eyes were puffy and her cloak was dusted with snow.

Vess scowled. "Even for one of us, you keep late hours."

"This was a mistake. We can't fight the Citadel. It was naive to ever think we could."

"Eh? You got the book. You got the magic. That was the plan."

"That makes one of us who can use the nether. How many do they have? Sixty? A hundred?"

Vess shrugged one shoulder. "So you get strong, then you find more like you and you train them. And when you are enough, boom. No more Citadel."

"That's exactly what I'm afraid of," Raxa said softly. "The only way to beat them is to recruit people like them. Train those people like them. *Become* them. If we do that, we've lost the very thing we're fighting for."

The other woman instantly grew thoughtful. "You speak like that, and you make sense."

"I've been going about this the wrong way. Mistaking anger for wisdom. Getting hold of the *Cycle* was a good idea. But the power inside it—I should be using that to protect my people, not to provoke a war against them." She had a sudden vision of the six children she hadn't risked seeing since she'd rescued them from the bowels of the Citadel. "No one else will ever care about them. It has to be us."

"Lots of talk. What's the doing?"

"If I was smart, I'd get the fuck out of here. Move the Order to Yallen. Or Setteven. Or all the way to Bressel."

Vess wrinkled her brow. "Would be smart. But you talk like you don't want to be smart. Why not?"

Raxa shook her head, wandering toward the middle of the snowy courtyard. "Why do people kill themselves? Why not leave the city? The country? The continent? Find out if there's something better out there?"

"I don't know. Why *not* do that?"

She turned to face Vess, frustration boiling up from her gut. That was the logical next question—she'd asked it of herself—but people *didn't* just leave, and their decision didn't feel wrong. Why? It wasn't a connection to the land, was it? That might be a small part of it, but it wasn't the main cause. Then what force could be so strong that it made you stay even when you were certain that staying would destroy you?

"Because we want there to be justice *here*," Raxa blurted. "If we run away, we admit that there isn't. And if there isn't justice here, why would we believe we can find it anywhere?"

"Oh, that's the worry? Simple answer: no justice anywhere. Deal with it."

"I'm going to try. In exchange for peace, I'll ask them for Cee. She was in bed with Gaits; literally, for all I know. She tried to get my kids killed. We can't have someone like that running their town watch."

"And we really can't have her escape the punishment."

"Naturally." Raxa began to pace. "But there's more to it than revenge. If they hand her over, it will prove they respect us—and fear us—enough to honor the peace."

"If they say okay, and you go there, and they betray you?"

"Then I kill them."

Vess rolled her eyes. "Just like the last time you tried that and ran away and barely lived?"

"I've got a new idea. Based on that fight."

"What if this new idea is also bad? What if this idea gets you killed?"

"Then I'm dead!" Raxa made herself take a deep breath. She lowered her voice. "And they have no reason to come after the rest of you."

Vess pursed her lips, taking a hard look into Raxa's eyes. "You think they're going to kill you, don't you? That's your plan. You sacrifice yourself, all our problems go away."

"I don't know what they'll do. All I know is that if I play my hand right, there's three outcomes, and we win each one of them. Either I die and the rest of you live. Or I kill them, and maybe we take this war after all. Or they give me the kidnapper and no one has to die."

"Except her."

"Except her."

Vess absorbed this, then chuckled. "Okay."

"That's it? No lecture about how stupid I'm being?"

"If I want to waste words, I'll ask my people to quit getting drunk so often. Always, you do what you do, and then tell me why it had to be so."

Raxa laughed wryly. It was the middle of the night, but she got straight to work on preparations. For one thing, she was already in the city. Beyond that, now that she'd made her decision, she couldn't stand to sit around waiting.

First thing was to speak to Gurles. She would rather have told no one at all, but the Order deserved better. He bore a flat expression as she explained that she was about to end the conflict with the Citadel—and it was going to be dangerous.

"If something happens," she finished, "I need you to hold the Order together. Don't elect a new leader until they're ready for it."

He looked her over. "You don't think you're coming back."

"I don't know. But for once in my life, I'm trying to be smart."

She put her endorsement of Gurles down in writing, then penned a letter to Galand laying out her terms and instructing them to meet her at the ruined fort the following night. She assumed he wouldn't be stupid enough to kidnap or torture the runner she sent to make the delivery.

After that, there was only one thing left to do. She hurried to the Pridegate, shadowalked through it, and slogged down the southern road, putting the city behind her. She stopped at the edge of the woods. She didn't think she'd been followed—she hadn't felt so much as a flicker of nether—but maybe all that meant was that he was too powerful for her to even notice he was there.

Heart racing, she cut into the shadows and ran into the forest as fast as she could. Five minutes later, with her juice running low and no sign of pursuit, she dropped back into the world.

Wind sifted through the snow-coated pine needles.

She walked for what felt like forever. Just as she was growing certain she'd gone in the wrong direction, the house appeared ahead. It was silent, shuttered, but the smoke trickling from its chimney attested that Herrick and the children were still there.

It was a couple hours before dawn, but it wouldn't be too outrageous to knock on the door. After the last few weeks, they'd be happy to wake up and see her. She could see their smiles, feel the warmth of the house spilling out around her, smell their hair. It would be so easy to make that happen. All she'd have to do was walk a few more feet.

Yet she couldn't get her legs to move. She counted down from sixty, willing one of them to open a shutter or walk out for more firewood. But after a minute had passed, the house remained still. She lifted her hand, then turned and walked back through the forest.

Feet crunched through the snow. Fear stabbed hard into her guts, but rather than lingering, it faded like a cramp. She knew why: whatever happened next, in just a few more minutes, it would all be over.

Hidden behind a crumbling wall of the ruined fort, she peered into the darkness, picking up their movement within the trees. Three of them. As they neared, she got a clear look at their faces: Galand, Blays, and Cee.

She drew her knife, tugged down her glove, and nicked the back of her hand. Shadows uncoiled from the rocks. Had they been left there by the blood of the long-ago dead? If there were shadows everywhere, did that mean there was nowhere in the world where a thing hadn't died?

She stepped from behind the wall. "That's close enough."

Down the slope, they looked up in surprise. Even Galand. Good. That meant he'd honored her demand that he not send spies ahead of himself.

"No need to draw this out," she said. "Hand her over and let's get on our way."

Galand gazed up at her. "Did you bring the book?"

Raxa reached into her coat and withdrew the *Cycle*. She unwrapped the oiled canvas she'd used to keep it dry and set it on a flat piece of wall. "Send her up. We'll walk away. Once we're gone, the book's all yours."

"There's one small problem." To his credit, he didn't smile. "I don't give up my people."

A dark spear winged toward her chest. He was fast, unnervingly so, but she'd been expecting it. She grabbed the *Cycle* and jumped into the safety of the shadows. The spear sizzled past her, a bright but harmless shaft of silver fury. The two men drew their swords and ran up the hillside. Blays dropped into the nether.

Seeing her there, he winked. "Don't suppose you'll come along quietly?"

She grinned back at him. "Hold still and I'll give you all the quiet you could ever ask for."

She backpedaled, drawing Blays ahead of Galand, who was high-stepping through snows that rose past his knees. Cee followed a ways behind the priest. She had a bow in her hands, but against the shadows, it was nothing more than a prop.

Raxa vaulted a wall, landing lightly on top of the snow on the other side. Blays was closing fast. Galand was yelling out for directions, but unless Blays dropped out of the nether, he wasn't going to be any help. All of which was exactly why she'd chosen the snowy, maze-like site of the fort.

She hopped a patch of rubble. Blays landed right behind her. Just as she'd been practicing since their first encounter where Galand had tried to do the same to her, she gathered the nether close, then shoved it into Blays as hard as she could. With an audible pop, he burst loose from the shadows, forced back into reality.

Raxa grinned and followed him out into the dimness of the night. Where the nether could be deadly again. Galand was nowhere in sight. She shaped the shadows into a killing blow aimed for the soft part of Blays' throat.

As she moved to unleash them, a woman stepped out of the nether right beside her. Something slammed into the side of Raxa's head. The night was cold enough to freeze the spit in your mouth, but all she felt was warm.

14

Dante crouched over the woman's body, wary that it was yet another ruse. Then again, if it was a trick, Raxa Dosse was doing an admirable job of not caring about all the blood pouring out of her head.

He dumped shadows into her skin. To his utter lack of surprise, her skull was cracked. Her brain looked all right, but the trouble with brains was that they could appear perfectly normal even while the organ's owner was laughing at the clouds and pissing themselves.

Deep inside the nether, he smoothed the crack in the skull and knit her skin back together. She was breathing deeply but peacefully. He turned her face to get her cheek out of the snow. She looked like a nice young woman. Nothing like the terror who haunted the streets of Narashtovik.

He wiped a bit of blood on his trousers and swiveled his head to glare up at Minn. "What part of 'take her alive' was so hard to understand?"

"I thought," Minn said in an annoyingly reasonable tone, "I would worry about hitting her with the correct level of force once she was no longer about to murder my husband."

"Thanks for that," Blays said. He sheathed one sword but kept the other out. "I'd promise to return the favor some day, but I'd really rather you not get into any almost-murders in the first place."

"Are you suggesting I should leave before she wakes up?"

"No way. When she wakes up, we're going to need every sword, arrow, and scrap of nether we can get out hands on."

As Cee climbed over a patch of rubble to join them, Dante checked Raxa's coat and found the *Cycle*. He opened the cover and discovered it was a fake. His first instinct was to strike her, but his second was to laugh. Fitting. They'd shown up with no intention of turning over Cee, and Raxa had shown up with a fake copy of the book. He checked her again and was unsurprised to find she didn't have the sword on her, either.

He sat back on his cloak with a sigh. "We'll have to talk with her."

"I've only got one word," Cee said. "'Die.'"

"Duly noted. Now in the interests of not having to explode her like a rotten pumpkin, would you kindly stand way over there?"

Cee gave him a dark look, then walked forty feet away. She kept her bow nocked, eyes fixed on Raxa. Dante focused on the nether around the sleeping thief. If she reached for it, he'd knock her out again, then repeat the process until she was spent and harmless.

That was the idea, at least. In practice, trying to keep a sorcerer safely in captivity was about as effective as trying to imprison a rattlesnake in your mouth.

Raxa's eyes opened, locking on Dante.

"Don't even think about it." He summoned a hundred spikes of nether from the air, hovering them inches above her body. "If you so much as move, I'll impale you from head to toe. Then I'll heal you and do it again. I'll be happy to keep that up until you get the idea — or go so insane you can't get any ideas at all."

Face stiff with tension, she glanced at Blays, then Minn. Seeing the other woman, Raxa made a face of sheer disgust. "Should have known."

Minn looked puzzled, then her jaw dropped. "*Saya?*"

"Saya?" Blays tipped back his face as if to beseech the heavens. "Don't tell me we have the wrong person again."

"We got the burglar who can walk through walls," Dante said. "If she isn't the *right* shadowalking rogue sorcerer, we're in more trouble than I thought."

"How do you two know each other, Minn?" Blays' eyebrows hopped upward. "Because she was at Pocket Cove. Where she learned to shadowalk."

"That is correct." There was no missing the edge in Minn's voice. "She was young then, and seems to have used a different name. But there's no forgetting that look in her eyes."

"The one where the caged tiger is imagining eating you bit by bit?"

"If I remember right, she always struggled with the nether. Was that why you ran away, Saya—Raxa? Because you were ashamed of your weakness?"

Raxa sneered. "You're right, I should have stayed. Until your people got me drowned. Or you tortured me until I went mad and flung myself down from the Fingers."

"We *have* to toughen ourselves. If we don't, Gask will destroy us. Who are you to complain? No one is taken to Pocket Cove against their will."

"And no one would go there if they knew what it's like." Giving Dante a baleful glance, Raxa propped herself up on her elbows to get a better look at Minn. "Which makes it a problem when you're never allowed to leave. Except, apparently, for you."

"That's different. My presence here helps keep Pocket Cove safe." Minn's face darkened. "I don't need to justify myself to you."

Raxa stared at her long enough to unload another ton of contempt, then shifted her gaze to Dante. "You have a problem. You can't kill me. Do that, and you'll never see your book and your sword again."

"Don't be so sure. I have powers you can't dream of."

"Sure you do, priesty boy. That's why you're freezing your ass off arguing with me out in the darkest woods."

He didn't know whether to sigh or to stab her. "What do you want?"

"Told you. You give me Cee, and I'll give you the book. The real one."

"What would you do with her? Kill her?"

"You don't have to worry about that."

"I'll take that as a yes."

"I'll even throw in your fancy sword. It's a fair trade. *More* than fair." Raxa glanced across the ruins toward Cee, who stood alone, bow in hand. "She can be replaced. A year from now, you won't even miss her. But if you've got your weapons back, think how much better you'll be able to protect the realm. That sword's already saved my life more than once. And as for the book—where do you think I learned to do this?"

She summoned a droplet of nether to her index finger. Dante tensed, preparing to beat it back with everything he had, but she blew on her finger, dispersing the shadows back to the dark places of the world.

Dante glanced at Cee. She was upwind of them and he wasn't sure she could hear their conversation; if she could, she gave no sign of it.

"No deal," Dante said.

"Come on. There's no way her life is worth as much as your artifacts."

"Probably not," he said. "But loyalty to your people is worth more than a mountain of gold. It's the glue that holds everything together. If I give that up, I'll lose the very thing I'm trying to protect."

She sighed, shoulders slumping. "Kill me, then. But spare the Order. We didn't start this war—*you* did."

Dante clenched his teeth. Even if he did have the stomach for torturing it out of her, if he tried, Blays would walk right out of Narashtovik. Threatening her children would likewise cause Blays to disown him; besides, if he did that, Raxa seemed like the type to throw herself at him in a mad frenzy, forcing him to kill her on the spot.

If he killed her and took some of her blood, he might be able to use it to trace it to other places she'd left bits of herself, stray hairs and so forth. But it wasn't at all likely. The connection would be so faint he'd probably have to be right on top of her stash before he felt anything.

He could send moths and beetles into the far corners of the city. But that could take years, and he'd have to be watching through their eyes all the while.

There were no good answers. But they'd figure something out. They always did. Pursing his lips, he moved into the nether that still hovered above her, preparing to send it swooping down.

"Wait." Minn held out her hand. "This is wrong. Those of the Cove don't kill each other. It's our most sacred vow."

"Good news," Dante said. "I'm not from the Cove."

"Does slaying her get your book back? Your sword? What does this solve?"

"It gets the city's most dangerous criminal off of our streets. Maybe things are easier in Pocket Cove, where the most trying decision you have to make is whether to eat the flounder or the perch, but in the rest of the world, you rarely get a perfect solution. Most of the time, the best you can do is go with the option that makes you vomit the least."

"She was one of my sisters. Even though she ran from us, that remains." She turned to Blays, making a sweeping upwards gesture. "He listens to you. Convince him."

Blays snorted. "He listens to me like a rock rolls uphill."

Raxa glared up at them. "Will you hurry up and kill me before I freeze to death?"

"There has to be something more valuable to you than murdering that woman over there." Blays tapped the point of his sword into the snow. "This was about those kids of yours, wasn't it? Bunch of orphans or whatever? Give us back our stuff, and the Citadel will take care of them."

"I take care of them myself."

"Then it's a good thing you've never done anything to endanger your life and hence your ability to keep caring for them. Who are they, anyway? Cousins?"

Raxa shrugged. "Just some kids off the street. The kind you see every day."

"Ah. Well, you missed a few. What about them?"

"Are you offering to house the others?"

Dante swung toward Blays. "*Are* we? With whose money?"

"The taxpayers, I suppose. I'm sure they won't mind throwing a few hundred silver at a project that'll result in the return of certain objects vital to the city's defense."

"We can't possibly house every vagabond child in the city."

"I know, it's an awful idea." Blays looked down at Raxa. "How many would it take?"

She frowned. "Do you mind if I stand up? It's hard to negotiate when your ass is getting soaked."

"The philosopher Kamrates said the same thing." Blays took a step back.

Raxa stood, knocking the snow from her trousers. "An orphanage is a good start. But you're going to have to do better than that. The sword alone is worth a kingdom."

Dante bit his teeth tight. "And how much is your life worth?"

"My life? I gave up on that the moment I set up this meet."

"Minn must have hit you harder than I thought. You seem to be forgetting the vital fact you're not selling me goods that you own. You *stole* them. From *me*."

"They're not yours until they're in your hands, are they?"

Her eyes widened. She reached for the nether. Dante grabbed for it, only to find that it was already surrounding him—that was why *she'd* drawn on it. If she decided to lash out with it, they were standing so close to each other he wasn't sure he'd be able to stop her.

"Enough!" Blays glared daggers at Dante, then turned them on Raxa. "You think some stupid sword is power? This man can annihilate you down to the burnt ends of your hair, steal a piece of your soul and turn it into a demon, then send that demon to devour everyone you've ever loved. And after that, he can travel into the afterlife to hunt you down and tell you all about it.

"With power like that, I'm sure it must be very tempting to abuse it. Gods know everyone else seems to. But we *try* to use it to make the world just a slightly less horrible place. You're currently delaying us from achieving that. For the good of the land, we ought to smear you and get on with our business."

Blays' face was red with cold and rage. He took a step closer to Raxa, eyes sparking like the clash of two steel blades. "You've done some bad things, haven't you? Enough to know how it gnaws at your soul. Maybe you've done so much harm that a part of you wishes we *would* kill you. I don't want to do that. I have to protect my soul wherever I can. It's already thin enough as it is. But maybe it's thin enough that I won't care about gutting you.

"We can find out. Or we can make a deal. You give back what you stole. We build you an orphanage. And the freakishly talented sorcerer over there trains you to wield *real* power."

Dante choked. "You want me to *train* her?"

"It's stupid to throw away a good tool. Besides, she's a thief and probably a murderer. We can't have her just running around the city, can we?"

"Much better idea to teach her to use the nether!"

Blays folded his arms. "She's a shadowalker. Apparently she's already on her way to becoming a nethermancer. You couldn't ask for a more perfect spy to install in Bressel."

It was Raxa's turn to gawk. "Spy? *Bressel?* I can't leave my people behind. I don't even speak Mallish!"

"Then you'd better start brushing up. You want to protect your merry band of criminals? Your urchins? Here's your chance to learn from one of the most terrifying people this side of the Woduns."

They all fell silent for a moment. Dante adjusted the clasp of his cloak. "Did you really learn to use the nether by reading the *Cycle*?"

"At Pocket Cove, I was never any good," Raxa said. "But once I had the book, it seemed to open something up inside me."

"That's how I learned, too. That, and a completely crazy old man."

"You're talking about Callimandicus?"

Dante nodded. "There wasn't another like him. That was the worst loss of the war."

Raxa had a distant look in her eye, as if remembering something from her youth, or listening to a story around a campfire. As fast as someone falling down, she regained her pointed gaze. "How do I know I can trust you? That as soon as you've got your things back, you won't blast me apart and feed me to demons?"

"That idea has occurred to me. But we need someone in Bressel. Other than Blays, you're the only shadowalker I've ever met outside Pocket Cove."

"And you know how *those* people are," Blays said. "The last time we were able to talk them into helping us, it required calling in a thousand-year-old debt."

Something moved across the stark field of Raxa's face. "What could I become?"

"I can't even guess," Dante said. "Part depends on talent. More depends on the work you put into that talent. And some depends on fate, or luck, or the will of the gods. All you can do is try, every day, and see how far it takes you."

"I need time to decide. Three days."

"Three days? Do you really need that long to scheme up a way to murder us in our beds?"

Raxa snorted. "You might be able to run off whenever you please, but I have people who depend on me. I have to make sure they're okay with me leaving them for a while."

"And if they're not, you'd give up your chance at this?"

"Dead truth is that I don't know. But I know I have to ask."

"Three days," Dante said. "I'll see you here."

She nodded to each of them, then took a last look at Cee, who remained apart, a picture of stoicism. Raxa departed so quietly Dante would have sworn she was shadowalking.

"Well," Blays said. "Did we just do something incredibly stupid?"

Dante tugged up his hood. "That depends. What exactly did we commit to?"

"'We'? Tragically, I can barely touch the nether. Minn's my witness to that. Teaching the wild helltiger to do magic is all your job."

"Thank you for volunteering me, by the way. I was just wondering how I could add yet another responsibility to my load."

"Think of it as training someone to make your life easier." Blays motioned for Cee to join them. "Moving along, if Raxa's going to infiltrate Bressel, she's going to need a partner. Ideally, someone who can do things like 'speak to the locals in their own language.'"

"I've already got someone in mind for that." Dante smiled. "And I think he'll like this even less than I do."

~

Sorrowen slouched into his offices with his shoulders hunched and his elbows tucked tight to his sides, as if he might be able to escape notice if only he could make himself small enough. Aware that he was being cruel, if only in a small way, Dante watched him enter in silence, allowing him to continue to wonder what this was about.

"Please." Dante motioned to a chair. "Sit."

Sorrowen followed orders, awkwardly scooting the heavy chair across the rug to pull himself closer to the table. He opened his mouth as if to ask a question, then thought better.

Dante gave him a level look. "I need you to do something you might have thought you'd never do again: return to Mallon. There, you'll infiltrate the Bresselian priesthood and attempt to locate a man named Gladdic."

Sorrowen's head gave an involuntary jerk. "Wait. *Wait*. You want...what?"

Dante repeated himself. "You'll have a partner with you. While you may need to coordinate at some points, I expect she'll be working separately."

"Er." The boy swallowed, pinched his eyebrows together, and looked steadfastly at the table. "Why me? Sir?"

"Because you're the right fit for the task."

"But I can't do a thing like that!"

"No," Dante said, "you're not *used* to doing a thing like that. But you made it here, from Mallon, by yourself. Just a couple of weeks ago, your quick thinking and ability to act in the moment saved Cee's life. You have the potential to be of great value. All you need is the opportunity to grow into the role. If I sound confident, that's because I was once in the exact same position you are now."

The boy scrunched his mouth to the side. "You don't think I'm too young?"

"Your youth is an asset. They're less likely to suspect you than someone older."

"How long will I be gone? Won't I fall behind in my studies?"

"Unless you plan to start a secret nethermancy school inside a

Mallish temple, probably so. But I'll be traveling with you until you reach Mallon. Along the way, I'll train you personally."

"Uh," Sorrowen said. "That is to say, you will?"

"It's a long journey. We'll need something to pass the time."

"Then I accept. Or I would, anyway, if not for the problem of other things that happened. Sir, I left the priesthood without permission. I'll never be allowed back inside."

"You let me worry about that," Dante said. "You have a month to get ready. If I have the time, I'll try to start your lessons before we leave."

Sorrowen stood, bowed, and practically ran from the chamber, as if wanting to flee the scene before Dante could change his mind.

With that out of the way, Dante sent for Olivander, Nak, and Blays. They took seats around the table, which was large enough for a dozen. Dante proceeded to lay out his plan to send Raxa and Sorrowen to infiltrate Bressel. Dante thought the idea and its execution were rather cunning, but as he finished, Olivander looked like Dante had suggested they dig a secret tunnel into Mallon using their teeth as shovels.

"Do you really think this is necessary?" Olivander said.

Dante leaned back in his chair. "We have to find Gladdic. If we hadn't intervened, he would have killed everyone in the Collen Basin."

"Are you trying to provoke war with Mallon?"

"Just because I'm always getting into them doesn't mean I *like* wars. Usually, I'm trying to avert them. But the universe has a bad habit of not listening to me."

"I see," Olivander said. "And you believe the best candidates for this job are a young boy and a woman who, until last night, was trying to kill you?"

"If they're caught, we can plausibly disavow both of them. One's a known criminal with a vendetta against us who thought she could go to Bressel to stir up trouble against us. The other's a Mallish boy who was sickened by what he was supposed to learn in Narashtovik and went running back to his homeland."

"Will you bring them back once Gladdic's been dealt with? Or will they be more permanent assets?"

"I hadn't thought of it. I suppose if they're still finding useful information, it would be foolish to bring them home too fast."

Olivander crossed his arms over his chest. "In other words, they'll be there until the end of time."

"Strange. You sound like you think you're saying the same thing I said, and yet every word is completely different."

"There was once a military philosopher named Andaral who said that until you sheathe your sword, you'll never stop cutting things with it. If you create an institution without defined boundaries, it will continue of its own accord, because you'll always find a new way to put it to use. Before committing people to the field, I strongly suggest we define our objectives."

"They're twofold. First, to locate and eliminate Gladdic. And second, to figure out whether Mallon has any immediate plans to do us harm. Once we've got those questions answered, we'll withdraw the spies."

"Very good. Nak, are you writing this down?"

Dante frowned. "Why would we want to put this in writing?"

"To hold ourselves accountable. You of all people should understand the power of ink."

"What if somebody steals the documents?"

"Like who?" Blays put in. "The unstoppable thief you just hired?"

"Bringing her aboard was *your* idea!" Dante said. "Besides, she's the perfect example of why we wouldn't want to leave proof lying around. We don't know what our enemies are capable of. The more I travel the world, the more I learn how little we know about what's lurking in it."

Nak pursed his lips, quill hovering over his parchment. "Am I supposed to write this damned stuff down or not?"

Olivander raised an eyebrow. Dante made a brushing gesture. "Oh, go ahead. Better make it short, though, because I'm making you carry it everywhere you go until I get back."

Nak's quill scratched over the page.

"If I'm through being interrogated," Dante said, "there's the matter of getting Sorrowen accepted into the Mallish priesthood. The problem is, he's already left it. Without leave. They'll refuse to let him back in."

Hunched over his work, Nak glanced up. "Why on earth do you think that?"

"That's what he told me."

"You're from Mallon. Don't you know anything about the priesthood?"

"I grew up in the middle of nowhere, knew nothing about the ether, and ran away almost half my lifetime ago."

"Ah, that's right, you went straight from nobody to nethermancer. Well, fortunately for us, while the Mallish priesthood does have a central governing body, its twelve orders are largely independent from one another. If I'm not mistaken, young Sorrowen was an acolyte of Taim?"

"That's right," Dante said. "Who do you think will be most likely to take him in?"

"Oh, anyone, really. Taim always gets the best and the brightest. The other orders will leap at the chance to take on a young ethermancer."

"Then we'll go for Gashen. If Mallon's planning for war, his priests will be jockeying for influence in the conflict."

"Excellent thinking. I'll tutor him in Gashen's ways before you depart."

"What *is* your timeline?" Olivander said.

"We leave in a month," Dante said. "That will avoid the worst weather in the pass and have us in Alebolgia by the start of spring."

"And your objectives in Alebolgia?"

"Finalize the Collen Basin's alliance with House Osedo, allowing them to shut the Mallish out of the port in Cavana. That'll require us to discover House Itiego's secret Tallas Route. Before or after that, we find Gladdic and we deal with him. Then we come home. I think we can be back by fall."

Olivander nodded. "And then perhaps your adventuring will be finished."

With the meeting concluded, Nak toddled off to locate Sorrowen and start on his lessons. Olivander went to draw up a timeline and logistics for the journey. Citadel business consumed the remainder of Dante's day. Tedious stuff, most of it, yet there was something pleasant about being able to make a score of decisions in a single day knowing that dozens of capable people would immediately set to work executing those decisions. It felt like all the world was a Nulladoon field and he was the player. The only one who could see the lay of the land and maneuver his pieces against the Citadel's opponents.

This was the height of power in action, the kind wielded by Moddegan in Gask and Charles in Mallon. And yet there was something hollow to it. It felt cloistered. Like a monk in his cell reading of great heroes, awful struggles, and glorious triumphs. Dante wanted to feel the wind in his hair. The cold on his face. To see places he'd never seen before and delve into their secrets.

That felt like *true* power. As he passed down judgments; consulted with Council members, monks, and nobles; and wrote down accounts of what he'd seen, done, and learned on his travels, a part of him was already impatient to get back in the saddle, ride for hundreds of miles, and sail into unknown waters in search of House Itiego's mysterious spice island.

As was so often true, wishes could be real sons of bitches. The day after his talks with Sorrowen, Nak, and Olivander, with one day remaining for Raxa to make her decision about whether to join them, Dante's loon pulsed. Frowning, he opened the line.

"Mr. Dante?" The voice was rough, barnacled with a maritime accent. "This is Jona, sir. Of the *Sword of the South*."

"I know who you are," Dante said. "Any news from Captain Naran?"

"Yes and no." Jona halted for three seconds. "You see, sir, three days ago, the captain made port in Tanar Atain. Now he's gone missing. Like he disappeared from the face of the earth."

EDWARD W. ROBERTSON

15

"Missing?" Dante's mouth went as dry as the salted cod favored by the *Sword of the South*'s quartermaster. "You're still in Collen, aren't you? And he's in Tanar Atain? So what exactly defines 'missing'?"

Jona grunted. "What I mean is we were supposed to speak yesterday afternoon. But we didn't. Nor yesterday evening, nor this morning. Now his loon's not working at all."

"But you're sure it was working prior to that, when he wasn't responding?"

"As sure as winter swells. There's a feel to the loons, ain't there? When I try to reach him now, his loon, it's like it's…not there. Like I'm talking into an empty room."

Dante ran across his chambers to gather his writing instruments and take notes. "Do you have any idea where he might have gone? Was he scheduled to meet anyone? Had he found any leads on Gladdic?"

"I'll tell you everything I know, sir, but I'll warn you, it ain't much. As I said, three days ago, the *Sword* reached Tanar Atain. The captain berthed in Aris Osis, the only port open to outsiders. The first day, no one's allowed off the ship. Inspections and tariffs and such. The second day, they're permitted to unload their goods. Captain Naran makes arrangements to tour a few warehouses, see what kinds of cargo he'd like to take on. The first visits were supposed to happen the next day."

"When he went silent."

"Dead on, sir."

"Do you know anything about who he was meeting with?"

Jona chuckled dryly. "This is Captain Naran, sir. Formerly Mr. Naran, quartermaster from hell. I expect he keeps logs of what time of day he takes his shits and how many times he has to wipe his—"

"That's wonderful," Dante said. "The names, please?"

"The first on his list was Oto LoMota." Jona spelled out the name. "Next was Undan Walan. And last was Iko DaNasan."

"Did Naran tell you anything about them?"

"He was angling to do business with people he thought might get him closer to finding Gladdic. According to him, LoMota's a bit of a black sheep who comes from a family of priests and so forth." Paper rustled over the loon. "Galan, she does business all across the interior, which the captain seemed to think is noteworthy. And as for DaNasan, it's rumored he has ties with an outfit called the Monsoon. Don't know who or else they are."

Dante paused while jotting all of this down. "Anything else?"

"Nothing that leaps between my ears. They'd only just arrived in port, sir. What do you think this could mean?"

"Naran might have left his loon on without knowing it, draining its nether until the connection collapsed. Or it could have been stolen by a cutpurse—it would resemble exotic jewelry."

"Is that where you'd stick your bets?"

"I would bet that someone's taken him prisoner. Either the authorities saw something suspicious on the ship, or Gladdic has people in the city. Either he was smart enough to be looking for Naran, or he's paranoid enough to interrogate anyone coming from Mallon." Dante spilled sand over his ink, blotting it dry. "Hopefully the captain will be questioned and released shortly. We'll leave as soon as we can. If you hear from him, or remember anything else, let me know."

Jona vowed to do so. Dante shut down the loon. He was about to run and find Blays, then remembered the advantages of his position and sent a page to summon Blays to him, along with Olivander and Nak.

They assembled in the room they'd met in the day before.

Dante didn't bother to sit. "I just heard from our contact in Collen. Captain Naran made landfall in Tanar Atain three days ago. Sometime between yesterday and this morning, we lost contact with him. It could be that something went wrong with his loon, but I'm operating under the assumption he's been captured—or worse. I intend to leave within three days."

Olivander thrust out his jaw. "To where?"

"To Javar's Bakery in Gallador. I can't stop thinking about his apple crisps. To Tanar Atain, obviously."

"There's a real chance that the captain's already dead. Or will be long before you get there."

Blays scoffed. "Do you think that makes Dante *less* eager to ride in and stomp it up? There's vengeance to be had, man!"

Olivander gave Blays a dark look. "'Stomping it up' sounds directly at odds with the idea of reducing our involvement in foreign lands."

"First, Naran might be jailed indefinitely," Dante said. "And thus in need of rescue. Second, even if he has been killed, we owe it to his crew to make sure they remain free."

"You owe it to your people in Narashtovik to stay out of harm's way. To keep *them* out of harm's way. What purpose does this venture serve? What's the value in saving the life of one sea captain—perhaps even his entire crew—versus the cost of your own life if you fail?"

Nak gave Dante a supplicating bob of his head that was only partially mocking. "It's a fair point, O Esteemed and Nigh-Invincible Bearer of Arawn's Wisdom and Might. Surely this friend of yours knew the dangers he was sailing into."

"Better than we do," Blays said. "But we have to go back to Collen and the Strip either way. While we're there, we might as well visit a strange new land, and then destroy it."

"Oh dear. You've fallen prey to Dante's adventurism, too?"

"When you're safe in this keep, isolated by a thousand miles of winter, it's easy to brush aside what happened in Collen. After all, it's none of our business, is it? People are fighting wars and killing people all the time, and we don't think twice about getting involved." Blays smiled, or grimaced, or something in between. "But I haven't seen those battles. I *have* seen the bodies in the caverns of Collen. I can't live with myself if I let Gladdic live. I will send him to the gods, and let them repent what they created."

"Ah," Nak said. "Well. Yes. There is the moral component. In that case, when would you like your horses ready?"

Rather than using the ruined fort all the way out in the forest, they met Raxa under the shadow of the spire of the Cathedral of Ivars. By daylight, and in the middle of the city, she looked like just another young woman out on an errand—off to one of the winter markets, or to place an order at the chandlery.

"Before you give your decision," Dante said, "our circumstances have changed. If you come with us, you won't have a month to prepare. You'll have three days."

She glanced at Blays, then back at Dante. "What's up?"

"It doesn't matter. It won't affect your involvement."

"If you want me to partner with you, I need to know if you're about to get yourself killed."

"I don't know enough to answer that question," Dante said. "But the person you'll be looking for might be responsible for our new haste. If Blays and I find him where we're going, that'll shorten the time you have to spend in Bressel."

"Least you're honest." It was snowing again and Raxa flipped a line of white from the folds of her cloak. "I'll go. But I'm amending our deal. You can have one item back now. The sword or the book, your choice. You get the other when you bring me back to Narashtovik."

"The terms of the deal were set. There's nothing to negotiate."

"Okay." She turned and walked off through the snow.

Blays gave Dante a squinty look, then shook his head and trotted after Raxa. "Quit being so dramatic. He's as stubborn as you are. If you walk away, he's only going to make your life miserable."

She stopped, back turned, then swore. "You need me more than I need you. What would you do if I walked away with the sword and the book and you never saw me again?"

Dante gritted his teeth. "I need the book to help teach you."

"Guess that makes your decision easy."

"And I need the sword to kill the son of a bitch we're going to hunt down."

She jerked a thumb at Blays. "He's the one who told me a sword is nothing compared to the almighty god-blasting power of the nether. You're asking me to put my life on the line for you *and* to trust you're not going to kill me as soon as you've got what you want. This is my insurance policy."

"What if you die in the line of duty?"

"Then you only have to hunt for one hidden treasure, not two."

Seriously contemplating an abundance of violence, he turned to Blays. "Help. Before I accidentally redwash the front of the cathedral."

"But the monks could stand to do a little honest labor," Blays said. "Look, if you were her, would you do any different?"

"*I* would trust the word and goodwill of my illustrious benefactor."

Blays cupped his right ear, tilting it to the sky. "Do you hear that? That's the sound of Cally laughing his ass off. I suggest we retreat to shelter until it crashes down."

Dante chuckled. At the mention of the old man, something shifted inside him. He had been young once, eager to learn. What would have happened to him if Cally hadn't taken him on and guided him down the path? Almost certainly, he would have died at sixteen, slain by the soldiers at Blays' hanging in Whetton. Even if he'd somehow made it through that, Samarand's agents would have gotten him soon after.

Instead, he'd been granted the chance to study under the guidance of one of the most intelligent and unusual sorcerers he'd ever known. And in the process, he'd advanced beyond any of his most secret hopes.

Maybe it was nostalgia. Or maybe it was the appeal of an unexplored form of arrogance: the role of teaching someone lesser, and shaping them into your vision of what they could and should be. Whatever the case, serving as mentor seemed to feel less like a burden and more like a privilege.

Nor did it hurt that sealing the deal would mean restoring peace to his city.

He favored Raxa with a critical eye. Regaining the sword had immediate appeal, but he wasn't even sure they allowed people to openly carry arms in Tanar Atain. From what Jona had said, they sounded unusually wary of outsiders. Besides, if he chose the sword and something happened to Raxa in Bressel, the loss of the true *Cycle* would be devastating. It was more than an object of power. It represented the legacy of Arawn in the north. A tradition that dated back over a thousand years. He wouldn't be the one that broke that honored chain.

"The *Cycle*," he said. "Three days from now, be at the Citadel gates at dawn."

She nodded. "That mean the war between us is over?"

"And if you want peace to remain in our absence, tell your people there can't be any more killings. No assaulting citizens, either. Now, if you want to rob the nobles, maybe they should hire better guards. But you might find it more interesting, and profitable, to look into certain Gaskan trade routes and warehouses. My friend Nak probably has a lot of information on the subject. I'll have to warn him not to accidentally drop a list outside the gates. Especially not at, say, ten o'clock tonight."

Raxa smiled. It was the first time she'd looked genuinely happy since they'd met. "See you in three days."

As the sun struggled to clear the heights of the Woduns, Dante waited outside the gates with Blays, Sorrowen, and four of Olivander's best rangers, who were mostly there to scout the route ahead, but would also help Dante keep an eye on Raxa.

That role was starting to look like it might be superfluous, considering there was still no sign of Raxa at all. Cold dread squirmed in his stomach like a ball of worms. If she didn't show—if this was yet another ruse—he would delay the trip until he hunted her down. And given that the delay meant additional risk for Naran's life, this time, Dante's mercy would be at an end.

As the first wan yellow ray poked out of the east, a lone silhouette walked lightly toward the gates.

"Hope you brought me a horse," Raxa said. "Otherwise, one of *you* is walking."

In fact, they'd brought two doughty raggies apiece, but were otherwise traveling light, intending to restock their provisions as they traveled through the Norren Territories and Tantonnen. Grooms helped Raxa into the saddle and redistributed her bulging pack into her two horses' saddlebags.

"I'll do my best in your absence," Olivander said. "Remember to know when to sheathe your sword."

As they rode out, Dante felt a twinge of guilt for leaving his city again so soon. Yet it helped to know that it remained in good hands. That, perhaps, was the most important thing a leader could do: assemble good people, and forge them into a group who could share the weight with you—and carry it onward after you were gone.

They headed south, clearing the gates and passing through the busy neighborhoods that had sprung up on the city's outskirts. As they left Narashtovik, Sorrowen glanced behind them, staring anxiously at the Citadel and the Cathedral of Ivars. Raxa didn't look back, but she did let her gaze linger on the forest ahead and to their right, a distant look upon her face.

Travelers had trampled a path through the snow. That day, they made excellent time. Yet by the point when the sun fell into the clouds hanging over the western hills, the road had already gotten worse.

"Mighty inconsiderate of Naran to disappear in the dead of winter," Blays said. "Next time he wants to get kidnapped or arrested, he better make sure it's spring."

Dante checked in with Jona, but the pirate still hadn't heard anything from Naran. As far as he could tell, the loon was dead.

They walked for half an hour past sunset, the rangers testing the way ahead, then got off the road to pitch their tents in the woods. While the soldiers gathered firewood, Dante called over Sorrowen and Raxa. He'd been thinking about this moment for the last few days, but finding himself in it, he had no idea where to start.

"If you're lucky," he said, "you'll have fifty days to learn. If I'm lucky, and the roads are fair, you'll have thirty. Either way, we'll barely have time to scratch the surface. So let's make each day count."

Feeling mildly foolish, he nodded at Sorrowen. "I know the

monks have drilled you on the *Cycle* until you must have wanted to turn it into book soup." Dante turned to Raxa. "But you haven't had formal training. Were there any parts of the *Cycle* you didn't understand?"

"Yeah," Raxa said. "Such as the first half."

"You've had the book for almost two months!"

"I could have had it for two years. Wouldn't change the fact I can't read Mallish."

Somehow, that had eluded him. It pitched his plan right out the window. "We'll have to remedy that. Besides, learning Mallish will help you do your job in Bressel." He rubbed his temples. "For now, it doesn't matter. The book already unlocked your talent. We can come back to its pages later."

He shifted his weight on the downed tree he was sitting on. "As long as you're willing to run away before you run yourself dry, a skilled sorcerer doesn't have much to fear from the average soldier. There's no armor that can save them from the nether. That means that one of the most valuable skills you can possess is the ability to defend yourself from other sorcerers. Both of you know the basics of deflecting an incoming nether strike, but let's see if we can't refine your technique."

"Er," Sorrowen said. "You're not going to shoot at *us*, are you?"

"You have ten seconds," Dante said. "Get running."

The boy paled and popped to his feet, running headlong into the forest, snow spraying from his boots. He was about to disappear into the trees when the laughter of the others brought him to a stop.

He trudged back to them, giving Dante a peevish look. "What did *that* teach me?"

"That you can't trust everything your teacher says." Dante brightened—he hadn't intended to say that, but it sounded just like something Cally would have said. "We won't aim at each other. The target will be the lower branches of that tree." He pointed out a pine sixty feet away. "I'm going to attack it. It's your job to deflect my attack before it hits home."

He walked twenty feet away from the others. He rolled up his left sleeve and got out his antler-handled knife. The blade was icy cold, practically sticking to his skin as he made the cut.

Checking that the two of them were ready, Dante shaped a handful of nether into an arrowhead, then sent it winging toward the designated pine tree. It was already a third of the way there before a black dart flew from Sorrowen's hands. The dart started strong, closing on the arrowhead, but then wobbled midflight, veering off course. The arrowhead smacked into the tree.

"You missed," Dante said.

"It was too dark to see."

"You don't want to try to watch it. Your eyes are too slow. Better to follow it by feel."

He sent another arrowhead straight at the tree. Sorrowen's counter dashed it from the air in a burst of silver sparks. On the third attempt, however, Dante put some spiral into his bolt and Sorrowen reacted too late. The nether crashed through the bough, sending it crunching into the snow.

Dante tried nine more times. Sorrowen only struck down a single one. His counters always seemed to be a little too slow, his adjustments a little too hesitant to overtake the looping arrowhead. Dante rejoined the others. Sorrowen looked like he was expecting to be smacked.

"You can't afford to be that slow," Dante said. "You know the attack is coming. That's an advantage you'll rarely have in real combat. Get the bolt up to speed, then worry about making adjustments to its course."

"But what if mine hits too hard?"

"No such thing. The whole *point* is to cause a wreck. Let's try again."

They got back in position. To Dante's surprise, after eight more bolts, Sorrowen apologized for being out of nether. He'd intercepted just one more strike.

"I don't understand," Sorrowen said. "I thought I was better than this."

"When the nether's flying right at you, I expect you are. We're working at a distance on purpose to develop your finesse."

"And to not kill you," Blays suggested.

The boy looked partially reassured. Dante motioned to Raxa. "Your turn."

They stepped apart. She called out that she was ready. He sent a straight shot at the tree, which was gouged and cracked from his earlier strikes. A blast of darkness shot from Raxa's hands and slammed into Dante's arrowhead, obliterating it in a spray of twinkling motes. He loosed a second attack and she knocked it down just as easily.

As the third flew toward the pine, Dante sent it into an irregular spiral. A great gob of nether overshot it, reversed course, and plowed into it from the other side less than three feet from the tree. Of the next three efforts, she nailed two and missed one.

"That's it," she announced. "Out of juice."

Dante let the nether dissolve from his fingers. "Already?"

"Was there supposed to be a lesson somewhere?"

He crunched back to the camp. The rangers had brought in wood and were striking a fire.

"You have good instincts," Dante told Raxa. "But you hit too hard. It's like you're dumping a bucket of water on a candle. Learn to conserve. Use as little as possible to achieve your goals. Often, defeating another sorcerer is a matter of wearing them down. Exhaust yourself in the first exchanges, and they'll rip you apart."

He ate and went to bed feeling good about having identified areas for them to work on. Yet after another three days of practice, having exhausted their supply of nether in each session, he couldn't feel the slightest bit of difference in their technique. During their fifth practice, they actually seemed worse: Sorrowen's hold was as wobbly as a toddler trying to lift his father's sword, and as for Raxa, in her insistence on doing her best to block every single one of his shots no matter the cost, she ran herself dry after a handful of efforts. On top of that, when she rushed in too hard, her counterattacks had such unsteerable momentum that it made it easy for him to slip under her guard.

"You better hope we fall down a crevasse and nobody finds us for twenty years," Dante said. "Because that's how long it's going to take for you two to learn to do this right."

Sorrowen flinched. Raxa just stared. Immediately regretting himself, and hoping the shadows and wavering light cast by the campfire would disguise his blush, Dante launched into a lecture about how they needed to imagine that his nether was a pigeon in flight while theirs was a plunging falcon with unerring aim.

Late the next morning, as they emerged from the forest into a stretch of rolling hills, one of Dante's loons twinged.

"O wise leader?" Nak said. "Is now a good time to receive a great deal of information that won't be useful to you for weeks?"

"As good as any." Dante tried to disguise his disappointment that it wasn't Jona with news about Naran. "I take it you've found something on Tanar Atain?"

"For various definitions of 'something,' yes. In the case of the history I found in the archives, the most important things to come out of Tanar Atain are the purity of its noble bloodlines, and the cleverness of the fashions they wore."

"Commissioned by the same royals he wrote about," Dante said. "Those books are always the worst. Makes me wish I could walk back through time and pay them to *not* write about the cuffs of their patron's jacket."

"I couldn't agree more. Yet once the author grew tired of chronicling the type and number of gemstones adorning that year's belts, or decided that even his patrons must have grown bored of hearing about the hems of tunics, he switched subjects to something the outsider might term 'interesting.'

"The history of Tanar Atain has been troubled, to say the least. It seems they've spent most of the last eight hundred years engaged in a series of dynastic successions, rebellions, and counter-rebellions, almost none of which can realistically claim to have ruled the entire area—or to have lasted for more than twenty years. In some cases, the ruling dynasty hasn't lasted twenty *days.*"

"Are they that war-like?"

"Not especially so, at least from what I can tell. The trouble, you see, is that Tanar Atain isn't land as you or I know it. The area is so swampy and boggy that the areas of usable earth are difficult to get to, let alone assault. Thus various regions and settlements were constantly breaking away from their conquerors. And if those conquerors attempted to reclaim the rebel territories, it usually weakened the attackers so greatly it left them vulnerable to an uprising in their home city."

Dante gazed down the road, which was so buried in snow that it was a matter of faith as to whether it still existed. "Sounds like finding Captain Naran might be harder than we bargained for."

"Perhaps, but perhaps not. You see, over a century ago, which is when this text was written, the Yoto Dynasty arose, unifying the region and keeping it under their control through a series of harsh but—the author is careful to stress this—necessary and ultimately beneficial measures."

"Who are the Yoto?"

"Little is said on that matter except that they are a branch of an earlier dynasty that was cast down by rebellion many years earlier. I get the impression the author covered the Yotos' earlier history in a separate volume."

"Which we don't have."

Nak tutted. "Regrettably, I failed to prioritize the archives' collection of Tanarian lore. I can glean this much: they're proponents of rules, and they take them extremely seriously. Assuming the Yoto remain in power, my advice is to hew strictly to all of their laws, customs, statutes, rites, and precedents."

"But Nak, we would never dream of breaking someone else's laws."

"Forgive me, master. You can't see me doing so, but rest assured I have fallen to my knees and begun the first of dozens of appeals to Arawn's mercy for slandering you."

"Have you found anything about the city of Aris Osis? I'm hoping that's all the further we have to go."

"It was only mentioned in passing. Sounds like a thriving place, and slightly less strict, due to the nature of ports. The author seemed to look down on it for this reason." Nak paused; across the loon, Dante heard the flipping of pages. "The book concludes on a curious anecdote relayed thirdhand from a wandering soothsayer. The soothsayer, in turn, claims to have heard the story from something called a noto, which from context appears to be some sort of traveling merchant.

"This noto, by name of Eko Abu, had a dangerous business delivering various herbs, roots, and barks between the coastal regions and the wilder reaches of the interior. One of these was a swamp known as Go Kaza; since all of the other noto refused to visit it, Eko Abu was making a small fortune bringing back the swamp's medicinal herbs.

"On one such venture to Go Kaza, Eko Abu was on his way to a raft carpet—don't ask me what that is—when he heard a scream from a small, densely wooded island. Against his better instincts, he tied up his boat and scrambled onto the island to offer assistance.

"Moving as quietly as he could, he stumbled upon a scene born from nightmare: a pale man, gaunt yet powerful, feeding on the neck of a limp young woman. Eko Abu gasped in horror. The pale figure detached from its victim, face dripping with blood, and leaped at Eko Abu, crossing forty feet in a single bound.

"The vampire fell upon him, knocking him to the ground. Eko Abu attacked it with his longknife, stabbing it in the chest, but as he withdrew the blade, the wound sealed behind it. The beast knocked aside the knife and plunged its fangs into Eko Abu's throat.

"Coldness swept through him. The world seemed to fall away, as though he were viewing it through a pane of dirty glass. He reached for his pouch, trying to find his jackknife, but in his haze, he opened his satchel of herbs instead, spilling his bundle of freshly collected roto ari leaves over the monster.

"The vampire recoiled with a scream, the flesh of its face sizzling wherever the leaves had touched it. Eko Abu threw another handful of leaves at the beast. With a shriek, it bounded away. Eko Abu ran to his barge, poling through the fetid water as fast as he could.

"As soon as he was away from the swamps of Go Kaza, Eko Abu isolated himself in another bog, convinced he'd soon turn vampire as well. There, he stayed in a makeshift shelter, eating the roto ari leaves in an attempt to purge his system of the disease. After ninety days and ninety nights, with no change in his body or his soul, he returned home to his wife and children.

"And whenever he went back to the swamps of Go Kaza," Nak finished with the satisfaction of all people telling the end of a good story, "he went wrapped in the leaves of the roto ari. He never saw another vampire again."

"I have so many questions," Dante said. "Like why the *hell* did you tell me this?"

"Because it's written in a book of history," Nak said. "And it's at the end of the book. The author must have included it for *some* reason." His voice shrank, sounding hurt. "Besides, this book is all that I've been able to find."

"But vampires aren't real."

"And neither are kappers, I suppose? Or the zombies you're so fond of raising when you feel like terrorizing your enemies? Those are nothing but myths too, are they? Excuse me for thinking that if you're traveling to a land where there *might* be vampires, *you* might want to know that you can protect yourselves by carrying roto ari with you."

"I'm sorry," Dante said, not quite believing that he was apologizing for Nak having told him a fairy tale. "I do want to know all I can learn about Tanar Atain. Even if it's nothing but myth. Oftentimes, the legends people tell can teach you a lot about them."

"Exactly as I thought," Nak said. "Now if you'll excuse me, I need to return to the archives."

One of the rangers returned to warn them that there was a group of armed and hungry-looking men in a grove of trees over the next hill. Dante was inclined to detour from the road: every delay was an annoyance, and besides, there was something troubling about the idea of riding into a group of people with the intention of baiting them into violence and then slaughtering them.

Blays, however, pointed out that if they *were* murderous bandits, by riding around them, they'd leave the bandits free to attack the next people who came through — people who would be much less likely to be able to defend themselves. Angered by the idea that a gang of thugs was preying on his citizens and travelers, Dante led the party onward over the next hill.

The bandits' attack was as predictable as its outcome: all the highwaymen died or fled into the wilds. Dante would have been happy to leave the corpses for the wolves, but Blays insisted on burning them. They left a roaring bonfire behind them.

A piece of him was happy to have made his land a little safer. Yet it reminded him that for all you did, your work would never be done: things were always breaking down, falling apart, dissolving into chaos. That was the lesson of the cracking of Arawn's Mill: even the gods couldn't make perfection that would last down through the years. In that case, why did mortals even try?

Behind them, smoke climbed to meet the clouds, the fluttering ashes of the dead mingling with the rising wisps of nether.

16

They made camp at sunset. Dante didn't really expect the bandits who'd fled the battle to try to take revenge—that was about as likely as a surprise attack by the offspring of the pigs in the sausage they ate for dinner—but he slew a pair of field mice regardless, assigning them to patrol a wide circle around the camp. Watching them begin their mindless circuit, he was struck with an idea.

"Tonight, we're going to try something different," he told Raxa and Sorrowen. "The fine art of infiltrating a place without having to be anywhere near it. Given what you'll be doing in Bressel, this is more likely to save your skin than learning to defend against a direct strike from the nether."

He paused to let this sink in, hoping it would provide them with an extra dose of inspiration.

"Nether rests in all things," he said. "Including the dead. If you draw on the nether in a body, you can connect yourself to it, allowing you to move the creature in question around—and perceive through its senses." He smiled at Raxa. "Like those beetles I sent to track you down."

She snorted. "You mean the ones I used to lure you into an ambush?"

"You mean the ambush where we almost killed you? We can compare scores later. Right now, it's time to conduct some pest control."

Normally, he would have taught them with bugs of some kind—they were typically more numerous, and he felt no guilt killing them—but the winter had already massacred them all. Besides which, insects were harder to control, requiring more precision. Fortunately, the field mice were plentiful, foraging for anything they could find. And though a mouse was cute when it was sitting in the open eating a seed, anyone who'd seen the horrors they could inflict on a larder—to say nothing of a granary—would carry their hate with them forever.

Dante nodded to one of them pawing through the snow at the edge of the firelight. "Strike it down, then I'll show you how to connect yourself to it."

Raxa poked herself with a knife, grabbed hold of the nether, and slung a bolt at the mouse. Rather than scaling it down to the size of her target, she used a bolt of the same size they'd been using to practice with. It slammed into the target so hard that the animal's head spun away, a burst of fur whirling over the bloody snow.

"That seems excessive," Blays said. "What, was it a convicted war criminal?"

Dante kept his face neutral, nodding at Sorrowen. "Why don't you give it a try?"

The acolyte stood straight, lifting his right hand before him. Nether webbed his fingers. He thrust his hand forward, shooting a dark needle at an oblivious rodent. The mouse squealed so loud that two of the rangers leaped to their feet in surprise. As it went on squealing, Dante put a quick but gentle end to its suffering.

He gave Sorrowen a dirty look. "Were you going to let it bleed to death?" He walked over to the fallen mouse and crouched above it, holding out his hand. "Watch close."

Moving slowly, exaggerating his actions the best that he could, Dante reached inside the nether contained within the tiny body. The shadows had settled to resting positions, requiring him to send them flowing through the mouse's organs and limbs. Holding these in place, he poured a dollop of his own nether into the body.

The shadows merged. The mouse stood.

Most times, his two students couldn't have carried themselves more differently. But as they watched the little undead vermin lift its snout to test the night air, the fascination on their faces was an exact mirror of each other.

Dante withdrew his nether from the mouse, letting it collapse. "Simple as that."

Raxa went first. With the nether settling inside the body again, she yanked it this way and that, trying to force it into shape. Dante gave her a steady stream of directions, but it took her twenty minutes to get the nether apportioned and circulating as it should be.

"Now connect it to yourself," Dante said. "Go easy—"

Raxa flooded it with nether, overwhelming the careful balance she'd made of its shadows. "Gods damn it!"

She booted the corpse as hard as she could, sending it arcing into the trees, then stomped off into the dark.

Dante raised his eyebrows at Sorrowen. "I suppose that means it's your turn."

Sorrowen went to work. He had the nether in position faster than Raxa had—he had more patience for fine tasks, and experience in general—but as he tried to meld it with his own nether, the shadows inside the creature seemed to slip away, as if he didn't have a tight enough grasp on them. Doggedly, he kept trying until his hold got so shaky he could no longer keep the nether in place.

"Good effort," Dante said. "We'll try again tomorrow."

He forced a smile and went to warm himself on the other side of the campfire.

Blays plunked down beside him. "Want some unsolicited advice?"

"The question answers itself."

"Right." Blays stood back up. "Continue to enjoy your failure, then. I know it's your favorite thing."

Dante exhaled raggedly. "Let's get this over with."

"You know why you can't teach them? Because you're too good at this."

"Of course. Just like how I can't run, because I'm too fast. Or breathe, because I'm too breathe-y."

"You definitely don't have to worry about being too thinky. How long did it take you to learn to throw the shadows around?"

Dante shrugged. "A few weeks."

"And that was *before* you met Cally. You were self-taught. You weren't even using blood yet. And you were still better than these two, who are using blood, and who've both had formal instruction in the past. You know how *I* had to learn? By practicing on a beach for months on end. And acquiring the help of a magic sea snail. Even then, I'm still terrible at everything but shadowalking. Learning the nether was so easy for you that you don't understand how hard it is for everyone else."

"So what should I be doing? Going back to the basics?"

"Beats me. You're the all-powerful sorcerer. I'm merely the guy who can throw just enough nether over your eyes for you to think a sunny day is overcast."

Dante spent the morning ride ruminating on this. By sundown, he'd come to the conclusion that he couldn't possibly do any worse by his students than he currently was, so what did it matter if he wasted a day or three exploring the fundamentals? Following dinner, he took Sorrowen and Raxa around to the other side of the fire, allowing them a small measure of privacy from the rangers.

"Tonight," Dante said, "I want to see how you summon the nether."

Raxa gave him a blank look. "You've seen us do that dozens of times."

"So tonight will make that dozens and one. The sooner you do as I say, the sooner we can move on to something more interesting."

Doing nothing to disguise her annoyance, she jabbed her shoulder, then brought the nether to her. Dante had her repeat this process three times, then made Sorrowen do the same.

Dante folded his arms. "If someone were to chop you two up and sew the best pieces into one person, you might make a decent nethermancer. Raxa, you rip the nether to you like you're tearing up weeds. When it hits you, it's raging like a flood. It's no wonder you have such a hard time controlling it, and that you use so much of it. As for you, Sorrowen, you're standing about like a helpless father waiting for his nine children to calm themselves down. You barely touch the shadows before putting them to use."

Sorrowen blinked. "But Brother Borrowen told us to let it flow like water."

"Then Brother Borrowen needs a dunce cap and a long sit in the corner. The nether may flow like water, but as a nethermancer, you're supposed to *channel* it. Like a funnel, or a canal."

Following his criticism, they were both staring at him like he'd passed out with his pants down.

"This is good," Dante said. "Because it means there's something to fix."

He cut his arm—on a whim, this time he chose his right one—and called to the nether, focusing it like water through a sluice or light through a lens.

"Not too fast," he said. "But not too slow. It might help to think of it as something alive. A dog of war, maybe. It has to be ready to obey you—but it also has to be hungry."

He released the nether, then brought it back, repeating the cycle until his students looked eager to try it for themselves.

Dante smiled. "Show me what you've got."

Sorrowen stepped forward before Raxa could move, face hardened with concentration. He held his hand aloft, fingers bent like winter-stripped branches. Shadows dripped from the nearby trees. At first they came slowly, as was his style, but then he bared his teeth, the cords in his neck flexing as he wrenched the nether to his hand. The shadows lurched forward, flinging themselves to his curled fingers.

"A little rough," Dante said.

Blays nodded, adopting a sage expression. "Then again, in a long relationship with the nether, it's good to keep things interesting."

Sorrowen repeated the drill time and again. The shadows started out reluctant to flow quickly, shuddering in resistance, but got a little smoother with each attempt. The practice was as basic as it got, yet Sorrowen was heartened by his obvious progress. When his strength gave out and the shadows refused to budge, he swore, kicking at the snow.

Dante jerked his chin at Raxa. "You're up."

She shook her hands as if to flick mud from them, then bent her knees, lifted her chin, and called to the darkness. The nether poured into her like an avalanche. Eyebrows flickering in irritating, she dismissed it, then tried again. Again, the shadows threatened to overwhelm her.

Blays scratched his jaw. "When we duked it out in the shadows, you came at me with a knife. Is that what you normally use?"

"You carry a sword when you want people to know you've got a sword," she said. "But a knife cuts just as deep—and no one knows you've got one until it's too late."

"Oh, I love all blades. But knives aren't about power, are they? They're about exerting the right pressure at the right moment."

She stared at him a moment, then held up both hands, palms out. A hazy cylinder of shadows swirled around her. This time, she seemed to be holding them back, damming the nether up through strength of her will. Arms trembling, she continued to hold it at bay, huffing steam as she sought some unseen sign. At last, finding what she was looking for, she nodded to the fringes of the light. A stream of blackness flowed toward her, forming a ball between her hands.

When she released it, Dante clapped his hands in triumph. "Do that every time, and you'll be a sorcerer before the year's out."

She tried again. A little shaky this time, but her third effort was better. Each time she repeated the summoning, she got a little faster and a little smoother. When at last the nether failed her, she grinned and stalked around the snow, walking it off like a tournament contestant who's just performed a great feat of strength.

"Now we're getting somewhere," Dante said. "Too bad we don't have anything to celebrate with."

"Yes," Blays said. "Too bad."

"Don't tell me you brought rum!"

"Okay, I won't tell you. The substance I'll be drinking with Raxa and Sorrowen is just...brown water. That makes us laugh too much and talk too loud. Must have come from a magical spring, this stuff."

He went to his saddlebags and fetched a leather skin that proved to be almost but not quite full of one of the Citadel's better batches. They sat by the fire and passed it around, sharing it with the rangers, who couldn't have been happier if Blays had discovered a pot of gold.

An hour later, Sorrowen poked at some embers with a stick, the brightening fire making his face look as stark as the canyons of the Collen Basin. "Is it true what they say?"

"Knowing 'they,'" Blays said, "whatever it is, it's a bloody lie."

"Then you didn't see the afterworld?"

"Oh, that? Yeah, we visited. Nice place."

Raxa had been staring into the fire. Hearing this, she swung her head about with drunken commitment. "You mean it's *real*? The hills and the stars and all that shit?"

Blays waved a hand about. "Oh, there's something beyond this. But as usual, the priests were completely wrong about everything."

Dante lifted his eyebrows at Raxa. "You don't believe in the afterworld?"

Raxa snorted. "Why would I? Everything the priests and kings have ever told us is a lie."

"Do you believe in the gods?"

"Have you seen any of them for yourself?"

"I might have."

She put her hand on her knee, pushing herself straighter. "You serious? Blays, pass that bag over here. I can't deal with this."

Blays complied. She swigged. Dante had always assumed there were nonbelievers out there somewhere. People were too different and too many for them all to believe the same thing; if you searched long enough, you could probably find someone who insisted the sun rose in the west. Even so, he couldn't recall ever having met a denier in person.

Then again, at that moment, he'd had enough rum that he couldn't recall much of anything.

Sorrowen licked his lips. "So what's it...like?"

"At first, you don't even know you're there," Dante said. "Then you get to live as you please for as long as you like. And after that...well, nobody knows."

Blays pointed at the boy. "Except all those dead people."

Sorrowen frowned, giving Dante a sidelong glance. "If that's what it's really like, then why does the priesthood tell us it's something completely different?"

"We didn't know," Dante said. "We've just been teaching what we were taught. What the *Cycle* tells us."

"Now that you know the truth, are you going to tell people about it?"

Blays laughed. "Can the High Priest of Arawn be a heretic to his own church?"

"Others have done it," Dante said. "It didn't go so well for Lyle." He reached for the skin full of rum. "Some day, I'll tell the people what we saw in the beyond. But they have to be made ready for it first. Their belief is who these people are. Challenge their identity with a new truth, and they'll hang you for it."

The following morning, Dante declared that it was time for Raxa to learn as much Mallish as she could. As they traveled, he, Blays, and Sorrowen spent hours pointing things out and naming them. Raxa didn't look thrilled, but she repeated the words dutifully. Seeing her dedication, Dante was almost but not quite convinced that she intended to hold up her end of the bargain, and that it wasn't just a ruse to find the right opportunity to murder him and Blays and skip back to Narashtovik. When they broke to eat lunch and swap horses, he started to teach her to read Mallish, too.

As night came, and they finished making camp, Sorrowen and Raxa resumed their training with an eagerness they hadn't shown since the first night. Dante spent a few minutes having them summon, dismiss, and resummon the nether. They still needed plenty of refinement, but each night of instruction was as precious as a gem. If they practiced their channeling as they practiced putting the nether to use, they could build two skills at once.

He got them started on intercepting bolts of nether again, but they were as clumsy as before. Even with their improved channeling, they were going to run out of strength before they'd had much chance to make any progress. He needed to teach them control, and *then* come back to interception.

"New plan," he said. "It's time for you two to learn to raise the undead. And do it right this time." He fished a few dead mice from his outer pocket.

Sorrowen gawked. "You...carry them with you?"

"It's easier than killing new ones every time I need them. Besides, in cold like this, they don't even smell."

He stamped down a patch of snow and laid out the bodies. Rather than having them squander their limited shadows trying and failing to raise the mice, Dante brought them to their feet with a wave of his hand. The rodents stared up at him, eyes as dark as the mouths of fish.

"Sorrowen. Bring the nether close. Be ready to use it."

Feeling the boy summon the shadows, Dante reached into the nearest mouse, locating the nether within it. To this, he attached a cord—or perhaps a pipe—of fresh nether, extending it outside the mouse.

"Connect yourself to it," Dante said. "You'll be taking it from me. Slow and easy. No need to rush."

Sorrowen nodded once. Extending a thread-thin tendril of nether, he attached it to the hanging cord, tested the link, then thickened it. As its diameter matched that of the cord, it winked out.

"I got it!" Sorrowen beamed, thrusting up a fist. "I—"

He staggered, collapsing on his side in the snow.

Dante ran to him, dropping into a slide. "Sorrowen? Are you all right?"

"Ohh." Sorrowen rocked on his back, pressing a palm to his forehead. Dante drove the nether into his body, but at a glance, there didn't seem to be anything wrong. Sorrowen sat up, laughing, and pointed at the mouse. "I can see through its eyes! Does it always make you this dizzy?"

Dante grinned. "Before you push yourself too far, try to—"

The acolyte jumped to his feet. Eyes flying wide, he spun and vomited into the snow.

Blays shook his head at Dante. "Why is there always so much

barfing when you're around?"

While Sorrowen was recovering, Dante prepared a second mouse. Transferring it to Raxa took a few tries, but learning from Sorrowen's experience, she'd seated herself, and only needed a short rest to acclimate herself to seeing through the dead creature's eyes.

Sorrowen, still a little green-looking, lowered his chin, bent his brows, and ordered his mouse forward. The creature dragged itself ahead, veering badly to the left, a single paw gripping into the snow while the others spasmed and kicked at nothing. A second paw found its way, followed by the remaining pair. Dante offered snippets of advice as Raxa manipulated her mouse, whispering to herself as she learned the basics of its command.

Within an hour, the two of them were able to make the mice run in whatever direction they liked. At a moment when the both of them had taken a step back to regard their little charges, Dante called them over to him.

"When people think of sorcery, they imagine raging fireballs. Hammers of force smashing down castle walls. A sorcerer striding into an enemy army and striking down soldiers by the thousands until their blood flows around his ankles.

"The nether can make you look like an avatar of the gods come to deal out wrath and ruin. But don't let yourself get so drunk on the vision of crushing and smiting that you forget the range of your power. Skilled nethermancers are more than a sledgehammer. They're also a scalpel. The nether can be used to solve any trouble you fall into—as long as you have the wit and imagination to put it to use."

He crouched down and held out his palm. Sorrowen's mouse scurried into it. Dante lifted the undead rodent up to eye level. "When you're alone in Bressel, and the enemy's closing in on you, remember that it doesn't always take lightning and hellfire to save your life. Sometimes, all it takes is a mouse."

The two students nodded. Dante set them back to their practice. They wandered into the edge of the firelight, following their mice.

"Smart advice," Blays said. "Who'd you steal it from?"

Dante laughed, but a flicker of doubt stirred in his chest. It was a thin line between wisdom and idiocy. Had Cally always been as confident as he sounded? Or had he been exploring as he went along, unsure of the truth of his statements until he'd seen his apprentices prove him right?

The next day, as they crossed a ridge, a band of norren hunters watched them pass, but made no effort to approach. After Raxa's lunchtime reading lesson, which was progressing slowly, Dante took a look at his collection of mice and decided that they were starting to look a little haggard and gruesome. He used the nether as a fine blade, flensing the creatures down to their bones.

That night, Dante instructed Sorrowen to use his mouse to build a block of snow, and for Raxa to have hers try to climb a shrub.

"Too easy," Sorrowen declared as his skeletal mouse packed a final paw-load onto the foot-wide cube of snow it had been raising and brushed the surface smooth. "That's barely any harder than making them walk."

Easy as the boy thought it was, Dante asked him to repeat the task until he ran out of strength. Smiling smugly, Sorrowen complied. Raxa had some initial difficulty getting the mouse's tiny claws to wrap around twigs, but by night's end, she had it ascending and descending the shrub with the grace of...well, certainly not a squirrel, but possibly a confused cat or a young child.

They entered a snowy plain broken up by boulders of dark rock. The steady wind kept the snow shallow, allowing them to increase their pace. Night came, bringing a sudden snowstorm. They huddled in the lee of a boulder.

"Last night, you proved you could build a block," Dante told Sorrowen. "Tonight, I want you to build a model of the Sealed Citadel. Including the outer wall."

Sorrowen's eyes darted from side to side. "Are you kidding? Sir?"

"What could possibly be funny about using a mouse skeleton to build a mouse-sized snow fort? Besides, you said your last task was too easy. I'd hate for you to get bored."

Grumbling, Sorrowen motioned his mouse to start gathering snow. Raxa got a good chuckle at this.

"Can't forget you," Dante said to her. "As for your task, you get to write out the first page of the *Cycle*. In Mallish. Using your mouse."

Her mirth died on her face. He provided her with a quill, an inkpot, and a palimpsest, then spread open the *Cycle*. The mouse hoisted the quill over its shoulder and began to write in shaky, uneven letters.

Dante watched until he got bored, then went to check on Sorrowen. The boy was having the mouse use a spoon to shovel snow faster. The Citadel's keep was already in place, though Sorrowen was neglecting its finer details. Dante watched the mouse pile up the foundation for the outer walls.

He returned to Raxa and leaned over the mouse scratching at the parchment with a quill big enough to be its pike. "How's it going?"

"I spilled the ink twice," she said flatly. "Then I thought, Maybe I should pack the inkpot down into the snow. So I did that. I haven't spilled it since."

"Excellent. Sounds like you're making real progress. And what about your alphabet?"

Raxa gestured to her pages. She'd written it down several times, in increasingly smaller and neater script. It still looked like children's writing, but considering she was copying a foreign language through the medium of a deceased mouse, her effort was deceptively skilled.

He kneeled next to her. "Are you enjoying yourself?"

Raxa squinted at him. "Would you be? I get why we're doing this, but that doesn't make it any less tedious."

"In that case, you should probably go rob Sorrowen. For the sake of your morale."

"Is that an order?"

He nodded. "To war!"

For a moment, she looked ready to call him stupid. Then her eyes lit up with mischief. She swiveled her head toward the mouse, concentration crinkling her face. The skeleton laid down its quill, bunged the inkpot, then slunk across the snow toward

Sorrowen, whose nose was buried in the process of directing his own mouse around his half-built walls.

Raxa's mouse slipped forward. Any sound it made was erased by the pop of the fire and the rush of snow in the wind. Like all of them, Sorrowen wore a thick cloak that hung past the backs of his knees. The mouse paused beneath him, gathered itself, and leaped high, snagging the hem of the cloak with its front paws. It kicked its back legs until they found purchase in the fabric.

Raxa collected herself, then guided the creature up Sorrowen's back. It reached a large pocket near his right hip and climbed inside, emerging a moment later with a packet of dried apples.

"Agh!" Sorrowen spun, slapping at his cloak. The mouse spun through the air and landed inside the model Citadel's walls.

Dante cupped his hands to his mouth. "You're being invaded! Protect your keep!"

Sorrowen glanced from him to the thieving mouse. With an affronted scowl, he pointed at Raxa's mouse, which was currently trying to jump up the foot-high snow walls. On the other side of the enclosure, his mouse raced along the battlements, flinging itself down at the intruder. They met with a brittle clack.

Raxa ran forward two steps, gesturing to her mouse. The two constructs ripped at each other, sending ribs and claws flying into the snow. Raxa ordered her mouse to spit out the packet of apple slices just as the enemy's oversized front teeth sank into its outstretched neck.

Raxa's creature collapsed in a pile. Sorrowen blinked in surprise, then stared down at his mouse until it looked like the sweat was about to pop from his brows. At last, the rodent rose on its back legs and did a victory jig.

Sorrowen picked up the packet of apples and returned it to his pocket. "Any further attempts to steal will be put down just as harshly."

"Next time, you'll never see me coming." For a moment, Raxa looked angry with her defeat—then she burst into laughter, gazing down at the remains of her mouse. "Is that the end of Captain Grabs?"

Dante leaned over the wall for a better look. "Afraid so. When they get too beat up, their nether leaks away, joining the residual shadows around them." He produced a small leather pouch and dumped out another pile of bones. "That's why it pays to carry replacements."

The evening's practice had been far more childish than anything the monks at the Citadel would have allowed, but Dante had never thought much of the traditional scholastic model. In fact, it was one of the many things about the Citadel he intended to alter or reform at some point in the future when he had free time—which likely meant when he was too old and frail to leave his room on voyages like this one.

For some reason, people believed that it was only real learning if it was boring, difficult, and unpleasant. For Dante, the best learning had always been when he was having fun. Sometimes, the subject itself was so compelling that it needed no other seasoning, but often, his interest in or ability to remember the details of that subject was due to the fact he'd had a blast while learning it.

With this in mind, he made certain Sorrowen and Raxa had more to do than listen to him lecture and then recite back what he'd just told them. He assigned them both a rotation of thiefly pursuits: getting Raxa's mouse to pickpocket the others in their group without being noticed; to scurry up trees, climb out on branches, and leap to others; to carry a small vial—the kind that might be used to contain poison—unstopper it, and pour it into a hole in the snow no bigger than a mouth or an ear.

Their favorite game was something they dubbed "the Little Gantlet," in which their mice were given a token to carry and protect across the landscape while Dante used his own mice to hunt them. Sometimes, Raxa and Sorrowen were on the same side. Others, they were in opposition. Sorrowen clearly preferred to work together, but Raxa didn't seem to care. The only thing she cared about was getting her mouse through the gantlet and dropping her token in the victory circle.

After two weeks of travel, the Dunden Mountains condensed on the horizon. With their time together nearly half over, Dante switched their lessons from the control of the mice to the creation of them. He soon ran into a challenge to his philosophy of making all learning and practice into a game, puzzle, or contest: they were bad at reanimating the dead, and there was no real way to turn their acquisition of these skills into a game. Or at any rate, to make a game more complicated than "whoever does it first gets to mock the one who failed."

Fortunately for their collective sanity, he'd already learned that it was counterproductive to lecture them as if they both had the same problems and solutions. Instead, he taught them individually. By the time they reached the mountains, Sorrowen was able to raise and command not just one, but two mice at once, if for limited periods of time.

Yet Raxa still hadn't gotten it. As they hiked into a blizzard, Dante had to divert most of his time and power toward clearing and reshaping the ground ahead of them. Three days into the Dundens, they stopped in the middle of the afternoon and made camp below the pass, meaning to try to cross it once they had a full day to work with. Dante hollowed them a shelter in the rock, complete with a small flue.

As the rangers struggled to get a fire going, Dante went over bits of the *Cycle* with Raxa. Particularly the sections involving Jack Hand, the adventurous sorcerer who'd used an army of dead rats to free himself from captivity. The original copy of the *Cycle* was far more than a book, and he was hoping exposure to these stories would jog something inside her or teach her something he couldn't. There was no guarantee she'd learn to use the little spies before they reached Bressel. If she couldn't, her chances of ferreting out Mallon's plans would drop sharply.

"Jack Hand again?" Blays got to his feet, brushing snow from his trousers. "Tell me when you get to the stories about his cousin Jack Ass. Until then, I'm going to make use of the daylight to scout the path ahead."

He exited into the falling snow. Dante finished up one of the passages about Jack Hand, then had Raxa try her hand on a mouse skeleton. After a few more failures, he switched back to reading the book. As he debated with Raxa about whether a single sorcerer could really command the number of rats the *Cycle* claimed Jack Hand had put to use, Blays materialized from nowhere.

"Shit!" Dante scrambled backward. "Don't *do* that!"

"If I didn't, I'd sink into the snow like an arrow fired straight down." Blays motioned in the direction of the pass. "I got nearly two miles ahead before I had to turn back."

"I could have sent a mouse to do that."

"Yes, but if you were off doing that, I couldn't teach your students, so from each their own and all that. In any event, the pass looks okay. Well, relatively okay. It won't *definitely* kill us." Blays waved a hand at the still air of the cave. "What were you guys doing in here, anyway? This place is swimming with nether."

"That's probably what I was going to clobber you with for appearing out of the blue. We were reading. There wasn't any nether involved."

"There was a second ago. It was flying around like a flock of crows the gods had forgotten to finish detailing."

Dante glanced at Raxa. "Were you drawing on the nether?"

She shrugged. "I'm saving it all for your gods damned mice."

Blays frowned. "Either you're mistaken, or my brain is in the process of freezing solid. As we always do, let's pray you're wrong."

He blinked out of existence. Now that Dante was expecting him, he could feel Blays' presence in the shadows. Blays took a couple of steps toward Dante, stopped, then moved to the open copy of the *Cycle*, which he seemed to stand over for a long time.

"Er," Blays said, returning to reality. "Turns out we're both right. Or wrong, if you're feeling cynical. The nether's still here. It's tumbling around like dust in a sunbeam in a barn—or like a stream flowing between you two and the *Cycle*. Thing is, it seems to be confined to the netherworld."

Dante examined the air in front of him and around the *Cycle*, but there were no more than a few particles of shadows drifting about, and nothing that came close to resembling a stream.

"I don't see anything."

Blays rolled his eyes. "Considering how poorly you use your ears, I'm not surprised your eyes don't work, either. You can't see it because you can't see into the shadows."

"What's the nether doing? Besides being there?"

Blays disappeared for another ten seconds before coming back. "Well, a lot of it's sinking into you. Although a bit is also going from you into the book."

Dante's skin tingled. "You're absolutely, one hundred percent sure of this?"

"That's what the book does," Raxa said. "You didn't know that?"

"You've seen this, too?"

A glimmer of self-recrimination crossed her face, as if she'd regretted saying anything. She eyed Dante, then glanced out at the storm outside the cave, seeming to relax.

"Yep." Raxa made a circular motion between herself and the book. "But only when I was inside the shadows. It doesn't react the same way to everyone, either. When one of my friends was reading it, she hardly stirred up any shadows at all."

Dante gazed down at the book. He was annoyed that they could see this phenomenon and he couldn't, but the darkness of his jealousy was already being replaced by the lightness of curiosity.

"It's still doing this right now?" He motioned to Blays. "What about you? Are you caught up in these streams? Or is it just me and Raxa?"

Blays held up a finger and blinked away again. When he returned, he was shaking his head. "It's sprinkling a bit of shadows on me. But it's dumping plenty on Raxa, and you look like you're in the middle of a filthy blizzard."

Dante was overtaken by that particular breed of thought where he wouldn't have been able to explain it to himself, let alone out loud to another person. Letting his inspiration propel him forward, he pointed at Raxa.

"Put your hand on the book." As she complied, he followed suit. He tried again to sense the flow of nether, but it remained hidden from him. "Watch what I do. When you feel ready, you try."

He got a bag of mouse bones from his pocket and dumped them on the cold stone floor of the cave. He drew the nether to his hand, matching his breathing to the slow expansion and contraction of the shadows. Thus synched, he waited for the nether to expand fully, then animated the skeleton. When the shadows shrank to their smallest, he withdrew the others from the mouse, collapsing it with a delicate rattle.

With each cycle of the nether, he animated and deanimated the mouse again. At first, Raxa watched him. Then she watched the mouse. At last, she seemed to be looking at nothing at all—or gazing through their world and into another.

She lifted her hand. Shadows swam from her fingers to the skeleton of the mouse. A bony tail twitched. Tiny claws flexed. The mouse rocked to its feet, turned around, and tilted its skull at Raxa.

They took the pass early the next morning. The snows were worse than Dante had expected, forcing him to tunnel through a short stretch of rock. They emerged into a blizzard so thick that he would have been lost if not for the dim shapes of the mountains around him.

There was nothing to do but press on. After two miles forward and a few hundred feet of vertical descent, the winds eased back. The snow changed from a stinging curtain to slow, cottony blobs that landed with little whispers.

After a quick shadowalk ahead, Blays returned to the group, mounted up, and maneuvered next to Dante. "Were you ever going to explain what you figured out yesterday?"

"Why would the wise master reveal all his secrets?"

"If I ever meet one, I'll have to ask him. Besides, the only thing you like more than being seen as wise is being seen as clever."

Dante smiled. "Typically, nether is visible in both the physical world and the netherworld, right?"

"As far as I know. But you can write everything I know about the nether on a husk of corn."

"Can you think of any forms of nether that aren't visible in our world?"

"No?"

"Funny, considering one such form repeatedly tried to eat you."

Blays tipped back his head. "Traces. What Gladdic used to make the Andrac. The little bits of you left behind when you die."

"That's the only type of nether I know of that would explain this."

"That would mean the original *Cycle* is full of dead souls."

"It's like the nether inside it is circulating through those who read it. Especially those who are talented with the shadows. I wonder if it's taken pieces from everyone who's ever read it. Then it mingles those bits with you, and takes a few from you to it, and this opens a channel."

"Sort of like the loons?"

"Sort of," Dante agreed. "This would explain why, when I read it, it seemed like I just learned to wield the nether out of nowhere. The *Cycle* was altering me—I just couldn't see it happening."

"You know what would be amazing? If the *ink* was made from traces. Now that would be style." Blays glanced over his shoulder. "This channel-opening, you think that's what showed Raxa how to make her pile of bones sit up and squeak?"

"Putting her in contact with my skills—and those of everyone in the traces—might have shown her how to do it. It could even have enhanced her own skills."

"Now that's interesting. If you and I tapped into the book, think it'd finally teach you how to land a wife?"

"Hilarious. The book's ability is exciting on its own, but there's something more going on here. I can't see it manipulating the nether at all. Only shadowalkers can—and as far as I know, the only people who can shadowalk are the People of the Pocket and their refugees. If I can figure out how to replicate the *Cycle*'s source of nether, I could hide my attacks from other sorcerers."

"Replicate it? You mean by taking people's souls and putting them into a staff or something?"

"Traces aren't souls, per se."

"We don't know that!"

"I'm just saying that we *could* do this," Dante said. "Apparently whoever made the original *Cycle* did it."

Blays gave him a crooked look. "Yes, and some others in your vaunted institution once raised a mountain range that nearly killed an entire civilization. Last time I checked, everyone still considered that a regrettable move."

They dropped out of the mountains and into the patchwork of plains and forests that made up the sparsely inhabited reaches of northern Mallon. Sorrowen was already versed in basic healing, but Raxa was unfamiliar with the techniques. Keeping the *Cycle* spread next to them, Dante had her healing small cuts by the end of the night.

Using the last of her energy, she sealed a nick on her palm, turning her hand back and forth. "How much can you do with this? If I cut Sorrowen's throat, could you stop him from bleeding out?"

Sorrowen scowled at her. Dante grinned. "I've saved people from worse wounds than that. Ether's better at this—it wants to restore things to the way they were—but the nether likes to grow things. Like veins, and flesh, and bones."

"Can you cure disease?"

"Everything I've run into. Well, almost everything. It's trickier than sealing up a wound, but a skilled priest can cure a lot of common ailments."

She sucked on her upper front teeth. "What about death?"

"We're still working on a cure for that one. As far as I know, once you pass into Arawn's hands, you're his for good." Next to him, Blays coughed. Dante kept a straight face. "Although people always like to tell crazy stories about people coming back from the dead."

A few days later, they spotted uncovered grass for the first time since leaving Narashtovik. Now that Sorrowen and Raxa were capable of raising mice by themselves, Dante had them use their undead minions to scout ahead for patrols, highwaymen, or other sources of potential unpleasantness. He had the two of them describe what they saw along the way. Raxa had a natural eye for detail. Sorrowen didn't—though he could sustain his mice for upwards of three hours while Raxa struggled to keep hers going for an hour.

As they neared Whetton, a column of black smoke climbed from the horizon. Dante took them close enough for a glimpse of the city. It now bore wooden walls, the gates closed tight. Something inside them was burning, but the fire appeared to be under control.

Wary of patrols, they traveled a good mile off the road before making camp. Dante used a spark of ether to light the firewood the rangers gathered.

He sat close to the fire, steam rising from his wet boots. "Have you figured out what you're going to do in Bressel, Raxa?"

She pulled her hair loose from the string she'd used to bind it back. "Thinking of hiring on as a messenger. They get sent to all kinds of important people. Nobody pays them much attention, either." She grinned. "Or maybe I'll find an outfit like the one I just left. Thieves know more about the comings and goings of the nobility than everyone but the courtesans."

Blays picked something from his teeth and spat it into the fire. "Try the Red Ghosts."

"Red Ghosts?"

"They're Bressel's version of the Order. Flash a few of your skills at them, and I'm sure they'll be happy to take you aboard. Only show your mundane skills, mind you. Show them you can shadowalk, and they're apt to drink your blood to try to absorb your power."

Dante raised an eyebrow. "How do you know about the operations of Mallish brigands?"

"Robert Hobble used to work with them, that's how. Any organization smart enough to work with the esteemed Mr. Hobble is going to be a great fit for our friend here."

As Blays and Raxa fell into a detailed conversation regarding the customs of outlaws in Mallish society, Dante took the opportunity to pull Sorrowen aside.

Dante removed a piece of mouse skull from his pocket. "Give me a dab of your blood."

Without missing a beat, Sorrowen got out his knife, scratched the back of his arm, and held it out for Dante. Dante smeared the piece of skull with a drop of blood, then sealed a layer of nether into the bone.

He extended it to Sorrowen. "Do you know what this is?"

The boy glanced at Dante, then down at the bone, then back at Dante. "Uh. I didn't know you made jewelry, sir. I'll wear it with pride."

"It's not just jewelry, you fool. It's a loon. It's linked to this one." Dante dangled his half. "Put it in your ear, and activate it like so—" He paused to illustrate. "And we can speak to each other from hundreds of miles apart."

Sorrowen gave it a try. When Dante's voice sounded in his ear, his jaw dropped, completely awestruck. Dante couldn't help laughing: there were few things funnier than a sorcerer who acted like he'd never seen magic before.

"Keep it secret," he said. "Don't even tell Raxa. And when you enter the priesthood, don't wear it around them—they might be able to sense it. You'll have to hide it somewhere. Only use it when you or Raxa has something to pass along."

Sorrowen bounced the loon in his hand. He licked his lips. "Are you sure this is going to work?"

"You just heard it for yourself."

"I don't..." Sorrowen pocketed the loon. "Nevermind. It's stupid."

"You're worried about your mission. You should be. You're about to be dropped into the lion's den. If you have a problem with that, you need to let me know now."

"But...I mean...what would it matter now? We're hardly two days from Bressel."

"Which gives you two days to decide you'd rather go back to Narashtovik."

"You'd let me do that?"

"I would," Dante said. "But first, I'd tell you that this *will* be dangerous. You could be hurt. You could even be killed. But I think you can do this. You're quick on your feet. That's one of the only two skills you need to survive anything."

"What's the other thing?"

"Resilience. The ability to take a punch, get back on your feet, and throw one back."

Sorrowen frowned. "You think I can do that?"

"You can find out in Bressel. Or you can return to Narashtovik, rejoin the monks, and never *have* to find out. Which life do you want?"

The boy was quiet for a few seconds. He glanced through the trees at Raxa and Blays, who were still laughing next to the fire, as if they'd burned all their worries along with the kindling. Sorrowen drew a wisp of shadows to his fingers. For a moment, he looked older.

"I'll go," he said. "It's what Narashtovik needs from me, isn't it?"

"Actually, I'm hoping you turn out to be worthless, because Mallon doesn't intend to do anything more threatening than wear those ridiculous pants of theirs."

Sorrowen laughed. They returned to the fire. Dante felt pleased with himself until it occurred to him that he'd never really believed that Sorrowen would have given up the mission to return to Narashtovik—and that if he had feared that outcome, he might never have asked at all.

Two days later, with the sun fading from the overcast sky, they gazed on the spires of Bressel.

"From here, you're on your own," Dante said. "I wish I had some final trick or lesson to teach you."

Blays shifted in his saddle. "I've got one: 'Never get in a fight with someone who can turn you inside-out.'"

"Try not to get in any fights at all. Especially not with their priests. Even if you think you're stronger, next to the nether and the ether, we're nothing but watery, helpless flesh. If you make a single mistake, you won't get the chance to make a second one."

Raxa sniffed. "Are you always this inspiring before you send your troops into battle?"

"This is why I encourage him to shut up and make things explode," Blays said. "Much better for morale."

Raxa grinned, gave the mounts that had carried her all this way one last pat, and walked onward toward the city. Sorrowen followed. When he was twenty feet from them, he turned and gave a hesitant wave.

"We're not sending them to their deaths, are we?" Blays said.

"Don't worry, this one's all on me," Dante said. "Although if they do wind up caught and executed, you really should have done something to stop me here."

He called the rangers over to him. He'd wrapped the *Cycle* in an oiled leather bag to keep it dry. He handed it over to Echels, who would lead the four escorts home to Narashtovik.

"If the pass isn't clear, wait for it to thaw," Dante said. "In fact, if there's ever a choice between getting the book home sooner, and getting it there safer, choose the safer option. If you run into any trouble north of the Dundens, the norren will help you. Otherwise, don't stop for anyone. Not even to help them. This book can't be replaced. Unless you're faced to decide between saving the book and saving the world, always go with the book."

"All right, Mother Dante," Blays cut in. "If you're ready to part with your precious child, perhaps we can get on with our job?"

Echels smiled, eyes crinkling. "We'll take perfect care of it, sir. We are aware that if we didn't, you'd use our skin for your bedsheets."

Echels secured the book in a pouch in his saddle next to his sword. With a clipped, birdlike call, he ordered his men to turn about and ride north. Dante tried not to think about how the *Cycle* would be on the open road for at least the next month. Anyway, safer with the riders than where he was headed.

They backtracked to a ferry they'd seen a few miles up the Chanset and crossed to the eastern bank. Once they were oriented southeast, meaning to hit the shore and ride straight along the coast and into Alebolgia, Dante sent a pulse to Jona's loon.

"Hullo?" It wasn't yet sundown, but Jona sounded well on his way to a good night. "That you, Dante?"

"In the voice," Dante said. "We're a few days outside of Collen, but we'd like to get to Tanar Atain as fast as possible. That means heading straight to Cavana. Can you ask the Colleners to meet us there?"

Jona chuckled roughly. "Wish all my jobs were so easy. The basin's already got a delegation in Cavana."

"Really? What are they doing there?"

"Diplomacy or some shit. You think they tell me anything? To them, I'm just a sailor who forgot which way the ocean is."

"Right," Dante said. "I'll let you get back to your rum, then."

Many miles east of Bressel, they came to the coast. The wind off the ocean wasn't as cold as it had been inland, leaving the way free of snow. They trotted along the pathway all the way to the inland sea Dante had created to block off the Mallish.

The Colleners had already established a small fort on the other side. They sent over a flat-bottomed sloop to transport Dante, Blays, and the horses to the other side. The Colleners were in high spirits, offering them food and drink, congratulating them in having secured the basin's freedom at last. Never one to pass up a feast, Blays talked Dante into staying overnight.

In the morning, they made all haste for the Strip of Alebolgia. After a stretch of desert, the starkness was textured with grape trellises and fields of low green winter wheat. They passed through the hills of Poloa and came to Cavana. Securing lodging at an inn, they sent a messenger to the Collenese delegation, who were apparently being quartered at House Itiego.

Within an hour of their arrival, a fist hammered on their door. Dante glanced at Blays, who shrugged and loosened his swords in their sheaths. Dante bit his lip until he tasted blood, gathering nether in his hands.

He opened the door. Lady Vita Osedo barged inside, her face clenched in wrath. She jabbed a thin, curved sword against Dante's chest.

"There's the liar from the north," she said. "Time to answer for your betrayal."

17

Raxa had always thought Narashtovik was the pinnacle of a sprawling, potent city. The kind of place you could get lost in. In her line of work, you couldn't ask for more.

But as she neared the capital's gates, she was starting to think you could fit Narashtovik into a single quadrant of Bressel. The city was big. Bigger than big. People scurried everywhere, tan and dark-haired, supplemented by a goodly number of others with light brown faces and hair as yellow as corn silk, and speckled by citizens and visitors who seemed to be from every limb of the world: pale, black-haired Gaskans; tall people with skin as reddish-brown as chestnuts; others with short orange hair and faces that were nearly as dark as charcoal.

Ahead, blue-shirted guards examined the flow of people coming through the gates, stopping everyone who hit their eye the wrong way. Her mission felt suddenly real in a way it hadn't during the long ride from the north. She'd taken Galand up on his offer for many reasons. Including a few she didn't fully understand. What she knew for sure was that she was tired of being hunted. Of feeling like a rat who had to dash for cover whenever one of the sharp-eyed and sharper-clawed agents of the Citadel came prowling by.

And maybe after Gaits, she'd been pushed away by disillusionment with what Narashtovik's underclass liked to call the "brotherhood of scum." Not that she was walking out on the Order. More like taking a break. While seizing the opportunity to learn how to not just walk in the shadows, but to kill with them. When she came back home, not only would the Citadel no longer be their enemy, but she'd be equipped to protect her people and her kids from anything short of a barbarian horde.

She passed through the gates. A pair of guards moved in front of her, eyes roving up and down her body. Maybe they were inspecting her for swords, or maybe they were just enjoying the benefits of a job that allowed you to look at whoever you wanted for as long as you liked without being criticized for it.

The shorter of the two guards raised his eyes to her face, then her hair. Unimpressed with what he saw, he said something, but it sounded like a foreign language.

Oh shit. It *was*.

Raxa tried to reconstruct the words in her mind. Something about…doing? No, about business. Was she here on business?

"Yes," she said in Mallish. "Business."

The guard looked at her like she was trying to stick her tongue up her own nose. He repeated himself, slowing the words. "What's your business?"

Raxa smiled, buying herself a few moments. Despite weeks of lessons with Dante, hearing Mallish spoken in real time and in a full vocabulary threw her for a loop. It was like she'd been taught to swim in a knee-deep pond and then been tossed into the ocean during a winter squall.

She took in the scene around her. They were letting almost everyone else through without question. Including a number of men whose clothes were as tattered as the Lady of Whispers' maidenhead—obvious vagabonds, if not highwaymen. Why were *they* being allowed inside? They looked like…

Mallishers. Like they belonged.

"Here to serve," she said, or tried to. Her grammar was awful, slapping words together like a drunkard hammering wooden cut-offs together in the hopes they'd form something chair-like enough to sit on. She smiled at the guards, playing up her naive innocence. "Family in the church."

They exchanged a look, then stepped aside and waved her in. She was well past them before she allowed herself to smile.

For there was one more reason she'd agreed to come to Bressel: to see new places, and cause them trouble.

The spires of temples jabbed at the gray, late winter sky. Blocky towers squared their shoulders against the city below them. The roofs weren't half as steep as in Narashtovik, and everything was so whitewashed it made her eyes hurt. Even so, while the forms were different, the function was the same. Tenements and public houses, markets and churches, makeshift buildings that had started as a cottage or barn and grown into an unholy mishmash of additions and expansions.

For the better part of an hour, she let herself walk the city, guided by nothing more than the want to feel the streets with her feet and inhale them into her lungs. Much like the buildings, Bressel's classes of people looked a little different than she was used to, but if you didn't get hung up on the small details, it was easy enough to recognize who was who. Shopkeepers and stall vendors calling out their wares. Beggars and the passersby who pointedly ignored them. Nobles and the rich rattling past in their sleek black carriages.

Best of all, though, was the greatest freedom of them all: being lost in a crowd. Anonymous and ignored, able to wander and observe without so much as a drop of fear. In Narashtovik, she hadn't been able to do that for a long time. She'd forgotten how much she'd missed it.

Somewhere, a bell rang, melodious but foreboding. Like it was warning the little people below it that judgment was always on its way. Raxa smiled again, adjusted her pack on her shoulders, and got on her way. Business was business. It was time to get down to it.

Blays had told her that the city's main liberators of imprisoned wealth were an outfit called the Red Ghosts. He'd claimed that the last time he'd spent time in Bressel, the Ghosts had favored the taverns of the Cutlery District. Raxa didn't know why the city *had* a cutlery district, to say nothing of why its cutpurses and cutthroats preferred to hang out there, but people like that tended to have warped senses of humor. Maybe they liked that it kept them closer to the knives.

The bigger streets had their names carved on posts set into

the corners, but she was even worse with written Mallish than the spoken variety. As she asked directions, she quickly discovered the locals didn't think too much of people who spoke broken Mallish in thick Narashtovik accents.

Ultimately, though, their politeness was stronger than their prejudice. An hour and only two wrong turns later, she found herself in a cobbled square of shops interspersed with pubs. Outside many shops, carved wooden forks and knives thrust up from the cobbles, taller than a norren, like the sacred idols of a lost dinner-worshipping kingdom.

Raxa wandered up for a closer look. Clever metal cutlery glinted behind glass windows, couched in dark velvet. Each set of gob-stuffers was unique: in one, the ends of the handles were shaped like seashells; another set bore the roaring heads of bears and eagles and cougars; others were more abstract, hewn from stark angles, or etched all over with delicate spirals. Pretty. Artful. But also one of the silliest fashions Raxa had ever seen.

She ducked her head into a public house. A glance at the normals inside told her more than enough. She moved on to a pub painted garish orange, its sign illustrated with a turtle standing on its hind legs with its front paws put up like a pugilist's. The Boxing Turtle?

Inside the dim common room, she spotted her own kind at once: sprawled in their booths and propped on their stools, they looked leisurely enough. But their eyes always seemed positioned to watch you and everyone else in the room, and their bodies, though momentarily relaxed, looked spring-loaded to run or fight at a moment's notice.

All that aside, the fussy hair and glittering jewelry was a dead giveaway.

A low wooden bar ran across the back of the room. She seated herself at it, glancing at the foamy mug of the man next to her and confirming Mallon knew the glory of beer. She ordered a mug. It was as bitter as a husband whose wife had left him for a man with straight teeth. Where was the sourness? She didn't know if she could trust a land that couldn't be trusted to make good beer.

The man to her left watched her with a smile. He wore a short brown beard that got thin over his cheeks, like a baker that had tried to stretch their dough too far. "Something the matter with your drink?"

Raxa summoned her words. "Do I make faces?"

"Like you're swallowing something that's still alive. Not what you're used to?"

"No. I am used to good."

He barked with laughter. He was about her age and he was handsome, in a slightly too intentional way. She wasn't big on men whose ponytails looked like they'd been coiffed in the king's stables. She preferred the type who looked like they cut their hair with their own blades.

He leaned forward, reaching for her mug. "Could be a bad batch. Better let me try." He hefted it, sipped, and swished it around. "Tastes good to me. I'll drink it if you won't."

She took it back. "I must get used to it. Or have no beer at all."

"Are you new in town?"

"Is my talk that obvious?"

"Speech," he corrected. "And I'm afraid so. Along with your eyes. And your hair. And the way you walk."

"You watch me come in?"

"Guilty. But you chose to sit next to me."

"I sit where there is chair."

She winced at the clumsiness of her grammar, but the man laughed as if she was the wit in a play. "What brings you here?"

"I look for work."

"What kind of work?"

"The work of this place." She gestured around the room. "The work that is done on nights and streets."

"You're looking for a brothel? I took you for a nice girl."

"Not a brothel." Raxa gave him a disparaging look as she searched for the phrase she'd made Galand teach her. "The merchants of the black market."

"Oh. That." The man took a long swig from his mug and set it down a little too abruptly. "We don't do that here. Sorry."

"Do I look like..." She searched for the word. "King's men?"

"The king's a cunning fellow. It would be just like him to enlist a Gaskan to waltz in and trick poor, innocent men into lives of crime."

Gaskan? Had the man never *seen* somebody from Narashtovik? She was about to scorn him when she realized he probably hadn't ever left the confines of Mallon. Giving him a second appraisal, she understood she'd snapped at the wrong fly. He was what the Order called a quiver-filler: the type you wanted to have plenty of at hand, but who was utterly replaceable—and expendable. He couldn't make recruiting decisions. He was probably under direct orders to deny the Red Ghosts' existence.

"I am sorry," she said. "I make a mistake."

He grinned. "Happens to the best of us. If you want to make it up to me, I'm happy to let you buy me a beer."

She begged off—not a good move, getting mired down with a quiver-filler when she needed a person who aimed the arrows—and left the Boxing Turtle, wandering for a while to clear her head.

She was working with steeper hardships than she'd accounted for. Limited as her speech was, it was hard to persuade. And impossible to be subtle. Among her kind, subtlety was a far more important skill than picking pockets or locks. A clumsy thief was a dead thief—or much worse, a captured thief who gets tortured until she gives up her friends.

But words weren't the only way to persuade. Often, what you looked like gave you more authority than the reasonableness of your words.

Raxa looked down at herself and pulled a face. At that moment, what she most resembled was a charwoman who'd lost a fight with a team of pigs. Hundreds of miles of travel had left her clothes rumpled, patched, and dingy. She spent a while wandering around the plaza and watching the comings and goings from the Boxing Turtle. When she was satisfied she had a general eye for their style, she toddled off to find a tailor.

Bressel had a full-blown garment district, but a few questions turned up the fact there was a small tailor's neighborhood just a few blocks from the Cutlery District. She hoofed it over. The shops displayed the latest in ruffian fashion. She settled on a young woman who looked eager for business. Raxa laid out what she needed, how fast she needed it, then haggled down the price. By modifying a few things she already had, the girl thought she might be able to have it done the following evening. Raxa gave her a down payment and went on her way.

She couldn't get anywhere with the Red Ghosts until she had her clothes. To make use of her time, she walked all the way to the palace. It was big. Impressive-looking. Palatial, even. Almost entirely stone, which she'd been expecting, but that was nice to confirm. She smiled at it, as if admiring it, while she assessed ways to break in.

Darkness came along. She found an inn and got a room. Downstairs, they were roasting chicken with potatoes and onions and carrots. Plain stuff, but they'd pinched some spices on it to dress it up. Anyway, after weeks of road food, it felt like a coronation feast.

Her room was on the fourth floor. The night was cool and heading toward cold, but she opened the window to flush out the smell of the previous tenant. Outside, the night was its usual mixture of friendly shouts, laughter, and drunken singing. Raxa knew she should be doing something useful with her time, even something as basic as going downstairs to have a drink and brush up on her Mallish, but hearing the clamor outside in a language that wasn't hers, a strange sadness sagged her shoulders.

Why had she come all this way? Why had she agreed to leave her people in order to meddle in the affairs of two countries she didn't give one shit about? To learn the shadows? Why? The ego of strength? She snuffed her candle, lifted her hand, and called the nether to her fingers. It was scary. Beautiful. Powerful.

But was it worth it?

By the time she woke up, she hadn't found any answers. But she didn't care, either. She'd made her decision weeks ago. She was here. She'd do her job.

She spent the day touring the city. Talking to locals. Goading them into explaining politics to the wide-eyed foreigner. She tried to poke the conversation toward wars and foreign affairs, hoping the people she was speaking with would spit out a few names worth spying on. The name Harald Walstone came up three different times. He was the Minister of the Eastern Reach, and it sounded like he was a hardass.

After a long day, the last light angled through the sky like it was passing through clear water. She headed back to the tailor. The job wasn't done yet, but the girl was happy to keep working — she was hungry, eager to prove herself. Raxa was happy to see it.

As the nine o'clock bells neared, the tailor handed Raxa a bundle of clothes and showed her to a private room to dress. Were the Mallish that squeamish about the sight of somebody else's smallclothes? Raxa stripped out of her old junk and pulled on a linen shirt, trousers that were rakishly baggy yet contoured to her shape, and a woolen doublet with sleeves that stopped at the elbow. Some of her ilk liked fancy footwear, but Raxa thought that well-worn shoes were a mark of your character. She'd kept hers.

All in all, it should have looked mannish, but the cuts and stylings kept it feminine. For her line of work, it was the perfect marriage of rebelliousness and practicality. On her way out of the tailor's, she felt enough swagger to be tempted to kick down the door.

She made her way back to the Boxing Turtle. Good cheer spilled from the shutters. Her entrance drew a few glances. She found an empty spot at a shelf on the side of the room and flagged down the serving boy for a beer. As she made her way through the bitter drink, she surveyed the room.

Didn't take long to find her mark: he sat at a table surrounded by confident young men and a few women who got a good laugh out of everything he said. His dark hair was swept back from his brow with an oil that surely smelled sweet, and when he gestured with his mug, he didn't spill a drop. Two types of people had dexterity like that: acrobats, and people who knew how to kill other people with swords.

If she wanted access to the Red Ghosts and their underground contacts, information, and resources, that was who she had to convince. Raxa doubted that words or the right outfit would be enough. She bided her time until he rose to use the privy. As he returned through the room, she stood and cut across the pub to intercept him.

The ol' bump-and-grab would be too obvious. He'd probably known that one since he was six. Knight-Saves-the-Lady? If she fell in front of him, he'd probably help her up—he had to look good in front of his crew—but if he caught on to her game, her attempt at something so obvious would be humiliating. Wreck her chances.

No, there was only one way for it: do something he'd never see coming.

He was halfway back to his table, smiling in the cocky, lazy way of people who think their success proves their superiority. Raxa curled her finger at the nether. It rolled out from under the tables and danced over to her hand. She tossed most of it aside. Using the finesse Galand had beaten into her during the trip, she sent a bug-sized dollop of darkness flying toward the man's head. It split apart, one half settling over each eye.

He stopped mid-stride, eyes widening against his sudden blindness. Raxa moved beside him. He reached out for balance, or perhaps to reassure himself that he was still conscious. His hand brushed Raxa's side.

She smiled, stepped away, and dropped the nether from his eyes. He stood there a moment, arms held a foot from his hips, as if ready to reach out and grab the world if it tried to slip away again. He muttered under his breath, then donned his cocky smile as if it had been a hat snatched by the wind.

Raxa bided her time, letting him get back into the swing of things. But he was drinking harder now. Rattled. Before he could get so drunk he got unpredictable, or started forgetting his promises, Raxa waited until someone on the opposite side of his table had launched into the telling of a long story, then headed over.

She stopped in front of him. He barely glanced her way.

"Excuse me, good sir." Raxa gritted her teeth, praying hard to Carvahal that she didn't sound as stilted as she felt. "You will hire me."

He swung his head around. A little drunk, but there was still some dagger in his gaze. "Fuck off."

"I can't in good faith fuck off, sir."

"I think you'll find it's quite simple. It's just like regular off, except you do it harder."

"But I can't. Because I find this." She held out her hand.

The thief-lord leaned forward. He gazed down at the gem-studded black leather bracelet in her palm, then felt his sleeved wrist. "Where did you find that?"

"On your arm."

"You stole my father's bracelet from me. And now you ask me for a job?"

He'd kept his voice low, but the entire table was staring at them. Raxa nodded. "So I can use my skills for you."

His hand darted out and crushed her wrist. He stood, taking the bracelet from her. His face was as red as if it had been struck. "You stole from me. In my own house? You have three seconds to get out before I steal your life."

Raxa sucked in a quick breath. "Good sir—"

"One. Two."

She turned and ran from the pub. As she flung open the door, the whole room burst into laughter.

Raxa jogged down the cobbles, then broke into a flat-out run. Not because she was afraid of pursuit—they'd gotten their laugh, that'd be enough—but because the pain of her disgrace was so intense the only way she could deal with it was to run until her body hurt worse than her soul.

A misty drizzle was coming down, slicking the cobbles and manure. After the second time Raxa slipped, she slowed and turned into the next alley. She confirmed it was empty, then hunkered down next to a stoop, raking her hand through her hair.

Part of it was just a bad turn of the cards. Instead of being appreciate of her skill and amused by her audacity, he'd taken it as a blow to his status. Even worse, it hadn't just been a flashy bauble, it'd been his fathers. Even so, Raxa might have been able to turn things around if she wasn't so bad with Mallish that everything she said came off arrogant or foolish. Surviving on the streets depended on being able to read the people around you. If Raxa couldn't present herself so they could read her correctly, she was as doomed as Irrolen in the Hall of the Bone-Eaters.

The rest of the night was a waste. Moping. Kicking herself.

Worst of all, she stayed up too late and drank too much and couldn't rouse herself until eleven in the morning.

Her first meet with Sorrowen was late that night. She spent the early afternoon eyeballing the palace some more. Could she insinuate herself as a servant? Thing was, in a place like that, even the servants were scrutinized to hell and gone. No way they'd take on a foreigner who didn't have a single reference. Earning that reference would take weeks, if not months. Long enough that by the time she had it, and was able to worm her way inside, Mallon could have already launched a new campaign against Collen.

Or Narashtovik.

Scratch that, then. Coming at it from the other angle, she scrounged around until she found a neighborhood full of blond-haired, tan-faced Colleners. She grabbed a seat in a pub and left her ears open. The other patrons didn't talk much politics until she ordered a second beer in a very thick and very non-Mallish accent. After that, they did some jeering of the Mallish for losing the war, and some speculating as to whether the king would call for a final invasion, but it didn't feel any more substantial than typical drunken commoner gossip.

Night came. Her old friend. She made her way past an arena, then a neighborhood of temples and monasteries and apothecaries, then old and rundown housing, then a park of statues of ancient dead men she didn't give a shit about. Sorrowen was already waiting for her. Knowing him, he'd probably gotten there thirty minutes early, then spent the wait worrying that he'd gotten the time wrong.

She came up on him from behind. "Hey holy man."

He started, banging his skull on the elbow of a beckoning statue. He turned, rubbing his head. "Why would you do that?"

"Because I could. How's it going?"

"Good, I guess. They accepted me into the priesthood."

"Already?"

He shrugged. "Dante was right. As soon as I showed them I could use the ether, they gave me my vows."

"Now all you need to do is assassinate your high priest, take his place, and mount a violent investigation to find his killer, using the ensuing confusion to commandeer all the information you can grab about Collen."

"I'm not...but why would they even appoint me?" He frowned at her. "Have you gotten anything from the Ghosts?"

Raxa tilted back her head. The night smelled like trees. "There's been a snag. I'm working on it."

"A snag? Like what kind of snag?"

"Like they've resisted my efforts to be recruited."

"But why would they do that? I thought you were the best!"

"It's complicated. Could be they're about to pull a job and they're wary about being infiltrated."

"Could you be pushing too hard?" He picked at a loose thread on his plain gray robe. "Maybe you should act like when you like a girl and she isn't so sure about you."

"How is that?"

"You know. Like you don't really care, but if she was smart, she'd go for a walk with you."

Despite herself, she smiled. "Hear anything from His Holiness?"

"Dante? Nothing really. They're on their way to Alebolgia."

"Where are you keeping the device?"

"Device? What device?"

"I'm supposed to report what I find to you. Therefore, you have a way to get it to Galand. A magic bird. A flying bottle. An incredibly loud whistle that only he can hear. Whatever it is."

"Uh," Sorrowen said. "It was entrusted to me."

"And if something happens to you, and I don't know where it is, I won't have any way to get in contact with them."

"I can't, Raxa. This is my duty."

She grinned. "All right, altar boy. Then you better not get yourself killed."

They set another meet for five days later. She spent a few days chatting up Colleners, hanging around public parks where angry people shouted at each other about politics, and, at night, seeing whether she could sneak into the palace. Not with dead mice. She didn't trust them. With herself.

Problem was, once you got through the outer walls, which had been converted from fortifications into the poshest shops and tea houses, you were then faced with an inner maze of private residences that were very obviously not supposed to be approached by anyone lesser than the fringe of the noble classes. Most of these were recent structures built from wood. By shadowalking, she could probably find her way through their maze in time, but she'd only have a few minutes to get inside the palace, look around, and get back out again.

Still, when you were digging out of prison, the only way for it was a few inches at a time.

As she made her rounds, she spun herself yarns she could tell if somebody caught her snooping around the palace or anywhere else she shouldn't be. She avoided the Boxing Turtle. She also did her best to avoid the feeling she'd had long ago as a girl alone in a hostile city with no friends and nothing in her pocket.

After four days of letting the Ghost's pub cool down, she made her way back to the Culinary District. The evening felt cool, but it was humid enough she was sweating into her shirt. A lone figure leaned against the outside of the Boxing Turtle. It was the guy she'd spoken with on her first try, the handsome young man with the too-thin beard. He tipped back a flask. The motion tugged his sleeve tight, outlining a knife strapped to his upper arm.

Changing plans on the fly, Raxa stopped twelve feet away from him. "Hello. I return."

The man wiped his mouth with his sleeve. "You sure that's a good idea?"

"There was a mistake. I come to apologize."

"Some things, it's better to get gone and stay gone."

"I know who your people are. I know that I can help them to be more."

The man took another swig, then tucked away the flask with a smooth brushing motion. "You don't have to convince me. You have to convince Errik."

He jerked his head down the alley. Most of it was dark, but at the far end, a candle burned dimly from somewhere behind the building. Low laughter crept down the passage. Raxa bent her left wrist, reassured as it bumped into the hilt of the knife tucked up her sleeve. The pub's door squeaked open, disgorging a man and a woman. They glanced Raxa's way as she followed the man into the alley.

It stank like piss both stale and fresh. The young man glanced over his shoulder. "Got a name?"

"Xara," she said.

He smiled. "I'm Tommen."

They reached a T-intersection at the back of the alley. Tommen turned to the right, bringing her before a group of three men who had a shared interest in hostile looks and stupid mustaches.

"This is Xara." Tommen grinned at them, putting a hand in the small of her back to guide her forward. "She's the one who was around the other night, yeah? One who nicked Errik's bracelet."

The man with the pointiest mustache smirked. "Oh, he's going to be happy with what you brought him."

Tommen thrust his fingers into Raxa's hair, entangled them, and pulled her head backward. She gasped in pain. He shoved his forearm across her collarbones, searching for her throat, but she was already blinking into the nether. She reappeared outside his grasp and pounded her fist into his left eye.

The others called out in surprise. Raxa devoted a fraction of a second to the idea of weaving herself in and out of the nether and her blade in and out of their throats. If not for the couple that had witnessed her entering the alley, she might have done it. Instead, she whirled and ran.

She splashed through the alley, the three men close behind her, Tommen staggering along behind them and clutching his eye. They yelled insults after her, but there was nothing about witchcraft or sorcery. Too dark for them to have properly seen what had happened. Brains had convinced them she'd just slipped loose. As for Tommen, she'd hit his eye hard enough that he wouldn't be seeing much of anything for a while.

She dashed from the alley, slipping on a clot of wet leaves. A short-handled throwing knife swooshed past her and clinked over the cobbles. Heart on fire, she picked herself up and ran on. If they'd been in Narashtovik, she could have lost them in any number of crooked alleys and secret doors that existed for situations exactly like this, but in Bressel, she could barely find her way back to her inn.

Then again, she kept a hidden door on her at all times. All she had to do was swerve down a side street, pop into the shadows before they came around the corner, then wait for them to run past.

She headed for the street on the south side of the square where she'd originally entered from. As she neared the corner, one of the men chasing her whistled two quick notes. Two men arose from a stoop on the corner and jogged toward her.

Raxa swore and veered to her left. The men behind her gained ground, just steps behind her. She ran pell-mell for the eastern street entrance. A pair of blue-coated guards wandered from it, breaking off their argument to glance at the chase.

Raxa swore again. How much bad luck could she eat in one night? She scanned the plaza for another way out, ready to make a break for it, then laughed out loud. She was so used to running from the city watch that she'd almost forgotten what they were supposed to be for.

"Help me!" she yelled, exceedingly glad she was in a foreign city where no one she knew would see what she was doing. "They attack!"

The guards drew their swords and jogged forward, the buckles jingling on their leather armor. Trying to bring tears to her eyes, Raxa thought about dead puppies and vagabond children trudging through winter with blue feet. The pack of thieves scattered, jeering at the guardsmen.

The younger guard pointed with his sword. "I know your faces!"

The other, an older man with dark hair and a red beard, motioned Raxa toward him. "Are you hurt?"

"I think I am fine," Raxa said. "I walk past the pub, and they come out and they chase me!"

"Animals." He raised his voice at the fleeing men. "And if I see you again, I'll bleed you like a cow!"

"Thank you." Raxa hugged herself. "I think they want to... hurt me."

"It's over now, ma'am. Come on then. Where do you live?"

She was about to name her inn, but was stopped by the flushed, proud look on the guards' faces. They'd just saved the helpless young woman. At that moment, if she'd asked to ride them home like they were horses, they'd beseech her to wait while they found a saddle. She racked her brain for one of the cover stories she'd patched together while contemplating how to get into the palace.

"I have no home," she said. "Not here."

The man made an O of his mouth. "Don't tell me you're sleepin' on the streets. I don't even like to *walk* them!"

"I come from the north. There, I am of a noble family. But I fall into trouble. I need to speak to the King Charles."

The two watchmen exchanged a look. The younger man gave a slight shake of his head. The red-bearded man pursed his lips and reached for Raxa's arm. "Milday—"

She pulled back. "Please, sir! I cannot be touched. This is the way in my land."

"No harm meant, milady. Follow me and we'll get this all sorted out."

She fell instep beside them. The bearded man asked her a few questions about where she was from and what had happened to her. Raxa allowed him a few details, including a name of Lady Yera, then insisted she could only tell the remainder to a proper authority. The irritable younger guard was visibly relieved when they came to a three-story stone guardhouse.

The red-bearded man brought her upstairs to a sergeant's office. "We're going to go get this sorted out, Lady Yera. You just wait right here."

He gave a short bow and exited. Raxa bolted the door, then shadowalked through the wall and followed the guard downstairs.

"Don't tell me you believe her," the younger guard grumbled. "Did you see her clothes? If she's a princess of some kind, then I'm the Queen of the Horse-People."

The older guard ran his hand down his beard. "I don't know what the hell's going on. When you don't know what the hell's going on, you don't *do* something about it. You pass it off to somebody to take the blame."

He buttoned his jacket and hustled out the front door. Frowning, Raxa returned to her room and spent a good hour thinking things through. She meant to stay awake and alert—if they came to arrest her, wanted to be able to do something to stop that—but her legs were worn out and her mind was, too. She nodded off in her chair.

A knock on the door jolted her awake. "Lady Yera?" The bearded guard called through the door. "Someone's come for you. Best come downstairs."

The wan light of dawn crept through the shutters. Foggy-headed, Raxa moved to the door. "Who has come?"

The guard didn't answer. Raxa unbolted the door, ready to launch herself into the shadows, but the hallway was empty. She descended to the ground floor. Two men in gold-trimmed blue uniforms were arguing with the watchmen who'd taken her in. A third man bowed to Raxa and showed her outside. There, a black carriage waited in the street, the horses snorting gouts of steam into the crisp morning air.

The guard swung open the carriage door. A middle-aged woman leaned out and beckoned. "This way, Lady Yera. The palace awaits."

18

Vita's sword poked against Dante's doublet. Four burly men piled into the room behind her wearing the orange of House Osedo.

"You think I'm a liar?" Dante said. "A betrayer? Maybe so. But not against you."

She snarled, tensing her elbow to ram the blade home. Dante shifted ever so slightly so the sword would miss his heart.

"We had a deal," she said. "And you cast it aside like an empty bottle. Why shouldn't I do the same with your life?"

Blays wandered forward, swords on his hips. "If you have to ask that sort of thing, you're not really going to kill him. So why don't we skip past the part where you bluster about the thinness of the slices you're going to reduce us to and get to the part where you tell us what this is about?"

"I should tell you of your own schemes? How should I know why your hearts are so black?"

"We don't have any idea what's happening," Dante said. "You could at least have the courtesy of telling us what crime you're accusing us of."

Vita's teeth flashed in anger. "More lies. You lie always. You sprout lies like a body sprouts maggots."

"We've spent the last three months traveling to, cleaning up, and departing from Narashtovik. We haven't spoken to the Colleners since then."

"He's telling the truth," Blays said. "Whatever's happened, we're exactly as dumb as he looks."

Vita's eyes scanned back and forth across Dante's face, as if reading the secrets of each line and tensed muscle. She grunted in annoyance, then spat on her sword—Dante had no idea what the gesture meant—and sheathed it.

"It was the turning of the year," Vita said. "The day after Embersday, Speaker Itiego announced the new taxes. Those of wines for export were doubled. The city of Poloa understood at once: Itiego and the Cavanese were growing jealous of the Poloan industry. Perhaps even threatened.

"Poloa announced that it would not pay. When Cavana boasted that it wouldn't reduce the new taxes, Poloa renounced the confederation. Its neighbor Julina leaped from the ranks as well; Julina had never wanted to join in the first place. There was talk of Poloan ambassadors swaying Hunedo to their side and forming a confederation of their own. If this had happened, many believed it would lead to the collapse of the Confederated Cities of Alebolgia, and Cavana would find itself alone against a powerful new enemy."

"Cavana had a simple play to stop that," Dante said. "Shut Poloa out of the port. If it couldn't export its wines, its strength would collapse in no time."

Vita shook her head, dark eyes somber. "This could not be. For the same reason Speaker Itiego denied your offer: the river of trade must flow. If Itiego had tried to dam the waters, he would have been hung in a cage, and shown what happens when all pleasures stop flowing—especially food and drink."

"So Cavana has to keep trading with Poloa even if they're enemies? What sense does that make?"

"The sense of there being many merchants who continue to wish to profit with Poloa, and who are wise enough to see that if the merchants of Poloa can be forced from the stream, the same could be done to them."

"But what about when they go to war? In that case, they're funding the enemy's troops!"

Vita gave him a scornful look. "If a city declares a Full War on another, then trade can be dammed up without consequence.

But the risk and shame of losing trade is why so few cities will risk the Full War. We are not so foolish as you think, Dante. Our system might confuse you, yet it keeps us at peace." She made a small shrug. "Or close to it."

"Much as I love hearing you two debate local politics," Blays said, "weren't you going to tell us why you were going to stab Dante?"

"All of this *is* the why. After Poloa and Julina renounced their membership in the confederation, Cavana threatened them with the Full War. This made Poloa ring with so much laughter it is said they heard it all the way in Collen. Their laughter ceased when the envoys from Collen arrived—and told them that unless they surrendered, they would be destroyed."

"Don't tell me Poloa fell for that."

She turned a cold eye on Dante. "The Colleners said that if they did not acquiesce, Dante Galand, the avatar of Arawn himself, would slaughter Poloa as ruthlessly as he had twice done to the Mallish in Collen."

"I have good news for Poloa," Blays said. "He's not much of a god. I hear his weakness is being hit by things that are sharp."

"It's too late. Soldiers from Collen and Cavana occupy Poloa now. For the Colleners' aid in maintaining the Confederacy, Itiego has promised to close his port to the Mallish." Vita lowered her gaze. "I needed our deal. And your people, they threw it away like the guts of a fish."

Dante ran his hand down his face. "We aren't any happier about this than you are. We'll talk to the Colleners. We'll find a way to make this right."

"You swear to this?"

"I do. And the Colleners are about to hear some swearing of an entirely different kind."

Vita made a slight bow of her head and left, trailed by her guards.

Dante closed the door. "I'm going to wait a few minutes before we pay the Colleners a visit. Otherwise, I might be tempted to introduce them to the window of the nearest tower."

"Pretty cunning move they pulled," Blays said. "If you'd thought of it, you'd be slapping yourself on the back."

Dante muttered something impolite. Ten minutes later, feeling no better about anything, he concluded the only way to be rid of his anger was to vent it at the cause of it. He and Blays strode through the brisk seaside streets to House Itiego, stopping at the manor's gates. A wrought iron albatross looked down at them with a single blue sapphire eye.

As Dante considered the merits of ripping the gates down, a figure emerged from the compound, thigh-high boots clapping on the cobblestones, collar flapping around his shoulders like boneless wings.

"High Priest Galand!" Gareno called. "Or is it Divine Lord Galand, Avatar of the Celeset? You must pardon my vulgar ignorance, sir, for I have no experience treating with deities."

"Shut up," Dante said. "Where are the Colleners?"

"Why, they remain the welcome guests of Lord Itiego. I am sure they would be overjoyed to share their luncheon with you."

"I can't think of anything I'd like more."

Gareno smiled happily and opened the gates, leading them to the same vaulted hall where they'd first met with Itiego. The Keeper sat alone at the main table. At a side table, several other blond Colleners stopped their conversation to stare at Dante and Blays.

The Keeper regarded them with her washed-out blue eyes. As Dante approached, she braced her gnarled hands on her thighs, arms quivering.

"No need to stand," Dante said. "I know how your knees bother you."

"I heard you were on your way." Within the stone walls of the sparse chamber, her voice threatened to boom like surf. "Did you achieve what was needed in your home city?"

"Do you actually care in the slightest?"

"Why would you ask such a question?"

"Because you don't seem to have cared about fulfilling our deal with House Osedo."

The old woman's wrinkled face didn't so much as flinch. "You heard about our change in fortune."

"I *heard* you threatened an entire city with annihilation—using me as the weapon."

"Opportunity presented itself. If we had waited until you returned to discuss the matter with you, that opportunity would have evaporated."

"There was no need to seize it at all. We had another way to close off the port!"

"And there was another way to deal with Senator Alder of Kaline," she said. "Yet you chose the method that would guarantee your course forward."

"There was no guarantee Poloa wouldn't call your bluff! What then?"

"What does it matter? We did as was needed to obtain everything that we needed. Our work is finished."

He jabbed a finger at her chest. "What you've done has sacrificed my city's future relations with Poloa and damaged my reputation with everyone else. Worse yet, you used me. Again."

She chuckled dryly. "It is easy for you to criticize our decision. It wasn't your land that sat with its flank exposed. There was no guarantee your gambit here would succeed, or that it would have been honored by the other party."

"We knew exactly how to get it done. As for the other party, at this point, I trust them more than I do you."

"I did what was necessary to secure the safety of the people I am sworn to serve. I won't apologize for saving them."

"I know," Dante said. "And I know you're happy to sacrifice us for them. You may have gained your security. But you've lost a friend."

The Keeper blinked. "What will you do? Will you tell Poloa the truth?"

"I haven't decided yet."

"If you do, you will undo everything we've fought for. The lives of everyone Gladdic killed in Collen will have been lost in vain."

He clenched his teeth so hard the points of his jaw ached. Hating her for her callousness toward her allies. Hating the fact that yet again, she'd used him like a figurine on a Nulladoon board.

And hating that she was right.

"I won't threaten Collen's safety." He stood. "And I won't see you again."

"I spend a lot of time thinking about where I'll end up," Blays said to her. "I can't see the future any better than anyone else. But I hope I never become like you."

Already on his way out of the chamber, Dante didn't see if Blays' words had any impact on the old woman's heart: but they cracked something in his own.

"I spoke to the Keeper," Dante said, keeping one eye on Vita's sheathed sword. "There's no undoing what's been done. Collen's deal with Cavana will stand."

Vita swore and paced about the room, boots punishing the wooden floor, her wedge-shaped cap pulled low over her eyes. Dante had requested to meet her somewhere more appropriate, such as the Osedo estate, or one of the city's more refined public houses, but she'd gone with his messenger straight back to the inn.

She stopped abruptly, turning on him. "Then I will also do what can't be undone. I will kill her."

She made for the door. Blays seemed to float between it and her. "Stupid question: what will killing her solve?"

"My anger!"

"If you really want her dead, I'm sure time will take care of that soon enough. Old as she is, it might get to her before we've got our boots laced up."

"Yet there is satisfaction in doing work with one's own hands. Step aside."

"You don't have anything to be angry about," Dante said. "We still need your help."

She thumbed her cap up her brow. "How so? Collen has won Cavana's friendship. What more does the Basin want from us?"

"We're not working for the Basin any longer. Your House owns a number of sailing vessels, doesn't it? We need to book immediate passage."

"I thought this friend of yours owned a ship. The dark man."

"Captain Naran left this area at the same time we did to look for someone in Tanar Atain. Six weeks ago, he went missing in the port of Aris Osis. We need to find him."

Vita gave her head a sharp shake. "This cannot be done. If he went missing in Tanar Atain, there will be nothing for outsiders to find."

"That's for us to worry about. Take us there, and I'll honor our original deal to find out where House Itiego is getting its spices."

"An offer of garbage is only tempting to the swine. Do you think I am a swine?"

"If so, Arawn's not going to like hearing about the atonement I need to do. What's wrong with our deal?"

"It's proposed by you. And you are either a liar yourself, or too foolish to know when you consort with one. Either way, I will not trust my family's fortune to your care."

"You have nothing to lose," Dante said. "Whether or not we find our friend, as long as you help us try, I'll find the Itiegos' source of spices."

"You do not understand. He who makes deals with known fools gets spat on by the gods."

Weary of guarding the door, Blays plopped down in a chair. "Tanar Atain's only a few hundred miles from here, isn't it? Why don't we just grab some horses and ride there? We'll get there sooner than we'll finish this ridiculous argument."

Dante raised an eyebrow at Vita. "Last chance. Turn us down, and we'll ride out within the hour."

She batted at the air. "Bah! You would never make it through the Hell-Painted Hills."

"Hills? We've crossed mountains so tall that your head gets dizzy from being so close to the fixed stars."

"They were full of monsters, too," Blays said. "Beasts like a horse made out of armored bears and also it was immune to magic."

Vita glanced between them, eyes narrowed as she hunted for signs they were mocking her. "I don't care who you are or what else you have done. No one crosses the Hell-Painted Hills."

Dante shrugged. "We don't have a choice. We have to find our friend."

"To suggest this only proves you are the fools I fear you are. You can't do this."

"Sure we can. And when we get back, we'll tell you exactly

how we did it."

She bit her lip, her youthful face creasing with worry. "If I could trust your intentions, I would take your deal in the flicker of a fly's wings. But I cannot, or the gods will see how I defy their law, and I will be cursed—along with the family I'm sworn to serve."

Dante forced himself to maintain a neutral expression. It sounded like she could be convinced, but that it was going to require the kind of favor-doing and trust-building that would take days or even weeks to accomplish. It had already been so long since they'd heard Naran had first gone missing. The thought of spending even more time letting him dangle in the wind—or rot in prison, or writhe under a torturer's blade—made Dante's stomach twist on itself like a sponge.

"Do you know about the Chainbreakers' War?" Blays said.

The corner of Vita's mouth twitched. "Wars are like the fire that burns down the forest. An ugly thing, but opportunity for new things to grow. Including commerce. Those of us who live by its flow know wars like a navigator knows the tides."

"Wonderful. Then you know why we fought the war?"

"To free yourselves from the yoke of the Gaskan Empire. And justly so: the torrent of trade it unleashed from Narashtovik and Gallador proves it was favored by the heavens."

"Yeah, that became part of it," Blays said. "But mostly, it was because of a promise we made years earlier to a single norren who'd helped us on our way: that we would free his people. If we kept a promise *that* absurd, why do you think we'd shrug off the one we're making to you?"

She straightened, heels tocking together, then swept her cap from her head and slapped it against her thigh. "Damn me! We will go. Our voyage is not long. I can ready our ship by the morning."

"Our?" Dante said. "We?"

"If we have struck a deal for you to find the Tallas Route, then you are my investment. And I always look after my investments."

Dante thought the plan to be loaded up, crewed, and ready to sail in less than a day was an optimistic goal, but by the following morning, they assembled on the *Finder of Secrets*, a single-masted cog with a deck, an aftercastle, and oar slots. By ten that morning, they'd cast off, maneuvered from the Cavana harbor, and struck south, keeping within sight of the rugged coast.

Vita had a cabin, but she preferred to observe their progress from the vantage of the castle. Dante joined her there to ask how long the voyage would last.

She glanced at the sails, then at the blue-gray waves slopping against the hull, which seemed to be flowing to the northeast. "Fair wind, a less fair current. I say it is four days."

"Is it that close?"

"You don't even know the location of the place you travel to?"

"That would be the deciding reason I hired someone to take me there."

Vita laughed brightly. Traveling seemed to agree with her. Then again, perhaps it was the rekindling of her dreams of smashing House Itiego's stranglehold on the tallas trade. Whatever the cause, she'd spent the early morning stalking about the *Finder of Secrets* yelling garrulous orders to the crew, and now that they were underway, she watched over her ship like a general about to send his troops into righteous battle, a gleam in her eye and a wind-painted flush to her tan cheeks.

"Come," she said. "I have something to show you. Maybe it will make you feel less like you are sailing over the edge of the world."

She led him down from the aftercastle and into her cabin. This was cramped and sparse, as they tended to be, though a window let in light and air. She moved to a wooden dresser nailed down on one side of the cabin and opened a drawer, shuffling through documents and maps. With a note of satisfaction, she withdrew one of the maps and spread it on the top of the dresser, which doubled as a table.

"Here, we see the world outside that window." She motioned to the glimpse of cliffs beyond the cabin, then down to the vellum map. "This is Alebolgia. Here is Poloa, south of Collen—to its great misfortune. Here is Cavana on the coast, and the other cities of the Strip."

She moved her finger southeast across a swath of short,

jagged bumps just south of Alebolgia. "These are the hills you wished to die within. And on the other side, Tanar Atain. Here is Aris Osis." Vita tapped a tiny illustration of a city on the Tanarian coast. "Three hundred miles from Cavana. An easy trip."

Dante leaned further over the map. Tanar Atain took up a roughly triangular mass between the hills to its north and something called the "Ashlands" to the south. If the map was at all accurate, Tanarian territory stretched for roughly a hundred fifty minutes along the coast, and extended inland all the way to the mountains that formed the southern extension of the impossibly vast Woduns. Its territory was covered in light scratches of ink that might have been trees or waves.

"Aris Osis is the only city?"

"Not at all." Vita indicated the large triangle of territory. "All belongs to Tanar Atain."

"But there's nothing there."

"When you look at a map, and you look out at the land it shows, are they one and the same? This map was not drawn by Taim or Silidus. It was drawn by one who could only record what they had been able to see. There is much to Tanar Atain that isn't Aris Osis. As to who and what this muchness is? The only ones who know are the Tanarians."

"The interior is closed to outsiders? Are they afraid of foreigners?"

"A person with the correct business in Aris Osis may berth in Aris Osis. But that is as far as we may go. The Tanarians are much like cats. You know cats?"

"Cats?" Dante said. "I think I've heard of them."

"Cat are friendly, pleasant to be around. Yet if you overstep yourself with them?" She jumped toward him, hand outstretched, fingers bent like claws. "They *pounce* you."

"What about the authorities? Will they help us locate Naran?"

"If he stepped over a line, don't be surprised if it is the authorities who have disappeared him."

She returned to the aftercastle to question the navigator about the weather. Dante watched the distant cliffs pass by. He had always enjoyed traveling, and especially sailing; the experience of being out in the middle of the sea made it easier to grasp the true size of the world and your place within it.

At that moment, however, it was hard to be on a ship without being reminded of the *Sword of the South*. During his acquaintance with the ship, it had already lost one captain. There was a chance it had already lost another—and that the ship itself had been lost as well.

The day passed unremarkably. The morning saw slack winds, but Vita promised they'd pick up as the sun climbed, a prediction that proved true. With the sun hanging high and the sail swelled, Blays swore loudly from the port side of the cog.

Dante jogged toward him, following his stare out to the horizon. At the sight of the hills, Dante's foot seemed to forget how to stay stuck to the ground. The pitch of the ship finished what was left of his balance. He landed on the deck, scraping his palms.

Across the water, the hills glowed red and yellow, shaded with orange and white and blue, as if they were aflame for miles. But there was no smoke. No flicker of fire, either. Rather than being rounded, the hills looked like they'd been pinched into peaks, like the dough of giant bakers, as craggy and sharp as the pocked black rock they'd seen in the Plagued Islands.

"Ah," Vita said, approaching. "So you see why one cannot simply ride into Tanar Atain!"

"Let me guess," Blays said. "The Peaceful Sheepy Hills Where Nothing Untoward Has Ever Happened?"

Dante gripped the wooden railing. "What caused this?"

Vita moved beside him, leaning her forearms over the rail. "It is said that, long ago, these hills were wooded, bountiful with animals and fruit. It was here that the Yosein lived. The ancestors of the Tanarians, the Yosein were peaceful shepherds and scholars. For generations, they roamed the hills, marking the arrival of each season with an offering of sheep to their gods.

"One year, there was a famine. A sickness of the grass that bloated the sheep until they fell dead and made the fruit fall from the trees before it was ripe. Though each month the famine worsened, still the Yosein made their spring offering, and then again in summer. By autumn, they walked like skeletons dressed in skin: even so, they made their offering. Yet by winter, they were so dizzy from hunger that they feared making the sacrifice would kill them. They asked the priests if they could wait until spring. The priests said the gods agreed, so the Yosein made no offering.

"A fortnight later, the skies filled with strange light clouds. The Yosein thought it was a storm sent to cleanse the grass, but they soon saw they were wrong. The strange clouds were a plague of enormous locusts, a million and a million of them. As pale as grubs and as large as dogs, they ate not the crops—but instead, the flesh of every living thing they could find. Sheep, geese, and human alike. Where they went, they left bones behind. The Yosein tried to flee, but the locusts followed, wolves with wings.

"Seeing that they would be hunted until they fell from exhaustion, and would then be too weak to fight, back the Yosein sent their greatest sorcerers back to do battle with the plague-beasts. Knowing that to fail would mean the death of all their people, the sorcerers held nothing back, smashing the locusts with pillars of fire, one strike after another, laughing as they too were burned by the powers they channeled against the pale horrors.

"For each locust they killed, another seemed to take its place. After forty days of fighting, with their own losses mounting, they knew there was only one way to stop the plague. And so they scorched the hills. Melted and blasted their homeland until poison belched from the rifts and killed the fruit trees and the animals that had fed the Yosein for so long. Still the sorcerers brought down their power, until the earth buckled and moved like the ocean, and the air shimmered with fire, and the sorcerers burned to dust that blew out to the sea.

"But the poison the sorcerers had called from the earth killed the locusts, too. Their bodies fell from the sky like the rains of nightmares. They were the last living things to touch these hills. The surviving Yosein descended to the swamps to the east, where they mingled with the people there, and became the Tanarians. They are the ones who called the hills 'Hell-Painted.' No matter how many years pass, the hills remain as poisonous as the first day they were fouled. All who enter? Dead. Dead like a fish taken from the water and tossed on dry sand."

Vita had a troubled expression on her face, as if she were considering ordering the helmsman to take them further out to sea in case any unseen fumes were rolling down from the hills. Dante frowned. The hills looked otherworldly, yet he wondered about their origin, and if they were as hostile as they looked at a distance. Even the great sorcerers of the Rashen, forefathers of Narashtovik, hadn't been able to cause devastation like that, or they would have in order to protect themselves from the marauding Elsen.

Which wasn't to say the land *wasn't* toxic death for all who stepped within it. Rather, he suspected the story of how it came to be was no more than a story. Then again, weren't the hills worth studying either way? If the story *was* true, such an ability would make for a far more effective barrier against your foes than the one he'd erected in Collen. Sure, apparently the process would require the sacrifice of a few monks. But if it was the choice between that and being invaded and destroyed utterly, he was sure said monks would be dedicated enough to make the right decision.

Past the hills, the air started to warm, arriving at the cool side of neutral. Dante killed the remainder of the voyage asking Vita about the history of Alebolgia and House Osedo. She was well-versed in both, which as it turned out was quite impressive, considering that the alliances between the Strip's cities shifted faster than island weather, and that there seemed to have been a new war, uprising, trade dispute, or replacement of the ruling dynasty every two to four years. It made his own turbulent history in Narashtovik feel a little less absurd. And made him jealous that, aside from the occasional Scour of Arawnites or war on Collen, Mallon had enjoyed centuries of a peaceful, almost boring tranquility.

In return, Vita asked him a great deal of questions regarding the Chainbreakers' War and his talent with the nether. He wasn't sure if her interest was because she enjoyed his company, or if she was thinking about how to bolster her House with sorcerers of her own.

The painted cliffs and hills ended abruptly, replaced by the flattest land Dante had ever seen. Forests sprawled to the horizon, disappearing in the haze. Through gaps in the thickets, wintry sunlight glinted dully from slack expanses of water. Vita announced they'd arrive in Aris Osis within three hours. It had been four days since they'd made way from Cavana.

Blays strolled out beside him on the deck. "Given any thought to our cover story?"

"We obviously can't be ourselves, the mighty rulers of Narashtovik," Dante said. "If Naran has gotten in trouble with someone—be it local authorities, or an outlaw outfit like Raxa's—they'll be tempted to kill us, or hold us hostage. We'll pose as ambassadors. Then they'll be afraid that if they hurt us, they'll call down the wrath of Narashtovik."

"If we put Narashtovik on their brain, somebody might recognize us for who we really are. We ought to say we're Naran's creditors and we're looking to find out what happened to our money. If he's in trouble, and they think we're just as mad at him as they are, they'll be freer with the truth." He glanced at a fish as it leaped from the waves, followed by a much longer and vicious-looking fish. "Not to mention less prone to think we're there to do something stupid, like breaking him out of prison."

"That's a genuinely cunning idea. How did *you* come up with it?"

"Don't forget I spent years trying to bankrupt the Gaskan Empire. Lord Pendelles became quite the expert on business and investment. As a matter of fact, if we ever retire from gallivanting around saving some people while killing some other people, I'd give some thought to becoming Narashtovik's lord of finance."

"You? Lord of finance? You spend more money than a crew of sailors making port!"

"Who better to decide how we use the city's money than the person with the most experience spending it?"

The *Finder of Secrets* veered slowly toward the coast. The forest pressed to the edge of the water, the trees propped up on dense, finger-like roots. At once, the land pulled inward, revealing a placid bay. Across the water, towers thrust into the sky. Not just the occasional spires of churches or keeps, but scores of them, as thin as reeds, the tallest more than two hundred feet in height.

"What's that about?" Blays said. "Don't like to get their feet wet?"

"In Tanar Atain, there is always more water than land," Vita said. "They must make use of every piece of ground they have."

She ordered her crew to strike the sails and row the cog into the bay. A rocky jetty extended from both sides, protecting the interior. A tower rose from the end of each jetty. Vita guided them to a pier at the base of the tower on the right.

Three men waited at the end of the pier, two of them armed with long bows and a rack of arrows that resembled thin harpoons. The third man was unarmed. All three wore pine-green tunics trimmed with white and plain jerseys beneath them. The buttons of their tunics were made of bone and the collars and sleeves of their jerseys were laced with finely braided strings of obvious quality.

All three had a faint green tinge to their pale faces that might have been a trick of the light. They had long faces, eyes that were almost colorlessly gray, and short but pointed chins. The soldiers' faces and hands were tanned from being out on the water, but glimpses of their sleeved arms and collared necks showed skin that was paler than Alebolgians, Colleners, or the Mallish.

The unarmed man cast them a pair of ropes, which the cog's sailors tied to the ship's cleats. The man grinned in a way that wasn't particularly happy, but nor was it threatening.

"Of the north?" His Mallish was lightly accented.

"Alebolgia," Vita said, injecting serious pride into the word. "I have been here before. I am Vita of Osedo, and this is my ship, the *Finder of Secrets*."

From his light coat, the man produced something that looked like a cross between an abacus and a small harp. With deft fingers, he tied tiny knots into a few of the strings.

"The *Finder of Secrets*," he mused. "Does naming it that make it better at its duty?"

"Perhaps it does. It can't hurt to try, can it?"

"What if its name makes you falsely confident in its abilities? If you think it's that great at finding the secrets you're after, won't you be more willing to overlook any mistakes you make along the way, justifying to yourself that it's destined to get there anyway?"

"If I am slack-witted, perhaps it could." She tugged down the end of her triangular cap. "But it can also serve as a constant reminder of my duty, honing my vigilance and always bringing me closer to my goals."

"Hmm. If a proud name brings you closer to your goals, shouldn't you call it *The Ship of Greatness That Will Bear Its Captain to Massive Riches and Eternal Glory*?"

Vita's mouth fell open in horror. "In my land, we depend on ships like a nomad depends on his horse. If you don't give your mount a respectful name, how can you ever expect it to serve you well?"

The official nodded deeply. "I've heard other people say that they talk to their ship or their bow or to their raft. And I think, if it talks to you, then it must be a person. And if it's a person, then shouldn't you let it go? Or at least pay taxes for owning slaves?"

Vita tilted her head a few degrees to the right, cupping her hand to her ear. "If so, my ship tells me that it is happy to remain mine, and that it does so of its own free will. And also that it wishes to make port."

The official narrowed his eyes, as if ready to say more, then glanced down at his abacus-harp. "Of course. Of what part are you?"

"I belong to the legs."

"What do you carry to Aris Osis?"

"Spice—and iron."

Eyebrows raised, the official added new knots to his record-keeping instrument. "Then you will be very popular. May I see it?"

She gestured to the deck. "Naturally."

He came aboard, accompanied by one of the soldiers. Vita showed him to the hold. Witnessing the ingots of iron there, he and the soldier returned up the stairs and crossed back to the pier.

There, the official handed Vita a yellowed bone the size of a knife handle. It was inscribed with a few glyphs Dante had never seen before.

"You are permitted entry for one week," the official said. "You are not permitted to travel inland from Aris Osis. Violating this dictate will result in your immediate imprisonment. If you need more time in the city, speak to the Bureau of Interlopers. When you are ready to depart from the city, please notify the same bureau."

"Naturally." She motioned to her sailors, who untied the pier's ropes from the ship's cleats.

"And if you'd like to tell me more about your talks with your boat," the official said, "then I will be right here."

Vita smiled in a way that promised she would do no such thing. The oarsmen pushed away from the pier and stroked toward the city's many docks, stirring brackish water and the scent of waste and rotten things. Greasy purple seaweed floated just below the surface.

"That," Blays said, "was one of the weirdest customs interviews I've ever heard."

Vita grunted. "Most of his questions had nothing to do with his duty. The Tanarians, they talk. And talk. And *talk*. At least when we Alebolgians get long in the tongue, it's due to wine. The Tanarians, they argue as if it were a sport."

A few other oceangoing boat were docked at the piers, yet the vast majority of the ships there were rafts, barges, and double-hulled canoes, with or without sails. Dante homed in on everything with a tall mast, checking for the *Sword of the South*, but didn't see the sleek vessel anywhere. The air smelled of raw fish and beached seaweed. Porters and stevedores unloaded cargo and lugged it into the city of towers. Most were human, but a few were neeling, small and gangly, their faces round and amphibian.

The *Finder of Secrets* eased in to an empty pier and tied up. Debarking, Vita showed the etched bone to another pair of green-clad watchmen, who gave the northerners a lingering stare before gesturing them down the pier. Vita strode forward, weaving through the schools of dockworkers with a shark-like momentum.

She drew a lot of looks. This in itself wasn't remarkable—she was one of few women on the docks, and was certainly the prettiest—but Dante, Blays, and Vita's guards and attendants were drawing nearly as much attention. Their gazes weren't overtly hostile, but they didn't appear particularly friendly, either.

Vita reached dry land and came to a stop in the shadow of a high warehouse. Dante took another gander at the docked ships, hoping against hope they'd find the *Sword of the South*, and Naran aboard it, with a sheepish story about how he'd dropped his loon overboard.

Instead, Dante saw nothing. He was abruptly aware that he was standing in an alien city in search of a man who they hadn't heard from in weeks. A man who had come here with the express purpose of hunting down Gladdic—quite possibly the most dangerous sorcerer Dante had ever encountered—and who owned a ship that could have sailed hundreds of miles away in the interim. The idea that they'd be able to find Naran suddenly felt horrifically naive. He was buffered by the squalling urge to climb back aboard the *Finder of Secrets*, sail to Cavana, and ride straight back to Narashtovik, never to see the Collen Basin, Alebolgia, or this place again.

"What's the plan, then?" Blays said. "Wait for Naran to fall out of the sky? Or stand here until someone takes a look at us gawking like idiots and decides that helping us is a good use of their time?"

Dante grinned, doubts dissolving like sugar in Galladese tea. "Let's get to work. You coming, Vita?"

She settled her cap over her dark hair. "I wish you luck. But I have business of my own."

She hiked off into the streets, which were paved with black mud bricks. In the strange city, Dante barely knew which direction was north, let alone where anything was, but he had the names of three people Naran had been in contact with: Oto LoMota, Undan Walan, and Iko DaNasan. Since they were merchants, there would be nothing strange about a well-dressed foreigner asking where to find them.

Dante was afraid they'd have to hire an interpreter, but as it turned out, most of the locals spoke Mallish, and those younger than thirty bore only the faintest hints of an accent, as if they'd grown up speaking it. According to the people they questioned,

LoMota was off in the capital, but Walan and DaNasan were right there on the wharfs.

Dante tipped both people who'd given him directions to the merchants' offices. Both times, the young men looked down at the silver coin in their palms with an expression of mingled excitement and anxiety, then hurriedly pocketed the money, as if it were contraband the town watch would take away from them.

Iko DaNasan's warehouse was the closer of the two. Dante and Blays headed down the street, soon coming to an arched brick bridge over a sluggish sprawl of brownish water. The bridge offered a vantage of several other waterways and bridges, revealing that the city was a mass of small islands. The shores were dotted with rafts, many of them sporting a slant-roofed shack.

At DaNasan's warehouse, stevedores lugged casks and crates through the tall double doors. Watching the men and women sweat with labor, Dante realized he hadn't yet seen a single horse, mule, or ox. No dung in the streets, either. Not of animal origin, anyway.

Blays found someone who looked cleaner than the rest and inquired about Mr. DaNasan. After a brief delay, they were brought to the back of the warehouse and onto a roofed wooden deck extending over the water. If it had been a warm day, the open walls and water flowing underneath would have kept it pleasantly cool.

A man rose from a brightly colored rug in the center of the deck. While most of the Tanarians wore a sleeveless sort of tunic that was cinched at the waist, covering their torsos before stopping halfway down the thigh, DaNasan was dressed in a pale orange robe that hung to his shins. A pattern of blue dots was tattooed on his forehead.

He gave them each a glance. "Mallish?"

"That's right," Blays said. "My name—"

"Do you think it's wise for a land to accept foreigners into it?"

"Foreigners into..? I'm not sure I take your meaning."

"It's an exceedingly simple question. Is a land made better by accepting outsiders into it? Or worse?"

"Well." Blays' cheery air deflated visibly. Hardly a moment

had passed before he lifted his chin and brightened his voice. "You'd have to think it's for the better, wouldn't you? After all, foreigners often bring goods and news that aren't available in your own land."

"That doesn't make their presence necessary. If we wanted those goods and news, we could travel to *their* land to acquire whatever we lacked. Furthermore, when it comes to goods, if they're not vital, then they're by definition not necessary. And if they are vital, and we allow ourself to depend on outsiders for them, that leaves us vulnerable to the whims of people who care nothing for us. Wouldn't it be much better to learn to create these goods for ourselves?"

"Difficult to argue with that one, isn't it? But if you're right, I can only hope the king doesn't hear about it until after we two foreigners have done our business here."

DaNasan tightened his mouth as if disappointed—or even insulted. "What *is* your business?"

Blays smiled and bowed his head. "My name is Pendelles, and this is my associate, Orson Smallhorn. Are you acquainted with a sea captain by name of Naran?"

DaNasan regarded them with sleepy eyes. "Why?"

"It's a simple question, sir."

"Mine's simpler."

"We represent his creditors. Captain Naran, you see, had only recently taken command of his ship following a period of…difficulties. To get his vessel back on its feet, so to speak, an infusion of capital was required. Unfortunately, while he was in the process of discharging his debts here in Aris Osis, we lost contact with him."

"Lost contact." DaNasan withdrew a pouch from a thong around his neck, withdrew a pinch of a reddish paste, and tucked it between his molars. "Sounds like you blew good money on a shit captain."

Dante cocked an eyebrow. "If so, that would imply we're idiots, wouldn't it?"

"Most likely, yes. But maybe you got lucky, and only invested in a bad choice because you were working on bad information. Either way, if he's run into trouble, shouldn't you be happy to hear he's gotten what he deserves?"

"*You* seem awfully happy to hear that Captain Naran might be in danger." Dante grabbed the collar of the man's robe and yanked him close. "Here is a piece of imagination you should treat as extremely trustworthy: if you don't tell me what's happened to him, I'll make sure that no one ever knows what I've done to *you*."

DaNasan took on a quizzical look, then sputtered with laughter. "Forgive me, good sirs! I forget that you're new to these swamps, and I've spent far too much time here."

"The air here makes you drunk?" Blays tilted back his head. "We'll make a fortune!"

"It isn't the air of the swamps, sirs. It's the air of the people. Are you not familiar with dana kide?"

"Afraid not. Is she your queen?"

"Dana kide isn't a person. It's a concept. The Tanarians consider it distasteful to educate barbarians about their ways, but I'm also from a foreign land, and will take pity on you. Let's say that we had met in my land, or yours. There, a polite greeting from me might be along the lines of 'Goodness, this rain sure is miserable.' You, being a polite chap, would agree out of hand — 'Sure is, my friend!'"

Blays glanced at a gaggle of Tanarians arguing on a nearby island. "That wouldn't be polite here?"

DaNaran shook his head, his thick chin threatening to wobble. "Hell, it'd be an insult! Here, a friendly reply to a complaint of rain would be, 'Yes, but it's good for the crops, isn't it?' Or 'Isn't it better to suffer a little rain if it keeps the mosquitos away?' And that is the idea of dana kide."

"Er." Blays ran his hand through his hair. "Why?"

"Oh, religious thing. Means something like 'heaven's voice.' The people here believe the truth is valuable *because* it's so hard to find. We can all see if it's raining, but if I claim that's a bad thing, there's no reason to take my word for it. Someone saying a thing certainly doesn't make it true. Could be they're lying. Or it could be they're a fucking idiot!"

Dante grunted. "I think that concept extends far beyond Tanar Atain."

"Difference is, here, they think it's your spiritual duty to argue with anyone who makes a claim of judgment. Doing that is the only way we can reach the truths hidden away by the gods. See then, you might be spitting away at a fellow, but if the two of you are bringing yourselves closer to the truth, what nicer thing could you do for a person?"

"This sounds like it has the potential to be extremely confusing. What if the two of you just hate each other?"

DaNaran made a dismissive gesture. "Then agree with every word he says. Will make him look like a total prick. And take care not to insult him, either. Some people take dana kide even further, believing a divine voice may speak through us at any moment, so it is our duty to speak every thought as we have it, and without fear."

Blays laughed. "They *want* you to speak whatever insults and cruelties flit between your ears? Did Aris Osis dredge all these canals to make it easier to get rid of all the murdered bodies?"

The merchant chuckled, rubbing his hands together. "Maybe they're so used to getting gored they no longer feel it. Whatever the cause, they have the skin of elephants. If you're going to do business with them, you'll have to grow the same." At this, he gave Dante an accusatory stare.

"I'm sorry for putting a hand on you," Dante said. "We're highly concerned about the fate of our business associate. Anything you can tell us about your dealings together could make all the difference." Though they were alone on the platform, he leaned closer, dropping his voice. "It could even save his life."

"You're sure he *wants* to be found?"

"Why wouldn't he?"

"You said you're his creditors. Say he takes a long look at his ledgers and decides he can't pay off what he's owed. He embarks on a trip to Tanar Atain. Oh, there's great money to be found there, he tells you. And then when he lands in Aris Osis, he just…" DaNasan pinched his fingers together, then spread them wide, blowing on them. "Disappears. Along with his debt."

"Ah," Blays said, still putting on the lackadaisical airs of a blue-blooded man of leisure. "If you know Mr. Naran, then you know he'd never welch on a debt, no matter how much he owed us. He's so stupid he'd rather keep his honor intact than the fingers and toes his creditors would take from him."

DaNasan looked ready to argue, then seemed to decide it wasn't the time. "Near two months back, Naran came to port with a cargo that only a drooling idiot wouldn't want to buy: Alebolgian wine, and even better—casks of iron nails."

"Nails? Like the little jabby bits? The ones you whack into things with the poundy stuff?"

"There aren't many iron mines out here in the swamps. To bind things together, Tanar Atain makes the finest ropes, twines, and threads you'll ever need. But sometimes, what you *really* need is a good nail."

"Were you two able to reach a deal?"

"Ha! Half the rats on the wharf were sniffing around his cargo hold. I made my offer, and when it wasn't good enough, I made another. I was still waiting on his decision when he went missing."

"Missing?" Dante said. "Where?"

"If I knew that, he wouldn't be missing, would he?"

"Yeah, you dolt," Blays said. He smiled. "Sorry, just trying to do as the locals would."

Dante muttered something impolite. "Is it possible he accepted a deal with another merchant and left port as soon as it was concluded?"

"It's not impossible." DaNasan glanced from the deck toward the middle of the waterway, where two rafts had bumped into each other. Their crews were currently engaged in a fevered skirmish of words that was threatening to explode into all-out war. This drew a few glances from people on the shores of other islands, but nobody seemed too concerned. "I wouldn't call us fast friends, but Naran and I have had acquaintance with each other since he was a deckhand. I don't know that he can fill Captain Twill's boots, but you're right that he's a man of honor. If he'd made another deal, he would have told me before striking out."

"Unless someone else was hot on his heels," Blays said. "Any idea what happened to the *Sword of the South*? Could it have been seized by the authorities? Or by its own crew, who shamefully mutinied, leaving their captain behind?"

"Either possibility is a constant risk for any trading vessel. And if either one had happened, there will be a record of it at the Bureau of Interlopers."

Dante folded his arms. "'Interlopers'? Does the state really keep track of every foreigner in the city?"

"Indeed it does—and it seems as though you should be grateful for it."

"'Grateful' has rarely described my encounters with bureaucracy. Will we need an interpreter? Or does everyone here speak Mallish?"

"Most speak two or three languages," DaNasan said. "But only the most backwards, raft-humping swamp-leeches don't speak Mallish. Children are taught by dint of law."

DaNasan provided them directions to the bureau, housed in a tower a half mile inland. Dante and Blays trekked across a series of bridges and islands, forced to backtrack twice when a bridge was lacking in the direction they needed to go. Trees sprouted wherever they could, forming dense green rings around the edges of each island. Towers dropped cold shadows across the city. Some were black brick, but the taller ones were hewn from big blocks of a curiously mottled orange and green stone. When Dante got a closer look, he saw the green spots were patches of mold. This grew on the trunks of trees, too, making everything look as if it had been here for ages.

After crossing a few islands and stealing plenty of glances at the locals, he leaned close to Blays. "Am I crazy, or do they not allow their women out on the streets?"

Blays gave him a sidelong glance. "If you can't pull your nose out of your books long enough to experience the real world, at least get a few with better illustrations. There are women everywhere."

As they passed a group of people clustered around a vegetable stall, Dante heard one of the hagglers speak in a clear feminine voice. Like that, the scales fell from his eyes. It wasn't that there were no women on the streets, it was that they shared the immediate appearance of the men: they were dressed in the same sleeveless garments; the men were beardless; men and women alike wore their hair clipped short, or shaved on the sides and longer on the top. Combined with their unfamiliar faces, his mind hadn't noticed the difference.

They were a slim people, but now that he knew what to look for, the subtler differences in musculature and hips stood out to him. Their garments and sandals were decorated individually, too—feathers, buttons, intricate stitching with colored thread, the occasional flash of a small piece of metal. Likely, there was meaning in the items on display that he was utterly blind to.

An orange tower loomed on the next island. Most of the dollops of land sported two to four towers, but this one stood alone, and was squatter and more military in appearance, with a thin watchtower rising from its roof. The bureau was just as DaNasan had described.

They crossed a final bridge and approached the tower's front steps. Outside, a man stood on a wooden box, its planks held together with artful loops of twine. A crowd surrounded him as he gestured and barked.

"...the last time we so much as *saw* Drakebane Yoto?" The man on the box was red-faced with anger—or from the contents of the wineskin in his left hand. "If he cares for us so much, why hide in the capital? Or worse yet, the deep swamps? I say the Drakebane forsakes us! That he must be replaced by a Bane who loves all the land equally! *I* say—"

"I say you're as ugly as hot vomit," a woman called to him from the crowd. "You don't smell much better, either."

The man swung his sharp chin to face her, unbalancing himself. He windmilled his arms to stay on the box. "The truth is ugly, isn't it? And the *truth* is the Drakebane doesn't give a fish's testicles for the people of Aris Osis. He should be replaced by someone who loves every city, float, and raft. Who loves every inch of this land!"

"How do you have time to stand about criticizing the Drakebane when you're still searching for someone to love both inches of *you*?"

The crowd erupted into laughter. The man on the box went so red Dante expected him to start sweating blood, but then he laughed loudest of all, bending at the waist and clutching his stomach.

"The Drakebane needs to be cast down," a second man said. He was young, but his black hair was already beginning to withdraw from his temples. "But not because it's been too long since he was in Aris Osis. Instead, because of his lies. He tells the bondsmen and the rafters they can own land, but how many have you ever seen free themselves from the lords' fields? He tells us we can serve the body as whatever part we choose, but how can we learn new trades when the masters keep choosing students from the same families year after year?"

The man turned in a circle, arms raised high. "What freedoms do we really have? The freedom to yammer and blather and turn on each other? All that does is divide us while the Drakebane laughs in his throne! He must be brought to the noose for his crimes—and replaced by one who will finally unravel the ropes of injustice!"

A few in the crowd raised their fists and made noises of agreement, but others looked silently angry.

"Other people's politics," Blays said. "Is there anything more boring?"

Dante pulled himself away from the scene and walked up the steps. A pair of green-clad guards stood watch in front of the doors, watching the argument below with tolerant amusement. Dante didn't know what was funny about hearing citizens calling for the death of their ruler. In Narashtovik, you could be jailed for such a thing. And that was widely considered lenient. In Mallon, you were likely to be tortured until you recanted your words and turned over any friends, family, or acquaintances who might harbor similar beliefs.

Granted, Mallon took things too far. It was important to give your people space to decide for themselves what they would worship, think, and say. That gave them the opportunity to come up with new ideas, and to test them against each other like knights on a tourney ground. Dante believed a large part of Narashtovik's renaissance was due to the fact he'd allowed the citizens much more latitude than most rulers did.

Even so, there had to be limits to such things. What good did it do for your land if you allowed your people to call for it to be destroyed? Didn't that just foment anger and unrest for no reason? What if dangerous ideas were, in a sense, like the traces: when you kept them confined to your own head, they were merely an inert unit, of no harm to anyone.

Yet when you pooled your dark idea with people who shared it, feeding it and growing it, if it grew large enough, it would create a demon.

As Dante neared the tower doors, one of the guards moved to stop him. He stated his business as briefly as he could—never a good idea to overexplain; it made you sound desperate, and the wider you stretched your story, the more chance that holes would appear. The guard told them to wait, then went inside.

Below, nobody was listening to the drunk man on the box anymore, arguing instead with the younger man who'd called for the so-called Drakebane's death. In contrast to the loud but ultimately convivial debate the drunk man had been having, this new discussion soon grew so heated that the second guard was obliged to jog down the steps and intervene. The young man was angry enough at the interruption that he appeared in danger of assaulting the guard, but before Dante could see the outcome, the other soldier returned from inside to let them know that the Minister of Guests had agreed to see them.

He and Blays were brought into a high-ceilinged foyer and led up three flights of stairs to a round hall thirty feet across. Light sliced through the open windows, bringing with it the not unpleasant scent of mingled waters.

A slender man awaited them in the center of the room, smiling pleasantly. The official's garment was tailored to his trim body, and as he shook their hands, its expensive fabric rippled like the surface of a wind-blown lake. Metal baubles adorned its hems, but they were tastefully few in number. It was clear that anyone in the city would find him impeccably dressed, yet to Dante's eyes, accustomed to breeches and trousers, the sight of the official's bare thighs made him appear childish.

"Welcome to Aris Osis," the man said in perfect Mallish. "My name is Yata Jon. By your appearance, you are not from here. Do you think you should have the same rights for petitioning this government as the citizens of Tanar Atain?"

Dante shrugged. "Who says we expect the same rights they

have?"

"A foolish assumption on my part! Do you believe that you should have *any* right to petition a government that you're not beholden to?"

"Do you ask this question to every foreigner who comes to you?"

Yata's eyes twinkled. "I do! It is useful to remind them of their standing, and me of mine. However, while your question is insightful, it's also irrelevant. Now would you be so kind as to answer mine?"

"As long as I'm here, am I beholden to your laws?"

"Naturally. If you were exempt from our laws, wouldn't that grant you more rights than our own citizens?"

"I didn't want to make any assumptions. I bet I'm held to the laws I don't even know about. Right?"

Yata looked him up and down. "There might be some judgment exercised depending on the nature of your offense. But yes, the strangeness of your own customs is no defense against violating our own."

"If I'm beholden to the punishment of your laws—including the ones I don't even know about—I should also have access to the protection of your laws. Including the ability to petition you, like I'm doing now, and ensure that I *am* acting within the law."

The official raised his eyes to the ceiling, smiling up at it. "You have been favored with a most convincing argument. How can I be of service?"

Blays introduced them as Pendelles and Orson, then jerked a thumb at the windows. "Are you aware you have a pack of seditionists outside? They seem unusually fond of regicide."

Yata laughed lightly. "Would that be Sober Rogi? I thought I heard him slurring."

"The fellow who seems to have lost his hand in a war and replaced it with a wineskin? It started with him, but he was soon replaced by an earnest young sort who seemed very concerned that young people aren't being granted free land and lofty guildships."

"Ah, a representative of the Righteous Monsoon. They insist with all their soul that there is a great hand crushing them down, yet when you ask them to show you the hand, they point at empty air—and insist that if you can't see it, then you must be a part of it."

"Are they any real danger? Or do they just like hearing themselves make big threats to big people?"

"I think they understand nothing of why our country is as it is, but have decided that the only explanation for its flaws is that it is run by evil men."

"When in reality you're probably just stupid."

Yata blinked. "You present me with a conundrum. Are you an outlander who thinks his insults are disrespectful? Or are they a sign of respect to our ways?"

Blays smiled. "Might as well get away with it when I can."

"It's one thing to let your people grumble about taxes," Dante said. "But it's beyond the pale to let them advocate for treason. What good does that do?"

Yata laced his fingers together. "We believe that the gods might speak through one of us at any moment. If there's truth in the words, they'll rise up from even the darkest waters. And if they're rotten, they'll sink into the silt." He lifted an eyebrow. "Does the loudness of our streets frighten you? If that's what brings you to my office, I can assure you it is all thunder and no lightning."

"We're here to find an associate of ours who appears to have gone missing. A fellow foreigner named Naran. Do you know of him?"

"Of course. It's my duty to know of every guest in our city."

"We were intending to meet him here. Do you know where he went?"

"Why, he was arrested."

"Arrested?" Dante blurted. "For what?"

Yata lifted his eyes in thought. "Crimes against the state? Yes, that was it. Crimes against the state."

"We need to speak to his jailers. Immediately."

The official got a good laugh from this, then grew thoughtful. "Sometimes, ignorance is sad; others, it's funny. Why is that?"

"If you can't take this seriously, the only thing that's going to be sad is your family, regarding your gruesome demise."

"Your threats are unlikely to elevate us to any special truths, sir," Yata said plainly. "Captain Naran was taken to the capital. Foreigners such as yourself can't leave Aris Osis. Foreigners can't speak to those outside Aris Osis. You have no recourse. The sooner you accept this, the happier you will be."

19

The civil servant's words hung in the air like the stink of an uncovered pot of week-old stew.

"I don't understand." Dante's head was buzzing. "He's being held in the capital, but we can't go there? Why not?"

"Because it isn't allowed," Yata said.

"I've gathered that much. What I'm having trouble with is the idea that any trouble could be caused by two men of commerce who are simply trying to find out what happened to one of their debtors."

"As I informed you, he was arrested. As for why you can't leave Aris Osis, we have decided that we have no need for outsiders in the interior of our country."

"Your people can call for the death of your ruler, but we can't travel to inquire peacefully about one of our partners?"

Yata nodded, earnest as a priest at his sermon. "Yes, because our people are our people, and you are a dirty foreigner."

Dante could feel his pulse hammering in his face. They were still standing across from each other—the Tanarians didn't seem to think much of chairs—and dressed in his tunic without any hose or leggings, Yata's pale thighs made Dante feel as if they were holding an official conversation with a man in his underwear. The absurdity of it versus the seriousness of their conversation made him want to start melting the walls.

"We're all reasonable people here." Blays folded his hands behind his back and paced leisurely around the room. "Or at any rate, you and I are, Yata; my friend Orson's sense of justice is so sensitive he's been known to pick fights with inanimate objects. Now, you said we can't go to the capital, or speak to people outside this city. But what if we hired an intermediary to take a message to the capital for us?"

"That can't be done," Yata said without hesitation. "The law forbids it."

"What if, in addition to sending a messenger, we also made a donation to your office? One that would surely outweigh any troubles caused by a temporary and one-time breach of convention?"

"You're trying to bribe me?"

"I wouldn't dream of it! This would merely be a way to help you cover the costs of running your institution. You could even use it to hire more guards, or keep closer watch on those sleazy foreigners. Why, such a deal would make your country safer."

"I stand corrected: you're trying to bribe me and proposing that we lie to the world that it is in fact a bribe. Sir, you have the moral character of a rutting cat. You show the very reason why foreigners are forbidden from the interior."

"It was just a suggestion."

"This can't be the first time something like this has happened," Dante said. "We must have some recourse."

"Yes," Yata agreed. "You can wait."

"Until?"

"Either he is released, or you stop caring about him."

Dante bit back a curse until he realized that, according to local tradition, he was being unholy. "You stupid pantless son of a bitch. It's vital that we speak to an authority and clear up what's surely been a misunderstanding. Otherwise, there will be grave repercussions for future trade between Mallon and Tanar Atain."

"No one here has the authority to countermand the law," Yata said mildly. "The capital of Dara Bode answers only to itself."

"Naran had a ship," Blays said. "The *Sword of the South*. Do you know what became of it?"

"It was informed that it should leave. It complied."

"Where was it headed?"

"That wasn't any of our business."

"We're not here to cause trouble." Blays planted himself in front of Yata. "Not for you, not for Naran, and certainly not for ourselves. If there's anything more that you can tell use, please contact us at the piers. We're with a vessel called the *Finder of Secrets*."

He all but dragged Dante out of the room. Yata watched them go. Once they were outside, Blays struck southwest in the general direction of the docks.

"Well, that's good news, isn't it?" Blays said.

"*Good news?* Which part? That Naran's locked in a cell in the capital? That we don't know why? Or that we can't talk to him or anyone about it?"

"At least we know he's alive."

Amazingly, this calmed Dante down. He crossed a bridge, gazing into the waters beneath them. "And we know what city he's in."

"I know that sound! That's the sound of someone who wants to get arrested."

"I doubt Naran was dumb enough to do anything genuinely illegal. I'm thinking he might have accomplished what he came here to do."

Blays tipped back his head. "You think he found Gladdic."

"Whether or not Gladdic's here, Naran's ship and crew were driven off. We're the only ones he has left. We have to free him."

"No arguments here. But let's be extra careful not to cause any more international incidents, shall we? Or if we have to cause them, can we at least blame them on the Mallish?"

Dante headed for the docks. In another port, it might have taken hours to locate the *Finder of Secrets*, but among the Tanarian sailing canoes and boxy longer-range vessels, Vita's well-kept cog stood out like the lone orange in a pile of apples. Dante found her overseeing the offloading of the ship's cargo.

"We've got a lead," he told her.

She glanced up from her work. "And you tell me this why? To brag?"

"The local government won't appreciate us looking into it. If something happens to prevent us from getting back here, I'll send my rat. It'll have a message tied to its neck."

"You have a trained rat? And you trust it to deliver a message to a place it has never been before?"

"It's exceptionally obedient."

"May I see it?"

"Uh," he said. "Maybe later. It's resting now."

She glanced across the city. "What are you getting into that might require the skills of an extraordinarily trained rat to bail you out?"

"Our friend's been arrested," Blays said. "We're going to un-arrest him."

"You don't sound very troubled about this task. Is it common for you to have to 'un-arrest' your friends?"

"Well yes. But it remains an open question as to whether that's because we have bad friends, or because the people who run prisons just can't stand to see exceptional people having a good time."

She smiled, running her finger along the brim of her cap. "If I didn't have a House to answer to, I would go with you. Stay out of trouble, yes? You still have a job to do for me."

Dante made a vague promise to be careful, then made his goodbyes and headed down the waterfront.

"Where are we going?" Blays said. "Please tell me it involves lunch."

"Back to see DaNasan. He seemed sympathetic to Naran. He might know how to get us in contact with the capital's magistrate."

As they made their way along the piers, he kept an eye out for anyone following them—Yata had claimed all foreigners were watched—but he was still having a difficult time telling Tanarians apart at a distance. As best as he could tell, there were no obvious spies.

DaNasan was out on business, requiring them to hang around for half an hour before he returned and invited them out back to his deck.

"So?" the robed man said. "Was the Bureau of Interlopers any help?"

"Naran's been arrested," Dante said. "He's being held in the capital of Dara Bode. Apparently, he committed crimes against the state."

Blays tapped the pommel of his sword. "In other words, the sort of thing you charge someone with when you don't like their face. I'm starting to think we need to pass a law banning laws."

"The bureau told us we're not allowed to leave Aris Osis. We can't even contact anyone in Dara Bode. We're going to need to—"

DaNasan held up his right hand palm-out. "Stop."

"You haven't even heard—"

"And I don't want to. It would only endanger me."

Dante gritted his teeth. "Do you want to know who's *actually* in danger? Naran! The one imprisoned in a forbidden city!"

DaNasan tucked his chin, glaring at Dante from beneath his eyebrows. In the gap in conversation, Dante heard an insult shouted from the shore of another island, reminding him that while they were removed from the eyes of the street, they weren't exactly in private.

"I owe you nothing." DaNasan's voice was quietly firm. "It would better me personally to hear you out, agree to help you, and then turn you into the bureau. My reward for such service would be substantial."

"But you won't," Blays said. "Because you're a good man with the heart of a modern-day Lyle."

"My gut isn't the only part of me that's soft." The merchant chuckled, then grew sober. "The truth is, I don't care for the bureau. Nor the government it's a part of. I find it needlessly controlling and opaque. Even so, I am no revolutionary. Just a man who enjoys grumbling. If you want someone who *will* help, speak to Undan Walan."

Dante scratched his jaw. "I know that name. Naran was in talks with her. I take it they're friends?"

"Safer to say your interests will align with hers. Now go. I wish you luck, but I don't want to see you again."

Dante shook the merchant's hand and left his property. The grounds of Undan Walan were located three islands further southeast along the sweep of the shore. Her docks bustled with double-hulled canoes and long, narrow rafts that didn't look remotely seaworthy.

Dante found a foreman and inquired after Undan Walan. He and Blays were directed to a gazebo next to the water. The finest netting Dante had ever seen enclosed the structure from the plentiful insects.

After they'd spent many minutes sitting around listening to stevedores insult each other, an older woman walked up to the gazebo and swept aside the netting. While DaNasan had been a foreigner—Parthian, maybe, though quite possibly from a land Dante had never heard of—Undan was a thin, pale Tanarian, her dark hair shot through with silver stripes. Her eyes had a particular smolder that Dante most associated with self-proclaimed prophets.

"Who are you?" She swiveled her head between the two of them. "You have the look of an iron fist hidden inside a velvet glove. Drakebane's men? But foreigners, so this can't be so. The personal swords of a foreign king, then. Mallon?"

"We don't represent King Charles," Blays said, happily falling into his routine of the casually decadent nobleman. "But we are representatives of another Mallish institution which, if I may be so bold, is hardly of lesser standing. We understand you're acquainted with one Captain Naran, recently of the *Sword of the South*?"

"The captain and I know of each other."

"We understand he's run afoul of some sort of trouble. Dreadful business—arrested and taken to the capital. Sure to be a simple misunderstanding. You see, we are in the service of his creditors, and would like to clear this up so that Mallon and Tanar Atain can get back to the business of making great heaps of money together."

"Creditors." She said the word as though it was the start of a magical incantation. "I have owed credit, and given credit, and in each case, I wonder: what do I *have*? What do I *owe*? In what sense does the debt exist? Can you point to it? Can you pick it up and put it in your purse, or lock it in a chest for safekeeping? No. Because it's no more real than a child's belief in fairies. Does that make you representatives of nothing?"

"If so, it's the most powerful nothing in the known world."

Blays brushed a speck from the front of his doublet. "Returning to the matter at hand, it turns out we have a problem."

"You can't go to Dara Bode," Undan stated. "Or speak to those who are there."

"Precisely. I understand this might be a delicate matter, but it was suggested that you might be of service in navigating this dilemma."

"You speak prettily. You powder your words and dress them in frills. These aren't the words the gods gave you. Speak plainly, or your words are as nothing as your credit."

Blays scrunched up one eye. "We need to get to Dara Bode. We'll pay you for it. And if we're snatched up along the way, we'll swallow our own tongues before we tell them who helped us."

Undan smiled toothily. "That feels better, doesn't it? Now tell me of Naran, so that I know you know him."

The two of them provided what Dante hoped was a credible amount of personal detail without veering too deeply and exposing that they were more than partners in trade. His fears evaporated when Undan began to negotiate a price. They arrived at a sum that didn't quite deplete everything Dante and Blays had brought with them.

Before they shook hands, Blays cocked his head. "As long as we're talking in truth-drenched god-words, I get the impression what we're proposing is highly illegal. So why are you willing to help us? Is it just the money?"

"If you get what you want," Undan said, "does it matter why I do what I do?"

"If you're doing this in service of a demonic master who's going to use our silver to fund his campaign to devour the world, then that might be relevant."

"When you choose to live among others, you choose to give up your freedoms. There is only one power that can regain those freedoms: the weight of money." The older woman flashed her teeth again. "Besides, the risk won't be mine. It will fall on my agent."

"Who's your agent?" Dante said.

"She will tell you her name for herself. She is young, and that makes her dumb. But that dumbness is good: if she was smart, she would never agree to this."

"How long will the trip take?"

"Four days, five. Depends on how clear the canallers have kept the water. You will meet your guide in two days at the Frog Vault. Arrive at dusk. She will have a boat, and carry a blue feather on the collar of her jabat."

"Jabat? Is that what you call your..." He gestured in a circle. "Tunics?"

Undan nodded. "I will send for your coin tomorrow night. If you miss your meet after that, your money is forfeit. We have never seen each other, and you don't know my name."

Dante shook her hand and left her pier. Dogged by paranoia, rather than heading right back to the *Keeper of Secrets*, he wandered inland from the docks, glancing behind them for pursuit. "She was a bit odd, wasn't she?"

"I think she's just the right amount of crazy: too skewed in the head to be trying to set us up, but not so insane that she'll forget to do everything we just agreed to."

"Do you suppose when you let people *speak* anything, it causes them to *think* anything? Resulting in the creation of more eccentrics?"

"I think you should test this idea in Narashtovik and find out."

Dante had no intention of doing any such thing, yet he hadn't spent more than a day in Tanar Atain and he was already beginning to question whether he might relax some of the strictures in Narashtovik. Particularly those around certain heresies. After all, his experience in the Plagued Islands had already proven that some of the church's beliefs were incomplete at best, and possibly flat-out wrong. It seemed less than saintly to punish people for holding different beliefs on other matters when he was no longer wholly convinced they were wrong.

And if there was a silver lining to all the running about he'd had to do in the last nine-odd months, it was that visiting new places had exposed him to certain imperfections in how he governed his realm. Despite the time he'd lost away from his people, when he returned, perhaps he could do a better job in ruling them.

Once he was convinced they weren't being followed, he quit meandering and returned to the *Finder of Secrets*. Vita stood on the deck swigging wine with her crew.

"We have a way to get to the capital," Dante told her. "But they'll evict you from town before we can get back from it. Can you get customs to extend the length of your visit?"

She tucked down the corners of her mouth. "They are strict. But I could return to Cavana, then bring more goods here, giving me a second stay. Do you know how long you will require?"

"Two weeks. When you come back, stay ready to shove off at a moment's notice. If things go the way they tend to, we'll be running all the way."

She offered them wine, toasting their journey. It tasted like crisp apples.

After a couple of cups, Blays motioned Dante over to the side of the boat. "Two weeks is enough to fetch Naran. But what if we find out Gladdic's somewhere out there, too?"

Dante let out a long breath. "We'll see what Naran thinks. The Collen Basin is safe. Gladdic's failed too much to have any sway left in Bressel. It might be better to get Naran out of here and walk away from the rest of it."

"Could leave Raxa and Sorrowen in Bressel until Gladdic comes home. She could get to him."

"Not too fond of him, are you?"

"On the scale of things I detest, he ranks somewhere between spider orgies and explosive hemorrhoids."

Dante frowned and drank more wine.

The following day was quiet. Two hours after nightfall, a man came around to collect Undan's payment. Dante handed over the money with the same oily pang he always felt when he wasn't dead certain he was spending wisely.

If it *wasn't* a scam, though, he was greatly relieved they'd finally run into a problem that could be solved through the direct application of cash rather than a convoluted scheme to depose or kill a rival, retrieve a lost artifact, or kick off a war. That was the result of how they'd presented themselves, wasn't it? If he'd swept into town as Dante Galand, High Priest of Narashtovik and nethermancer supreme, Undan no doubt would have asked him to resurrect her dead husband or overrun an enemy merchant with a horde of zombies.

But since he'd arrived as a simple financier, money was all they thought to ask from him. Barring life and death danger, he pledged not to reveal his powers to another soul until it came time to extract Naran.

The following afternoon, Dante and Blays made their way to the Frog Vault, a small island whose north end featured a particularly slack and shallow portion of water. The croak of the frogs drowned out the din of arguments and insults from the surrounding islands. Dante and Blays waited in the shadow of a yellow-trunked tree that was propped up on its roots, as if it was trying to escape the pungent waters.

The daylight in Aris Osis had a blurred, dull quality, and as the sun neared the horizon, blocked by towers and haze, it felt like the city was sinking below the surface of a vast, shaded pool. As the minutes went by, Dante grew concerned that DaNasan had decided to turn them in after all, or that Undan's love of silver had talked her into running off with their money and giving them nothing in return. After all, if she'd reneged on a conspiracy to commit a crime, what recourse would they have to get their money back?

Before his stomach could knot itself too tightly, a gentle paddle stirred the water. A canoe resolved in the gloom and glided smoothly toward shore, lodging in the mud there. Seated in the hull, a girl of about eighteen years regarded them with curious, unafraid eyes. Two blue feathers hung from the collar of her jabat. She was as slender as a child's first hunting bow, but her arms and shoulders had the look of pale cuts of wood being shaped into something that would last.

"You two don't look as dumb as I thought." She lobbed a packet at Dante. It bounced off his chest. Blays caught it before it could fall into the murky water. The girl jerked her chin at the packet. "One bulb each. Chew them good."

Blays fished out two purple-spotted plant bulbs, passing one to Dante.

Dante held it to his nose, smelling onions and capers. "What is it?"

"Eni rio. We'll need it to get out of here."

Blays crunched his down. Dante followed suit. The bulb tasted so strongly of onions—though a strange kind Dante had never encountered before—that it made his eyes water.

"What's it do?" Blays said. "Give you strength to paddle longer?"

"Nah," the girl said. "It kills you."

Dante stared at her, then spit messily, but he'd already swallowed almost all of it. He stuck his finger down his throat and gagged.

The girl rolled her eyes. "Idiot. If I meant it *kills*-kills you, would I tell you before you were dead? Eni rio makes you *act* dead. When the Watchers of the Water look you over, you'll be so dead-faced they'll pay me to haul you away." She slapped the side of the canoe. "Now get in. And if you tip us over, then you have to ride underneath."

Dante scowled at her. "Have you done this before?"

"If I said no, would you walk away?"

He grunted, waded into the water, and climbed over the side. It was an awkward maneuver and he probably would have spilled them if the girl hadn't planted her paddle in the muck for balance. Blays hopped in as lightly as a dragonfly alighting on a cattail.

She pushed off, spun them around, and paddled leisurely toward the northeast, making no more sound than the occasional drip of water. Low laughter drifted from islands and collections of rafts moored together; people lived on their boats, Dante realized. Likely, that was true of all the laborers who couldn't afford a scrap of land.

Once the fullness of the night had crouched down on the city, the girl paddled toward a stone bridge, veering toward its abutment. Crossing under its shadow was like sailing into another world: water echoed on all sides, smelling as musty as a cave. The girl pulled the canoe parallel to the abutment. There, a shelf of stone rose a few inches from the water.

"Get out," she said.

Blays tipped back his head at the arch above them. "Oh, are we in the capital already?"

"Change into these." She got a sack from under her bench and tossed them each a jabat. "Two dead outlanders smells like three-day-old fish. But two dead hari won't lift an eyebrow."

"Hari?"

She made a searching gesture. "Foreigners who stayed. Trash-people. No one cares if their bodies stop living."

Light spilled in from either side of the bridge, giving Dante enough visibility to undo various laces and clasps. And for the young woman to stare at them with utter shamelessness as they stripped down. To Dante's annoyance—which didn't make a ton of sense, considering he had no intention of romancing her—she seemed far more interested in Blays.

With an inner sigh, he adjusted the jabat on his shoulders and cinched its thin rope belt. As stupid as it looked, it did circulate the humid air rather well. He strapped on sandals and returned to the canoe.

Blays tied his belt in a stylish loop and jerked his chin at the girl. "Now that you've seen my ass, you could at least tell me your name."

She grinned. "Volo. Back aboard before the eni rio hits you."

Blays reembarked. They wadded up their old clothes and hid their swords beneath it. Volo resumed paddling, faster this time. Soon, though her arms didn't seem to be working any harder, they seemed to be going faster yet, the lanterns on the shores leaving long trails of light behind them. Dante's tongue felt huge in his mouth.

"I think," he said. "The bulbs."

"Lie down," she said without looking back. "If you fall in, you won't be able to swim."

He eased himself back, elbows shaking beneath him. Blays did the same; the canoe was built for multiple people, but they had to do some rearranging to reach a point where there weren't any feet in faces or elbows in ribs.

As soon as Dante quit moving, he felt as relaxed as the moment when you fell asleep. For a minute, it was immensely pleasant, like flying might be; the canoe skimmed through the water without so much as a single jolt. He wanted to laugh, but he didn't seem to know how.

The world got faster and faster. He tried to blink, but his eyelids wouldn't budge. Towers raced past them. The only thing that wasn't moving far too fast was the stars, so he fixed on them. His breaths grew further and further apart. So did the beats of his heart. Among his last clear thoughts was the realization that if someone was going to kill him, he would be utterly powerless to stop it.

Towers and bridges blurred past them. He felt as cool and still as a stone at the bottom of a lake. And then—were they stopped? A man's voice called out, half bored. They *were* stopped.

A light neared. A man stood above them on a stone walkway carrying a spear and a lantern, dressed in a green jabat. "Who's in the water?"

"Volo of the Maggots," the girl said. "Got a delivery."

"What've you got tonight?"

She shrugged. "Pair of dead hari."

The sentry leaned close, shining the lantern into Dante's face. "You didn't kill 'em, did you?"

They both laughed.

"Smelled bad *before* they died," Volo said. "Thinking I'll take them to the Garu Marsh."

"Why bother? D'you think they have souls?"

"Hari? They look like people. Must have souls of some kind. But they're probably bad ones."

The guard laughed again, the light of his lantern whirling. He crouched down for another look at Dante, crinkling his nose. "Why would the gods give them souls they knew were bad?"

Volo looked down at the "corpses" with mild disgust. "Maybe they're not so good at making souls. Some of them come out bad. Have to put 'em somewhere."

"But most of the world is *worse* than hari. That means the gods must be awful at their job!"

"And our leader says he's appointed by the gods. Makes you think."

The guard nodded sagely. Looking preoccupied, he leveled

his spear and poked Dante in the ribs. Pain ripped across his side. If he could have screamed, he would have.

The soldier scrunched his mouth and stood. "You're right about the smell. Get 'em out of here. Clear waters."

"Clear waters," she said back.

She paddled away from the wall and toward a high stone arch, letting herself coast to a stop. In Dante's peripheral vision, he saw a net being drawn away from the mouth of the arch, opening the way forward. Volo waved in the direction of a lantern and paddled through the gate.

All towers and structures disappeared, replaced by blank sky. Within a short period of time—Dante still couldn't gauge it any better than that—dark branches grasped together, crowding out the stars. Insects whirred so loudly it was as if they'd burrowed inside his skull.

The lights were long gone behind them. Things weren't speeding by so fast anymore, but even the stars seemed to be moving now, hovering below the trees, winking on and off. As Dante fought to understand how this could be so, one of the stars drifted over the canoe. Volo batted at it: it was a bug, carrying its own light, as if it had a torchstone embedded in its ass.

He might have fallen asleep for a while. When he came back to himself, his limbs and face were tingling. He found that he could blink. Beside him, Blays was twitching. Overhead, the branches weren't moving at all. The insects were still whirring. Out in the darkness, something splashed softly.

"Keep wiggling," Volo said.

"Will it help?" Dante slurred.

"It'll help stop you from being eaten by everything that wants a piece of you."

He wiggled harder. As his floppy limbs and wobbly joints began to cohere into something resembling a functional body, Volo chipped at a flint, spraying sparks onto a wooden cage. Something caught inside, lighting with a soft oily whoosh. Though the lantern was mostly made out of something that looked like wicker, only the parts that were supposed to burn were currently doing so. Volo hung it from a pole in the prow of the canoe.

They were floating in a clearing of sorts, a patch of open water surrounded by thick-trunked trees. Hundreds of wicker cages hung from the black boughs. Inside, white bones rested in untidy piles. Other bodies still carried flesh on them, the skin sloughing off, what lay beneath glistening darkly.

Blays sniffed. "Wish my nose had stayed paralyzed."

"What is this place?" Dante said. "A prison?"

Volo gawked at him. "You imprison your dead?"

"Of course not. We bury them. Don't you?"

"You *bury* them? In ground? That's disgusting!"

"Oh yes, much cleaner to hang them in gibbets to get eaten by bugs and drip juice on you when you pass under them."

"Ground is for growth, not death. Here, we elevate the dead above the waters so they don't have to be afraid anymore."

"Is that what you do?" Dante gestured at the cages, then in the direction he thought might possibly be Aris Osis. "Ferry the dead here?"

"That's right. I'm a Maggot."

"Hey now," Blays said. "You seem like a perfectly nice person."

"It's an honor to be a Maggot. I'm one of the only parts of the body that isn't of the body." Volo gave them a look up and down. "You two aren't merchants, are you? You're soldiers."

Dante kept his expression neutral. "What makes you think that?"

"You have swords. And you're doing something you're not supposed to. Something you could get killed for. Merchants don't put their lives in danger. They use money to get other people to do that for them."

"You're right. We're soldiers for the same people Captain Naran works for."

"Not like those common ones, though," Blays said. "We're the elite. Double-elite, really. The normal elite would have you believe otherwise, but that's because they're jealous."

"Like the Knights of Odo Sein?" She considered them. "Does that mean you're going to kill me?"

"Why would we kill you?"

"So I can't tell anyone who you are. Or maybe you only became soldiers because you like killing people, so you'd sword me just because you can."

Blays flexed his hands, working out the last of the sluggishness. "If we were the type to do that, would it be a great idea to plant that thought in our heads?"

"It doesn't matter. You've already thought of it." Volo narrowed her eyes. "And you wouldn't tell me what you're really doing here, either. Are you going to kill the Drakebane?"

"We barely know who he is," Dante said. "Why would we want to kill him?"

"Because he tells people they're free, and then he enslaves them."

"I have about as much interest in getting dragged into the affairs of Tanar Atain as I do in spending any more time hanging around beneath these thousand corpses. We have a job to do, Volo. Let's get to it."

She looked disappointed—Tanarians seemed to have endless patience for conversation—then got out a stoppered gourd. Using a piece of reed, she scooped out a portion of spicy-smelling red paste.

She shoved it under Dante's nose. "Eat this."

"What is it this time?"

"Keeps the bugs away. Unless you want the bugs to come."

"Why would I want to attract insects?"

"Don't ask me. You're the one who doesn't want to eat it."

He swallowed the paste. It was spicy enough to singe his tastebuds, but that didn't seem to be masking any unpleasant flavors. Or poisons.

"These are the rules of the water," Volo said. "Don't leave the boat. Don't make splashes. And don't eat any bugs."

"I don't think you need to worry about us eating any bugs," Dante said. "Ever."

"Then you've never been hungry." Volo picked up her oar and started paddling, leaving the cages of the dead behind them. "Watch for patrols. If they catch us, they'll arrest you for trespassing."

"How are we going to be able to move around the capital if we'll be arrested on sight?"

"Are your ears decorations? When you're in the capital, you

can go where you want. You'll look like just another hari."

Blays eyeballed a large blue frog croaking away from the banks of an island little bigger than their canoe. The frog's eyes were downcast, almost rueful. Seeing it, Dante felt a sudden and inexplicable sadness.

Blays tore himself away from the sight. "Why stop us from traveling around, anyway? What are your leaders afraid we're going to do? Accidentally spend money on your goods?"

Volo went quiet for three seconds. "I shouldn't say. It's a crime."

"We're already committing bundles of them, aren't we? What does one more matter?"

"They say it's for your safety. That the swamps are too dangerous."

"And is hiring guides considered unholy?"

"Yes," she said, deadly serious. "Because that would let you see how things really are here."

She fell into a moody silence. The swamps rang with the cries of birds, frogs, and insects. Sometimes Dante heard the whine of mosquitos, but none of them seemed to be landing on him. Either the red paste was doing its work, or the mosquitos didn't like foreigners any more than the people did.

His eyes darted to every furtive splash. The place was spooky, he'd give it that. Yet over the next hour of travel, he didn't see anything that looked especially dangerous. At least not to anyone who wasn't in the habit of sticking everything they saw into their mouths and swallowing it live. Once, he saw a large pair of cat's eyes gleaming from the branches of a tree, but it didn't look like they could be attached to an animal any larger than a badger. Whatever danger the king was worried about befalling foreigners out in the wild, his fears appeared overblown.

It was immediately clear, however, that if anything happened to Volo—or she decided to abandon them—he and Blays would be completely and utterly screwed.

The canopy was too dense to make out more than fleeting stars; he couldn't glimpse a single constellation to get his bearings by. When morning came, he could orient himself to the sun, but even then, he had no idea which direction Aris Osis was. The only thing they could do was paddle south or west until they struck the coast. Assuming they still had a boat. If they didn't... well, he supposed they could steal one from an innocent person, but he didn't want to go down that line of thought.

He had no idea how dedicated Volo was to keeping them alive. Probably, she saw this as a job, nothing more. Certainly nothing worth putting her safety at risk if they got into a mess. Quite suddenly, her continued well-being vaulted to the top of Dante's priorities.

A few minutes after he'd reached this conclusion, Volo directed the canoe to a wedge of turf barely keeping itself above the water. She ran them aground and hopped out.

"Time to kiss some dirt," she said. "Help me set up camp."

Dante looked around them. "We're stopping already? If you're tired, one of us can paddle."

"Just needed to put some distance between ourselves and the city. Not good to travel at night. The light attracts things."

"Like what? Bloodthirsty moths?"

"Want to find out?"

Frowning, he brought ashore bundles of cloth that turned out to be hammocks. Volo went to work stringing them up.

"Hammocks?" Blays said. "The ground isn't so sacred we can't sleep on it, is it? Otherwise, you're going to want to have a word with the worms currently befouling it."

Dante tied a rope around a branch, testing his knot. "I imagine there's less snakes this way."

"*Less* snakes? Meaning there are still some snakes?"

"I expect it's better to have a few snakes around than having to deal with a bunch of snake-eaters."

Dante tied the other end of the hammock and gave it a tug, wincing as the movement tore something in the spot where the guard had poked him with the spear. He'd thought about healing it with the nether, but Volo seemed fairly sharp-eyed. The last thing he wanted was for her to pick up on the fact that his wound was mysteriously healed.

Fortunately, it was only a small cut, but he was so used to healing any bruises and nicks he'd picked up over the course of the day that the small pain felt magnified and strange. Beyond that, he'd spent all of his adult life not particularly concerned about any wound short of a lethal blow. To be reminded of the vulnerability he'd once felt—one that nearly everyone else in the world lived with—was unsettling.

They ate a meal of dried fish and a bready fruit Volo found on the little island. As she chewed, she flicked a piece of rind into the water. Something broke hard against the surface, vanishing as quickly as it had struck.

"We won't be alone tomorrow," Volo said. "People of the teeth will be out fishing. Legs will be out delivering goods. And the eyes will be on patrol."

Dante fished a seed from between his teeth. "What do we do if we run into a patrol?"

"You can hide. Or we can poke out their eyes."

He stared at her, completely uncertain if she was serious, or just letting her mouth express every idea that crossed her mind. "For now, let's stick with hiding. There's going to be enough trouble as there is."

"Then what if that's a sign that we should cause more?"

"It isn't."

She gave him a reproachful look. "You say no too fast. When you kill all of your ideas while they're still infants, none can grow up to work your paddies—or defend your castle."

Dante crawled into his hammock. He was soon asleep. During the course of the night, he woke more times than he could count. It was more than the chorus of creatures. He felt uneasy, as if something were slowly drawing closer, and every time he nodded off, it took another step forward. Was it the green crush of the forest? He didn't think that was it. He'd been in intensely wooded areas before. The jungles of the Plagued Islands were so lush you couldn't traverse parts of them without following game trails or hacking your way forward a foot at a time.

It was more than the claustrophobia of a forest. It felt like the swamp was breathing. Like it was alive.

Volo rousted them at first light to pull down the hammocks before anyone could see them. They'd barely gotten the canoe underway when voices bleated out ahead. Two men were arguing heedlessly, voices ringing through the trees. Something about nets; fishermen, likely berating each other about whose turn it was to untangle the skein.

Before Dante and Blays could conceal themselves, a raft swung from behind a shaggy stand of trees. Two men pushed it forward with long poles, paying much more attention to their discussion than to where they were planting their staves.

"Can't be so," the older man said. "Ain't no way that Sadi Lono, the man who caught the wind with his bare hands, is sluggish enough to let himself get netted."

The younger man swatted at something. "But say it's Ura So doing the netting. She smiles at him, dazzles him with her ruby teeth, then catches him up."

"Right, and what happens when he snaps out of her spell? He goes at the net with the Knife That Can't Be Sheathed."

"Won't help. The weave is too tight."

The old man guffawed. "You're telling me the knife that cut a hole through the earth can't cut a net?"

"This is the net that dragged down the moon! There's no way —" Finally noticing Volo's canoe, the man broke off mid-sentence.

Volo paddled onward, skirting around a snag protruding from the water like the hand of a drowning man. As the raft sailed by, the two men stared at the foreigners. Dante did his best to look like an obedient servant.

"I say he's stuck fast," the younger man muttered, turning back to his partner. "As if she's going to just stand there while he fumbles about for the knife?"

Their voices faded into the forest. Volo made a thoughtful noise. "If the wrong person sees you, they might turn you in. Next time, you should probably try to hide."

Though it was still a couple of weeks until spring, the air was warm, intensified by the heavy dampness of the air. Ropes of vines and threads of moss hung from the trees. Another canoe emerged from behind a lumpy little island; again, it was too close for Dante and Blays to try to hide themselves in the bottom of their boat. The man inside the other canoe glided past, watching them from the corners of his eyes.

They'd barely started out and Dante was already doubting

they could reach Dara Bode without someone turning them in to the authorities. He considered killing one of the many, many flying bugs and sending it ahead of them to scout the way, but there wasn't a singular path forward, meaning he'd have to maintain a small fleet of flies to cover whichever way Volo took them. Anyway, if he *did* see a patrol coming their way, he couldn't alert Volo without exposing his abilities.

With no better option, he and Blays flattened themselves against the bottom of the canoe and covered themselves in hammocks. Water thumped gently against the hull. Dante felt jumpy and irritable. Blind. More than that: like he'd lost both his arms. He was so used to being able to call on his powers that being without them made even simple tasks feel abruptly overwhelming.

He dozed on and off. Early that afternoon, Volo guided the canoe out of the main waterway and found an outcrop of ground where they could stretch their legs and eat lunch.

"I don't suppose there's another way to the capital?" Blays said. "Preferably something that ends each day with an inn, a fire, and kegs of exotic beverages?"

"There are some towns along the way." Volo glanced at a fish leaping from the water. "But the problem with towns is they're full of people."

Too soon, they were back in the canoe. Dante took his time in lying down. Before, there had been any number of gaps in the growth, but here, the trees, brambles, and vines had grown into an interlocking wall. They were traveling more or less down a tunnel. One that looked as though it only existed due to constant maintenance.

He dozed off. Some time later, something jabbed him in the ribs. Before he could yell out about snakes or swamp rats, a hand clamped over his mouth.

"Trouble ahead," Blays said. "Dressed in green."

Dante peeked over the gunwale. They were stopped at one end of a hallway through the trees. At the far end, roughly five hundred feet away, a house-raft had been stopped by a double-hulled canoe bearing what appeared to be a roof. This would have been puzzling if not for the green paint on its hull and the piles of soldiers spilling from it onto the raft. It was a military vessel, and the roof was a shield against arrows.

Dante rubbed grit from the corner of his eye. "Can we go around?"

"No other routes. Growth's too thick." She curled her lip. "Just how they want it."

"No sense trying to hide. They're searching that boat."

"We could always act like we have nothing to hide," Blays said.

"And pray that they've chosen today to quit enforcing their laws? The ones they're clearly in the process of enforcing right now?"

"You never know when someone's going to make a mistake on your behalf." His tone went arch. "Besides, if they look at us cockeyed, we can always just kill them all."

For Volo's sake, Blays presented the idea as a joke, but Dante took his meaning clearly: they could, if necessary, brute-force their way through the situation. But that would mean revealing himself, not to mention massacring a score of soldiers, an event that was likely to be investigated by an even larger force of soldiers.

"We can't turn around now. It'll look like we're fleeing them." Dante gripped his temples. "When they're done with the raft, will they come over to inspect our boat? Or are they holding a static checkpoint?"

"Sharp eyes don't sit still," Volo said. "They'll come for us."

"Then Blays and I will swim over to the shrubs and hide there until they check the canoe. There will be nothing for them to find and they'll be on their way."

"But you don't get in the water. Not unless there's no other choice."

"Ah," Blays said. "There isn't."

At the far end of the tunnel, the soldiers had climbed off the raft and back into their war canoe. It was already paddling forward, heading toward their much smaller boat. Dante grabbed his sword from the bottom of the canoe and rolled over the gunwale.

He landed with a soft sploosh. The water was the same temperature as the air. He'd expected to be able to touch the bottom, but his feet kicked through empty water. He dropped below the surface. It was so murky he couldn't see anything except a vague sense of the light above him.

He swam hard toward the gnarl of trees hemming them in to the right, keeping one hand in front of him to ward off any submerged branches or rocks. His fingers caught in something slippery. He jerked back his hand, giving a short, bubbly shout.

He kicked on until he was out of breath, then broke the surface. The war canoe was shockingly close, as if it had teleported halfway across the tunnel through the trees. Praying none of the soldiers had spotted his head, he dropped back under the water. He passed under the deeper shadow of the wall of shrubs. Stray twigs and thorns dangled in the water, grabbing at his arms as he broke through them.

He emerged into an oval of relatively clear water surrounded by trees and undergrowth. Blays popped up next to him. Bits of leaves and flowers tumbled from the branches in a steady shower. Across from him, a giant fallen log rested in the water, its bark coated with green moss and orange mushrooms. Out in the waterway, the war canoe was backbeating its oars as it approached Volo, who now looked very alone and very small.

Dante was treading water; try as he might, he couldn't avoid making a few small splashes. With no dry ground in sight, he pushed toward the log. Most of its bulk was underwater, but at twenty feet long and close to four across, it could easily support both his weight and Blays'.

He grabbed a knob on the log's side, searching for a nub of branch to haul himself up with. Despite the time it had spent soaking in the water, the log's scaly bark was so hard it nearly cut his hands.

"What the..?" Blays whispered. "Stop!"

Dante glared at him. Blays was gesturing hard for him to back off. Baffled, Dante turned back to the log. A yellow circle had appeared near one of its ends, barely above the waterline. In its center, it was marked with a smaller black circle.

He was staring into a giant eye.

The beast jackknifed, lunging for him. He saw fangs, a gaping throat like a hole through the fabric of the earth. He grabbed for the nether, but the jaws were already snapping closed around his chest, pulling him under the surface of the water.

20

The black carriage rattled through the streets, its driver yelling and swearing at any pedestrian who dawdled in its path. Inside, Raxa settled into the velvet seats. The air was awash in rosy perfume.

"My apologies for the wait you had to endure." The woman across from her spoke Gaskan at a rapid clip. She sounded like one of the aristocrats from back home, but to Raxa's relief, she bore a light Mallish accent. "The guards who were assisting you were under the perverse impression that I value sleep more than the execution of justice. Needless to say, they're being flogged as we speak."

"Ah," Raxa said. "Thank you."

"My name is Maura of Boscayne. I am going to ask you some questions. And then I am going to help you."

The carriage's sashes were open, letting in plenty of light. Lady Maura was fifty years of age and her face was tan even by Bresselian standards, but as she gestured, Raxa caught glimpses of lighter skin around the collar of her dress. Spent a lot of time outdoors for a noble. She had thin, quick fingers. Deep laugh-lines entangled her mouth and eyes, although she looked and sounded like the sort who never belly-laughed, and settled instead for a constant state of low-level amusement.

Raxa had no idea who she was, but she could already tell that the lady would want something from her.

"You are from Gask," Maura said. "But Gask is so large its own weight caused it to collapse. Which fragment of the whole is yours?"

"Dollendun," Raxa said. "The Jorrelun family."

"Unfortunately, it has not been my pleasure to make their acquaintance. Most of my summers in the former empire have been spent at the lakes of Gallador. A picturesque place. Do you know it?"

"When I was younger. But not in years. Like you said, Gask is a big place."

"Large enough that one could tour it for decades without running out of new sights. Why, then, would one need to travel to Bressel?"

"It's not a pleasant story."

"Most true ones aren't. But in the sharing of them, we understand that we are all bent beneath the same burdens."

The carriage rocked through a pothole so deep Raxa's rear left contact with the bench. "My husband is the youngest of four brothers. With no fortune guaranteed to him, he had to make his own. The war that cracked Gask into fragments—as you put it—also opened the door to opportunity. You know about norren art?"

"Know it? In Bressel, I am its champion! I'm an avid collector of norren line paintings. My favorites originate from the Broken Heron Clan."

Raxa nodded as if she knew who that was. "I'm less than an expert myself. But my husband seized on the bossen trade. Started selling it across every corner of Gask. He did well. Well enough to get ambitious. Last year, he brought a caravan of norren goods to the Collen Basin."

Maura wrinkled her nose. "Why would an upstanding and well-blooded Gaskan want to do business with the Collen Basin? They care for nothing but spears and hoes."

"In Gask, competition is fierce. Others had already established markets in Mallon. My husband thought that if he was the first to open up the Collen Basin, he'd make all three of his brothers envious of his wealth."

"Spiting one's family is such wonderful motivation."

"When he first got to Collen, he sent me letters weekly. Three months ago, the letters stopped. I waited as long as I could. And then I came to find him."

"What? All by yourself?"

"I brought ten men-at-arms," Raxa said. "Along with two of my husband's men who knew the way to Collen. Bandits ambushed us in the woods north of Bressel. Killed everyone."

"Outrageous. *Outrageous*. Did they really think the woods' cover would hide them from the gods? How did you come to elude them?"

"When it was clear we couldn't win, one of my guards grabbed me. He tried to sell me to the bandits. I had to..." She looked down, biting her lip. "To stab him. I ran then. Hid in a stream while the bandits hunted for me, shouting what they'd do to me. It was so cold. I think I fell asleep for a while. When I came to, I went back to the site, but all my guards were dead. They'd taken everything but a few clothes." She gestured at herself, smiling wryly. "This was the best I could do."

"And then? You came to the city with nothing?"

"I didn't know what else I could do. Last night, I was trying to find someone to take me to Collen when I was robbed. If the town watch hadn't saved me, the thieves would have killed me in the street."

Maura regarded her for several seconds. Raxa had the idea it was the longest the woman had gone without talking in some time.

"Your story is dreadful," the woman said. "I consider it an affront to the reputation of the entire city. How can I help you reattain your footing?"

"I've heard the Collen Basin is at war with Mallon. Is it true?"

"Collen has rebelled. Again. This time has been more successful than past efforts, thanks in large part to the aid of a grotesque sorcerer who summons abominations to use as weapons."

"Collen broke free? Will Mallon go back to war?"

The woman made a flicking gesture. "The rebellion makes King Charles look weak. His pride might lead him to strike back, even as others in the palace wonder if we wouldn't be better off without the troublesome Basin."

Raxa gazed at the floor of the carriage. "I can't travel there to find my husband alone. I'll write home. And find a way to care for myself until my family sends my men-at-arms."

"Nonsense. There's no need for you to care for yourself. You'll be staying with me."

"But we've just met. Why would you help me?"

"Because I have a keen interest in all things Gaskan." Maura smiled, crinkling the corners of her eyes. "And because I am a person who enjoys ruffling feathers. I think your story will turn some heads at court."

Raxa smiled hesitantly, then gratefully. The carriage passed under the shadow of a wall: they had entered the palace grounds. All the secrets of the kingdom were no more than a short walk away.

Lady Maura, her husband, and their staff were housed on the third floor of one of the Fadrians, the wooden buildings ringing the palace. Their apartments were stuffed with fancy rugs, plush furniture, all the usual rich person junk. Raxa's room had beeswax candles and a feather mattress. As she sank into bed for a nap, enveloped by the cloud-soft bedding, Raxa wondered if once she was done spying on Mallon's plans for Collen, she could find a way to stay and spy on someone else as well.

When Raxa woke, Maura took her for a stroll around the mall between the palace and the Fadrians. The shade trees were starting to push out new leaves. Upwards of fifty people were out enjoying the temperate morning, all of them well-dressed, all of them useless. How much silver did it cost to dress them in linens, to feed them beef and quail eggs, to house them in their lordly quarters? Why didn't the peasants rise up and take back what these leeches had bled from them?

With that thought, she stiffened. She'd always considered herself to be fighting against these people. Now, she was working for their equivalent in Narashtovik. That was the way, wasn't it? Whatever you thought you were, the world corrupted you.

She set her jaw. The mall was only a small fraction of this gathering of parasites. The palace and the Fabians must be filled with hundreds of courtiers and nobles. Finding the few of them who knew what she needed would be rough.

The afternoon was spent fitting her for court-appropriate dresses. By the end of it, Raxa felt martyred. At twilight, the door flew open, admitting a man of fifty whose hair and beard were frosted with silver.

He seemed to close on Lady Maura with a single step, hugging her tight. "Nothing best terminates a woeful day like the embrace of one's wife." He noticed Raxa, his bushy eyebrows climbing. "Ah. We have company?"

"This is Lady Yera of Dollendun," Maura said. "She is currently suffering from a surfeit of bad luck. We are going to reverse that trend."

"We are?" He sized Raxa up, then smirked at his wife. "A northerner bearing a story of sorrow. Tell me, this wouldn't have anything to do with your dispute with Loris?"

Maura smiled thinly. "It is purely an act of altruism. If that act also has the consequence of thwarting Loris, I can only ascribe it to the gods showing their approval for my good deed."

Lord Boscayne winked at Raxa. "Well, Lady Yera, please see that my clever wife doesn't get herself into too much trouble."

Raxa smiled back at him. If they thought she was a pawn, she was happy to let them. Because Maura was a mark. And the key to working a mark was to find out what they want from you, then pretend to give it to them. As long as she could do that for Maura, she'd have the run of the palace.

They ate. It was opulent. Raxa tried not to enjoy it as much as it deserved. After, she declared she was tired and retired to her room.

She moved to the window and gazed across the dark mall, where young courting couples now wandered in the night, working up the nerve to kiss. Raxa could only slum around in the shadows for a few minutes per day. Unless she knew the exact time the king's ministers were slated to discuss their plans for Collen, and then showed up at the precise moment they quit the pleasantries and got down to policy, she had no real chance of hearing what they intended to do about the Basin.

She'd need to steal documents. She supposed she should start with the Lord and Lady Boscayne—try to figure out what they were up to, whether Raxa was getting herself into any trouble. She'd already made an assessment of the apartments. After napping, she crept out into the moonlight hallway and headed for the lord's study.

The door was locked. Interesting. Hadn't been earlier. She had it open in seconds. She moved to the writing desk. The surface was scattered with blotting sand. She picked up a page and held it to the moonlight.

And saw it was written entirely in Mallish. Which she couldn't read. Cursing herself, she set it down and returned to bed.

The entire morning was spent having her hair done and modeling for the finishing of her dress. Once it was done and on her, she was paraded in front of a mirror. The woman who stared back at her looked very elegant and nothing like her.

That afternoon, Maura took Raxa around to tell her story to a few friends. Raxa played her part. The other women looked suitably horrified. Raxa could tell Maura was sowing the seeds of gossip, but she still wasn't sure what the game was.

On their way back to their apartments, Raxa asked, "Is it possible I learn to write Mallish?"

Maura cocked her head. "We're going to be quite busy. Why would you wish to learn the writing of Mallish?"

"Because to not know it and to be in Mallon is to look like you are stupid."

The lady laughed warmly. "The fight against ignorance is our noblest war. I will secure you a tutor."

Meaning Raxa would soon have access to all the writing materials she needed, too. During dinner, she did her best to not sound too distracted. She was due to meet Sorrowen that night. After days of trying to figure out a way to break into the palace, she now found herself trying to break out of it.

As midnight neared, she changed into her old clothes, bolted her door, opened the window, and slipped into the shadows. She dropped down to the balcony on the second floor, grabbed its rails, and lowered herself, dropping lightly to the ground. Still in the nether, she sprinted across the cobbled span between the Fabians and the outer stone wall. She ran right through the wall, found a dark street, and returned to the normal world.

She jogged most of the way to the park. Even then, she was late. Sorrowen didn't mention it.

"Well?" he said. "Did you make it into the Ghosts?"

"I stopped trying to join them when they tried to kill me."

"They tried to *kill* you? But if you can't get in with them, how are you going to find out if there's going to be another war?"

Raxa shrugged. "Thought I'd get into the palace instead."

The boy laughed, trailing off as he saw she was serious. "The palace? Like the palace where the king lives? How?"

"Ask the lady who's housing me there. I'll pick up what gossip I can, but the good stuff's going to be in the ministers' documents. I think I can get to them, but there's one problem: I can't read them. I'm going to start learning to read Mallish tomorrow."

"Why would you do that?"

"So that I can read Mallish."

"You don't have to do that. Just copy them and bring them to me."

"You can read them. Because you were born here. And spent years in the priesthood." She grinned at him. "Quit making me look like an idiot, will you?"

"I wish *I* was in the palace. They have me chopping wood and reading about Gashen's victories all day long. It's so boring. He always wins!"

"Picked up any dirt yet?"

"It mostly just seems normal." Sorrowen tilted his head. "But yesterday, I was going in to sharpen my axe when I heard two of the masters talking. Master Jameson said..." The boy closed his eyes, remembering. "'If the war brings the foreigners to us, I wonder how merciful they'll be after all?'"

Raxa snorted. "They can't seriously believe the Collen Basin's going to invade them. Galand's not sure the Colleners can keep their own borders safe. That's the whole reason we're here."

"Maybe so, but Master Waymore thinks they might counter-invade, too. He replied, 'They will spare us. They need us to keep peace among the people. Remember that it is our only chance for reform.' Then I dropped my axe on my foot and yelped and they stopped talking."

"Well, pass it along to the bosses. Then if they get it wrong, they can only blame themselves. Heard from them lately?"

"Early this morning. They're nearly to Cavana."

"Let them know we're in position. That it's only a matter of time until we'll have what they're looking for."

He peered at her, his eyes lit like the candles of a scholar working late into the night. "How did you get like this?"

"Like what?"

"So...sure of yourself."

"By having been through much worse. Now let's get out of here before somebody sees a young male monk fraternizing with an older female roughneck in the middle of the night."

Raxa went back to the Fabians at a jog. Despite her haste, by the time she got home, she'd been out for nearly three hours. When a servant came around in the morning to see to her, Raxa was so thick-headed from exhaustion that for a moment she couldn't remember where she was.

The day was filled with more gossip-mongering. Maura emphasized that Raxa's husband had chosen to do business with the Collen Basin over Mallon, implying that it was because of the unfavorable tariffs Mallon placed on northern goods. Even so, sensing some resentment toward Collen, Raxa was careful to guarantee Mallon's bluebloods that her husband had *wanted* to come to Mallon, but the dictates of business had thwarted him.

The day after that, she got her writing tutor. Along with enough parchment to cover the sails of a ship, and enough ink to dye them. Within minutes of starting her lessons, Raxa was incredibly bored, but she gritted her teeth and did her best. Combined with the bits and pieces she remembered from Galand's lessons, she learned fast.

Maura assured her that she'd requested audiences with several ministers who could apprise Raxa of the situation in Collen, and how she could best look into her husband's disappearance there. She also gave Raxa a flippant warning about how long such requests could take to be fulfilled.

Several days drifted past, a tasteless porridge of court chatter, writing lessons, and strolls around the mall. At least this gave Raxa a good look at the palace. Each night, she catnapped, then got up in the darkest hour to slip outside and shadowalk into the palace itself, getting to know its escape routes and its exits.

A handful of them, anyway. The palace was gigantic. A town unto itself. She could only spend a few minutes inside it each night until she had to hoof it back home before she ran out of juice and got kicked out of the shadows. Using dead bugs, she tried spying at a distance, but she had a hard time hearing anything the people were saying. It was like she didn't know how to get her ears to work with the bugs' ears. She tried to hone her skill, but it was slow going. And any energy she spent on the bugs was juice she couldn't put toward shadowalking.

She preferred to do her work in person anyway. And as day after day passed with no word from the royal cabinet, Raxa was starting to think she'd have time to memorize every stone in every room of the palace.

"I possess good news," Maura announced one morning after breakfast. "The Minister of Foreign Dignitaries has agreed to see you this afternoon."

"This afternoon?" Raxa said. "But I've only waited twelve days. Is he sure he doesn't need twelve more to prepare his office for my arrival?"

"You can make japes now. Your Mallish is improving. Shall I inform the Minister that you will be there? Or would you prefer to pout that the men you need to speak with because of their importance also have concerns that don't involve you?"

Raxa smiled. There was no denying that Maura was a cold-blooded aristocrat who couldn't imagine anything better to do with her wealth than try to make more of it. As Lady Yera's story had rippled through the court, Maura had begun to openly question whether the newly-opened Galladese Passage was enriching the Middle Kingdoms at the cost of Mallon's coffers—and if so, whether the king had any choice but to reduce tariffs on all goods out of the north. Raxa had zero doubt Maura had only taken her in to use her as a political bludgeon.

Yet Raxa liked her anyway. "Tell the Minister I'll see him."

"And thank him for his attentions on this matter."

"And thank him for his attentions."

Servants helped Raxa garb herself in various undergarments and the dress Maura had had made for her to wear to any such audiences. At the appointed time, Maura accompanied Raxa into the palace, where a royal servant delivered them to a modest-sized hall.

A man rose from a table. He was dressed in a pine green doublet with floppy sleeves cinched at three points along the arm, making them resemble a string of moldy onions.

He bowed. "I am Odden Laxley, King Charles' Minister of Foreign Dignitaries. I am sorry to hear the conditions that brought you here, but I am glad to meet you nonetheless."

Raxa thanked him and grabbed a seat. Laxley had already heard her story, but he prompted her to tell it herself.

"I'm waiting for my soldiers to come from Dollendun," she concluded. "Anything you can tell me about the situation in Collen will help me find my husband."

Laxley frowned, the ends of his long mustache hanging past his chin. "It is not advised that anyone should travel into Collen at the present time. The locals have savagely murdered many of our people. They have made raids across our own border. There is even talk of witchcraft."

"But I must find him. If there's to be another war, I have to get him out before anything happens to him."

"It is not not known whether our king will dedicate more resources to quelling rebels who may be incapable of accepting civilization. However, we do possess certain assets within Collen. They might make inquiries of your husband on your behalf."

Raxa did her best to pry more from him, but either he truly had no idea about Mallon's plans for Collen, or he had no intention of revealing them to a northerner. She did a careful dance around the Mallish spies he'd implied were working in Collen, but he stonewalled her there, too.

"He wasn't altogether unhelpful," Maura decided once they'd returned to the Fabians. "But I assume a woman like yourself is not satisfied by the assurances that strangers will ask questions on your behalf."

"Not in the slightest," Raxa said. "I need to know more."

"I will inquire of Harald Walpole. But it will mean more waiting."

"Fine by me. The longer he makes me wait, the more time I have to spread my story."

That drew a smile from Maura.

Once Raxa was alone, she killed a spider, painstakingly reanimated it, and sent it on the long crawl toward the palace. When Laxley concluded his day, it followed him to his chambers. That night, Raxa snuck into his rooms, rifled through his writings, and spent hours copying down a page from each. If Sorrowen found anything interesting in one of them, she'd go back for the rest.

At her next meet with Sorrowen, Raxa told him that Mallon had spies operating in the Basin. He told her that Galand and Blays had diverted to a place called Tanar Atain—something about one of their other people getting arrested while snooping around. She didn't know whether to be concerned that Galand's other spies were getting snatched up, or relieved that he was bothering to rescue them.

Sorrowen paged through the copied documents she'd brought, repeatedly shaking his head. "Some of these talk about Collen, but it's just about keeping track of which Mallish people of note are still in the Basin. I don't think this guy gets much of a say in things."

Raxa had been afraid of that. Over the next two weeks, she made another couple of trips into Laxley's quarters, but nothing she turned up seemed significant.

She had just about given up on seeing the Minister of the Eastern Reach when she was summoned to his presence.

Harald Walpole was a tall man with a craggy beard, a frown carved from granite, and eyes that looked like they could see your secrets. When Raxa entered the hall, he barely nodded.

"Lady Yera," he said. "I know your story. Why should I care?"

She raised an eyebrow. "My husband is missing, milord. He might have been taken hostage. Or even..." She trailed off, letting her voice quiver.

Walpole's rock-like expression didn't budge. "Your husband is a northerner who means nothing to me. Thousands of my men have died in Collen. For the moment, the fighting has stopped, but the slightest nudge could cost me thousands more. So I will repeat myself one time. Why should I care that your husband went somewhere he shouldn't have?"

"Want the truth? You shouldn't."

This got him to raise his eyebrow. Raxa was surprised it didn't creak.

"Let me guess how this normally goes," she went on. "Woman walks in with a tragic story. She beseeches you. Cries at you. And demands you make it *your* business to make it better."

"Wrong," he grunted. "It isn't just women."

"You should care about me because you don't have to do anything for me. I'm taking care of this for myself. The only thing I need from you is to know what I'm getting into."

He'd stayed on his feet and hadn't offered to let her sit down. Still standing, he crossed his arms. "What do you need to know?"

"When I go to Collen, will I be walking into a war?"

"Can't say what the Colleners will do."

"I'm not asking what the Colleners will do."

"Then you're asking me for state secrets."

Raxa sucked her upper teeth. "My men will get here one month from now. Will there be fighting by then?"

Arms folded, tapping his right upper arm with his left hand, Walpole turned his back on her to regard an oversized map of the region mounted on the wall. "Collen's bunged themselves up like a keg. An outsider looking at the situation would conclude that it would take months for anyone to mount an effective attack on their defenses."

She smiled. "Thank you, Lord Walpole."

He dismissed her with a nod. This time, she'd brought her spider with her. She let it crawl down her dress and onto the floor. Walpole soon left the hall they'd met in, the spider hitching a ride on his trousers. He retired to a high tower in a room by himself. He worked well past dark. He took no visitors.

Raxa ate dinner. Drank wine with the Boscaynes. Napped. At midnight's bells, she woke and slipped outside.

The tower was deep into the palace. Raxa ran as hard as she could, deep in the shadows, the stars overhead burning like white coals. She entered the building, following the path she'd laid out for herself to minimize the distance she'd have to travel. Even at this late hour, guards stood silent, polearms in hand.

She dashed up the spiral steps to Walpole's tower. Shooting through the wall, she threw herself back into the real world. The run had taken several minutes. She'd have enough juice to make it home, but not much more.

The chambers included a larger study and a smaller room furnished with stuffed chairs and a cabinet stuffed with stout liquors. A window in both rooms looked down on part of the palace roof, a secret courtyard of flowers and shrubs chopped up into animal shapes.

Raxa got out her parchment and went to work. The room was laden with documents. Way too much to get in one go. She copied the first page of everything that mentioned Collen—one of the few Mallish words she recognized instantly—then moved on to everything recent. It was laborious work. Time-consuming. She'd deactivated her spider long ago—couldn't suffer the drain on her powers—so she kept one ear cocked to the stairwell, straining for any sound above the scratch of her quill.

Finished, she dried her ink, the smell of which she was starting to hate, rolled up her pages, and ran fast as hell back to the Fabians. Climbing was easier in the shadows, but even so, her grip on the netherworld was starting to quiver by the time she had scaled the balconies up to her window.

Two days later, she brought what she'd found to Sorrowen. In the darkness of the park, he shuffled through her copies.

A third of the way through the stack, he swung up his head so fast a lock of hair flopped down his forehead. "You got it! Raxa, you—!"

She reached out and bopped him on the side of the head. "Keep your voice down, you idiot. We're holding our own death warrants right now."

Sorrowen rubbed his head, still grinning. "This is a payment order. For enough money to raise a small army!"

"Is that what it's for? An army?"

"It doesn't say. It doesn't say who it's for, either. All it says is that it's about the east. About the coming fighting there."

"There were other pages to this. If I get them for you, can you tell what the crown is paying for?"

"Well I can't know that until we have the rest of it!"

"I'll bring you the rest two nights from now," Raxa said. "I've spoken to the man who runs the eastern reaches. Tell Galand war is coming. It's not a matter of if, it's a matter of when."

She spent the next day fending off a steady dose of nerves. When midnight finally came, and the uninteresting people were snoring in bed, she climbed out the window, ran across the mall, and reentered the palace. The entire hall smelled like roast grouse with rosemary; scullions were still cleaning up the mess.

She ascended the tower to Walpole's private offices. These were dark, but down in the rooftop courtyard, lanterns glowed and courtiers laughed, crystal glasses glinting in their hands.

Raxa lit a candle, keeping it back from the window. She moved to the desk and opened the top drawer. Half of the parchment she'd gone through the day before was gone. She pawed through what was left. The payment order was missing. Heart pounding, she opened the drawer below and found another stack. Recognizing them from the day before, she paged through them until she found the order.

It was three pages in all. She got out her stuff and started copying. She was just moving on to the third page when a key scratched in the lock of the door.

21

Teeth scraped against his ribs. The beast's jaws squeezed him on both sides, threatening to crush him. It felt like his head was spinning—because it was; the monster was rolling in circles, dragging him under, meaning to drown him.

He called out to the nether, feeling it surround him, drawn to the blood leaking into the water. He shaped it into a spear and drove it blindly into the creature's midsection.

It relaxed its jaws. Pressure relieved, with his face momentarily above water, Dante gasped for air. He'd barely gotten a breath in when the creature clamped down again. His assault should have blown straight through its body, but it didn't seem weakened at all.

He was back under the water and its jaws were forcing the air from its lungs. He gathered a second strike and hammered it toward the beast's middle. Yet the black bolt seemed to waver, impacting sidelong. Dante felt it do little more than scrape across the bark-like scales.

The monster squeezed harder yet. He felt a crack, a gush of pain that made his vision go white. He forced his mind to return to its tethers. The nether swirled around the edges of his eyes, as if impatient to be put to use. He formed a third bolt and rammed it into the top of the beast's head. He held tight to the bolt all the way through, guiding it home, yet it felt like trying to punch someone underwater, the attack's strength sapped away.

His lungs were screaming now. So were his ribs. As it rolled him over again, he waited until the light brightened, then drove up his head and fought for a gasp of air, but a slug of water came with it, choking his lungs. He coughed, tasting blood.

He tried to draw the nether together for another strike, but he was coughing and writhing and drowning; trying to shape the shadows was like trying to shape dry flour. His pain and anguish peaked until he thought he couldn't stand it, then withdrew like a boat leaving a pier.

In his state, he could hardly think, yet he knew exactly what was happening: it was ending. A part of him embraced it—an end to this pain, yes, but also to all the strife, the loss of friends and mentors and innocence, and all for what? To make things slightly better? Or too often, just to keep things from getting worse? The gains were so small and the costs were so big: better to have been a farmer, a fisherman, a scribe for a kindly monk in a backwater village.

Anger. Anger like a thunderclap. A great hand reached down through his mind, plucked up these thoughts, and shook them until their skinny spine broke. He wouldn't let it be over. He had touched the world, and he'd made it better. He'd freed people. Saved lives. Exposed fetid lies and learned soaring truths. He had rebelled against kings and resurrected a friend.

And his power was too great to let it end here.

He pumped nether into his own body, strengthening his ribs, bolstering his blood. He sent it charging into his lungs and it wasn't air yet it was enough to let him see and think and move again. He tried to reach for his sword, but it was pinned against his thigh by the monster's teeth. He pounded his fists against its head, scrabbling for an eye.

It grunted, a blast of foul air bubbling over his body, then spat him out. Dante knew he was still in incredible pain, but the removal of the crushing pressure felt like being reborn, and inhaling a full breath of air felt like winning a war. Through watering eyes, he watched as Blays withdrew his sword from the monster's back, then stabbed it beneath two overlapping plates, wrenching one loose.

Dante forged the shadows into a dark blade and rammed

them through the hole Blays had cut in the creature's hide. Blood showered into the trees. He ripped the nether toward him through the inside of the monster, shredding the flesh in a vortex of destruction. The creature reared back its neck in an S-shape. The nether exploded from its mouth in a hail of blood and teeth and pink goo.

The monster went slack, collapsing into the water with a splash. Including its thick tail, it was thirty feet long, an enormous lizard with a broad, snake-like head.

Blays stood from its back, chest heaving. "Did we just slay a dragon?"

Dante tried to answer, but his voice wouldn't work.

Blays hooked a hand under his armpit and hauled him halfway up the corpse. "Get on top of it. If they kill our guide, we're as dead as this beast."

Seeing Dante was in no immediate risk of drowning, he dived off the side of the monster. Through the trees, Dante glimpsed soldiers in green jabats firing arrows at Volo's canoe. She was nowhere to be seen.

Something tugged at Dante's leg, which was still dangling in the water. He jerked his foot away, but the tugging repeated, followed immediately by more to his other leg. It was like something was pinching him with its fingernails.

Or with little mouths.

Swallowing down the urge to vomit, he scrambled for a handhold. The water frothed around him, red with blood. Silver scales flashed. A small fish darted for his hip, only for a whiskered red fish to dart forward and snatch the smaller fish in its teeth. Unseen others continued to tug at his legs. He grabbed tight to a knob on the beast's flank and tried to pull himself up, but the pain in his ribs was so punishing he slipped. He poured nether into his side and heaved again, kicking his way up to the top of the monster's back.

He looked down at his legs and fainted.

After a period of warmness, he could see again. No thoughts yet, just a dull sense of confusion. People were screaming, but it wasn't him, was it? Right: his legs. They were still bare, but they were now pocked with dozens of red divots. Some ran deeper than they looked. He tried to wiggle his toes. His left foot did fine, but his right wasn't responding very well.

Beyond the screen of trees, a man yelled out in triumph. Dante turned in time to see Blays falling from the roof of the war canoe and diving into the water. But he was still holding onto both his swords: good sign of life. A few bodies in green uniforms were floating facedown by the canoe, the water around them boiling with fish.

Others in the canoe took aim with their bows, trying to pick Blays out from the dim water. Dante gathered the shadows in his hands and packed them into a ball. He sent it skimming along the water to plow though both hulls of the enemy vessel just at the waterline. Splinters twirled through the air. Soldiers yelled out.

One leaned over the hull to inspect the damage. Volo popped up from the arrow-riddled prow of her boat and loosed a slim arrow. It took the man in the ribs, dumping him into the water. Soldiers fired back on her, forcing her out of sight.

Blays reappeared inside the war boat, stabbing a man in the back. Volo stood again, shooting a soldier as he charged at Blays. Dante gestured to the nether, meaning to rain hell on the remaining enemies, but his vision went gray and he crumbled to his side.

He was bleeding heavily, inside and out. Woozily, he sent nether streaming to the holes in his legs, filling them with drops of darkness. He'd mended countless cuts and broken bones, but replacing lost flesh took ten times the effort. After healing a few bites, he stanched the bleeding in the rest and turned his focus toward the damage to his chest.

His jabat was hanging off him in shreds. A row of puncture marks traced his upper chest, with another cutting across his hips. One by one, he erased the cuts in his skin, then delved beneath to mend the punctures to his organs. Once these felt stable, he glanced back at the war boat. Only a handful of soldiers were still standing. With Blays blinking in and out of the shadows, and Volo sniping them from her canoe, the enemy would be wiped out within the minute.

Though his torso wasn't fully mended, Dante switched back

to the gouges in his legs, fearing they might never be healable if he didn't take care of them now. Shadows rolled to him in great waves and sank into the ragged bites, filling them with pale new flesh that left his legs spotted and dappled. Sweat broke across his forehead. Head swimming, he finished his right leg and moved to the left, starting with any damage deep enough to hobble him.

His hold on the nether grew looser and looser. As he neared the end of his powers, he made a rough pass of the remaining bites, stopping up the remaining bleeding.

Hearing a splash behind him, he turned. The boat was silent, bodies draped over gunwales and floating in the water, jerking as fish plucked at them from below. Volo stood in her canoe, looking forlorn. There was no sign of Blays. Dante tried to stand for a better look, but the corpse of the monster bobbed beneath him and his wobbly legs gave out.

Blays snapped into being in front of him—he'd shadowalked across the waters to avoid the storm of fish within them. Blood spattered his limbs and clothes.

He cracked a smile. "Don't suppose you've got any arrow medicine left?"

He wavered. Dante's eyes lowered to his torso. A broken stick projected from the right side of Blays' chest. A branch? How had he gotten a branch stuck to himself? And there was a second one in his stomach. Both spots sopped with blood.

Realization flooded over Dante's reeling mind, horrific and ashamed. They weren't sticks. They were snapped-off arrow shafts.

Dante reached for the shadows, but it was like trying to pick up the floor. He tried again, then a third time, working with the patient deliberateness of a barber shaving the king's neck. His next efforts were increasingly frantic. On other occasions, he'd been able to channel beyond his capacity at the cost of damaging himself, but he had nothing left to prime the pump with. As he understood what he was facing, cold panic prickled up his spine.

His throat closed on itself. "I'm out."

"Ah," Blays said. "Well, don't let Volo stick me in one of those cages, will you? There's no room to build a statue underneath."

Blays fell to his knees, clutching the broken shaft jutting from his stomach. He slumped backward, bent awkwardly. Volo was calling to them from the other side of the trees, but Dante barely heard it. Bile crept up his throat. He had nothing left. Too wrapped up in undoing the horror that had befallen him to imagine the others might wind up hurt, too. Sick anguish curled around his bones. For all that they'd been through, all of the ludicrous odds and fearsome powers they'd defeated, they'd been undone by a patrol of common soldiers, a wild animal, and a school of fish.

He had healed himself quite thoroughly. But in that moment, he wanted to draw his knife, open his veins, and sink into the warm darkness. He would be alone in the Pastlands, but once he muddled his way through to the Mists, he could rejoin Blays on their next journey.

A memory snagged in his mind. The whiteness of the Mists, glimpses of mountain and ocean through the gaps in the fog. The light that came from everywhere, because everywhere *was* light.

He closed his eyes, inhaling deeply, exhaling through his nose. Light shined through his eyelids. He blinked. A glowing speck hovered above his bloody palm. It was smaller than one of the fireflies they'd seen dancing in the night, but the dot expanded with every breath, growing to the size of a marble.

His focus shuddered. The light twinkled, growing translucent, shrinking on itself. Dante stared into it, his will hard enough to shatter steel. The light steadied. Became opaque. And swelled to the size of a plum.

Holding the light in his hand and mind, he saw the shape of what Blays had been, unhurt and whole. The ether yearned to restore it. That was its entire purpose: to hold fast to order no matter how hard the storms of chaos battered against it. Just as Dante was doing as he gazed down on his dying friend.

He nodded. The ether streamed toward Blays, moving not with the turbulent torrent of the nether, but with linear precision, exactly like a shaft of sunlight beaming through a knot in a barn wall. It gathered around the base of one of the arrows and absorbed into Blays' skin.

The broken shaft pushed free from his chest and rolled to the side, landing on the hide of the dead beast. The arrowhead was a cruel wedge of shaved bone. Dante sat back. While the nether was something you guided and channeled, he now saw that the ether was a process that unfolded on its own, like the blooming of a flower. Or better yet, like a magical book where, if you opened it to the page you wanted, it would begin to read itself.

Carefully, he pointed the ball of ether down toward the arrowhead in Blays' stomach. The light sank toward the wound, entering it. Though Dante didn't need to guide the healing process, while it was ongoing, he did have to continue to maintain the ether itself.

This maintenance was demanding—almost frighteningly so. Fresh sweat beaded his temples and chest. His hands quivered. He could feel the core of his being wearing out, ready to collapse on itself. Already, he was nearly done for, the ball of light evaporating down to a hazelnut, then to a delicate firefly.

Dante was shaking like a leaf in a storm. But with a calm mind, he rode the winds. And hung on to the light.

With a fleshy pop, the second arrowhead extruded from Blays' gut.

A pall of silence rolled across the swamp. It was the silence of the space between breaths, the silence of the moment after creation, the silence of a mind gone still in the wake of exhaustion.

Blays coughed himself upright. He spat blood, looking impressed at the volume of mess he'd created, then grinned at Dante. "That was just a joke? 'Oh yeah, sorry about you bleeding to death, but I'm totally out of nether.' You asshole!"

Dante tried to smile, but he couldn't seem to feel his face. The world was tilting. As he fell, his last thought was the hope that he wouldn't roll into the water.

A bird was screeching like it had just been robbed in the street. He woke piece by piece: first his ears to the cry of the bird; then his nose to the smell of mud and flowers and decay; then the sweet ache of his muscles and the jabbing pain in his legs.

He was lying in a hammock suspended a hand's span above the ground on an island barely twenty feet across. He didn't see the canoe anywhere. The other hammocks were strung between the voluminous trees, but there was no sign of Blays or Volo. His shredded jabat had been replaced with an older and shabbier one.

He made a tentative gesture toward the nether. It responded cheerfully. Still feeling thoroughly banged up, Dante made a second pass at the worst pains in his chest and legs. There were a few shallow grooves in his left leg, but he no longer looked like a grub-riddled log.

He stilled his mind. Nothing came. Refusing to let any annoyance or emotion of any kind disturb the pond-like placidity of his thoughts, he stared into his palm. A light glowed within it.

Focusing on a single divot on his leg, he envisioned how it had once looked. And willed the ether to make reality match his memory. His skin tingled. The divot began to fill, but stopped short of disappearing entirely. Yet he felt like he still had a hold on the ether. Why couldn't he finish the healing? Because he lacked the skill? Or because the further removed in time an object got from its ideal state, the less the ether could do to restore it? Maybe it was—

Something crashed down from the tall blue-leafed tree in the middle of the island. Dante shot to his feet and reached for his sword, but it was no longer hanging from his hip. Blays dangled from a branch, swinging back and forth before letting go and landing in a crouch.

"You're awake," Blays said.

"You're stating the obvious."

"In that case, you smell bad and you're as pale as a fish's ass. You all right? There was enough blood on top of that lizard to fill a keg of really bad beer."

Dante took a few steps around, bending his arms and legs. "I appear to be remarkably well, considering I was partially devoured twice."

"As nice as it is to have anti-insect paste, what these people *really* need is something to ward off the enormous lizards."

"Where is Volo, anyway?"

"Taking a peek ahead. We're starting to run low on a few little things. Like food."

"We're low on rations? How long was I asleep?"

"Hmm." Blays did some counting on his fingers. "Well, first there was the first day. Then there was the second day. I was never much for schooling, but I'd say that makes two days."

After the chaos of the encounter, Dante found the loss of time wasn't particularly disturbing. "What was that thing? The lizard?"

"Volo called it a swamp dragon."

"Interesting. The only problem with that is that dragons aren't real."

"Then apparently you got your ass kicked by your own imagination. I understand the act of getting swallowed can cloud your thinking, but did it ever occur to you to try killing it?"

"I did. It was resistant to nether."

"Like the kappers?"

"The kappers seemed impervious. This was more like I had to hit it with ten times the force to do one-tenth the damage. I've never run into anything like it."

"This reminds me." Blays' pack was hanging from a branch of a tree. He opened it and retrieved a cloth-wrapped item a foot long and two inches in diameter. "Volo said you should have this."

"What's this?"

"Swamp dragon penis."

Dante dropped it on the ground, skipping back a step. He swore. "Is it actually a penis?"

"It's a horn. Volo said that anyone who kills one of them should take it and carry it around. Sign of courage and all that. Supposed to protect you from evil, too. So be careful not to burn yourself with it."

Dante bent to pick it up. The horn was black and slightly tapered, coming to a point at one end. "Someday when I'm looking up at this mounted on my wall, I'll smile and remember the day we finally left this awful place."

He sat in his hammock, turning the horn in his hands. He brought a tendril of nether to him and probed the horn's surface, meaning to see if he could determine how it had shrugged off his attacks—and, with any luck, discover how to nullify its defenses on the chance they ran into another lizard.

The probe sank a fraction of an inch into the surface before coming up against an unyielding screen. Blank. Smooth. Matte. But undeniably nether, coating the horn from one end to the other.

The shadows were stuck fast. Like they were frozen. He could neither withdraw them from the horn nor add to them. That appeared to explain the animal's toughness: this embedded nether was deflecting anything that came at it. You could wear it away if you struck the same spot hard and often enough, but the amount of force required would exhaust most nethermancers before they broke through.

He was still examining the horn when Blays croaked like a frog, indicating a boat was inbound. Dante moved to the north end of the island. Volo paddled toward them, bringing the canoe up onto a muddy landing.

She hopped out the front and gawked at Dante. "You're a sorcerer!"

"You're deluded," he told her. "You must have hit your head during the fighting and mistaken the stars you saw for magic."

"I know what I saw. You blew a hole right through their ship!"

"They hit a rock."

"When Mr. Pendelles swam to you, he had two arrows sticking out of him. When I helped him get you into the canoe, he was fine. And so were you—but there was blood everywhere." Her young face twisted with anger and hurt. "I'm not stupid. If you wanted me to not see, you should have blinded me with your sorcerer's tricks. And if you can't let me know the truth, you should kill me right now."

She stood across from him, feet apart, empty-handed. Dante grimaced. "I need you to swear that this secret stays with you."

"What right do you have to tell me what to do with my own knowledge?"

"I attained that right when I entrusted you with our safety—and our ability to complete our mission. If you have any honor in you, swear you'll keep this secret."

"A smart person once told me honor is just something that

powerful people use to stop you from acting in your own interests."

"In that case, we part ways here. Since you were paid to get us to Dara Bode, we'll take the canoe." He squelched through the muck toward the boat.

"Fine!" Volo said. "I swear to keep it secret. Bloody scales, do all sorcerers talk like you?"

"Like what?"

"Like you rule the world."

"Pretty much," Blays said. "Although he makes something of an art of it."

Volo gave Dante a quizzical look. "How many people can you kill at a time?"

Dante rolled his eyes. "That depends on how many stupid questions they ask."

"It's a lot, isn't it? Why would an investor send someone like you to chase down some dirty old sea captain? Aren't you worth much more than he is?"

Dante glanced at Blays. Blays said, "You're right. That wouldn't make sense." He lifted a finger into the air. "But if we're not soldiers, what makes you think the sea captain is really a sea captain? There are mysteries at work here, Volo. Mysteries *within* mysteries. All shall be revealed when the time is right."

She regarded him solemnly. "Is this a test sent to stretch my understanding? To remind me that what I'm told — even what I see — isn't always the truth?"

"Could be. That's all part of the mystery, isn't it?"

"What say we discuss this on the way to the village?" Dante said. "I'm starving."

Blays tilted his head. "We're still doing this?"

"Think it's a bad idea?"

"Some might say that being attacked by a dragon, a squadron of soldiers, and a swarm of carnivorous fish might be the gods' way of telling you it's a good time to turn back."

"We're alive. And we're not holding back anymore. We can do this."

They packed up their things and shoved off from the island. Dante killed a dragonfly and sent it whirring ahead of them.

Compared to the moths and beetles he was used to dealing with, it was as nimble as a falcon.

"The fish that attacked you," Volo said. "Ziki oko. World-eaters. That's why you stay out of the water. Well, that's *one* of the reasons."

Dante gazed down into the brown murk. "Are they common?"

"Wherever blood is shed. So you might be seeing a lot of them."

His airborne scout spotted a number of canoes and rafts, but nothing that resembled a patrol. Within three miles, sleepiness draped itself over Dante like a soaked cloak. He sat up straight, arching his back to ward it off, but his body was still recovering.

"Dante." Time had passed; someone was shoving his shoulder. "We could be in trouble."

He swung upright. They were emerging from the shadow of the trees into a sunny clearing. In its center, dozens of rafts were lashed together. Green crops grew from the water. Four earthen mounds had been raised up, one of them supporting a formidable stone tower.

It had the look of a thriving little community. Yet the only sounds on the air were those of the swamp: the frogs, the bugs, and the birds.

Dante brought the nether to him; it came easily, sheathing his fingers. Two concentric rings of wooden posts encircled the village, extending two feet from the water. As Volo approached them, Dante made out a mesh net stretched between each pair of posts. Volo came to a gate, opened it, and paddled inside. An inner set of posts and nets still separated them from the settlement.

"What's this?" Blays leaned over to close the gate behind them. "Keep the fish out?"

"The outer net keeps the bad fish out. The inner keeps the good fish in. And the space between is filled with tigerfish."

Dante caught a glimpse of something orange and whiskery drifting away from the boat. Volo came to the second gate and ferried them inside. To left and right, low dirt walls enclosed paddies of green stalks sporting a handful of oversized, teardrop-shaped leaves. The earthen walls were flat on top and wide enough to walk down, running to a wooden dock fronting the collection of rafts.

A few trees provided shade from the sun, which was otherwise plentiful, making the settlement smell less miasmic than the swamp around it. Volo brought them to the dock and tied up the canoe. They got out, sandals thumping on the boards.

On the other side of the dock, bodies bobbed gently in the water.

Others were sprawled on rafts, limbs trailing over the sides. Two hundred at a glance. Dante ran across the dock to the nearest of them, grabbing the woman's jabat and heaving her up onto the boards. Water streamed from her pale face. Her eyes weren't blinking and her skin was the same temperature as the water. A deep gash across her stomach threatened to spill her cooling organs across the dock.

Volo slapped her hand to her forehead. "I was just here!"

Dante scanned the wide clearing. "How long ago? Did you see anything out of the ordinary?"

"Such as a massacre taking place? It was fine! They were working! Fishing!"

Blays put a hand on her shoulder. "Did you know any of them?"

"I knew *all* of them." Her reddened face crumpled. "I knew..."

She broke into tears, sinking to the dock. Dante watched for a moment. Aware there was nothing he could do for her, he went to the bodies instead. He'd seen enough massacres to know that there were often a few survivors, but most of these people had been dumped into the water. Even if they hadn't bled to death, they would have drowned.

After he'd been investigating the bodies for a few minutes, Volo recovered enough to help the search. They went from raft to raft. Nothing but corpses. The front of the stone tower hung open. Dante sent a dragonfly inside. Blood spattered the first and second floor. On the top floor, bodies lay in a heap against the back wall.

Dante went up to check them in person while the others kept watch on the grounds. The corpses were women and children. No survivors.

He returned to the sunshine of the late morning, wiping his nose and eyes, as if that would cleanse them of the sight and smell of the blood.

"Whole village," he said.

Blays nodded. "Soldiers?"

"Animals would have chewed them up. Dragged them off. Had to have been people."

"Injuries almost look animal, though. All the puncture wounds."

"Spears," Dante said. "They don't have a lot of iron here. Even their soldiers were using bone-tipped arrows."

"And what about the ripped-up guts?"

"That I don't know. Maybe we should ask—"

"Over here!" Volo shouted. "*Help!*"

They ran toward her, jumping from raft to raft. She kneeled inside a shack, hand on the back of a young boy, his eyes staring blankly. He looked to be about twelve, but every Tanarian looked younger to Dante.

The boy said nothing as Dante checked him over. He showed a few scrapes and bruises, but nothing to be concerned about. Volo spoke with him in soft, quick words, mixing Mallish with a local dialect. Within a minute, he was making shy eye contact with the three of them.

"His name is Tap," Volo said. "I knew his family."

Dante gazed down at the boy. "Do you know who did this?"

The boy glanced up quickly, then spoke in a soft, worn-out voice. "The soldiers. They came in their boats and they told us to gather on the dock. They wanted to know, they asked, Who killed the others? But nobody knew what they meant. The soldiers, they kept asking who did it. And the people kept telling them they didn't know. Then one of the soldiers said…" He lowered his eyes, thinking. "He said, 'This is punishment for your treason.' That's when they started to…"

Tap choked up. Dante gave him a few moments to recover. "How did you escape?"

"I hid under the water. I breathed through a reed we use when we're spearing fish."

"Was there anyone else with you?"

The boy shook his head.

"Let's get him out of here," Dante said. "There's nothing more to see here."

Volo swung her head to the side. "You want to leave?"

"No, I want to get the food we came for, and then leave."

"They butchered these people. We have to find them! You can kill them!"

"And then what? Another group of soldiers is sent to slaughter another village in retaliation?"

"This isn't fair. These people did *nothing*." She advanced on him, jabbing her finger at his chest. "They died because of what *we* did!"

Dante squeezed his eyes shut. At that moment, he would have rather taken a swim in a tub full of ziki oko than get roped into another internecine bloodbath, but he had no idea how to express that without sounding like a complete asshole.

"He's right," Blays said. "We've seen this a hundred times. If we go after the culprits, the crown will fall on you like a drunken mountain. These people are dead—and we're going to honor their deaths by not doing anything to get more innocents killed in the name of vengeance."

"But justice is only what we make of it," she said. "If we sail away, what does that make us?"

Dante could only shake his head. Years ago, he'd harbored the same burning wrath she was feeling right now. If he'd been ten years younger, he probably would have gone ripping off into the swamps to track down the killers and chum the waters with their guts.

He told himself that path led only to more ruin. But did he reject it because he was wiser? Or because after he'd risked everything to help the Collen Basin, only for them to turn on him the moment it was convenient, he no longer cared about anyone's troubles but his own?

A tear slipped down Volo's face. "It makes us cowards."

But she went with them nonetheless, gathering food from the village and stashing it in the canoe. As they padded away, the sun shined warmly on the waters and the dead alike.

~

They moved onward with cold purpose, and the grim knowledge that even if they found Naran, and executed Gladdic, they would walk away from Tanar Atain leaving some crimes unavenged.

Dante scouted the way ahead with a small armada of dragonflies and water striders. Following the sinking of the war canoe and the massacre at the village, soldiers prowled the swamps constantly, forcing Volo to backtrack and detour down obscure paths barely wide enough to permit their canoe. As they squeezed through the shrubs, ticks gathered on the tips of the branches and flung themselves at the warm human bodies.

Sometimes when a patrol neared, there were no alternate routes for Volo to flee through, requiring Dante to harvest a solid wall of brambles around the canoe, hiding them until the threat had passed. They kept Tap with them—Volo had a friend in the capital who she wanted to hear the boy's story—but the boy made no trouble. If anything, he was so quiet and pliable Dante worried that the things he'd seen in the village had cored what was vital inside him, leaving behind a shell of flesh that could only sometimes remember that it had once been something more.

When he wasn't securing their path, Dante studied both the swamp dragon horn and the ether. No matter how he approached it, the horn's nether remained immobile. Yet its presence reminded him of the shaden. He had a wild idea that if he learned how to access the stored shadows, he might be able to make himself resistant to nether, just as the dragon had been, but for the moment, that remained no more than sheer speculation.

He had better luck with the ether. He could still only command a highly limited portion of the light, but he seemed to have unlocked a more precise control of what he had to work with. The night after they'd gotten back on their way, he broke a small twig, leaving it dangling from the branch, then let the emptiness fill him. The twig glowed, straightened, and reattached itself to the tree.

The following day, one of his dragonflies entered a clearing.

Another raft-village was spread across a broad expanse of paddies and docks, protected by the two-part net fences. A team of soldiers watched from the shade as villagers waded into the shallows, cast strange plow-like objects into the water, and dredged up loads of silt, constructing a new paddy.

Every time a worker crawled out of the water, leeches spangled their legs and trunks. The soldiers watched impassively. If a worker took too long resting in the shade, they were dragged across the dock and shoved back into the water. Dante didn't tell Volo what he'd seen.

Dawn came slow, the sky oppressed by black clouds. The air was as still as crystallized ether. Two hours into the day's voyage, the clouds opened as if they'd been slit. Rain slammed through the canopy, battering Dante's scouts to bits. He tried slaying a small pink fish and sending it ahead of them, but it couldn't see far enough through the water to be worth the effort.

Abrupt flashes of light speared through the rain-racked trees, followed by the boom of thunder. Rain gathered in the bottom of the canoe, obliging them to bail it out with a bowl.

With hours of daylight left, Volo guided them onto the shore of a nondescript island. "You get out here."

"No offense," Blays said, examining the trees, "but your people didn't choose a very glamorous spot for their capital."

"The capital's two miles from here, fool. That's why you have to get out now."

"You'll have to forgive me. When we hired you to take us to Dara Bode, I stupidly assumed that meant you'd take us to Dara Bode."

"If I did that, they'd catch us. And all three of us would wind up in the dungeons. Or was that how you planned to meet your friend?"

Dante brushed a strand of damp hair from his brow. "Why don't we try the same trick we used to get out of Aris Osis?"

She gave him a look like he'd suggested an archery contest using themselves as targets. "Is your head full of mud? What business would I have bringing two dead hari into the capital?"

"Then what are you going to do instead?"

"Tell you to get out and wait here. Only I hadn't planned on you being defiant and ruining everything."

Dante pressed his lips together and debarked, bringing his gear with him. Once he and Blays were ashore, Volo gave them a nod and shoved off, disappearing north into the driving rain.

They strung their cloaks between some shrubs and huddled beneath them. After an hour, Dante went down to the banks, slew a water strider, and sent it skimming a few hundred yards in the direction Volo had gone. As it surveyed the waters for incoming boats, Dante cursed himself for not sending a fish to follow Volo into the city.

Their cloaks sagged with rain, dripping on them. A short while later, one tore free from the shrub, exposing them to the downpour.

Dante sighed, crouching in the muck. "How long do you suppose we should wait here?"

"That depends," Blays said, "on how long it'll take you to build a boat."

"Why am I the one doing the building?"

"Would you trust *me* to build a boat? I'd probably build the keel on the top and the deck on the bottom. In fact, I don't even know what either of those words mean."

Thunder rumbled sporadically, like the rantings of a drunk man who kept falling asleep mid-sentence only to snap awake and continue his ravings a few seconds later. As the gray skies dimmed, a large outrigger canoe appeared in the water strider's sight. The boat was painted bold yellow and trimmed with pale blue. It sported a figurehead of an angry-looking fishing bird with a crested head. Lean men in yellow jabats paddled on through the rain.

The outrigger came to a stop within a hundred yards of their island. The captain of the vessel stood and peered about. He bore a delicate mustache. Wispy as it was, it was the most facial hair Dante had seen since entering Tanar Atain.

"Sirs Pendelles and Smallhorn!" the man announced. "My name is Bo Tuin. I have been sent by Volo to retrieve you." He gazed across the hazy swamp. "I'm getting soaked, sirs. Might want to come out before I decide to go home and dry off."

Keeping the nether in easy reach, Dante moved from behind a

tree. "Over here."

The canoe made landing. Bo had brought clean jabats for them, powder blue with a shovel-shaped icon on the breast. They changed behind a shrub. They came back to find the captain gazing up at the rain-lashed branches.

"The trees protect us from storms such as these," Bo said. "Give us fruit and such, too. You could say the trees seem to care for us. If so, suppose we've got any obligation to care for them?"

Dante and Blays exchanged a look. Blays cleared his throat, deciding it was his turn to handle the dana kide duties—or, possibly, he just wanted to. He did seem to get a kick out of discussing things he didn't care about in the slightest.

"Depends, doesn't it?" Blays paced thoughtfully, sandals squelching in the mud. "If a man comes by my house and steals some old firewood I'd been meaning to get rid of, he's done me a favor. But do I really owe him anything for it?"

Bo pursed his lips. "So we'd have to figure out if the trees *intend* to help us. I'll have to ask them sometime!"

He grinned, opening a knapsack. The greeting seemed to be over already. Either Bo wasn't much for formalities, or he didn't think they had time to indulge in them. He produced a pair of looped ropes.

"Pardon the shackles," he said. "But you're escaped hari, being returned to the estate of Do Riza, your master." The man grinned wider. "Don't worry, sirs. The Do is a very merciful man."

Frowning, Dante allowed himself to be bound. Men with the bearing of bodyguards helped them into the canoe. The bodyguards tossed Dante and Blays' cloaks into the water and slipped their swords onto their own belts.

In soft Gaskan, Dante said, "Are we being arrested for real?"

"These days, I've been arrested enough that it doesn't bother me," Blays said. "But if he says he's sorry, but he has to pretend-kill us, that's when I'll complain."

The rowers pulled hard, racing to the north. Once they were underway, Bo made his way back to them, holding onto the mast for support. "Stay quiet through the gates. Your questions will be answered at the Do's estate."

Dante nodded. "Who is this Do Riza? What's his interest in

us?"

"I am but an agent of the hand, sir. Have you ever seen a talking hand?"

"One time," Blays said. "I've sworn off Galladese gin ever since."

Dante sat back and resolved not to worry about anything until they'd arrived at their destination. The way forward soon grew littered with rafts and the half-sunken wreckage of them. It was still raining hard as the trees opened before them and they looked on the great city of Dara Bode.

The city was composed of a series of concentric rings. The outermost was a stretch of open water about four hundred feet across. Where it touched the forest, the branches were neatly chopped back. Large round areas were enclosed with nets; Dante suspected they were fish pens.

They came to another ring of two net-fences. A gate stood across the outer net, wide enough to allow the entry of one of the big barges they'd seen wallowing through the waterways. Bo spoke to the green-uniformed guards there, who gave Dante and Blays a close look, then added a few knots to the little string-board they used to keep records.

The guards waved them through the two sets of gates and into the next ring, a sprawling patch of aquatic farmland. Paddies of the teardrop-leafed plants alternated with stands of short green-trunked trees growing in tight clusters. These bore extremely long, rectangular leaves, some of which had tattered into thin strips. Squat green fruit grew in heavy bunches—bananas. Dante had seen them in the Plagued Islands. Even in the rain, a skeleton crew of laborers was out among the plants, using bone-headed hoes to uproot purplish roots from the paddies. Others inspected the banana trees. Wherever they spotted fruit starting to turn yellow, they hacked down the entire tree and cut loose the bunch.

The canoe navigated through the farms and into a manic sprawl of rafts. People sat under roofs of banana leaves, sheltering from the rain as they passed around bowls of food, tossed dice (which seemed to exist in every land Dante had visited), and fooled about with cubic wooden frames strung with innumerable threads and shiny glass beads. If not for the rain, the noise of their boisterous arguments would have been deafening.

Dante crinkled his nose, but the smell of the city was oddly minimal, and largely overpowered by the scent of the rain. Clear lanes were maintained through the raft-slums. They sliced forward, coming to another ring of wooden platforms supporting simple homes and shops. There was a general lack of smoke. In the few places it was rising, people waited in line carrying covered clay pots and strings of uncooked fish, waiting to make use of the communal kitchens.

After so long on the water, Dante could smell the damp earth ahead. Past the platforms, manors of dark brick stood on artificial islands, protected from unwanted traffic by brick walls. Wooden watchtowers rose from the corners of the islands. Further ahead, stone towers defied the stormy sky. The canoe pulled up to an island dock. The men hopped out and helped Dante and Blays, who were still shackled, debark without falling into the water.

They were brought through a wooden gate and into a courtyard of ludicrously-hued flowers. There, Bo passed them off to a servant named Ki, who brought them to a sparse sitting room and informed them that the Do would see them shortly. Ki removed the ropes from their wrists, but didn't yet return their swords.

Blays took in the pastel hangings and the bamboo benches along one wall. "This room's a little too nice to hack us to bits in, isn't it?"

"Whoever the Do is, he hasn't brought us here to murder us," Dante said. "He'll want something from us. Something he can't do for himself."

"Pick his own crops?"

The door opened. A guardsman entered, followed by a slim Tanarian in a tailored yellow jabat and black sandals with straps that rose to his knee. A second guard brought up the rear. Dante offered a shallow bow to Riza, but the man waved him off.

"What good does bowing do for anyone?" Riza said. "I know my place. Do I need you to show it to me? If I need you to bow, doesn't that imply I wouldn't be a lord if you didn't? Doesn't that grant *you* power over *me*?"

"Sure," Blays answered. "Right up until the moment you remember the extra special power granted to you by the armed gentlemen you brought into the room with you."

The lord smiled. "I am Do Riza. And I expect you're wondering why you're here. The answer is simple: I desire more connections with Mallon. I understand you carry some very strong ones."

"We don't represent King Charles," Dante said. "Nor any of the major lords."

"Glad to hear it, since I was to understand you work with merchants. Just as you had trouble getting into our nation, some of us have trouble getting things out of it. I'm not talking about anything untoward. I'm talking about simple trade."

"You can't do this through Aris Osis?"

"I should be able to, shouldn't I? They're my goods. I should have the right to sell them where I please."

"That's what most of us believe."

Riza clasped his hands and paced across the room. "Yet shouldn't a king have the right to govern what comes in and out of his kingdom? When there's a dispute between these rights, shouldn't the king's will prevail?"

"If I answer yes," Blays said, "does that mean the two of us illegal foreigners should leave? Forgive the suggestion, but isn't this the sort of thing you should have worked out *before* you smuggled us into your manor?"

"I'm about to make a vital decision. How can I be sure I'm making the right choice if I don't test my beliefs against other arguments?"

"Well, let me know when you've worked it out. In the meantime, got any wine?"

Riza smiled thinly. "I have decided that a king doesn't necessarily make decisions based on what's best for his kingdom. Sometimes, he makes decisions based on what's best for himself. We will proceed. Regarding Aris Osis, trade through its port is highly regulated. For a person in my predicament, it's made much easier if outsiders approach my agents seeking trade."

Dante nodded. "What if our employers were to come to Aris

Osis looking for something only you can provide?"

"Then I would be well-positioned to secure the right to provide it. We can start small. Once the stream's flowing, it'll be easier to divert it into other areas."

"Our superiors would be happy to expand their reach into Tanar Atain. But isn't it dangerous for you to be working directly with a pair of outlaw hari who've infiltrated the capital itself?"

"That depends on what you intend to do here."

Dante was suddenly aware that he didn't know how much Riza knew. "Right now, we don't even know why our associate was arrested. Once we've determined that, we might be able to broker a deal with the authorities. But we'll need a go-between."

"Or I could get you a permit to speak with them yourselves."

"There are permits for this? Why didn't they tell us this in Aris Osis?"

"Because it requires the favor of a Do, which I'm guessing you lacked. Even then, it would have been difficult to acquire until you were here in person."

"Get us our permit, and we'll get you your partners in Mallon."

Riza grinned and entwined his fingers with Dante's in a way that suggested the braid of a rope—either this was the Tanarian way of shaking hands, or Riza was crazy. He made various promises about beginning the process of securing them a permit, then left them in the company of Ki the servant, who showed them upstairs to a pair of rooms decorated with dyed pieces of glass and wall hangings that vaguely resembled harps made of dangling knotted strings.

"Okay, I'll ask the obvious question," Blays said once they were alone. "Do we trust him?"

Dante picked up a green glass figurine shaped like a rearing swamp dragon. "He was awfully fast to help."

"That makes you *less* suspicious?"

"There are political rifts here. We've seen them firsthand. If we're lucky, we just might be able to get Naran out of here without a fight."

"Are you betting on that vanishingly unlikely outcome? If so, hold still while I find some dice so I can part you from the rest of your money."

"I'm not counting on it. In fact, I'm going to explore other options right now."

Dante sent for Ki, asking where foreign prisoners were typically held. After Dante repeatedly reassured Ki that he wouldn't use that information to go running around the city unescorted, Ki informed him that foreigners of note were kept in the Blue Tower, which was within bowshot of the Bastion of Last Acts, all of which was a little bit to the north. Before leaving, Ki noted that even if Dante *did* try to sneak out, he would find it impossible to reach the tower.

Dante's mattress was elevated on a short wooden platform, presumably to reduce his exposure to bugs. He poked around underneath it and found an oval-shaped red beetle. He killed it with a pin of nether and bound it to himself. He was afraid it was going to have to make the journey on foot, but when he opened the shutter, he discovered the rain had slowed to a manageable rate.

He sent the beetle north. It gained altitude slowly, fighting hard against the rain. It trundled over sloped rooftops speckled with water barrels. Dante had seen a number of cities from above in this way and the view never ceased to delight him: the way the neighborhoods blended and shifted, the patches of greenery, the spokes and veins of the streets (or, in this case, waterways). What it exposed was that there was no single unifying plan, yet there was order nonetheless, one that emerged as the people who lived in a place built on the past and each other, forming everything from miserable slums to the soaring spires of cathedrals.

Ahead, the islands and manors stopped cold. They weren't in the innermost ring of the circle. There were three more: a narrow band of dirt, another stretch of open water, and then, in the very center of the city, a walled fortress several times larger than the Sealed Citadel.

This, presumably, would be the Bastion of Last Acts. A dock extended from its front gate, but even though there was no real way to deliver siege engines to it, the painted iron doors looked strong enough to outlast time itself.

Rather than the brick used elsewhere in the city, the fortress' walls were made of faintly blue granite blocks. There was both an inner and an outer curtain wall, regularly spaced with towers, along with a generous bailey and an intimidating keep. It was all very impressive. Really, given the general lack of large-scale fortifications elsewhere in Tanar Atain, its scale struck Dante as a little ostentatious.

As soon as he looked for it, the Blue Tower was obvious: a tall building of stone so blue it had to be dyed. It was set apart from the main fortress by a span of twenty feet. A wooden crane-like object had been erected on the Bastion's nearest tower. It appeared capable of lowering a wide plank across the gap to the Blue Tower.

Windows ringed the tower's periphery. Little more than slits, but plenty wide enough for a beetle. Dante went from cell to cell. In Narashtovik, the dungeons only held a handful of souls at any given time, but here, each cell held at least one prisoner, and usually two to four, which hardly give them the space to all lie down at once.

Dante only had to travel one floor down to find him. Naran sat alone against the back wall of his cell. He looked as gaunt as a desiccated lemon, his eyes open but unmoving. Cuts scattered his face, arms, chest, and the soles of his feet. They had been precisely drawn.

"Found him," Dante said in a low rasp. "They've been hurting him."

Blays' jaw tightened. "Bad?"

"Nothing that can't be healed."

"Ah, good. Can I kill them anyway?"

"No more incidents. If we can't talk or bribe him out, we're grabbing him and getting the hell out of here."

"That sounds so reasonable," Blays said. "And yet I have the uncontrollable urge to dull my swords on jailers' skulls."

Dante flapped the beetle back and forth in front of Naran's face, but the captain didn't so much as glance at it. Or blink. Suddenly afraid he was sitting up dead, Dante landed the beetle and confirmed Naran's chest was rising and falling. This accomplished, Dante turned the beetle in a circle, searching for anything small he could pick up, but the cell was swept clean.

Dante trundled under the door and into a neighboring cell. Those with three or four people inside were scattered with dried reeds to soak up any fluids the cellmates might find objectionable enough to start screaming about. Dante grabbed a shred of reed in the beetle's jaws, laboriously dragging it under the door and back to Naran's cell.

Naran still hadn't looked over, but Dante was already planning to go so far as to spell out his entire message, then bite Naran's foot with the beetle. He sent the bug out for a second mouthful of reed, then a third. He had almost finished spelling Naran's name when footsteps whispered in the hallway.

A key chittered in the lock. The door swung outward. A tall man stepped inside, a plain gray robe swirling around his long limbs.

Gladdic cranked his cadaverous face into a smile and turned it on Naran.

22

Less than two miles away, Dante choked on his own spit. "He's right here."

Blays made a show of looking around the guest room. "Thoughtful of Naran to save us from—"

"Gladdic! *Gladdic!*"

In the cell, Gladdic tucked his hands into his sleeves and gazed down at Naran. "Are you aware that the *Ban Naden* considers it an offense to keep every promise that one makes?"

Naran said nothing. Gladdic took a step toward him, lips slightly parted to show the tips of his teeth. "You are receiving spiritual wisdom, sirrah. It is polite to not interrupt. But it is rude to not listen."

Naran's eyes shifted toward the priest.

Gladdic waited a moment, then nodded. "Taim grants the measures. Among these is time, and it is a property of time to change things. When one makes a promise to do something, that promise is specific to the context in which it is made. Yet later, when it comes time to fulfill that promise, time will have changed the context in which it is now to be fulfilled.

"Sometimes, it no longer makes any sense to honor that promise—but men will do so anyway, mistakenly believing that this serves their *own* sense of honor. The *Ban Naden* states that this is a falsehood, for time has changed things. Since Taim has purposely allotted time to enact these changes, when you defy time, you defy Taim."

Gladdic allowed Naran to absorb this, then went on. "Thus, to honor Taim, I do not keep all of my promises. In fact, I scorn those who do. But I kept this promise: I have returned."

"Nothing has changed." Naran's voice grated like an iron plate dragged over cobbles. "If you wish to get from here to the Isle of Fanshain, that I can tell you how to do. But I can't tell you how they destroyed your demons."

"You believe this is about me, don't you? You pox-cocked sailor. This is about the *world*."

"And your wish to control it."

Gladdic went still for five long seconds. "How strong is your friendship with them?"

Naran snorted, eyes flashing. "Do you even understand friendship?"

"Answer my question or answer to the knives."

"I consider them my friends. I hope they think the same of me."

"Then I think we will test this. We shall see that they know where you are, and then see whether they care to come get you. What do you think of this?"

"I think—"

As Naran spoke, Gladdic glanced directly at the beetle. Dante severed his connection to it, senses returning to the room in Riza's manor.

"Gladdic's in the cell with Naran," he said. "They've been torturing him. Trying to get him to tell them how we fought the Andrac. Either Naran doesn't know, or he's got a spine of steel— but he looks broken."

"Then it's only fair that we break something of Gladdic's. Should we start with his face and work our way down?"

"The good news is he has no idea we're here. He wants to use Naran to lure us down here, then get the answers out of us."

"So he can fix up his demons and take a second run at obliterating every native citizen of Collen?"

"Presumably. We're going to have to think of a way to off him without ruining our efforts to petition the rulership."

Blays gave him a level look. "The petition's out the window.

Gladdic's paranoid enough that if he hears foreigners are speaking to the Drakebane, he'll pop by for a look. When he sees us, he'll bring the throne room down on our heads."

"So we grab Naran, then take a run at Gladdic?"

"Or just grab Naran. Either way, we can't tell Riza to call off the petition. It wouldn't make any sense. That means we need to get this done before we get invited in to see the officials."

"Then it's a good thing it takes less time to grow a new orchard than it does to schedule a meeting with high officials." Dante paced around the room, head tilted up at the ceiling. "So how do we get to Naran?"

"Well, you can start by telling me anything at all about the place we're breaking into."

Dante described the general layout of the Bastion of Last Acts. "The Blue Tower shouldn't be that hard to get into. This isn't the High Tower of the Tauren. It's just your ordinary pile of stone. It's surrounded by water, but we could always swim out to it."

"Swim?"

"When you're in the water and you move your arms and legs because you suspect drowning might be unpleasant?"

"Do you suppose a ruler who builds a giant castle surrounded by an even gianter moat isn't going to fill that moat with the plentiful water-horrors these swamps are literally swimming with?"

"Right. So how do we figure *that* out? Other than dipping a toe in the water and seeing if we pull back a stump?"

Blays shrugged. "Rat?"

"Rat?"

"Rat."

"Ah," Dante said. "Rat."

He called for Ki and received permission to go take the air in one of the island's many courtyards. While he pretended to admire a topiary of pink flowers trimmed in the shape of a thick serpent, he surreptitiously murdered a rodent digging at the base of the house. Once he'd revived it, he sent it scampering to the north end of the island, where it jumped into the water and continued swimming until it reached the ring of earth enclosing the Bastion.

Dante lowered its head close to the moat. The water was cloudy from all the rain, but he could make out the outlines of several placid, carp-shaped creatures lurking around and not causing any particular trouble. He backed the rodent up a few steps, then ran forward and leaped into the water with a rat-sized splash.

Through its beady little eyes, the Blue Tower looked as tall as a mountain and as distant as the moon. It churned its paws, holding its nose above the water out of habit.

Something tugged at it from below. Dante sighed and instructed it to keep going. A few seconds later, another tug jerked it to the side. The water frothed madly. If the rat had been capable of feeling pain, it would be squealing loud enough to make the dead wake up and tell it to shut up.

Within a minute, its bones were sinking to the bottom, taking Dante's spirits with them. His link to the creature fizzled away.

"Ziki oko," he muttered. "Swimming's out."

"Unless you want to try scaring Gladdic to death with our spooky skeletons." Blays thumbed his chin. "What *about* the skeletons?"

"Seeing as our flesh and guts require those skeletons to move around, I think it would be unwise to separate ourselves from them."

"Not ours. The rat's. Do the fish eat the bones?"

"They might. It wouldn't surprise me if they'd eat a steak, the bone inside it, and the plate beneath it."

"Would it be too much trouble to find out?" Blays said. "I mean, if you're not too busy petting the flowers over here."

It took him a few minutes to locate another rat. Blays kept watch while Dante flensed it. Once it was down to bloody bones, Dante reanimated them and lobbed them into the water. They sank into a dark, burbly confusion. Once it touched bottom, Dante sent it dawdling forward, stumbling over roots and unseen debris.

An hour later, it nosed up onto the banks of the rampart enclosing the moat and looked around. Seeing no nearby observers, it ran across the dirt and jumped into the ziki oko-filled waters. A few silvery fish darted up to it and took exploratory nips at its flanks and limbs, then drifted away, uninterested.

"Bones work," Dante said. "So what? How do we get Naran out of there with a measly rat skeleton?"

Blays plucked a black flower and sniffed its center. "That depends on whether Volo can get us a rope."

Dante made an inquiry with Ki, who informed him that Volo was currently out on business, but that he would see she got Dante's message. As the clouds dimmed, they were summoned to eat in a wood-paneled dining chamber. Pink and white fish were served on plates of powder blue glass. They were also brought frogs' legs, which Dante privately designated as tasting of the worst parts of both chicken and fish.

"I've made my initial inquiry," Riza informed them. "It wasn't rebuffed. Assuming everything proceeds smoothly, I expect to attain an audience within two weeks."

"Two weeks?" Blays said. "You Tanarians move with the swiftness of stallions. In Bressel, I'm still waiting to hear back on some inquiries I made three pairs of boots ago."

Preoccupied though Dante was, the meal was a highly pleasant one, with Do Riza asking any number of penetrating questions about Mallish politics and commerce. Through a combination of vagueness, fabrication, and the odd fact, Dante and Blays skated their way through the discussion. When the ice they treaded grew thin, Blays pushed the conversation onto Tanar Atain, and what Riza might be able to offer a trade partner. Riza waxed at length about Dara Bode's glass industry and the multiple workshops he operated.

"The wealthy are always happy to throw silver at exotic new baubles," Blays said after Riza had claimed Tanarian glassblowers were the best on the continent. "But while their fickleness can be a virtue when it allows us to conjure up new trends from thin air, it also makes them apt to flee en masse when something spooks them. Your country is fascinating, but I've detected an undercurrent of..." He gestured searchingly. "Conflict."

Riza smiled. "Then you're not blind. There is dissatisfaction among some of my countrymen. They believe the Vanguard of the Drakebane enforces ways of life that haven't been necessary in generations. They argue that years of peace and plenty have proven that the old strictures are outdated. But does this necessarily follow? What if we have peace *because* of these strictures, and this proves the Drakebane in fact does his duty very well?"

"Fine questions all around, but here's the one my superiors will be concerned about. Are these divisions serious enough to disrupt trade?"

The lord made a rolling motion with his shoulders. "If the Drakebane misreads the current, his opponents could become disruptive. But the swamps are deeper than anyone knows. In hidden waters, there are always other paths."

They moved on to other matters. When dinner concluded, Ki informed Dante that Volo had arrived. She was waiting for him in a courtyard that seemed to serve as a foyer for those who weren't good enough to enter the manor itself.

"We need a rope," Dante told her. "Of highest-quality Tanarian fiber."

She gave him a dubious look. "The best rope comes from the Hana Oso family. And it goes for an ounce of silver per foot."

"Correction: we need a rope of second-highest-quality Tanarian fiber." He handed her a small sack of silver. "Just make sure it's light and strong."

"Those are the only qualities good rope has."

"If you're such an expert on ropes, then I'm sure you'll get me a great one. I need it by tomorrow night. Then we're also going to need a ride to the Bastion — and out of Dara Bode. Can you do that?"

"If this is what I think it is, I can do anything you need."

She jogged off into the darkness. Dante spent the next day surveilling both the Bastion of Last Acts and the Blue Tower. Right after dawn and shortly before sunset, the crane-like contraption on the nearby turret was lowered, creating a bridge between it and the Blue Tower. During these times, guards and servants arrived to serve food, swap buckets, and clean out cells and the occasional corpse. Otherwise, the prison tower was left to itself.

That night, Riza provided them a Tanarian spirit called adda yin. It was made from adda, the plants they grew in the paddies. The liquor was a cloudy purple and tasted mildly sweet. Dante drank as sparingly as he could, but by the time the house went quiet, and he and Blays stole down to the dock to find Volo, his head was still a little loose on his neck.

Volo waited in her canoe. They nodded to each other and embarked. She paddled away with the stealth of someone who'd spent her life on the water. The night smelled like rain and mud and snails frying in nut oil. It was raining again and they only passed one other canoe on their way to the Bastion.

Volo guided them up to the mound encircling the fortress. A brick retaining wall rose to a height of four feet. Carefully, Blays stood, got a hold on the top of the wall, and pulled himself up. Dante followed. They flattened themselves to the dirt as Volo pushed off, heading for the lee of a nearby island.

The moat was two hundred feet across to the front dock of the Bastion, but the distance to the Blue Tower was half that. Dante had brought a pillowcase with him. He upended it, spilling a cohort of skeletal rats to the dirt. They looked up expectantly.

He set up a coil of rope and nicked his left arm. Moving his mind into the inner retaining wall, he opened a narrow hole in one of the bricks, burrowed half a foot into the hard-packed dirt beyond, then turned and ran parallel to the wall's surface. After two feet, he looped back toward the wall, emerging through a second hole two feet from the first one.

He nodded to one of the rats. It took one end of the rope in its teeth and lowered itself down the wall, reaching one of the holes. It scampered inside, dragging the rope behind it. A few moments later, it emerged from the second hole. As Blays leaned over the side and tied the rope fast, Dante sealed the dirt and bricks tight around it.

With one end secured, he motioned to the team of rats. They bit down on the free end of the rope, pulled it to the edge, and plopped into the water. On the bank, the rope uncoiled inch by inch as the submerged rats dragged it forward.

A nerve-rackingly long time later, dim white shapes appeared at the base of the Blue Tower. Dante coaxed a finger of stone from the side of the building. Using the rats' eyes for guidance, concentrating with everything he had, he wrapped the prehensile stone around the end of the rope. Barely able to feel what he was doing, he slid the rocky finger—now a loop—up the blue granite. Once it was eight feet up the side of the tower, he pulled the rope into the thick wall, embedding it firmly before clamping the rock down as hard as he could.

"Well," Blays said. "Now to find out if you should have sprung for that Hana Oso rope."

He unpocketed a short length of finger-thick cordage, looping it over the main rope and through the belt of his jabat. Once it was knotted tight, Blays spit on his hands and shimmied out on the rope, hanging beneath it. As he advanced, the rope sagged, lowering him closer to the black moat. Dante's attention darted back and forth between the two sections of brick and dirt anchoring the rope, seeking any sign they were about to crumble.

Hand over hand, Blays crossed to the other side, hunkering down on the narrow lip of earth surrounding the base of the Blue Tower. Dante had sobered to the exact wrong point where his head was still muddled, but not so much that it gave him any extra courage. He tied himself to the rope, grabbed on, and swung out over the moat.

Cool air floated from the water. The rope was neither rough enough to hurt his hands or smooth enough to make him lose his grip. It was light and strong, too, without too much give to it. Really, it was remarkably woven. As he climbed forward, he had the rather absurd thought that he should try to import some to Narashtovik.

A third of the way across, he glanced down. Flecks of silver moved on the surface. At first, he attributed this to the moonlight, but he'd never seen moonlight swim in expectant circles. He cursed and continued on. Halfway across, with the rope sagging him within two feet of the water, something splashed beneath him. Looking down, he glimpsed a fish spring into the air, tail flapping, jaws snapping. He would have sworn he could count every one of its arrowhead-shaped teeth.

He hurried on, gaining a few inches in elevation as he came closer to the tower. Another minute, and he swung his feet down to solid ground. He made doubly sure that his footing was solid before he untied himself from the rope.

Blays flashed a grin that looked a little too close to one of the ziki oko, then vanished. Dante listened to the frogs. Moments later, Blays reappeared a quarter turn around the outside of the tower, beckoning Dante over. Dante joined him, flicking the scab off his arm to feed the nether anew. He nearly squeezed a drop of blood into the water to taunt the fish; imagining the sound of the entire moat boiling, he thought better of it, and proceeded with the business of creating an opening through the wall of the tower.

The smell of sewage wafted from inside. They entered a room of barrels and boxes, pausing to let their eyes adjust to the near-total darkness. The skybridge to the Blue Tower had been pulled up hours ago and Dante was virtually certain the interior was unguarded, but he sent one of his skeletal rats bounding up the stairwell, placing a second to stand guard in the portal he'd opened to the outside.

He took the lead up the dank stairwell. Pale, chubby lizards clung to the walls. Dante exited on the penultimate floor. Behind one of the doors, a man sang softly to himself, voice dimming to nothing, as if the man had forgotten where he was, before resuming with the next line.

Naran's cell was clasped shut. Dante struck the lock with a blade of nether and stepped inside. The singing stopped—it had been Naran, singing a song of the sea, a sea he'd feared he'd never see again.

"Oh no," Naran said. "I've finally gone insane."

Blays strolled forward. "If we're the best your fevered brain can come up with, you really need to meet some more interesting women. Unless they don't interest you at all, in which case I'm flattered."

Naran grinned and tried to stand, but he couldn't get his feet beneath him.

"No, sit there all night." Blays extended a hand. "It's not like we're in the middle of a jailbreak."

Naran clasped Blays' wrist. The captain pulled himself halfway up, then fell back. Gritting his teeth, he strained his legs, neck bowing with effort. He rose.

Naran gave them a severe look. "Took you long enough."

Blays laughed and wrapped him in a hug. Naran burst into

laughter, too, deep gasps of it that veered toward anguish before resolving into relief. Dante hesitated a moment, then hugged the captain as well. Naran smelled ghastly, but Dante only felt anger. The sailor's once-strong body had been reduced to a dry stalk.

Naran withdrew and placed a hand on each of their shoulders. "I don't know what I've done to deserve such friendship. But I will work to earn it."

"My life has always depended on my friends," Dante said. "And they can always depend on me."

"Anyway, don't thank us yet," Blays said. "Not until you see what you're going to have to do to get out of here."

Naran quirked a brow. "After the last few weeks, I wouldn't care if we have to walk across hot coals."

"Let's make this a little easier on us." Dante called to the shadows and sent them over the captain, healing his cuts and erasing his aches.

Naran cocked back his elbows, nodding once. "Ready when you are."

They left the cell. Dante thought about using the ether to restore the broken lock, then thought it might create more confusion among the jailers to suspect Naran might have had help from one of the Bastion's own guards. As they descended the stairs, Dante found himself having to slow down to avoid outpacing Naran.

"So what are you going to do first?" Blays said. "Eat? Drink? Or eat and drink and eat?"

"I think," Naran mused, "that I will take a bath."

At the doorway Dante had opened in the base of the tower, he surveyed the Bastion and the distant rampart, then stepped outside. "Can you help him across?"

Blays rubbed his palms against the side of his tunic. "We'd better hope so. If his life depends on your arm strength, he's got a better chance trying to jump across."

Naran didn't have a belt and they hadn't thought to bring another. Blays looped the thinner cord over the rope spanning the shores, passed it around Naran's waist, and tied it off. Naran gave him a disgusted look, untied the knot, then redid it with a sailor's aplomb.

Blays secured himself to the rope and took the lead. Naran followed shortly behind him. Initially, it looked like it would be an uneventful crossing, but Naran soon slowed. A quarter of the way across, he stopped altogether, breathing hard as he let the cord around his waist support most of his weight. His breathing slowed. He advanced after Blays, but only made it a few more feet before exhaustion forced him to stop again.

Pressed against the tower, Dante frowned. If the rope pulled loose, or one of them fell, what could he do? Try to slaughter every fish in the moat? Raise an island under Naran and elevate him above the feeding frenzy? Wait, there was a better route: rather than worrying about saving them from disaster after it happened, he should worry about preventing that disaster in the first place. He could simply refresh Naran's muscles, allowing the captain to advance without getting tired out.

As he was about to execute this plan, Blays flipped around, grabbed Naran's collar, and pulled him along toward the other side. Dante laughed silently. He'd been out-clevering himself. Sometimes, the mundane solution was all you needed.

The two of them reached the other side and climbed up to solid ground. Dante hurried across the rope, giving the silver fish following beneath him a disapproving look. He got to the rampart, checked that the other two were okay, then moved to the outer retaining wall, draping his arms over the edge and waving slowly back and forth.

A canoe materialized from the darkness. Dante and Blays helped lower Naran down, then joined him in the boat. Volo shoved off from the wall.

"You should know something," Naran said. "Gladdic is here."

Dante grunted. "I saw him threatening you. Do you want to leave Dara Bode right now? Or do we stash you with our ally and go back for Gladdic?"

A shadow passed over Naran's face. "I can't ask you to do that."

"But you want us to."

"I do. But I also believe that if you leave him be, he'll come for you. He is obsessed with learning how to strengthen his demons.

I believe he thinks that if he can cure them of whatever weakness you exposed, he would become unstoppable."

"Better to hit him before he knows what's coming than to wait for him to hit at us. Blays?"

"We already had a personal and a moral reason to go after him," Blays said. "At this point, he's practically begging for us to detach his head from his body."

Dante had a number of questions for Naran, but there would be time to ask them when he was back. Or after they were all dead. They continued in silence to the dock at Riza's manor. Above, the house was quiet.

"Best if you two stay here," Dante said. "We can get ourselves back to the Bastion. Volo, if we're not back by three o'clock, take Captain Naran to Aris Osis. Naran, wait for the arrival of our friend from House Osedo. She'll take you wherever you need to go."

"I've seen too many storms to share your full faith in the gods," Naran said. "But if they care for this world at all, they'll be with you tonight."

Aware they might find themselves on the run and in desperate straits, they took their packs with them, carrying a small amount of food and necessities. Riza kept two small canoes at the dock, unadorned vessels meant for servants' errands. Dante and Blays climbed into one and headed north. Though it was now after midnight, lanterns burned in the windows of several island manors.

They came to the brick retaining wall, securing their boat and climbing up to the top of the dirt. Dante heard paddles churning somewhere in the distance, but the moat itself was silent. They crossed their rope over to the Blue Tower and entered its base. Dante had left his skeletal rats there as lookouts. He scooped all but two into his pillowcase, leaving one inside the bottom floor of the tower and sending the other scampering up the steps to scout.

The tower remained as silent as a blown-out candle. They came to the top and exited through a hatch. A soft breeze coursed through the night. Exposed on top of the tower, with no trees above them and no water within eighty vertical feet, Dante took a deep breath. Ever since leaving Aris Osis, he'd been trapped beneath the trees, confined to a boat, and surrounded by water filled with creatures that wanted to drink his blood, eat his flesh, and lay their eggs in his bones. This was the first time in days he hadn't felt claustrophobic and on edge.

Blays was clubbing him with a look that roughly translated to "Quit sightseeing and go murder our worst enemy." Dante glanced between the fortress and the city. In the brief time since they'd left Riza's estate, nearly all the lights on the other islands had been put out. The Bastion was just as dark.

Dante moved to the edge of the roof and faced the crane-like structure on the tower across from him. He'd spent a good deal of the previous day studying it—along with other aspects of the Bastion of Last Acts, such as the location of Gladdic's quarters. He removed one of the rats from the pillowcase, wound up, and hurled it across the gap in a high arc. It came down in the middle of the crane, claws snagging on a twist of rope.

The undead vermin got its bearings and climbed down to the crane's controls. In truth, it was more of a trebuchet than a crane, albeit a very low-powered one. The rat found the appropriate rope and started gnawing for all it was worth. A minute later, the last strand popped. A counterweight fell on one side, swinging a long wooden platform down toward the top of the Blue Tower.

Dante and Blays moved to see if they could cushion the racket of its impact without getting crushed. It came down on their uplifted hands with an uncanny lack of weight, as if it was made from a wood of cork-like lightness. They lowered it to a depression in the rim of stone hemming in the rooftop.

Blays climbed up on the platform, extending his right foot beyond the roof and pushing down on the lightweight wood. It neither snapped nor creaked. Blays made an expression so dour that he might as well have been walking into his own grave—remembering Blays' fear of heights, Dante bit his teeth together to stop himself from laughing.

Mumbling curses the way some men might pray, Blays hitched up his pack and walked onto the platform. The boards jogged under his weight. He altered his gait so his feet swept a fraction of an inch above the platform. The good news was this stopped the platform from jogging up and down. The bad news was it made him look like an idiot, and took twice as long as walking like a normal person would have.

Eventually, Blays reached the other side. He hopped down next to the contraption and folded his arms impatiently.

Dante rolled his eyes and started out. The platform was a full three feet across. If he'd been walking down a forest lane three feet wide, it never would have crossed his mind to worry about falling down, but now it was all he could think about. Ironic that after his days-long bout of low-key claustrophobia, he was now hampered by some rather serious agoraphobia. He really needed to teach himself how to fly.

He came to the other tower and stepped down beside Blays, who was happy to turn his back on the bridge across the sky. Dante pulled on a rope handle, lifting a trap door set into the roof. He motioned his rat ahead. It hopped down from step to step.

Dante nodded to Blays and started down. They reached the bottom of the tower without incident, emerging into the lawn between the outer curtain wall and the inner. After a quick glance around, they walked to the inner wall. Blays shadowalked through it. Dante opened a narrow passage for himself. Guards overlooked the bailey and the keep's front doors, so they moved to the rear of the keep instead. There wasn't a door, but they didn't need one.

They found themselves in a dark room that smelled like books. Odd. Dante hadn't seen a book or so much as a quill since coming to Tanar Atain. Interesting though this was, it had nothing to do with the heinous blasphemy he was about to commit against Taim. He'd already mapped his route out for himself and had no trouble finding the servant's stairs. They ascended to the sixth story and crept out into the hall.

They were halfway to Gladdic's room when the shouts sounded from outside the keep.

Dante pressed himself to the wall, straining his ears. "Tell me that's not about us."

"Someone could have seen the bridge was down to the Blue

Tower."

The shouts were growing louder by the moment. They'd passed an intersection a moment before. Dante backtracked and moved to the southern window, which had a view of the walls, the moat, and the city beyond.

Torches flapped from the entrance to the moat. Canoes were streaming into the water. Dozens more waited to follow them. Flames bloomed in two of the leading boats; flaming arrows darted forward, lodging inside a lone canoe speeding out to meet the disturbance.

"Strange," Blays said. "If I didn't know better, I'd say that was a revolution."

Dante wanted to deny this out of hand, but guards were racing along the outer walls, shooting bows down at the water. Lanterns flared to life in the towers. Dante had a clear view of the gates through the inner curtain wall. Against all reason, these were currently cranking open. Guards rushed in from the sides to push them closed, only to be fired on from the top of the wall.

Dante pressed his knuckles against his forehead. "Couldn't the people have waited to liberate themselves until tomorrow?"

"On the other hand, it makes for great cover for an assassination. We have to hit him right now. Before someone comes to bring him to the fight."

They hurried away from the window and toward Gladdic's room. As they neared his door, Dante bit the inside of his lips and surrounded himself in great clouds of nether. He ripped the door open and charged inside, flooding the room with pale light. The room was as sparely furnished as everything else in Tanar Atain had been. It took no more than a glance to know that Gladdic wasn't there.

"Ah." Blays' voice was thick with disappointment. "Back to Riza's with us, then."

Dante nodded numbly, hating the taste of the idea, but knowing that he had no choice but to swallow it. Just in case Gladdic was using sorcery to hide himself, he sent probes of nether to every corner of the room, but he felt nothing.

He closed the door and headed for the servants' stairs. "The Blue Tower's away from the fighting. If we hurry, we can get out the same way we came in."

Blays opened his mouth to reply. A door banged open. Sandals clapped down the hallway. Before Dante could tell which way they were going, four men spilled into the corridor across from him.

Two were dressed in the green of Tanarian soldiers. Another wore a long white shirt and white trousers, both of which were baggy and flowing. And the fourth was a tall figure in a gray robe with the sunken eyes of a man who saw evil wherever he looked.

Dante's heart took a flying leap from his chest. Before anyone could say a word—before any sense of recognition had entered Gladdic's eyes—Dante hurled a swarm of black blades at the Mallish priest.

Beside him, steel flashed as Blays drew swords. Gladdic's head jerked back. He lifted his right hand. Piercing white light blazed down the hallway. The shadowy blades slammed into the priest's ether, obscuring the hallway in black sparks, white shards, and gray dust.

The maelstrom of thwarted energy winked away. The floor and walls were blasted with grayscale streaks. Gladdic stood with his feet together, left hand at his waist, his right hand lifted in benediction.

"Galand and Buckler," he said. "Why are you here? Is that which is foul so obsessed with spoiling that which is pure?"

Blays spun his sword in a circle. "You're pure now? Is that as in, 'I'd like to purify the Collen Basin of everyone who lives there'?"

"I would have brought peace. You, however, are true servants of the nether. You bring nothing but death and war. Just as you have brought it to this place."

Dante locked eyes with the man in white, who he suspected was a local priest. "Do you know what he is? This man you work with?"

Gladdic scoffed. "*You* are the font of lies. The decay that rots not only flesh, but souls."

"He likes to be seen as the sword of the faith. The storm that will wash the heresy from the world. But when he thinks no one's watching, he uses the nether to create monsters—and commit acts that would sicken the gods. He *is* the heresy he fears."

Gladdic's face tightened like a fist. A transparent cube of light shimmered beneath his right hand.

"It's true, isn't it?" The priest in white turned a doleful eye on Gladdic, then smiled. "And that is precisely why we need you."

"These men are working with the rebels." Gladdic narrowed his eyes. "Every second we waste talking is another second their comrades spend slaughtering the innocent. For the heart!"

He splayed out his hand as if he was releasing a dove. Radiant lines shot down the hallway. Dante slung bolts of nether to intercept them, showering the ceiling with dark and fast-fading stars.

Blays charged forward, dropping into the netherworld. Gladdic lifted his palm and crushed his fingers together as if he were squeezing an orange. Blays stumbled bodily out of the shadows, crashing into the wall and sliding to the floor. Seeing him exposed, one of the soldiers lunged, jabbing toward Blays' ribs with a thin, quick sword. Still on the floor, Blays shoved off from the wall and rolled to the side, hacking across the back of the soldier's ankle. The man spasmed and dropped. Blays thrust his sword into the man's heart and popped to his feet.

The second soldier turned and ran down the hall. The priest in white dropped into a low stance. Ether lanced from his right hand, nether flowing from his left. Gladdic followed this with a blast of crystalline light that glinted with rainbow facets. Blays scrambled back, diving past Dante as Dante met the assault with a brute wall of nether. The energies collided with a thunderous whoomp, scorching the floor and sending everyone staggering back.

So far, the battle had been little more than a raw back-and-forth of power. The Tanarian priest was only moderately skilled, but Gladdic could turn back Dante's efforts with finessed doses of ether, while Dante was forced to club down Gladdic's attacks with awkward torrents of shadows. In a war of attrition, he'd be on the losing side.

He reached into the stone beneath Gladdic's feet, meaning to wrench it open and drop Gladdic to the story below. Gladdic snapped forth with snake-like speed, ripping the nether apart. The priest in white smiled and strolled forward, harrying Dante with a flurry of low-strength but constant attacks.

After two exchanges, Dante had picked up the man's pattern. He waited for the third flurry, then counterattacked with an arc of darkness that split apart as it neared its target. Blays, poised for an opportunity, speared forward, ready to gut the priest while the man was distracted by the nether.

Gladdic thrust needles of ether directly at Blays. Blays swore and dropped into the shadows, the light shredding into the wall behind him.

Blays reappeared beside Dante. "I'm no use here. I'm going for help!"

Blays turned and ran. For a moment, Dante felt Blays sliding through the shadows, but he lost all feel for him as Gladdic and the Tanarian hurled dancing geometries of ether down the hallway. Dante lashed out at each shape and line, casting the passage into a pall of dark mist. As Gladdic held his ground, the priest resumed his advance, decreasing the time Dante had to deflect his attacks. This was a sword that could have cut both ways, but Dante was too busy fending off Gladdic to make a serious offensive against the priest.

Dante fell back a step, then another. His foes pressed harder yet, flakes of deflected ether dashing against Dante's face. As the Tanarian took another step toward Dante, Gladdic paused to gather a mighty pillar of ether. The hair stood up on Dante's arms. When the blow came, he wasn't sure that—

Blays stepped out of the wall right beside the priest. His right-hand blade wheeled through the air. The priest yelled out in surprise and anger, the sound abruptly silenced as Blays' sword cut through his throat and spine. Blood painted the ceiling. Nether swarmed to the toppling body and the stump of its neck.

Gladdic's face grew long in surprise. He loosed a symmetrical storm of ether at Blays, who sprinted back toward Dante as fast as he could, his eyes bulging with effort and his face streaked with blood. Dante met Gladdic's assault and diverted it into the walls, battering them so hard that dust shot down the passage.

"Beheading?" Dante said.

Blays snapped his sword to the side, whipping off the blood. "I've spent enough time around sorcerers to know how to deal with you. I'd have cut him in half if I could."

Rather than slamming Dante with the column of ether he'd been gathering, Gladdic let most of it disperse, beginning a thoughtful and measured assault. They tested each other, feinting and probing, searching for holes in the other's guard.

Yet no matter how subtly or misleadingly Dante structured his attacks, Gladdic turned them aside before Dante had had the chance to develop them. Blays made a few trips into the nether, trying to flank Gladdic, but each time, Gladdic ejected him nearly instantly. While Dante had to look out for both light and shadow, and was thus unable to fully commit to defending against either, Gladdic seemed attuned to the slightest twitch of nether.

Dante quashed a smile. Swatting down an incoming beam of ether, he pulled the pillowcase from his belt and dumped his skeletal rats out on the floor. He motioned toward Gladdic. The rats bolted forward, claws skittering on the stone before gaining traction.

At the same time, Dante pressed hard against Gladdic with a chevron of shadows. Piece by piece, Gladdic carved apart his attack, then turned to the rats, who were almost upon him. With a small twist of nether, he severed their connection to Dante. The bones tumbled apart, sliding over the stone.

Dante flung a second wave of shadows at Gladdic, exchanging thrusts, parries, and ripostes, guiding the nether to dart and weave in complicated, near-random patterns. As Gladdic concentrated on picking off the screen of black darts, Dante quieted his mind. Touched the ether. And asked it to remember the rats' prior form.

Scattered bones swept together, cohering into complete skeletons. Focused on Dante's efforts with the nether, Gladdic didn't even seem to notice. The rats raced at Gladdic, throwing themselves at his legs and climbing up his trunk, biting and rending, blood staining their fleshless jaws.

Gladdic screamed in fear and revulsion. He slapped at the rats in panic, dashing one of them, then blasted three apart with shaky gusts of ether so overdone that the rats' bones sprayed against the walls. The remaining rats burrowed harder, drenching him in blood as he gathered a second round of light.

Dante yearned very badly to gloat, but that could wait until he and Blays were kicking Gladdic's head around like kids playing sally-ball. Gladdic had wriggled away too many times already. He reached for the nether.

And felt nothing at all—as if every shadow had vanished from the world.

23

Dante's mind locked up. Reaching for the nether and finding nothing was like trying to place his foot on a step that wasn't there. Like grabbing hold of a door handle only to discover the door was painted onto a solid wall. Down the hallway, the light snapped off from Gladdic's hands. He looked startled, then began to laugh raucously, bashing at the gnawing rats with hammer-like fists.

"Er," Blays said. "What?"

Dante scrabbled at the shadows, but they wouldn't budge. Neither would the ether. He drew his sword and ran at Gladdic. Gladdic's eyebrows hopped up his brow. The priest got to his feet, tiny bones tumbling from the folds of his robe, and hobbled down the hall, leaving smears of blood behind him.

Sandals smacked against the floor. A crowd of men swerved from around a corner. The soldier who'd fled the encounter had returned, but all Dante could look at was the two warriors he'd brought with him. Their faces were concealed inside helmets that resembled eyeless heads of swamp dragons. They wore mail vests, bracers, and skirts, but rather than being made of metal, or the lacquered wood he'd seen a few warriors wear in the Plagued Islands, the knights' armor appeared to be made of black scales.

In their left hands, they carried small shields shaped like black half-moons. In their right, they bore curved black swords lined with silver. The pommels ended in thick black spikes.

But even more commanding than their arms and armor was their sense of stillness. Their presence felt like the distillation of the dead of night in the dead of winter, when even the wind has found somewhere warmer to hide. At once, Dante knew that whatever force was blocking his access to the nether, they were the ones behind it.

Gladdic laughed again. One of the rats had gouged open his forehead and painted half his face with blood, tracing the creases of his crow's feet. "You know nothing of this land. How does it feel to know you'll die here?"

His knees buckled. A soldier grabbed for his elbow, helping him hobble away.

Dante pointed the tip of his sword at the knight across from him. "You're harboring a man who killed thousands of innocents in the Collen Basin. Step aside and go defend your gates."

The knight stared back at him, eyes hidden behind his helmet. "Are you servants of the Eiden Rane?"

"We don't even know what an Eiden Rane is," Blays said. He made a "let's get on with it" gesture with the tip of his sword. "Out of the way, will you?"

"Do you choose arrest? Or death?"

Blays sighed. "I should start carrying the heads of my enemies around so you guys will know I'm serious. But I'm not sure where I'd get a big enough wagon."

He lifted his swords in a guard. Dante kneeled and picked up one of the bloody rat bones, then edged beside Blays to cover his flank. Dante himself remained a fair swordsman—better than most, but lacking the training or instincts of a true expert—yet the possibility that the knights outskilled him didn't bother him in the slightest. Blays had skill enough for them both.

The knight nodded once, then brought up his sword along his center. The blackness of it seemed to be moving, like a river on a moonless night. Out of habit, Dante called out to the nether. Its absence made him feel naked. More than naked—more like he'd lost his arms and legs.

The lead knight swung a diagonal blow toward the intersection of Blays' neck and shoulder. Blays twitched up his left-hand sword, meaning to catch the enemy's blade and guide it past him as he drove his right-hand weapon into the knight's torso, a maneuver Dante had watched him execute a hundred times.

The black sword hit Blays' blade with a high-pitched metallic chink. Blays' eyes went wide. The knight's weapon sheared through Blays' steel, sending half his sword spinning away. Blays grunted, jerking his hips forward and his shoulders back, yanking his head away from the incoming strike.

The black blade hissed past his head. A lock of blond hair fluttered to the ground. Blays danced back two steps, gaze shifting between his severed sword, the lock of hair, and the knight's sword, which was now outlined in purple, shadows rippling across its surface. The pair of knights drew their shields closer to their bodies and advanced.

"Run?" Blays said. "Yes. Run!"

He turned and fled down the hall. Dante matched him step for step—this time, it wasn't a ruse. The knights gave chase, slowed by their armor. Blays grabbed a lantern from the wall and flung it in front of the two men. It smashed open, the oil going up with a blast of air, shooting light and heat down the corridor. The knights didn't make a sound, simply backed up and waited for the fire to fade.

Blays swung down a long hallway, breaking right at the next intersection. A few steps in, it became obvious it was a dead end, but turning around would expose them to the knights. His eyes fixed on an open door to a dark room. He rushed inside, Dante on his heels, and closed the door as silently as he could, enclosing them in near-total blackness.

For just a moment, Dante could feel the nether around him again. As soon as he tried to reach it, it once more clamped down tight.

"This is the plan?" Dante whispered. "*Hide?*"

"Why not? They'll have to go deal with the rebels eventually." Shouts and the ring of iron poured through the window, punctuating his claim. "Or I suppose we could climb out the window."

Dante moved toward it, then clasped his hand over his mouth and nose. "No we can't."

"We'll just knot together some sheets or something. Climb

down to the window below."

"Is that before or after you rip the iron bars out of the window with your bare hands?"

Blays rocked on his heels, then walked to the wall and reached out to feel the dim, X-shaped metal bars running between the corners of the window. "Lyle's twisted balls. Why would they bar a bedroom window six stories off the ground?"

"How should I know? Maybe they have a problem with giant bats. It's not—"

He cut himself short as footsteps sounded in the hall. They advanced without haste, steadily approaching their door, as if the knight could somehow see through the walls.

Blays held out his hand. "The horn."

"The what?"

"The swamp dragon horn! Do you still have it?"

Dante unshouldered his pack and opened the compartment where he kept his more interesting and precious items. He passed Blays the horn. "What are you doing?"

Blays gripped the horn like a knife. "Ambush."

Dante was about to ask what the hell he was talking about, but the footsteps had just arrived outside their door, stopping there. His torchstone rested in the same compartment he'd taken the horn from. He plucked out the small white stone, holding it up between his forefinger and thumb. Blays looked at it blankly, barely able to see it in the gloom, then nodded in recognition.

Blays crept closer to the door. The handle began to turn. Dante gripped the torchstone and brought his fist to his mouth. As the door swung inward, Dante blew into his palm, covering his eyes with his other hand. Blays looked down and away.

The torchstone flung piercing light to all sides. The knight paused halfway into the room, jerking his shield up to protect himself from being dazzled. Blays sprung forward, driving the horn toward the man's exposed armpit. The knight whirled and lashed out with his sword. Blays adjusted his attack into a block. As the black blade struck the horn, purplish sparks spat into the air.

The horn held.

The knight, anticipating that his sword would cut through

whatever it was wielded against, was already leaning forward, attempting to continue a strike that was now stalled. Blays slipped inside the knight's guard and speared the horn into the side of his neck. As blood showered into the air, Blays jerked his elbow back as hard as he could, ripping out the man's windpipe.

The knight reeled backward, dropping his sword and clutching at the loose tubes flopping down his chest. Blays flipped the horn to his left hand, took up the sword, and slashed it into the knight's ribs. The armored vest seemed to slow the sword a little, but it still passed halfway through his chest.

Someone shouted a question from down the hall; it sounded like a name. The query repeated, more insistent.

Blays closed the door, muffling the other man's calls. "There's blood all over the hall. They can't miss it. Don't suppose you've got your nether back now that this bastard's dead?"

Dante shook his head. "Think that sword can cut through the bars?"

"It snipped *my* sword easily enough."

Blays hustled to the window. He drew back his arm and swung. With a sharp metallic ping, the sword clipped halfway through the bar. Another swing severed it. As Blays chopped through the other bars, Dante dragged the knight's body in front of the door.

Blays took a final swing, sending the bars tumbling down into the night. "Say what you will about these pricks, but they have excellent taste in swords."

Dante leaned out the window. They were on the east side of the keep, lacking a clear view of the southern bailey the rebels had stormed through. Fires flickered to his right. Some yelling and screaming was going on, but it sounded stifled, as though it was happening within the lower floors of the keep.

He and Blays were currently fifty feet above the ground. If he'd had the nether at hand, he could have built them a staircase down the side of the keep. Or simply massacred the horde of people who were currently thundering down the hallway toward their room. Faced with nothing but mundane solutions, he had no idea what he was supposed to do. Die?

Blays was busy slicing up a sheet and knotting the thick strips together. Dante tied the other end of the makeshift rope around a stump of the iron bar that remained in the corner of the window. As Blays continued to work on his end, Dante picked up a bench and added it to the corpse-barricade at the door, supplementing this with a low, compact desk.

"I got blood here!" a man yelled directly outside the door, startling Dante back. "They're inside!"

Blays tied another strip to the rope, pulling it tight. "Bad news. I'm out of sheet."

"That's it?" The rope wasn't quite thirty feet long. Dante gritted his teeth and tossed the free end out the window. "Climb down as far as you can."

"It isn't long enough!"

"So Minn tells me. Now go!"

Blays' hand went to the hilt of his sword, as if he was ready to argue they'd have a better chance fighting off the small army that was even now starting to push on the door. Seeing the look on Dante's face, he calmed down, grabbed the rope, and jumped out the window. As Dante grabbed the sheets and swung his legs outside, someone banged into the door, jarring the debris he'd thrown in front of it.

Blays slid down the rope, looking about for other windows they could climb into. "There's nothing here!"

He reached the end of the line. Dante stopped just above him. The air smelled smoky. The clamor of battle echoed throughout the bailey. He'd overestimated the length of the rope: it would be a fall of close to thirty feet, directly onto hard ground. He glanced up. A pale face protruded from the window. The man produced a bow, nocked an arrow, and rather awkwardly drew it back.

"Jump!" Dante yelled.

Blays looked up at him like he was crazy, then noticed the archer drawing down on them. "Well that's just rude."

Dante coiled his feet against the wall, pushed himself off, and let go of the rope. Blays did the same. An arrow whistled past them and thumped into the dirt. Dante's head dizzied as he fell into empty space. He threw his mind in all directions, beseeching and berating the nether. The ground raced to meet them—

and smash them apart.

Like the lighting of a candle dispelling the darkness, the oppressive stillness vanished. Heart beating so hard he couldn't form coherent thoughts, Dante dived into the nether in the ground beneath them, softening it, letting water flood in from beneath. The two of them splashed down into a pool of thin mud.

Disoriented, he fought his way to the surface. The bow twanged above them, the arrow slapping into the muck. Dante reached the edge of the pit and pulled himself free. Blays got out beside him, covered from head to toe in blackish mud that smelled of rotten eggs. The color made for the perfect camouflage as they ran across the bailey.

Blays slicked mud from his face. "How did you know you'd be able to reach the nether again?"

"I didn't," Dante said. "But I figured that I could heal our broken legs once we dragged ourselves away from whatever was blocking it. How did *you* know the knight's sword wouldn't cut through the horn?"

"Because my intelligence is matched only by my keen powers of observation." Still running, Blays held up the knight's sword and the severed horn. Next to each other, it became obvious that the sword's pommel *was* a swamp dragon horn. "Did you see the nether on the blade? The knights use the shadows the same way you do: to cut through things steel can't."

"They're powered by nether. Since the swamp dragon's hide was hardened against nether, you thought the horn would turn the sword aside."

"You're the almighty wizard, you tell me. I'm just the guy who swings a few pounds of metal to make enemies dead."

Dante swerved around a dozen bodies strewn in the grass, half of them wearing the green of the crown. "Right now, I think we should both be the people who run as fast as they can from whatever the hell's going on here. I'm all but spent."

They made for the looming inner curtain wall. Reaching it, they walked briskly along it until they came to the gap Dante had opened through the stone. Blays took the lead through the narrow passage. He walked out into the wide avenue between the inner and outer walls and stopped short.

Across from them, a squadron of un-uniformed soldiers jerked to attention, brandishing a motley assortment of spears, short bows, and a single sword.

"Just who we're looking for," Blays said, keeping the point of his black sword pointed at the ground. "You're the rebels?"

The man with the sword cocked his head. "Rebels?"

Blays pointed back toward the keep. "The not-those-guys?"

"We're not 'rebels.' We are the liberators of our country. The fighters of the tyrant who beguiles us with illusions of freedom while knotting our bodies in traprope. And we are here to cut those bonds."

"Excellent! As you can tell by choice of mud, we're unsophisticated foreigners, and we're very confused about what's happening here. Would you be so kind as to ferry us across the moat so we can leave you to your glorious revolution?"

The rebel considered them, face slowly darkening. "What are foreigners doing in the Bastion of Last Acts?"

"Trying very hard to get out of it."

"Or pretending to. I think you're tools of the Drakebane. Spies sent to beseech our aid, and then take advantage of our pity by undermining us from within." He motioned to the other soldiers. "Arrest them."

Blays smiled and backed toward the gap in the wall, which he might be able to defend interminably, or at least until someone came up with the idea of attacking him from both sides at once, or shooting arrows at him. The soldiers trained their weapons on him and shuffled forward warily.

As Dante reached for his sword, the gears clicked into place. He let his hand fall to his side. "Is Do Riza here?"

The rebel lieutenant stiffened. "What do you know of the Do Riza?"

"I know he likes drinking expensive adda yin. And that he has a very nice estate."

"Though the beds could be more comfortable," Blays said, dropping his voice to a gossipy tone. "Then again, enough adda yin, and you could sleep on the point of a spear."

The rebel shifted his weight from foot to foot, then gestured to his troops. "Take them to Soulcast Tower. I'll find Do Riza."

Six soldiers escorted Dante and Blays to a staircase in the outer wall, delivering them to the domed top floor of a stout tower overlooking the southern approach to the fortress. Though they could still hear the clamor of fighting further into the bailey, along with the nearby groans of a makeshift physician's ward, the tower itself was serene and secure, its interior painted with pastel geometry, along with murals of knights in dragon armor doing battle with hideous creatures of all kinds.

Dante found a bench and picked off the patches of mud that were starting to harden on his skin. Blays seemed perfectly content to leave it be, leaning back against the wall and whistling an old Mallish drinking song.

They didn't have to wait long before Riza joined them. His hair was a bit bedraggled, and his jabat sported a few dabs of blood, but otherwise, he looked hale and untroubled. He dismissed the sentries, along with the pair of secretaries and bodyguards who'd accompanied him.

He stood across from them, face unreadable. "Did you accomplish your goals tonight?"

"One of them," Dante said. "The other one got complicated. Did Volo tell you who we are?"

Riza smiled like a Nulladoon player admiring the opponent's move. "Don't blame her for it. I could see the guilt in her face from the moment she arrived with you. When I questioned her, she did her best to hold back."

"How did you convince her?"

"I simply spoke the truth. That if what you were here to do could upset the balance of our plans, we'd lose everything."

"*Was* that true?"

"It could have been."

Blays sighed. "Are you two *trying* to talk like a pair of old lovers?"

"They've had this attack planned for a long time," Dante said. "I presume it wasn't scheduled for tonight, but they had to move it forward after Riza discovered we were going to break into the Blue Tower."

"Correct." Riza moved to the northern side of the tower for a better look at the keep. "If you'd succeeded or failed, it could have prompted the Bastion to enhance their defenses even further — and to investigate their soldiers for signs of disloyalty. Additionally, as your sponsor, I might have been implicated. Either event would have spelled disaster for our movement."

"Which is?"

"Why, the overthrow of the Drakebane Yoto dynasty, of course. What were *your* goals here?"

Dante glanced at Blays. Blays shrugged. Dante said, "To kill a priest."

"What was his crime? Heresy?" Riza's eyes twinkled. "If so, should I fear for the safety of the entire realm? None of us believe in your squabbling northern gods."

"Do you believe in the extermination of the Collen Basin? If not, we should be all right with each other. But we need this man dead. Do you think you'll take the keep?"

"I don't have to wonder. We've already done it."

"The man we're after is named Gladdic. He's a sorcerer, and an extremely dangerous one. You need to hand him over to us."

Riza's amusement left him as neatly as if he'd tucked it into his back pocket. "Your warning is appreciated. Once I better know who you are, I may decide to make him yours. Until then, I have business to prosecute."

He left them in the tower. As it turned out, there was no decision to make: along with the Drakebane, his cabinet, and his coterie of knights, Gladdic had fled from the city and into the swamps. No one knew where they had gone.

"I see." Naran lowered his eyes to the table. "If we try to follow him into the wilds, are we cutting the gray?"

Blays wrinkled his brow. "Are we whatting the what?"

"It is a sailor's term. When a captain finds himself on the fringe of a storm, if he's skilled, he can harness the winds to his benefit. But if he's not skilled, or he's too reckless, he can find himself overtaken and wrecked by that storm. We call that 'cutting the gray.'"

"We landlubbers have a term like that, too. We call it 'having a dumb idea.'"

The three of them were seated on rolls of fiber that were apparently used as chairs in the more formal parts of the land, such as the secondary dining hall in Do Riza's manor. Outside, starlight glinted from the dark waters. Smoke bleared the sky where it rose from the Bastion.

Lanterns burned across the city, with patrols of armed commoners paddling around in canoes to scout the waters for signs of resistance, but the city was oddly peaceful. If someone was to wake up for a glass of water and glance outside, they would have no idea an insurrection had just thrown down the government.

"This whole thing feels strange," Blays went on. "We have no idea where Gladdic is headed. I've got a bad feeling that if we try to find out, we're going to find ourselves sucked into a maelstrom of awful."

"What if we did know where Gladdic went?" Dante said.

"Then I'd like to think I wouldn't have said otherwise."

Dante reached into his pocket, withdrew a rat bone the size of an apple stem, and set it on the table. One of its knobs was stained red. "That's Gladdic's blood."

Blays grinned. "You can follow it right to him. Though that still leaves the small matter of navigating a bunch of swamps that were deadly enough before a civil war broke out amongst them."

"I think we can talk the locals into giving us a hand. They want this Drakebane captured or dead. If Gladdic stays with him, I can lead Riza straight to him."

"Sounds like that's enough to buy us passage. I'm in. Naran?"

Naran thrust out his lower jaw in thought. "As long as we confine ourselves to Gladdic. I have no issue with the Drakebane or these rebels."

"The rebels clearly have popular support," Dante said. "And from what we saw on our way here, they deserve it. Even so, I have no intention of getting involved in their struggle. If Riza tries to twist our arm into fighting for them, we'll make our own way."

As far as Dante could tell, Riza wasn't the chief conspirator, but wherever he stood, he was far enough up the pecking order that he would likely be embroiled in strategic talks for the rest of the night. Dante stressed to Ki that he had information that could deliver the Drakebane to the rebels.

Even so, it was close to an hour before Ki returned and instructed them to get into one of the Do's canoes. Ki brought them to the Bastion, where rebel eyes gazed down at them from the battlements and troops sang drunkenly in the bailey. The front steps of the keep were darkened with blood. They were led through a great hall into a smaller adjoining chamber furnished with a few low tables and a rack of seating-rolls. The air smelled of the fresh smoke of wood and the stale smoke of an unfamiliar herb.

Riza entered a minute later. His face looked tired, but his movements were energized. "You say you can bring us to the Drakebane. How can you know our land better than we do?"

Dante shrugged. "Magic."

"What do you care if we find the tyrant?"

"I don't. I care that he's traveling in the company of my enemy."

As Dante spoke, Riza leaned closer, craning his neck owlishly, watching Dante's face as if concerned that a predator lurked beneath it.

"This man is a priest, yes?" Riza said. "A man of your gods? What has a holy man done to make you want him dead so badly that you would travel into Tanar Atain and gamble your own life for the chance to take his?"

"He killed one of our friends." Dante squared his shoulders to the lord. "And in the Collen Basin, he killed thousands of civilians."

"Unprovoked?"

"During a war."

"Isn't one of the properties of war that when it comes, people will die? Guilty and innocent alike?"

"By definition, the innocent are innocent. Those that murder them have to be punished for it, if only to dissuade others from doing the same thing."

"What were his reasons for war? Were they just?"

"His goal was to pacify a region that wanted to govern itself, then kill everyone there and replace them with colonists from his own people. Even a Tanarian couldn't argue the justice of that." Dante might have said more, but Riza was leaning in again, staring into Dante's eyes as if they were texts that could be read. Dante drew back his head. "I'm sorry, but do I have something on my face?"

"You will forgive me. I'm merely attempting to ascertain if you've laced your claims with rido ashe."

"Rido ashe?"

Riza twirled his right index finger. "A manner of insidious sorcery. What you might call black magic."

"Impossible. Nether can't touch words."

"I don't claim that it can. I claim—I *insist*—that words themselves are rido ashe. That they can be used to cloud your mind, to trip it and ensnare it, to confuse it and turn it against what is right. You see, we already know what is true. All we have to do is turn our ears away from the babble around us and towards the words waiting in our hearts.

"This is why the Drakebane tells us it's so important for the people to say anything they like. So that the people, and in particular the people he designates to do so, can flood us with lies and nonsense. He fills the land with so much empty water that when we try to swim down toward the truth, we'll drown before we ever reach it."

Dante frowned. "You think giving people the freedom to speak their minds is a *bad* thing?"

"When those minds have been swept out on a tide of ideas as poisonous as sea water and as treacherous as the swamps? Absolutely. Thus we must limit what can be said—dike the seas, drain the swamps—until the truth thrives once more."

"This sounds like it could be a belief of convenience." Dante fully believed this, but tried to couch it in the casually interrogative tone employed whenever Tanarians engaged in ritual debate. "Couldn't this just be a way for you to protect yourself from having to listen to their arguments?"

Riza pulled back from Dante's face as if it had just split open with oozing sores. "That is the exact manner of falsehood that threatens to wash the truth out beyond anyone's finding. It's pure rido ashe. The very reason we must put a stop to it."

The room was suddenly very quiet.

Dante lowered his chin a fraction of an inch. "You'll have to pardon me. I was attempting to participate in dana kide."

Riza looked unconvinced. Blays cleared his throat. "This thing about rido ashe. That's why you're out to stick the Drakebane's head on a pike?"

"It's but a symptom." Riza's anger pivoted back toward the crown; Dante silently appreciated Blays' gambit. The lord strode across the chamber. "In obscuring and diluting the truth, our great master is better able to hide any number of unfortunate facts about his empire. Primarily, the fact that our citizens don't *really* have the freedoms they're promised, and are instead kept subservient through a number of cunning systems.

"Among the most wicked of these is the idea that anyone can build and own land. Is this true? Well, yes, I'm sure it's written into the law. But a whole spiderweb of related laws comes with it. The raising of land requires the payment of an initial tax that most laborers can't afford. Even if you can afford it, and spend the time and effort necessary to create your plot of land, it is then taxed even more heavily. Given that it can take years to make a piece of land profitable, most would-be freeholders wind up bankrupted by taxes. At which point the land is forfeited to the state."

Blays grunted. "Did they set it up to work like this on purpose?"

"Does it matter? Either way, the outcome is the same: what the peasants lose, the crown gains." Riza snorted archly. "This hasn't even broached the subject of the Body of the People. We are told that we each have our part and that each part is vital to the whole. Perhaps so, but some parts are clearly more vital than others—and rewarded in kind. The crown's answer to this, of course, is so what? Anyone can become whatever part they wish!"

"Now, I'm no genius, but I'm picking up the idea this might not strictly be true."

"A few people attain their desired part, yes. But most aren't allowed beyond the simplest trades, following the same rut laid down by their fathers and mothers. It is believed that just enough of us are allowed to drag ourselves out of the swamps to convince everyone else that it's possible."

Riza stopped his pacing and turned to regard the three of them. "I'm not particularly concerned whether our reasons satisfy you, because they are for us, not you. But this is why we fight."

"Our only concern is Gladdic," Dante said. "We won't interfere with your business."

"Which doesn't mean we want any part of yours. You came here under the guise of merchant enforcers from Mallon. To Volo, you revealed yourself as sorcerers. Where are you really from and who do you represent?"

"I'm from the north. And I represent myself."

"That's not good enough. My time is valuable. Continue to waste it, and I'll see you out of the city."

Dante exhaled through his nose, searching for the right admixture of truth and omission. "I'm from Narashtovik. I'm a priest of our holy order—but my involvement here is purely personal."

"Narashtovik." Riza tipped back his head, mouth pursed. "The city where the dead are on constant march against the walls?"

"Such reports are highly exaggerated."

"Fortunate for you. If your interest is merely personal, why should I be concerned with it myself?"

"Oh, because of the demons," Blays said. "Gladdic makes them, you see. And we know how to kill them—assuming he hasn't come up with anything worse in the meantime." He drew the black sword, purple light crackling silently along its edges. "Though this might help even the odds."

Riza's lips parted. "Where did you get that?"

"From the body of a man who was trying to turn *us* into bodies."

"That came from a Knight of Odo Sein." The nobleman put his right fist into his left palm, clasping them over his navel. "We will pursue the Drakebane. If you can help us find him, Gladdic is yours. We leave in two days."

24

The key scraped for its hole, metal on metal. Raxa's heart threatened to blast out the top of her head. She stuffed the stopper into the ink bottle and swept the documents into the desk's top drawer. She stuck her thumb and forefinger in her mouth, then snuffed the candle with a quick sizzle. As the tower door swung open, Raxa tumbled into the shadows.

Harald Walpole entered the room. He wasn't carrying a candle and from inside the shadows, the silver pools of his eyes seemed to be looking right at her. He held a dagger against his thigh. In perfect silence, he moved across the room, pressed himself to the doorway to the sitting room, and swung inside. A moment later, he returned to the larger chamber, sheathed his dagger, and went to the window overlooking the rooftop courtyard and the happy party that laughed on below.

He glanced back and forth between the festivities and the wall opposite the window. He'd been below, hadn't he? He'd seen light in his quarters, and rather than sending a servant or a sentry, he'd come to investigate for himself.

He made a noise low in his throat and walked back out. He closed the door. Locked it. Raxa waited for the shuffle of his first step, then eased from the shadows. Whispering a curse, she reached for the desk drawer.

The footsteps reversed. The key clicked into the lock. Raxa jumped back into the black and silver. Walpole reentered and moved to the desk. He leaned over the snuffed candle and sniffed. Reached out and felt its wick. He drew back to stand in brooding darkness.

Raxa could feel each second sapping her stamina. Should have grabbed up the papers rather than stuffing them into the desk—she'd been blindsided by haste, moving too fast to think things through. Now, she'd shifted in and out of the darkness twice, sucking away her juice each time. She could walk out right now, but if she did that, she'd leave the documents behind. Including an obvious half-finished copy. If Walpole found it, he'd take the original somewhere else. Or, from what she'd seen of him—decisive, hard-nosed—he'd destroy it.

Walpole exited to the hallway, leaving the door open. He returned with a candle and lit the one on his desk. He sat, planted his elbows on the desk, laced his fingers together.

From his bearing, Raxa wouldn't be surprised if he stayed there until dawn. And every second she wasted waiting for him to go away brought her that much closer to a rude boot out of the shadows.

She moved into the sitting room. Weak candlelight fanned through the doorway, but the walls lay in darkness. Raxa emerged into reality, opened the drink cabinet, and smashed a bottle of brown liquor in the corner. As the sweet smell of rum gushed through the room, she dived into the shadows and ran past Walpole as he charged into the room, dagger drawn.

She moved to the desk, flicked back to the real world, and stole the papers from the drawer, both the original and the copy. She closed the drawer with a tight wooden squeak. Vaulting back into the nether, she booked it through the stone wall and into the hallway.

The shadows were already getting slippery. Wouldn't have nearly enough to get her all the way back to the Fabians. Needed to get away from Walpole and out of the nether as fast as she could. She thought about climbing to the top of the tower to hide and sneak down later, then growled to herself and loped down the stairs. She'd barely gotten one floor down before Walpole's boots racketed on the steps above her.

Within a few turns of the stairs, she could see him coming

down behind her, his eyes shining like pockets of angry quicksilver. She knew the base of the tower was flush with the roof. On the last floor before the descent into the larger palace, she veered directly toward the wall, praying she had her orientation right and wasn't about to fall down the side of the palace. She emerged through the wall onto a flat stretch of roof. Tucked behind a row of shrubs, she returned to the world.

Hands shaking, she caught her breath, smoothing out her dress—she'd chosen something court-worthy, just in case of a contingency like this, but also unencumbering enough for her to work with if it turned out she needed to do any climbing or tumbling.

Not a hundred feet away, partiers exchanged witticisms and compliments, flattering each other like idiots, their drunkenly healthy faces aglow in the pool of light cast by the lanterns. A stone block rose behind them, housing the stairwell down to the interior. Raxa checked her hair with her hands. Seemed relatively intact.

She straightened her spine, tipped back her chin, and walked forward. Nearing the wash of light, she beckoned to a servant carrying a tray of goblets. He hastened to bring her one. Prop in hand, she slowed to an unhurried pace, meaning to draw as few eyes as possible on her way to the stairwell.

The door to the stairs banged open. Two soldiers spilled out, scanning the mingling courtiers. Down on the grounds, a guard yelled out an order, his voice echoing through the courtyards.

Walpole had already spread word throughout the palace. They'd be stopping anyone of lower birth than a prince.

The rooftop garden was fenced on one side by an iron railing overlooking a lawn of trees, grass, and flagstones. Raxa made her way to the rail. Keeping her hand inside her pocket, she folded the pages into a tight packet. She leaned over the railing, as if drinking in the cool night breeze, and let go of the creased parchment. They fluttered on the way down, threatening to snag in a tree, then landed on the paving stones by the base of the wall.

She lifted her glass of pink wine and took another drink.

Smiling, she moved toward the door to the stairs. One of the guards moved in front of her.

"Ah," he said, as if he hadn't thought about what he'd actually say until this moment. "There's been...an incident, milady. No one can leave unless they've been...checked."

"Checked?" She arched her eyebrows. "For what?"

"I don't know," he admitted with tangible relief. "Just come with me. Please. Milady."

Raxa did some requisite scoffing, then followed the soldier downstairs to the front hall. A business-like servant with the imperious bearing of a minor lady took Raxa into a side chamber and asked her to turn out her pockets. Raxa protested just enough to make it look like she cared about her dignity, then relented. Finding nothing on her more suspicious than a jackknife, the woman delivered her to the palace doors.

"Please wait here," the servant said. "I'll find a soldier to escort you home."

"No." Raxa's denial had been a little too fast. Her wit put a knife to her brain's throat and demanded it provide a reason. "I couldn't possibly. You need all your men here to help you in your search."

"But Lady Yera—"

"I live at the Fabians. If I can't walk from here to there without being assaulted by brigands, then I don't fear for myself. I fear for the *city*."

She'd been around the nobility long enough to inject this with enough arrogance that the servant had no choice but to smile tightly and let her go on her way. Raxa strolled across the mall. Soldiers were posted in a loose ring around the palace, holding lanterns up to watch the night. Was Walpole always this paranoid? Or were the secrets in his quarters just that serious?

She reached the facade of the Fabians, then turned and walked alongside them until she provoked a rat out of hiding. She pointed at it. A black bolt sizzled from her finger to its head. As it spun away, she was afraid she'd blown it to pieces, but it was still mostly intact. Crouching over it, she called to the nether. It hung back, then dislodged from its hiding spots, reluctantly filling her hand. Gathering the dregs of her strength, she sent it into the rat.

The rat shuddered. It lifted itself to its feet, collapsed, then forced itself upright, gazing at her with its dead and glassy eyes. Feeling disgusted with herself, yet powerful, she sent the rat scampering across the mall.

Watching through its eyes made her want to barf. She sent it onward, past a stationary guard, who glanced at the rodent and shook his head, muttering something foul. The rat crossed a paved space, approaching a high wall. Raxa searched for ten minutes before she found the folded papers. The rat picked them up in its mouth, then trotted back across the mall. When it returned, Raxa pocketed the papers, went upstairs, and collapsed into bed.

"Eventful night?"

Raxa looked up from her breakfast—breakfast in the sense that it was her first meal of the day. By the bells' reckoning, it was eleven in the morning. Maura had appeared to her right, gliding across the carpet without making a sound. At least not one that Raxa had been able to pick up over the clamor of her own chewing.

Raxa dabbed egg from the corner of her mouth. "Should it have been?"

"I couldn't say myself. There were some who considered it the event of the month."

"You mean the party. The one on the roof."

Maura rolled her eyes. "Don't tell me there was more than one."

"I couldn't sleep. I had the window open and I could hear them laughing. I'm sorry, I don't know what came over me—I just wanted to ask what it was for. I didn't think they'd invite me up."

"The only thing you have to apologize for is thinking I wouldn't want to go with you. Next time, yes?"

Raxa smiled. She spent the day convinced someone was about to kick down her door, tear her room apart to the floorboards, and drag her off to a dungeon. Instead, it was as quiet as the morning after Falmac's Eve, when hungover farmers stayed huddled under their covers, emerging only to grumble at their children to go see to the chickens.

She didn't bother to copy Walpole's order sheet. There was no point trying to return the original to his desk. After the last night, it was so creased and rat-nibbled that its return would be more obvious than its absence. Anyway, whatever it was for, it was too big to cancel just because someone else had found out about it. She tried to read it, but the combination of cramped handwriting and fancy words was too much for her.

At last, midnight. She put on her trousers and doublet, tucked the orders into her pocket, and shimmied down the balconies to the ground. The night before had been a tough time. The kind of thing that would scare some people into lying low for a while. She'd always thought that if you gave into the fear too often, one day, you'd go to ground and never find the guts to come up again. The only thing was to get back out there the very next day and prove that the last time was nothing. That the world should be afraid to run into *you*.

On the off chance someone had been watching their meets, she and Sorrowen had arranged to rendezvous at a different park not far from his monastery. As usual, he was already there waiting for her. Without a word, she handed him the two sheets of parchment.

As he read, raw glee spilled across his face. Raxa made a note to invite him to play cards with her some time; he had so little control over his expressions she'd take him for every penny in his pocket.

Finished, he jerked his head up from the orders, waving them around like they were on fire. "This is it! The order!"

"For what? Weapons? Mercenaries?"

"I don't know."

She gave him a pained look. "I thought you said this was the order."

"Yeah, but it doesn't say what it's *for*. Other than so much money that these people should be ashamed they're spending it on a war and not a cathedral to the glory of the gods. But it does tell us where the goods are supposed to be delivered." He peered down at the page. "Keller's Pier. Three nights from now."

"They're making the exchange during the night?"

Sorrowen bobbed his head. "Two in the morning. That's...

weird, isn't it? Sounds like something you'd do."

"And I deal in things I've taken from other people. Makes you wonder what they're buying that they don't want anyone else to see it?"

"Camp followers?"

Raxa was too exasperated to smack him. "What about you? Heard any prime dirt? Or just the usual stories of the gods being awful to each other?"

Sorrowen looked perturbed by her borderline heresy, then rolled back his eyes in thought. "There is one thing. But it's a little strange. The masters have been preaching about the return of Daris—and the need to kill him." He chuckled heartily. "Can you believe it?"

"What's a Daris?"

"Raxa! Have you never even set foot in a church?"

"Not since I learned to walk on my own."

He swayed back from her, as if afraid of breathing the unclean air that surely surrounded her, then sighed. "If Dante hears I had to tell you this, he'll make sure you spend the next decade locked in a seminary. The story of Daris is told in both Mallon and Narashtovik. Do you at least know about Carvahal and the fire?"

"Who's Carvahal?"

"Oh, for the love of—!"

"He stole the fire from Taim," Raxa said. "Who was keeping it for himself like a greedy asshole. Carvahal's the one who brought it down to humans."

"Correct. Except for the part where you called Taim an asshole. Although I guess in this story he kind of is, because the first thing he did when he saw the theft was gather up his army to go kill Carvahal. Carvahal could see he was going to get clobbered, so he passed the torch of flame to Eric the Draconat, the greatest dragon-slayer in the world, so *he* could climb up to the heavens, fight Daris—Daris being a dragon, you see—and make Daris join his side."

"Why the hell would Daris join Eric if Eric was trying to kill him?"

"Because...I mean...that's how honor works."

"Oh," Raxa said. "No wonder I've never thought much of it."

Sorrowen blinked, then plunged onward. "Eric beat Daris, so Daris and all of his other dragons had to help Eric and Carvahal go fight Taim. After the biggest fight the world had ever seen, Taim slew Daris, and the whole world tilted. But just as Taim was about to win the day, take the fire, and thrust humans back into darkness, Eric stabbed him in the heart, forcing him and his allies back into the heavens.

"So we kept the fire. And it's kept us warm and defended us against the night ever since. Eric is the big hero of this story, but as you can see, he couldn't have done it without Daris' aid. I mean, doesn't this seem weird to you?"

"That the father of time went to war against a giant lizard to get back his torch?"

"Daris was a hero. But when the masters discuss his coming return, they warn us that we'll have to stand against him. Now why would they think that?"

"Because they love Taim?"

"I think it's because of his origin. Before he died and Jorus took over, Daris was the sole ruler of the northern kingdom. Which, given what the people down here think about the north, marks him as untrustworthy at best, if not downright evil. I think the priests are trying to get people used to the idea that they have to fight the north—to fight Narashtovik."

"Mallon can't even beat Collen in a fight. So you think that for their next move, they're going to declare war on Collen *and* Narashtovik?"

"Maybe they're going to retake Collen, then turn against Narashtovik for helping Collen. That's what Dante's afraid of. That's why it's so important for us to stop them in Collen."

"I know what we're here to do," Raxa said. "But I don't know anything about your holy books. You'll have to run all this past Galand. Anyway, let him know we might be about to break open Mallon's plans. I'll scout the pier where they're dropping off the goods. Meet me back here at midnight in three days."

With her night's work expanding before her, she jogged east toward the river. As she neared the docks, the smell of cool fresh water drifted through the streets, along with chatter from the wharfside pubs. She entered the first she found, ordered a drink, and asked where to find Keller's Pier. She had a story all cooked up about what her business there was, but the drunk next to her didn't care about anything except that she was sitting next to him.

She stayed a few minutes in gratitude for the information, then headed north along the mile-wide river. Most of the piers were silent and dark, but at a handful of them, stevedores wheeled goods into waiting warehouses. Keller's Pier was blocked off by the bars of a tall iron fence. A dozen docks extended into the lapping black waters. Raxa toured around the fence to the other side. Several big warehouses occupied the grounds. Big enough to hold just about anything you could ever want to buy.

As she turned around for another pass, a watchman wandered out from one of the warehouses. Raxa headed on past and didn't come back.

Back at the Fabians, she kept her head down. Three days went by like nothing. The evening of the deal, she sat down to supper without much appetite. She didn't know what was going to go down that night. Could be they'd stumble into bad luck, have to run out from Bressel and not look back.

She found her eyes kept drifting to Maura. Raxa knew the score. A mark was a mark. When you were done with them, you tossed them aside like a spent corn husk or a shoe too worn to mend. The night before, she'd kept Maura up late drinking so the lady wouldn't bat an eye when Raxa planned to say she was tired from the previous day's festivities and meant to bed early.

They'd gone through a bottle of good wine apiece. In the middle of making good headway on a third, Maura had leaned back in her chair—or, more accurately, lolled back in it—and the typically arch if currently sloppy look on her face had been replaced by something thoughtful.

"I have a confession to make." Maura pronounced each word carefully, separating them from each other like she was plucking bay leaves from a stem. "When you first came here, I didn't come to your aid because I am a nice person."

Raxa moved to object, but Maura waved her off. In the dim candlelight, she suddenly looked too small for her chair. "No, Yera, I am an *effective* person, and the core of being effective is understanding your limitations. Mine include the fact that I'm not nice. But since you've been here, I wish that I were, because perhaps it would cause more people like you to be a part of my life."

Now, sitting at the dinner table a night later, Raxa felt an unexpected sadness. Tonight might be the last night she heard Maura's proper modes of speech, her crooked little sense of humor. Raxa had always hated the nobility, but if she'd been born into it like Lady Yera was supposed to have been, she and Maura would have been friends.

She stayed at the table a while longer, stretching out the moments, then stifled a yawn, smiling in embarrassment. "I'm sorry, I think I had a little too much fun last night."

She excused herself to her room, undressed, then blew out her candles. Sitting in the darkness, she *was* terribly tired, but she made herself stay up until it was time to climb down to the street and get her ass to the park.

That night, with a mission on the line, she was the first to arrive. Sorrowen showed up five minutes later, looking mildly spooked.

Raxa assessed him. "You're nervous?"

"No," he said. "Yes."

"Good. We're about to put ourselves in danger. You work with someone who isn't afraid of that, and they'll *put* you in danger. But the enemy won't know we're there—and if they find us, they'll have no idea what we're capable of."

The strain on his face eased marginally. "I keep the loon in a hole in the oak tree up the lane from my monastery." He described the exact spot and how to use her blood to active it. "If anything happens to me, you'll need it to speak with Dante."

They headed toward the river. Sorrowen was dressed in the clothes he'd traveled to Bressel in, plain sturdy coat and trousers. They didn't look like predators or prey and drew no attention. At the docks, rats scurried for spilled grain and scraps of fish. She and Sorrowen each killed one, returned them to whatever weird not-life the nether provided them, and pocketed them.

Lanterns were already glowing from the docks of Keller's Pier. Guards patrolled, swords on hips, but rather than the blue of the king, they were wearing plain brown clothes. Raxa hunched beside a warehouse, watching them make their rounds. Nobody seemed to be patrolling outside the iron fence.

They circled around the back of the neighboring warehouse. Raxa helped Sorrowen climb up to the roof. He was terrible at it. Almost dashed his brains out twice. She prayed they wouldn't have to make a daring escape. They crawled across the gently sloped rough wooden shingles, setting up against a stone chimney with a vantage of the docks.

They'd left their rats down on the ground. They sent them meandering through the iron fence, moving from shadow to shadow until they were positioned near the base of the piers. Raxa still couldn't hear much through her rat's ears, but at least she could see everything that it could.

They waited, listening to the wash of the river, the crunch of the guards' boots, and the thunderous peals of laughter from the pub down the way.

An hour later, carriages clattered through the darkness. Three vehicles arrived at the rear gate to Keller's Pier and were allowed inside. The carriages stopped at the front of the warehouses and disgorged a surprising number of men. A tall man got out, broad-shouldered, folding his arms as he watched his soldiers arrange themselves across the grounds and his servants unload heavy boxes from the backs of the carriages.

"That's our man," Raxa whispered. "Walpole."

Sorrowen nodded, so earnest that she had to look away or burst into laughter. As another man scooted out from the carriage, arranging his gray robes around himself, Raxa's grin died on her face.

"*Shit*. Kill the rat."

"What? Why?"

"Kill it now!"

She slashed the connection to her rat. A flash of darkness filled her eyes, then blanked out. Beside her, Sorrowen jerked. He squinted, then turned to her, young face bent in confusion.

She pointed. "See the priest?"

"You think he would have sensed us?"

Raxa nodded. "And now I'm wondering what they're doing that requires the skills of an ethermancer."

The priest fussed with his robes a moment longer, then moved to stand alone, slowly swiveling his head to watch the grounds. Servants milled about, coagulating into small groups. As minutes crept past, Raxa shifted position against the hard shingles.

A soldier pointed upstream, calling out an order. Servants drifted toward the docks. Raxa followed their gaze up the river. White squares cohered from the gloom. Sails. The hulls were patches of blackness against the starlight shimmering on the river. A small armada came to bear, sidling up to the docks and tying fast. The ships were long and slender, riding low in the water.

A woman debarked and made her way to land, long loose hair flapping down her back. Walpole moved before her. They clasped hands. She talked for a while as Walpole nodded gravely. Sailors came to shore, gathering to the side. In time, the woman gestured to the pier she'd walked down. She and Walpole made their way to one of the ships, climbed aboard, and disappeared belowdecks.

They were gone for several minutes. When Walpole emerged, he gestured to a cluster of soldiers waiting at the foot of the docks. They fanned out, going from boat to boat. Walpole moved on to a second ship, pacing its top deck before descending to the hold.

Once the inspections were done, Walpole and the woman from the ships met on dry land. Teams of servants lifted the heavy boxes and brought them before the two officials. Walpole flipped open a lid. Heaped silver shined in the night.

The woman clapped, calling to her sailors. They loaded the chests into two of the ships. The woman talked with Walpole a while longer, then returned to her crew. The pair of ships they'd taken the cash into cast off and started rowing upstream, leaving the many other boats behind at the docks.

A few of Walpole's people went into the warehouses. Most returned to the carriages, which exited the gates at the rear, hoofbeats fading into the night. Within minutes, the piers were quiet again, patrolled only by a trio of sentries.

"Need to find out what's in the boats." Raxa propped herself on her elbows. "Ready to knife some watchmen?"

"You want to kill them?"

"That's typically what knives do." She let him twist a moment, then grinned. "No knives. Not unless something goes very wrong. I'll sneak onto the boats while you keep watch."

They climbed down the back of the warehouse and walked two piers north of Keller's. Raxa ran Sorrowen through the plan, which was as simple as they got: she'd shadowalk onto the docks and check out the ships while he made sure nothing came up on her while she was belowdecks. They edged south along the river bank, stopping one pier away.

Sorrowen hunkered down in the shadow of the dock. Raxa stepped into the shadows. The river and its reflected stars were already silver and black; in the netherworld, they glowed with the intensity of a black sun. She ran forward, stepping lightly over the mud at the edge of the shore. The iron fence ran all the way to the water. She crossed the shallows, the water feeling as thick as sand beneath her feet, then jumped up the side of the closest dock, grabbing the edge of its decking and swinging herself lightly up top.

The three sentries remained in the yard, mostly watching the fence while casting occasional glances at the dark piers. Raxa hurried past the nearest pair of boats berthed at either side of the dock, putting a little more distance between herself and the guards, then jumped aboard the next ship she came to.

The deck was clean and bare. She found the ladder belowdecks, dropping to the bottom and landing in a crouch. After a glance to all sides, she fell out from the shadows. She stood in a square of starlight. The rest of the hold was as dark as death. It smelled bilgey, but also strongly of pinewood and pitch.

She let her eyes adjust. The hold was mostly empty, a few barrels and crates secured against the walls. Raxa moved from the ladder, got out her flint, and lit a candle. She pried open the lid of a barrel, releasing the odor of potent beer. The one next to it held salted fish. Several others were empty. She checked from stem to stern, even knocking on the bulkheads near the front and back to search for hidden compartments.

Finding nothing of interest, she ascended to the deck. A breeze tousled her hair. The grounds between the docks and the warehouses remained quiet. Dropping into the shadows just to cover her advance to the next ship felt like a waste. She crossed to the dock, crawling on her belly to the boat across from her. Its hold was every bit as uninteresting as the first one had been.

A sense of unease dripped into her stomach like sour liquor. She moved on to the next pair of ships at the end of the long dock. Their cargo was yet more salted fish and bitter-smelling beer whose odor was surprisingly similar to the planks of the hull. Bare essentials of sustaining a crew during a voyage. Nothing to justify the expense in Walpole's order.

Had they already carted the goods inside? Raxa ran the scene back through her mind: Walpole and a few of his people had gone onto the boats; Walpole had paid the woman; she'd left with her people; Walpole and all but a few soldiers had left. No stevedores had entered the ships. Either the goods had been small enough for Walpole and his soldiers to remove themselves, and they'd brought down a whole fleet to protect those goods from pirates, or the cargo was still onboard.

She climbed back up to the deck. Not wanting to take any chances, she hopped into the shadows, ran down the pier as fast as she could, hit land, and moved on to the next dock. She jumped aboard the closest ship and down the hatch to the hold. As soon as her feet hit the boards, she bounced back to the real world.

She lit her candle, grabbed the iron crow from its pegs on the wall, and slid its flat end under the lid of a crate. The nails held fast. Raxa bore down on the bar, grunting with effort. With a wrenching squeak, the lid flew open. She stumbled back, the iron crow flying from her grasp. Before it could clang to the floor, she threw herself forward, catching it and landing with a thump.

Heart beating harder, she leaned over the top of the crate. It was filled with dried apples. She swore, the words echoing closely in the damp, piney hold. She sniffed the air, then frowned down at the foodstuffs. She lifted her eyes to the ceiling. What if she wasn't finding anything because there wasn't anything to find? What if the order—

Shouts sounded from outside. One was a man with a deep voice. The other was Sorrowen.

She clambered up the ladder and peered over the gunwale. The gray-robed priest stood on the dock halfway toward the boat, back turned to her. Sorrowen moved toward the foot of the dock. A spark of ether shimmered in the priest's hand.

"Get out!" Sorrowen's command quaked with nerves. He gestured as if to ward the man off, but his eyes were pointing down the dock. Toward Raxa.

He wanted her to run. To get out so that someone could tell Galand what they'd found. Sorrowen was clearly scared—as the ether grew in the priest's hand, the boy's widening eyes mirrored its size and brightness—but he was still walking forward, commanding the priest's attention. He was young enough that he probably thought his death would make any difference.

Light seared from the priest's hand, trailing an incandescent stream. Sorrowen's arm squiggled forward spasmodically, shadows spraying everywhere in an undisciplined spurt. Raxa glanced at the dark waters. A quick dive into the shadows and the river, and she could be out of Keller's Pier without anyone having known she'd been there.

Yet something held her back. Maybe it was that Sorrowen was young, no longer a child but not yet an adult, and she'd never been able to let the young get ground up in the gears of the world.

Or maybe it was the latent urge to push her new powers. And learn what she could really do.

Couldn't shadowalk up on the priest. He'd feel her coming, boot her out. Probably when she was so close that he'd rip her apart before she had time to defend herself. She bit open her lip and ran forward, the dock's boards bouncing under her feet. She spread her hands wide to scoop up every shadow she could find. Nether streamed to the warm blood sliding down her chin.

She bent it into a big black scythe and hurled it at the priest.

He continued to hammer at Sorrowen, straight rays of light blasting into the younger man's whorl of shadows. Her blade sped toward the priest's back in perfect silence. She held her breath, waiting for it to pass through him and for his body to slide in half.

He whipped his head around, pushing his right palm forward. A tight line of whiteness glared from his hand. It struck the scythe in the center, shattering the shadows. A few quick pokes of ether took care of the few shards of nether still coming his way.

Raxa had sent a whale of a strike at him, and he'd deflected and destroyed it with a few precise counter-thrusts. Because he was more skilled? Or because that was simply the way the nether and ether worked? Galand had talked about this stuff, but she couldn't remember what he'd said.

She lobbed a needle of shadows at the priest. Harried on both sides, he barely had time to shape his counter. A finger-sized rod of light lanced toward her needle, obliterating them both. So it was a game of quickness and subtlety. Rather than broadswords, they were dueling with thin, twitchy blades.

She smiled. Sorrowen locked eyes with her, grinning back. A blast of ether illuminated his face, yanking his attention back to the priest. Raxa jabbed at the enemy from her side, obliging him to turn to her before he could set up a killing sequence against Sorrowen.

Face reddened with wrath, the priest came at her with a flurry of attacks. It was too fast for her mind to follow, but somehow, her hands spun out one answer after another, taking on a rhythm like fencing—or no, more like *music*, like listening to it or like inventing a song as you played, the notes and nether bending in ways you could never have predicted, but which always sounded right in hindsight.

She became lost in it. Like the nether was wielding *her*. Everything in front of her grew sharper and brighter while everything around her dimmed out. Time slowed. And then it was something deeper than music. Deeper than thought. Like she imagined the animals felt, the wolf out on the hunt or the owl in flight.

She'd never felt much for religion, no more than a light stirring or the occasional yearning toward something more. Yet as she wielded the shadows, she knew what it was to believe: and better, to speak with powers greater than herself.

They'd only been dueling for a matter of seconds, but already, the nether was getting sticky, slower to arrive at her hands. Across from her, Sorrowen's face was taut with effort. The priest looked tasked, too, but there was no telling how much juice he had left in the squeeze.

She couldn't seem to get past his defenses. But she could still disrupt them. She flicked a needle at his head and followed this with a denser wedge of shadows. As he gestured to parry the first strike, she sent the wedge driving downward, hammering into the planks a few feet from him. The boards splintered apart and upended beneath his feet, dropping him half a foot. He yelled in surprise.

Sorrowen jerked his hand forward, as if swatting at a spider. Darkness zipped into the priest's back. He cried out, jerking forward, still caught in the broken boards. Raxa drove a black spike into his forehead.

Sorrowen grinned, then grimaced in horror at the sight of the slack body. No time for feelings. Soldiers were already streaking from the warehouse toward the docks. Raxa flicked bolts of nether from her hand like throwing darts. They converged on the lead soldier, cartwheeling him to the dirt. She grabbed Sorrowen's sleeve—he was still staring at the dead priest—and pulled him along the pier toward the river.

An arrow hissed past them, splashing down in the water. Raxa skidded to a stop at the end of the pier. There, a rowboat bobbed in the current—Raxa had spotted it while checking out the boats, noting it in the space in her mind dedicated to making sure she always had another way out, if not two or three. She shoved Sorrowen inside and untied the rowboat's rope from the cleat. They shoved off, Raxa rowing hard, the current sweeping them downstream from Keller's Pier.

"His body was just..." Sorrowen said. "He was *gone*. Like a shank of beef."

Raxa dug her oars into the water. "Yep."

"But how can that be right?"

"He shouldn't have gotten in a fight with us. You okay?"

"Yeah. Yes. I think. Are you?"

She nodded, gazing back at the pier. The soldiers were swarming into one of the smaller warships. Within moments, they were free of the docks, oars punishing the water. They'd be on the rowboat in another minute.

"Got much juice left?" she said.

"Juice?"

"Nether."

"Uh. Some." He glanced back at the advancing ship. "Not enough to fight an army!"

"We only need a little. In a few seconds, I need you to put a shadowsphere on the rowboat. Extend it past the gunwales, but don't cover the whole boat—leave the stern uncovered."

"You want me to hide us so they can still see us?"

"Just do it, okay?" Behind them, a man called out, spotting them. Raxa rowed on, giving them a few more seconds to catch up. "Now!"

They were swallowed in darkness. For an instant, she was afraid she'd been shot in the head with an arrow and was now dead, but she could still smell the river, feel the water tugging at the oars, hear the soldiers calling out in suspicion. She pulled in the oars.

"We're going over the side," she said. "Keep your head low and the sphere up. Follow me toward the closest dock. Us aweigh!"

She rolled over the side, plunging into the water. It was cold enough her whole body went tight. She swam underwater toward the west, pulling free of the dark sphere, then surfaced, keeping no more than her nose and eyes above water. Sorrowen surfaced right in front of her, making her flinch back. They were almost parallel with a dock fifty yards back toward shore. Avoiding any splashing, Raxa paddled for it.

The rowboat drifted downstream. The warship cut past them, oars bubbling through the water. Archers stood in the prow, bows bent. Men yelled out to the rowboat. Getting no response, the sergeant gave the order to loose arrows. They thunked into the rowboat's hull.

Raxa came level with the dock, pulling herself along it. Nearing the shore, loose flaps wrapped around her ankles. She kicked at the weeds and pulled herself dripping onto the firm mud. Sorrowen was right behind her, looking like a half-drowned cat.

She pointed toward the streets. They took off at a run, stiff from the cold swim. Water squished from their boots.

"Dry clothes first," she said. "Then we need to go to the loon."

"You found the cargo? What was it?"

"Nothing."

"Nothing? Okay, *you* get to tell Dante that one."

"They weren't delivering goods," she said. "They were delivering the ships."

Sorrowen stared at her like a cow. After a moment, his eyes popped wide. "Dante cut off overland routes into the Collen Basin. So Mallon built a fleet to invade instead."

"Did you see their hulls? Flat-bottomed. They can land anywhere. If we don't warn Collen, they'll never see the invasion until it's already behind their defenses."

25

The claws of the rats gouged his skin as they climbed up his body. Some stopped on his torso, pawing to his organs like a dog digging into sand. One continued up his neck and came to his face. Compelled, Gladdic opened his mouth. The rat reached inside his mouth with intelligent delicateness, took hold of his tongue, and tugged.

The tongue pulled away as easily as dough with too little water.

He awoke from the dream sheathed in sweat. He lay in the bottom of a war canoe. Stars and clouds fought to be seen through the wicked branches of the trees. Before the dream could fade, he held it in his mind, remembering the pain of his mutilation and the feelings that had arrived with each hurt.

He did so in part to punish himself, but also to tease out the dream's meaning. There were some who believed that dreams could hold visions sent by the gods. Pagans thought they were the dreams of dead spirits passing through you—or worse, that they weren't the spirits' dreams, but their experience in the afterlife. Others yet held that dreams were utter nonsense.

Gladdic thought none of these things. He believed that dreams were missives from the soul.

The rats had been Galand's. It would be simple enough to conclude that he was simply afraid of the sorcerer hunting him down again, but the primary emotion he'd felt on being eviscerated by the rats hadn't actually been fear. Not of physical violence and pain, at least. Rather, he'd felt as though he was being judged—and he'd feared that he deserved it.

Drifting on the waters of the swamp among the splash of the oars and the scent of the night, he let his mind drift as well. Galand dogged him everywhere he went. The man's pursuit extended beyond all reason. What if that was because he *was* beyond reason? Perhaps he wasn't in command of his own faculties. He might have been possessed by the gods to punish Gladdic. How else to explain his willingness to leave the land he ruled and risk his life so many times?

Not long ago, Gladdic would have considered these thoughts of his persecution first with self-pity, and then with rage. But he had changed, hadn't he? Yes. He had. He knew guilt. In truth, it had always been there. Yet his calling in Collen had been so righteous that he'd locked away his guilt like a filthy criminal.

Now, it rushed through him like the Celeset. It was strong enough to have compelled him to roll out the side of the canoe into the waters and their vicious fish, or to blast a beam of ether between his ears.

But he was now on a quest of far greater gravity than what he'd failed to do in Collen. The thought struck him like a thunderbolt: likely, the gods had cursed him in Collen *in order to return him to Tanar Atain*. And *that* was the truth within the dream of the rats. For rather than fearing them, he had accepted their terror, knowing his path was just.

He would carry that same acceptance into the depths of the Go Kaza. No matter the pains and horrors that awaited him, he would make his stand against the evil that brewed in the shadows.

Either way, he would find peace. Either he would bring light to the darkness that would consume the world, and know redemption. Or what awaited him at the Wound would put an end to this wretched life, where gods played with men like toys, and evil stood proudly on all sides.

He sat up in the boat. They were sailing in brute darkness, barely able to see what lay ahead.

In the Go Kaza, it was better that way.

~

The armada struck out from the captured city, oars churning the stagnant water. Dozens of canoes bore hundreds of soldiers away from Dara Bode. It wasn't the most overwhelming war band Dante had ever seen, but to the rebels' best knowledge, they easily outnumbered the forces that had escaped with the Drakebane.

The goal would be to run the enemy down before they could gain recruits from other towns and garrisons.

Dante sat in a double-hulled canoe next to Riza. Holding the mouse bone in his hand, a steady pressure built in his forehead.

"Northeast." He pointed inland, adjusting his finger. "Straight ahead."

Riza called the directions to Commander Barain, an older man with a piercing, hollowed-out glare, then turned back to Dante. "Do you know how far?"

Dante closed his eyes, examining the shape of the pressure hidden beneath his brow like a third eye. "Fifty miles from here, give or take. But they're on the move, too."

He'd tried more than once to send a dragonfly to shadow their foes, but whenever the insects had drawn close, his connection to them had been severed. He didn't know if that was the doing of Gladdic, the Drakebane's sorcerers, the so-called Knights of Odo Sein, or another force entirely.

He had too many questions and too few answers. Do Riza had been so busy organizing the pursuit that Dante hadn't had the chance to speak with him since reaching their agreement. But now that they were underway, Riza appeared to have few immediate responsibilities.

"I know how to deal with Gladdic," Dante said. "But I don't know how to combat the Knights of Odo Sein. What can you tell me about them?"

Riza took a seat on a rowing bench, gazing ahead into the trees, vines, and clouds of gnats. "The Knights of Odo Sein exist outside the Body of Tanar Atain. Rather, they are its sword. They are devoted. They are potent. And they are vicious."

"When we fought them, they seemed to be able to stop all sorcery in its tracks."

Riza chuckled. "That is precisely what they were created to do. Above all else, they are the reason Tanar Atain lives in misery. Many years ago, an order of sorcerers sought to topple the Drakebane dynasty. To their credit, they succeeded. To their disgrace, when the deposed tyrant returned from the wilds with the Odo Sein, the sorcerers had no answer to their powers."

"Do they use artifacts to suppress the nether? Or can they do this through a magic of their own?"

"If I knew a secret like that, they would have killed me long ago."

"Is it safe to assume they'll be traveling with the Drakebane?"

"Oh yes. They are his bodyguards, servants, and executioners."

"How many will there be?"

The nobleman shrugged lightly. "The Odo Sein keep their ways secret. Their numbers, too. Personally, I'd count them at no more than a score, but the Odo Sein have always been more interested in the hinterlands than the cities. Who knows how many more they have lurking out in the Deep Swamps?"

"And they were created to stop sorcery?"

"The Drakebane will tell you that our own sorcerers forged them to defeat the Dragon of Ages and his manifold demons. But the Drakebane *would* say that. In the old ways—the ways that were drowned out in the babble of a billion beliefs—there *was* no mention of the Odo Sein. Our defeat of the dragon was always a temporary victory. And it was told that, one day, for all our efforts, we would finally lose."

Dante was immediately intrigued: he knew almost nothing of Tanarian religious beliefs other than that they didn't seem to believe in the Celeset. Such a thing was bizarre, almost eerie. Gask, Narashtovik, Gallador, Houkkalli, and Tantonnen all more or less followed the same tenets. Mallon denied Arawn's status, but otherwise recognized the same gods and goddesses. Collen and Alebolgia emphasized things that were simply wrong—or beside the point, if you wanted to be charitable—yet the questionable branches of their faith extended from the same trunk Narashtovik grew from. Hell, even the Wesleans believed in a system that had its roots in the Celeset.

Every corner of the continent believed in some form of the Twelve Gods. Well, except the norren, at least, who followed their own ways, as they always did. But Dante thought that human and norren beliefs could coexist without contradiction: it made sense that different races could be overseen by and responsible to different gods.

But as far as he knew, the Tanarians were human. It was harder to see how their beliefs could coexist with the fact of the Celeset. Regretfully, he didn't have time to explore that just now.

"I know I can put Gladdic down," Dante said. "But the Odo Sein are another matter. If you can think of anything that could help me deal with them, we'll all be in a better position to do less dying."

He turned and waved his arms over his head, signaling Volo to bring her canoe beside Riza's vessel. They'd been offered space in one of the command ships, but Dante had thought it wiser to maintain some semblance of independence. Volo matched the double-huller's speed and course, drawing within inches of it. Dante hopped across.

He explained what he'd learned. Blays listened with a single-mindedness he rarely displayed outside of their strategy sessions. Naran paid close mind, too, although he sat with his hands folded and his spine straight, as if he were an attentive student.

Dante nodded at the sword sheathed at Blays' hip. "The short of it is that, right now, the only weapons we have to fight the Odo Sein with are one of their own swords, and a dirty lizard horn. We have to come up with more."

"None of your skills worked in their presence?" Naran said.

"I couldn't so much as touch the nether to put it to use. It was like it was locked behind a glass case. Same with the ether."

"Same here," Blays said. "I couldn't shadowalk. Couldn't get a bridge going."

The captain frowned at the looted sword. "Yet you say their weapons displayed unnatural powers."

"Their swords were crackling with so much nether they were as purple as a twisted nipple."

"That's a damn fine question," Dante said. "Why do the swords work when nothing else does?"

The question lingered in the canoe like an odor no one wanted to claim. Blays brushed off a cobweb they'd just passed through. "Do you actually expect us to be able to answer this? While I'm at it, should I also explain why bad things happen to good people?"

"I expect you to try to help." Dante reached out his hand. "Here, give me the sword."

Blays unbuckled it, passing it over sheathed. Dante drew it slowly. Initially, the metal was a dull black, as inauspicious as a sleeping body, but once it was free of the scabbard and exposed to the light and air, bolts of silver-black nether sizzled from its cross-guard to its tip, turning purple and then fading from sight, only to be replaced by a new wave of shadows.

Dante followed them down to their apparent source: the grip, crafted from a swamp dragon's horn. Yet the tough chitin deflected his efforts to move inside it. He could have used the nether to scrape a hole in it, but with extremely little desire to accidentally destroy their only working artifact, he turned to the swamp dragon horn instead.

Wielding the nether like a carver's chisel, he chipped away at the horn's armored exterior. Minutes later, he broke through. He was expecting a reaction of some kind—a blast of shadows, or even, for some reason, a small explosion—but nothing happened at all. The hollow interior was nothing more than an empty chamber roughly the size of an index finger.

Dante turned the horn in his hand. "There's nothing there."

"Maybe it's only a useful vessel," Blays said. "Try cutting into the one on the sword to see what's in it."

"What if I damage it?"

"So what? If you break it, can't you use the ether to restore it?"

"That's just..." Dante was about to call it "idiotic," but once he stilled his metaphorical knee, he rubbed his chin in thought.

"A good way to learn how to fight back against our lethal and mysterious foe?"

Rather than verbally conceding Blays had a point, Dante carefully worked away at the pommel of the sword, leaving the blade sheathed. As the horn's outer shell thinned, Dante quieted his mind, preparing to send the ether to reverse his work. But on boring to the center, he found it was hollow, too.

He gave it a good inspection with the nether, then sat back with a scowl. "Empty. I'll refrain from comparing it to anyone's skull."

Naran cleared his throat. "You're certain that when the sword is in active use, the nether is coming from the horn?"

"I'm not certain of anything. When you approach a problem, certainty is the enemy of the solution."

"Could this be similar to your loons?"

"I've been thinking about that," Dante said. "But if a nethermancer watched a loon in action, even if they didn't understand how it worked, they'd still be able to see the shadows powering it. With this, I'm not seeing anything."

He drew the sword again. Dark lightning shimmered along the blade. This was an encouraging sight, as it meant he hadn't ruined anything—yet—but even with the hole dug into the horn, he still didn't see any source for the power. The weapon wasn't drawing nether from outside itself, either. He spent a good minute passively observing, then a long span poking, massaging, and vigorously eyeballing every square inch of the weapon.

Satisfied that there was nothing to see, and highly dissatisfied that that was so, Dante became thoughtless, asking the ether to restore the item to its original purity. The hole in the horn faded.

He sheathed the sword. "This makes no sense. It has to be coming from somewhere. Nether can't just appear like magic."

Blays looked stupefied, then grinned like a kid who's discovered where his parents hid the cake. "Yes it can."

"If that's what you believe, it's no wonder you can barely conjure up enough nether to dab a quill in. The shadows are always there."

"True enough. But you can't always see them."

Dante leaned back. His mind spit out the answer like a lemon pip. "Like the *Cycle*. You think?"

"I do my best not to, but sometimes I can't stand to watch you flail about. So let's find out. Hand over your torchstone. The horn, too."

Dante rummaged through his bag and handed over the stone and the horn. Blays picked up the sword, whisked it from its sheath with a flourish he'd obviously spent many hours practicing, and disappeared.

Volo paddled on. The canoes were approaching a narrow gap through the trees; captains hollered orders, directing the armada into a double-file line. As soon as the force passed through the gap, they dispersed once again.

Blays returned with a self-satisfied smile, the torchstone shining in his hand. He sheathed the sword and held the stone up to the hole in the horn. "Take a look."

Dante peered inside, but the core was no longer hollow. Instead, it was filled with six black stars a couple of inches across, stacked one on top of the other. "Traces?"

"That's what they look like to me. Then again, I'm just the humble sell-sword who sometimes has to do your job for you."

Dante laughed; nothing raised his spirits like making progress toward an answer. "What if the Odo Sein are able to clamp down on the shadows in our world, but their ability can't reach into the netherworld?"

"So if you're drawing on something from the netherworld—such as the traces—their ability can't stop you. Hence they get to wave around these amazing glowing swords."

Dante gazed in at the motionless black stars. "There are enough traces in here to form an Andrac. Why aren't they merging?"

"Maybe swamp dragons don't like having soul-eating demons sprout from their horns."

"I could draw on these to fight the Odo Sein. They wouldn't be able to stop me."

"Yeah, unless they think about using their nethereal swords to bat down whatever you throw at them." Blays drew the stolen sword a few inches, letting the ambient sunlight fall into the abyss of the blade. "There isn't much nether in one of those horns. Rather than wasting it on a few black arrows that are spent as soon as you've used them, I say we make another sword."

Dante held the weight of the horn in his hand. He'd meant to use it to learn how to battle the knights, but he supposed that forging it into a killing weapon would satisfy that goal rather well.

But there was one large assumption looming over that plan: that he'd be able to learn how to craft such a weapon before they ran into the Drakebane and his army.

Yet there was nothing else to do but get started. Using the nether as a scalpel and a crowbar, he sliced and pried the wooden handle and leather wraps away from the tang of his plain sword. Once the steel rod was revealed beneath the cross-guard, he carved a slot into the flat end of the horn and wiggled it over the tang, forming a new handle.

The fit was already quite snug, but deviled by paranoid thoughts of the blade slinging itself free mid-swing, he stilled himself, allowed the ether to begin to mend the slot, then cut off the light's progress as soon as it had started to close off the hole he'd cut in the horn's end. Dante tested the handle and found it gripped so tightly that none of them could budge it.

He had hoped this process would take long enough for his mind to gin up the solution to how to make his sword do what Blays' did, but his hope was sadly misplaced. He drew the looted Odo Sein sword, observing the now-visible traces flow up from the handle and into the blade, then turned to his weapon and instructed the traces in his dragon horn to follow suit.

They moved, but there was nothing crackling or purple about them—they moved less like lightning and more like viscous oil, which they were about as sharp as. And rather than circling of their own accord, as soon as he stopped guiding them, they quit whatever they were doing and returned to the hilt.

As he experimented with various configurations of the traces, he didn't seem to be making any progress whatsoever. But sometimes progress was just a matter of trying dumb things until you stumbled on a smart one. Early that afternoon, the pressure in Dante's forehead began to increase slowly but steadily: they were catching up.

At the rate it was going, he feared they might reach the deposed ruler—and Gladdic—by the next morning, but as the sun tumbled toward the hazy horizon, the pressure stabilized. The enemy was on the move again.

He took a break to clear his head. He'd tried to loon Sorrowen a few times over the last two days, but hadn't gotten any response. This time, the young man answered within moments.

The boy told him that he and Raxa were on the verge of unraveling what seemed to be a major Mallish military investment. One that was being overseen by Mallon's Minister of the Eastern Reach. All signs pointed to the renewal of hostilities with Collen. Sorrowen didn't know the nature of the investment, but seemed to think they'd have the answer within a few days.

"Let me know as soon as you've found it," Dante said. "We won't directly intervene in Collen again, but if Mallon's planning a final push to retake the basin, we can still warn them."

"I think this is about more than Collen." Sorrowen hesitated. "I think they're starting a drumbeat against Narashtovik, too. The priests are saying strange things—beliefs that didn't exist when I left here a few years ago."

The boy recounted the priests' stories of a resurgent Daris, Lord of the North. Dante listened with a furrowed brow.

"You might be right," he said when the boy concluded. "But scriptures and parables are often designed to be impenetrable to people who aren't steeped in your beliefs. Keep your ears open. We need to learn more."

He closed the loon's connection, relaying what Sorrowen had told him to Blays.

"What if Mallon's preparing a third invasion?" Blays said. "Are we still going to leave Collen to face it on their own?"

"We can't run off to Collen every time they're in trouble. Not without forsaking our own land. If things had been different between us, maybe I'd return a third time. But they decided they didn't need our help. Let's see if they're right."

"That's a bit cold." Blays stared down at the murky water. "But I don't think I disagree with you."

"Anyway, Gladdic's the architect of the Mallish plan. If we kill him, interest in fighting the Colleners might collapse."

As soon as Dante spoke these words, he wondered if they were true, or merely the balm of wishful thinking that allowed you to turn your back without the sting of guilt. Either way, he couldn't spend time worrying about what might befall Collen. Not when he had his own troubles to tend to.

He turned back to the matter of the swords. He thought to ask Naran whether Gladdic had ever said anything about the Odo Sein during his interrogations, but Naran was curled up on a tarp next to a bench. The captain had been sleeping—and eating—a lot since being plucked out of the tower.

Other than that, Naran seemed healthy enough in both body and mind. According to him, his arrest had been sudden and unexpected: he'd been making inquiries among his merchant contacts at the docks and must have said something indiscreet in front of the wrong ears. Next thing Naran had known, he'd been snatched up by a gaggle of soldiers in green jabats and informed that he'd committed the crime of sedition for prying into imperial business.

After a round of questioning, they'd whisked him off to Dara Bode, where they'd tossed him into the Blue Tower, questioned him again—these had focused on his interest in foreigners inside Tanar Atain—and then largely forgotten about him for multiple weeks.

It hadn't been until Gladdic's arrival that the Tanarians had resumed their questions, more forcefully than before. This time, they'd seemed quite concerned to learn that Naran did most of his business from Bressel, asking repeatedly what he knew about the Tanarian enterprise in the city. At last, Naran confessed that he'd come looking for Gladdic, the Mallish priest. Which had only prompted them to cut him up a bit more and ask if that was *really* the only reason he'd come to Aris Osis?

Other than the few days at the start and finish of his captivity, however, Naran had mostly been left to himself. If Dante had been trapped in a dingy cell with nothing to read and nothing to do, he would have spent each day practicing with the nether (assuming, for the sake of the scenario, he couldn't use it to open the walls or blast the entire tower apart). He couldn't imagine what it had been like to be so alone—and worse, to be separated from all of your interests, studies, and pursuits.

With these dreary thoughts sliding around his mind, he alternated between studying the authentic Odo Sein blade and trying to make his copy imitate it. As the afternoon wore on, a sluggish, mild nausea crept over his body. He tried to push through it, but soon found himself on the verge of vomiting and passing out, not necessarily in that order. He put away the swords and tried to soothe himself with nether, but it didn't seem to help.

At sunset, the commanders ordered the canoes to a halt. Some of the soldiers bivouacked on small islands while others bedded down in their boats. There was almost no chance of an attack, but the troops seemed less rowdy and argumentative than any group of Tanarians Dante had witnessed up to that point. After a dinner of fish and root paste, Riza sent a messenger to summon Dante to his island.

Riza greeted him with no pretense of dana kide. "How far?"

"It's not precise enough for me to say for sure," Dante said. "But we're closer than we started the day. Maybe as much as five miles."

The lord stared into the north, face pinched. "I fear we won't catch them for many days."

"I thought they'd be recruiting help. Won't that slow them down?"

"Mustering their loyalists is only a part of their plan. I believe they're making for the Go Kozo—the land's wound."

"Sounds cheery."

"They'll hope we won't follow," Riza said grimly. "It might be wiser if we didn't. But I don't think they're traveling to the Go Kozo to hide where we dare not follow. I think they're going there to summon something unholy to their cause."

"Gladdic's demons?"

"Maybe. Or maybe something worse."

Dante tried to press him for more, but Riza had fallen into a dark mood. Dante returned to his island camp. Was Riza trying to sway him into supporting the rebels against the Drakebane's heinous tactics? It was hard to say for sure; perhaps he was only venting. Yet a subtler approach was always more effective at convincing a neutral party to your side than it was to preach at or berate them.

Whatever the case, he didn't care. Caring was Riza's job, along with the other leaders of the movement of the Righteous

Monsoon. Dante didn't even have to care if the Righteous Monsoon won or lost. With that thought, he fell asleep with a smile.

Morning came. The pressure in Dante's brow told him the enemy's northern path was drifting eastward. Hearing this news, Riza looked unhappy but unsurprised. As they set out, an unsteady rain beat at the waters.

Whatever illness had afflicted Dante the day before was long gone, so he resumed trying to duplicate the captured sword. After an hour of getting nowhere, he sat back and got out the other artifact he'd successfully reproduced: the loon. The loons worked for two reasons: they used their own internal source of nether, requiring no input from him—in fact, they could easily be used by someone who had no talent with the shadows whatsoever—and their function was based on qualities found in the objects they were made from. In order to hear from and be heard by someone else, you built the loon from the skull bones of a creature that had once been able to hear.

Being such a poor user of ether, he'd never tried to make a torchstone, but he understood the concept was similar. By using a base of azamite, a particular kind of cloudy gemstone that could focus ambient light into a brighter, condensed illumination, and imbuing it with ether, you could cause the stone to magnify and even *create* light.

By comparison, it seemed as though the nether in the Odo Sein blade could magnify the cutting strength of the sword. But how to access the sword's inner virtue of sharpness? The ability to cleave? To take a whole and sunder it into two?

In the afternoon, the flotilla came to a stop. Their force had been skirting the settlements they'd passed, but the scouts reported that a nearby village appeared empty. Fearing the Drakebane had orchestrated another massacre, the Monsoon diverted to investigate.

The adda paddies had been ripped up, the roots plundered. The docks were intact, but most of the houserafts were gone. There were no bodies. It was as if everyone there had picked up and left—or been taken.

They gathered food from what little remained and moved on. Dante had hoped the interruption would jar an idea loose from his mind, but he felt thoroughly stalled.

"Volo," he said. "Do you know any stories about the Odo Sein?"

The girl laughed. "I got more stories about those bastards than a frog has pollywogs."

"Are there any involving their swords?"

"You mean like the Red Tide of Falo Loc? Before I was born, the Drakebane's father Evo Yoto decreed his soldiers needed more adda so they could fight back the interlopers from the Deep Swamps. He said that when harvest time came, he needed ten percent more from each village. Well, the people of Falo Loc worked hard to meet their quota, but halfway through the growing season, a blight killed five out of every six plants.

"Harvest came, and Drakebane Evo sent the Odo Sein to collect the empire's share, but Falo Loc couldn't meet their obligation. So the Odo Sein killed everyone. Chopped them into bits!"

Dante waited for more, but Volo's laughter indicated that was the end of the story. "What the hell does that have to do with the Odo Sein's swords?"

"What do you think they used to kill the villagers?"

Blays shrugged. "The shame of not meeting their quota?"

"I'm looking for something that gives me insight into anything unique about their swords. I'm already well-versed in the notion that swords as a class are capable of cutting people up."

Volo stuck out her lower lip, swerving around a bare branch reaching out of the water. "Well, that's about the only thing the Odo Sein do."

"Know what? Tell me any story that comes to mind. You never know when something vital's going to spring up."

Volo launched into a string of tales, starting with the story of how the Odo Sein had created swamp dragons as mounts and ridden them to battle to expand the Tanarian Empire across the marshland. After several successful campaigns, however, the dragons had escaped their masters. They'd been living in the swamps—and killing innocent travelers—ever since.

Next was the legend of Ro Woto, widely regarded as the greatest swordsman of all the knights of his time. For years, his loyalty was as unparalleled as his skill. One day, he and several other knights were sent to travel into Yataga, a lesser kingdom that had been at war with the fledgling Tanar Atain. The knights were ordered to pick up a large group of Yatagan children orphaned after a recent battle. Once they had their young charges in their war canoes, the knights started back toward their homeland, where the orphans would be resettled.

Ro Woto was supposed to return by himself to Dara Bode to inform the Drakebane of their success, but he'd only gone a short ways before spotting a group of Yatagan warriors ahead. He turned back to warn the others, and witnessed his fellow knights tossing the Yatagan children into the open swamp, then canoeing away as the ziki oko feasted.

Seeing this, he was overcome with black wrath. He flung himself at his former brothers, striking down one after another until their bodies lay so thick on the water you could walk across them without getting your feet wet. It wasn't until seven Odo Sein surrounded him on the central platform of a war canoe that they were able to wound him. Even then, he fought on, his sword crackling against theirs as he slew first one, then two, then four.

But in the effort, the surviving three wounded him a second time. Ro Woto collapsed to the deck. As they closed on him, he was too weak to lift his sword arm. Yet he reached inside himself and his soul streamed forth to his sword, and it lifted of its own accord, dancing between his foes like a skipperfish. When it finished, all three enemies fell dead. Then Ro Woto smiled and died — but his soul stayed always with his sword, and whenever it was carried by another Knight of Odo Sein, the bearer was inspired to help the helpless.

After that, Volo told three quick stories about the Pacification of the West, where the Odo Sein were deployed to put down an insurrection in the western territories that had been spearheaded by a division of Mallish priests sent to gain a foothold in Tanar Atain. The knights were described as whirling through the enemy's soldiers like tree-nodders — a type of local windstorm that made the trees seem to bob their heads.

When the priests came forth to stop the slaughter with their magic, the Odo Sein called upon the Stillness of Rocks in the

Stream. When both light and dark were fastened in place, the Odo Sein lifted their blades, which blazed with shadows forged of the knights' own spines. The priests looked on in terrified wonder, spending their final thoughts to ask their gods why their magic had failed them while the enemy's swords whistled down upon their necks, uniting them with the awful darkness.

"That's as morbid as something out of Dante's diary." Blays eyed Volo. "You said your people tell that story to children?"

"It's the truth." Volo cocked her head. "Do you foreigners lie to your children?"

"We practically make a sport of it! How else are you going to get them to do what you want?"

"Have you tried the truth?"

"Truth doesn't work on them."

"Not when you've trained them to be unable to tell truth from lies, and why it matters."

Blays gave her a dirty look, sputtering for words. "Dante, help me out here. You justify lying to people all the time."

"We lie to them to control them," Dante said. "And because we're so frail we can't imagine that they're not. When we lie to them, it isn't really to protect them. It's to protect ourselves. To allow us to pretend that *they're* the weak ones."

Volo had stopped paddling, her head twisted around to watch him. Her face had the stunned, almost alarmed look of a worshipper hypnotized by a sermon. "Do you really believe that? Or is that just dana kide?"

"I don't know. I wasn't even thinking about it until I said it."

"That's the sign the gods are speaking through you." She narrowed her eyes. "At least, that's what the Drakebane *wants* us to believe. But we all know we already have the truth inside us. So what do we need the gods to tell us anything for?"

Before Dante had the chance to respond, she turned and drove her oar into the water, stroking hard to regain her place in the loose formation of boats. Dante was momentarily annoyed by her withdrawal from a debate she'd started, then remembered that he didn't give a damn.

Instead, he silently recapped the stories she'd just told them. Usually, he thought he had a good ear for what was historical fact and what was myth, but in Tanar Atain, the borders of truth felt as foggy as the Mists. Even so, he thought he might have a lead. In both the last stand of Ro Woto and the massacre of the Mallish priests, the stories had said the Odo Sein had drawn on something inside themselves to lend strength to their swords.

He handed the knight's sword to Blays. "Take that into the shadows, will you? Watch it close and tell me if you see anything like you do when somebody's reading the *Cycle*."

"Like nether flowing between me and the sword?"

"Yes. But don't limit yourself to *only* looking for that. That's a good way to miss what's right in front of you."

Blays blinked from sight. Through the ripples in the shadows, Dante could feel him moving in slow, deliberate motions, like he was practicing a new sword form. Two minutes later, he reappeared in the canoe.

"The traces are moving around like crazy." Blays rolled his wrist, twisting the sword back and forth. "But I'm not seeing anything coming out of me."

"You're sure of that?"

"Why do you need me to test this? Do you think the sword's drawing on another trace? One we haven't seen yet?"

"I think that's a possibility."

"Then we know how to test that, don't we? Give me the torchstone." Blays reached out. Dante handed it over. Blays walked into the shadows again. This time, he was back within a matter of seconds, the torchstone glowing in his hand. "Just lit myself up good. Now watch and tell me if *you* see anything."

Blays propped a knee on a seating bench and tilted his sword through a chain of techniques. The ether shining from the torchstone threw each mote of nether into sharp relief. Shadows gushed up from the handle of the sword, jagging along the blade before returning to the grip. As far as Dante could tell, however, none of these shadows were coming from Blays himself.

He watched for another couple of minutes, then cursed, pressing his fingers into his brow. "There's nothing I hate more than having a great idea refuted by stupid reality."

Then again, just because it didn't appear to be the traces, that didn't rule out all forms of nether. What if they'd been powering the swords with the common nether inside their own bodies? Dante lifted the sword he'd been working on, reached inside himself, and summoned the shadows from his blood and bones. It looked and acted no different from the nether he could have called out of the water or the mud, but it was always possible that it contained properties he didn't know about. He sent it into the traces in the sword's handle.

This accomplished nothing. Except, he supposed, that it ruled out one more possibility for how to craft the swords. This might have been useful, except that he suspected that the ways to *not* create the swords were infinite in number.

He was getting frustrated again. Frustration was the enemy of discovery. Before it could poison his mind, he set down his sword and picked up the Odo Sein weapon. As the nether swept out of the handle and coursed along the blade, it sizzled and jerked, flowing and branching as unpredictably as turbulent water.

Yet the longer he watched it, the more convinced he became that there were small patterns within the chaos. Or if not patterns (for they didn't repeat themselves exactly), then tendencies. It was like watching water pour down an uneven slope: while it looked like it was going whichever way it pleased, and often did just that, over time, it was prone to follow the same routes.

He didn't think the nether's course along the blade had to do with the shape of the sword itself. At least not its physicality; nether could pass straight through the steel without knowing it was there. Why, then, did it follow these patterns? And if it wasn't following the physical planes of the sword, what *was* it following?

As he turned these questions over in his mind, a dull ache formed in his head. His stomach started to toss and turn like a young soldier whose fear of the coming battle won't let him sleep. He found it more and more difficult to concentrate. Bad airs from the swamp, probably, but when he tried to cleanse his blood with nether, it didn't help in the slightest. Blays and Volo appeared unaffected. Even Naran, thinned and weakened by captivity, slept peacefully.

If it was a bad air, it seemed unusually interested in him. And come to think of it, it only seemed to afflict him when he was handling the Odo Sein blade.

"Do me a favor?" he asked Blays. "Will you hold the sword for a while? My wrist's getting tired."

Blays shook his head in disgust. "Should I find a pillow for your delicate ass, too?"

"Just trying to find a way to make you useful."

Blays took up the sword. Dante resumed observing the shadows snapping along the blade, sketching out any tendency that repeated more than twice. He'd run out of ink many days ago, and the Tanarians didn't seem to use writing instruments at all, just their string-harp things. This had required him to fill his ink pot with a small quantity of his own blood. Running low, he paused to refill it.

Blays made a gagging sound. "That's easily among the five grossest things you've ever done. And I've seen you stick your hands inside corpses like you're looking for prizes."

"You're afraid of blood now? What do you think is the red stuff that comes out of all the people you stab?"

"I just set it free. I don't...*play* with it."

Dante rolled his eyes and continued sketching, filling one page and moving on to the next. The effort helped distract him from the illness he felt, which was slow in fading. After ten minutes, Blays was making swallowing noises. After fifteen, Dante glanced up and saw that his tan skin was ashy, with sweat beading across his forehead.

He set down his quill. "Something the matter?"

"It feels like I've been stricken with a hangover. If so, I'd really like to know where I found all those spirits, so I can do it again."

"How long have you been feeling this way?"

Blays shrugged. "The last few minutes. It came on fast."

"How would you describe it?"

"I'm not a physician, but I'd say it's a general shittiness of the head, followed by a shittiness of the gut. Feels like something's sucking the strength right out of me."

"Have you experienced something like this before?"

"Like I said, hangovers." Blays frowned. "Hold on, you're deducing something! Were you expecting this?"

"I think," Dante said, "that the sword is consuming our traces."

"What do you mean, our traces?"

"The one each of us carries inside. The one that's left behind in the shadows when we die."

Blays swallowed again, then glanced in horror at the sword and flung it to the bottom of the canoe. As soon as he let go, the purple nether vanished from the now-inert blade.

"You mean it's been sucking my soul?" Blays wiped his hand on the side of his jabat. "When were you planning to tell me?"

"Once it happened."

"What if that part of my soul's gone for good? I'll turn into you!"

"Lyle's balls, will you calm down? The same thing happened to me yesterday and I'm fine today. It happened again about an hour ago and I'm already feeling better. Slightly."

"Slightly."

"When you spend nether, it tries to return to wherever you called it from. It just takes a little time. I'm betting the traces are no different."

Blays ran his palms down his face. "It's immensely comforting to know that my soul will *probably* come back to me *eventually*. You couldn't have waited until tomorrow to confirm this on yourself?"

"Always better to confirm a phenomenon's existence by using a second subject." Dante picked up the blade. As the nether began to whirl about its edges, he sheathed it, then pointed to the hilt. "The stored traces aren't getting used up. They're circling back and forth around the blade, providing its cutting power. But what powers *them*? In the legends Volo told us, when the Odo Sein needed to, they were able to draw nether from within themselves and channel it into their swords."

"But we looked for this exact thing earlier and couldn't see it."

"We thought that proved it couldn't be the traces, but we fell victim to our own egos. We couldn't see the traces in action, but that isn't hard proof they aren't part of the process. All that proves is we might be morons. Here's what we know for sure: the sword isn't consuming its own nether. Meanwhile, it's draining something from us. And there's a historical record of it doing the same to others."

Blays burped in discomfort, then winced. "Then you can only use it for so long each day before it starts to kill you?"

"Seems like. Although it's possible it doesn't have to be powered by the wielder's trace. Maybe when you kill someone with it, it can use their trace instead."

"Er. You suppose that's where the traces in the lizard's horn came from? The people it's killed?"

"That's possible."

"So what happens if you run through your own trace? Does the sword break?"

"Could be," Dante said. "Either that, or you do."

Logically, the next step was to locate his own trace within himself. However, given that his trace had already been depleted to the point of illness, Dante thought it best to carry on with that line of exploration after he'd recovered. Instead, he studied his sketches, searching for anything that could help him understand how to guide or align the traces trapped in the swamp dragon's horn.

Throughout the day, the pressure in his head inched steadily upward. By the afternoon, it was increasing rapidly. Some time later, the enemy began to move northeast again, but the Monsoon was still gaining ground. Or water, as it were.

Dante made sure that Riza knew this. Which made it all the more surprising when Commander Barain called for the flotilla to stop and make camp shortly after four that afternoon.

Blays frowned. "We're stopping already? There's still nearly two hours of daylight."

Volo made a murmuring noise. "We're about to enter the Deep Swamp. Bet they want to spend as few nights there as possible."

"What's in the Deep Swamp?"

"Things that make you want to stay out of it."

Dante helped make camp, then got back to his sketches. He'd made around fifty. Flipping through his parchment, the images seemed to be suggesting something—but if so, the message was too subtle, or he was too dim to understand it. That night, little green lights bobbed over the waters. He thought they might be fireflies, but sometimes the lights faded, darkening away to nothing. Other times they held perfectly still, as if watching the soldiers sleep.

He awoke to rain falling on his face. He hadn't had time to stop being angry about that before Riza called him over to the nobleman's island. Servants scurried about packing up tents and rolling up down-stuffed mattresses made from a Tanarian fabric woven so tightly that the feathers' quills couldn't stick through.

"Sorcerer." The Do's eyes skipped from tree to tree, occasionally dipping to the water, which was swirled with rainbow-colored oil. "Be on watch today."

"For what?" Dante said. "The enemy's at least twenty miles ahead of us."

"The Deep Swamps lie ahead. The creatures there are rarely disturbed."

"Duly noted."

Riza shifted, glancing at Dante and then back to the trees. "Yet even these reaches aren't uninhabited. If you see anyone traveling without a boat, warn me at once."

"How would they get around without a boat? Are there no ziki oko?"

"They're much rarer here."

"Is the water that shallow? Or do the people swim around?"

Riza cranked his head around to meet Dante's eyes. "Do you doubt my words?"

"The better I understand what we're getting into, the better I can protect us."

"Protecting us is my duty. Your duty is to abide my orders. Am I understood?"

Dante nodded and returned to his island.

The flotilla advanced into the bog. The color of the waters shifted from a rich brown to an ocher laced with metallic ribbons that gleamed dully beneath the overcast light. With this change in water, the trees changed too, the singular boles replaced by irregularly braided orange trunks, as if several plants had congregated together for safety. Rather than willowy, draping branches, their boughs were angular and jagged, sporting slender black leaves. Some wore clumps of a dark matter that looked like sticky fur.

Nearly a third of the craft were deployed as scouts, keeping close to the fleet and within sight of each other. Dante slew a few dragonflies and beetles and dispatched them a mile or two ahead. As he paged through the sketches, warming up his mind, one of the dragonflies blanked out. A minute later, motion attracted him to the eyes of a beetle. A bat with the jaws of a tiny wolf swooped toward it. Its mouth opened wide. An instant of darkness was followed by a glimpse from between rows of needly teeth. The connection was roughly severed.

Dante considered making some fish or bats to do his bidding, but he couldn't spare the nether. Not until the sword was forged. If they had to fight their way through the Odo Sein with a single blade and no shadows to call on, they'd never get to Gladdic.

Suddenly glum, he turned back to his sketches. And stopped in the middle of flipping over one of the sheets. Hurriedly, as if the idea might escape him if he didn't jot it down, he unstoppered his ink pot of blood and, guided by the patterns in the sketches, distilled them into an arrangement of seven red dots, roughly t-shaped.

He blew on the markings, drying them, then shoved the parchment in front of Blays. "What does this look like to you?"

"A sword." Blays traced his finger from point to point. "Blade, cross-guard, hilt."

"It *looks* like a sword. But it isn't, is it?"

"No," Blays said slowly, "it's your own blood dabbed on a square of cow skin. Are you being pedantic on purpose? Don't tell me you've bought into norren philosophy."

"I think it's more like a constellation."

"All right, it looks like a constellation. What does this have to do with anything?"

"The Odo Sein blade has seven traces in its horn. When you watch the nether move around the blade, it appears to flow chaotically, but it always flows through the same seven points. I think this is the underlying structure of the sword. Like its skeleton. Or its soul."

Blays was looking at him like Dante was trying to sell him a block of wood painted like beef. Rather than fighting to explain something he wasn't sure he understood himself, Dante set his sword-in-progress on a rowing bench and sent his mind into its hilt. His horn only held six traces, not seven, and as he lured them out with a few dabs of blood, he dearly hoped that the precise number wasn't vital to the operation of the sword.

Working partly on the example of the Odo Sein sword, and partly on intuition, he dabbed his blood along his sword, spacing it out in six points. The six traces stopped their slow circulation, each one settling on a different blot of blood. But by channeling them between dots manually, they flowed in a manner almost identical to the Odo Sein weapon.

As he paused to think, he glanced out the side of the canoe and locked eyes with a pair of yellow cat-eyes floating on the surface. These were attached to a scaly lizard as big as a fully-grown man. Unlike the swamp dragons, its snout was as long and narrow as a sight hound's. It watched him pass by, then sank below the surface.

He returned to the sword. He thought he'd found its underlying structure, its bones or its soul. Yet it was still missing its blood, so to speak. He instructed Blays to wield the Odo Sein sword again, watching every speck of nether as closely as he could. Just like before, he couldn't discern which of the shadows powering it were coming from Blays: it was too stirred up, as cloudy as the orange waters they were paddling through.

Volo's story of the swordsman had specifically mentioned him delving into his spine. Dante closed his eyes and turned his focus inward, finding his spine and the nether within it. If there was a trace there, he couldn't see it. Even so, he mixed it together, withdrew a fraction—if he *was* fooling with his trace, the last thing he wanted to do was pull the whole thing out of his body—and sent it into his sword.

His sword sat there, pointedly doing absolutely nothing.

Blays scratched his temple. "Shouldn't that have worked?"

"Unless I'm not getting any of my trace," Dante said. "Or if the common nether it's mixed with is nullifying it somehow."

He tapped his front teeth. Traces left by dead people tended to stay put unless you used blood to goad them into action. What if he removed all of the normal nether from his body? Would the trace be exposed? He did this excessively slowly, wary for any sign of the sickness overtaking his body and indicating he'd accidentally stripped himself of his trace, too. After a few minutes, with his body entirely void of nether, he couldn't feel any aches or nausea, but he couldn't see the trace, either.

He was getting nowhere. He squeezed his eyes shut and leaned against the gunwale, trailing his fingers in the water. Almost instantly, he thought better of it, jerking them out and wiping them dry.

"This is ridiculous," he said. "Narashtovik has fielded dozens of generations of priests and nethermancers across hundreds of years of travel and study. Not a single one of them could have figured this out for me?"

Blays settled his elbows on his knees. "If they'd done that, you'd be complaining about how there was nothing left to discover."

"Couldn't they have at least left me a hint?"

"They didn't need to." A note of impishness had entered Blays' voice. "You already know how to access the trace."

"Interesting," Dante said. "Because no, I don't."

"No? Then what's happening when you wield the Odo Sein blade?"

"But I don't know *how* it's drawing on our traces."

"Who cares? Cheat!"

Dante lowered his chin, gazing at the stolen sword. "It will draw out the trace for me. If I divert that into my sword, it might be enough to power it."

He set the blades beside each other on the rowing bench, keeping one hand on each hilt, the Odo Sein blade black and wreathed in what might have been purple lightning, his sword shabby plain steel in comparison. Streams of nether rippled around the black blade. He activated the traces within the pommel of the steel one, sending them coursing along the stars of their bloody constellation.

The river of traces didn't want to leave the Odo Sein weapon. But water's strength — its adaptability, its willingness to carve new channels, its relentless need to move forward—was also the key to controlling it. Working carefully, Dante guided a finger of nether away from the purple-black flow and channeled it into the traces calmly circulating the steel sword.

Blackness welled from the guard, unreeling up the blade like spilled ink. Dante's heart galloped. The inky substance spread upward, reaching the tip and enclosing the blade.

Blays leaned forward. "Did you—?"

Dante shushed him. Nerves thrumming, he withdrew the trickle of nether from the Odo Sein blade. His own sword remained black. He sheathed the knight's sword.

Blays looked at him, eyebrows lifted.

"I think it's drawing from me," Dante said. "But something's still missing. The nether isn't crackling along the edge like it should be. It's like I've built a body, but I still haven't given it life."

"Okay, then what does life need?"

"Air. Water. Food."

"I don't think you need to feed your sword a rasher of bacon to get it going."

"Nether doesn't eat," Dante said. "But it does need sustenance."

He lifted the sword and drew its edge along his left arm. A red line appeared along his skin as if by magic—and purple-black light erupted from his sword like a bruise of fire. Still touching his skin, the madly whirling nether ripped into his arm.

He yelled out and jumped to his feet, flinging down the sword. His motion rocked the canoe. Volo swore; Dante stumbled against the gunwale. Naran, jolting from sleep, grabbed Dante's right arm and pulled him down into the bottom of the boat.

The sea captain scowled, rubbing his puffy eyes. "Are you aware you're bleeding?"

Blood coursed down Dante's arm. Around him, strange trees twisted together like muscly orange snakes while bulbous flies drifted about with scorpion-like claws dangling from their upper bodies. He was traveling into a nightmare, yet he felt as free as a hawk on the wind.

~

It was one thing to create a weapon. It was another to learn how to use it.

While the swords wouldn't simply chew through whatever you touched them to, the nether along the blade exaggerated the force of a strike many times over. Even a relatively gentle swipe would cut deeply and harshly into its target. Dante had some experience with this property from wielding the bone sword, but the bone sword was a heavier weapon.

And to Blays, the blade's ability was largely foreign. He spent much of the day performing a number of subtle exercises with his sword, practicing for a minute or two, then sheathing the weapon for as long as half an hour before attempting another set of maneuvers.

That evening, as soon as they made camp, Blays motioned Dante to a clear spot on the edge of the little island and drew his sword. Black light glowed in the gloom.

"Whipping motions," Blays said. When Dante shrugged, Blays spun to the side and snapped his wrist, swinging his sword at the braided trunk of a sapling. The blade clicked right through, sending the tree-collective to the ground in a whisper of long leaves. "You see?"

"What did that tree ever do to you?"

"You don't have to spend much strength to cause a lot of damage. That means you can be quicker, less committed. A snap of the wrist is all it takes."

He motioned for Dante to draw his sword, then began to fence with him, leading him through a few techniques at quarter speed. The techniques were subtle but uncomplicated: engage the enemy's weapon, flick it aside, then whip the point of your blade at your foe.

Too soon, they began to feel sickly. Blays stepped back and put away his sword. "When we're in the thick of things, don't overthink it. Thinking makes you slow and we don't have enough time to train these skills into our bodies. But these aren't normal swords. If you can fight with them like they're meant to be fought with, you'll be the one left standing at the end." He tipped back his head, thoughtful. "Although the downside of that is you'll be the one who has to mop up the mess."

In the waning light, Dante practiced for a little longer, keeping the sword sheathed as he repeated the simple forms Blays had shown him. With his footwork taking him near the edge of the island, he took a fleeting glance at the water, then gasped.

A pale face had lifted itself clear of the surface to stare at him, its eyes blank wells of darkness. Dante did a double-take, but by the time he looked again, the face was gone. The water wasn't troubled by so much as a ripple. Shaken, he sent a tendril of nether into the depths, questing after whatever he'd seen—a person? Some bizarre fish?—but found nothing.

The night was a quiet one. When he woke, the pressure in his head indicated their quarry had returned to a northerly course. Riza accepted this information indifferently enough, yet when they started out, the commander barked out a pace that left the oarsmen huffing and straining. Until that day, Volo had done almost all the paddling—she insisted, as if it were a point of pride—but the fleet was now moving so fast that Dante and Blays had to spell her regularly.

At noon, they broke to eat and rest. Dante boarded Riza's war canoe and nodded to the Do. "We've been gaining on them all morning. At this rate, we'll be on them by tomorrow."

Riza made an approving noise. "Encouraging news. We might have reclaimed the capital from the Drakebane's dynasty, but I won't trust that our nation is safe until his flame has been snuffed."

"Then why haven't we been traveling this fast all along?"

"To preserve our strength for the coming battle."

"Has something changed? Things suddenly feel...urgent."

"This isn't a part of the swamp we wish to delay in," Riza said. "Speaking of which, I believe we've rested long enough."

The fleet got underway. Within half an hour of Riza's cryptic warning, men shouted ahead. Scouts paddled back through the trees, faces taut with the strain of their haste.

"Boko mai!" The trooper's voice was nearly a scream.

Three canoes darted forward. Archers stood up on the decks propped atop the twin hulls, nocking arrows to their short but strong Tanarian bows. Beyond, scores of dark, slender shapes raced through the branches of the trees. They moved so fast Dante initially thought they were flying. Rather, they leaped from bough to bough with frightening agility.

"Loose!" a sergeant bawled.

Arrows slashed into the trees, but it didn't so much as slow the boko mai. As the swarm closed on the lead boats, the archers released a staggered volley. Their arrows crashed into the branches and exploded in shocking bursts of fire. The air thundered with the noise of the blasts.

Smoking bodies fell from the racked branches, the beasts squealing as they plunged into the water. A few of the survivors scattered, but the others were undeterred, dropping onto the decks of the canoes. They ripped at the soldiers with scything claws, carving away chunks of meat and dashing away with their prizes.

Men stabbed at them with spears and loosed arrows at the marauding creatures, but the boko mai twisted their lithe bodies, dodging nearly everything that came their way. Dante's instinct was to unleash a hellstorm of nether at the attacking vermin, but he held back. This wasn't his fight. If he exposed his abilities now, they'd expect him to use them whenever they ran into trouble. Worse, they'd look to reel him into their conflict against the Drakebane.

He watched with no particular discomfort as the beasts returned in a second wave, hacking off hunks of flesh. Was he wrong for not intervening? If you could help, and didn't, wasn't your negligence as criminal as those committing the act itself? Then again, if a person was wrong for not acting, then so were the gods. And if you couldn't expect the gods to be good, why should a mortal be expected to be better?

Arrows and swords dropped a few more of the boko mai. The rest disappeared in the trees, leaving bloody decks and sobbing men. The Tanarians temporarily converted two of the more barge-like ships into floating physicians' tents, then continued north.

Within the hour, the trees grew taller, the leaves pressing out the light as if the sun had been wounded in a chase and was being dragged away by some great predator. Crags of narrow, angular rock sprouted from the swamp, spattered with moss in all shades of green. Buildings, or what was left of them. The ruins of walls jutted from the water like broken bones. Others lurked just below the surface, ready to disembowel any boat that tried to sail over them.

Commander Barain ordered the fleet into a double-file procession. The sailors in the leading canoes thrust long poles into the water ahead of them, feeling for submerged ruins. Wherever their poles jabbed into rock, they dumped a thick blue dye over the surface, where it clung fast to itself, barely troubled by the paddles of the passing canoes.

Dante's head swiveled to follow an upthrust of stone that might have once been a tower. Its lower reaches were blue, but its upper section was blackened and slagged. Moss grew on the blue stone, but wouldn't touch the melted segment.

"What was this place?"

Volo eyed the gnarled arm of rock. "Some people say it was the home of a bunch of people who went someplace they shouldn't have. Others think it was people looking to free themselves from the Drakebane dynasty."

"Which do you believe?"

"That people tell whichever story best fits their hate."

Rain sifted through the leaves. Within seconds, it strengthened to a spatter, then to the roar of a waterfall. Dante spent the rest of the day bailing out the boat. They made camp two hours before sunset, though the clouds were so dark it already felt like twilight. The swelling in Dante's forehead was getting harder to ignore, beating like a slow heartbeat under his skull.

Some time before dawn, his loon pulsed. It was Sorrowen. His voice was ragged with exhaustion yet pitched up with fearful excitement. He explained what they'd seen at the docks. Dante asked him a few questions, then thanked him and shut off the loon.

Blays was sitting up, a lump in the darkness. "Well?"

"Mallon's built a fleet of warships," Dante said. "They're flat-bottomed. They could sail into the inlet we made in Collen, or land on a beach somewhere behind the Colleners' lines."

"How dare they react to our reactions! So now that we know they're planning another attack, does that change our stance?"

"I still plan to do nothing."

"That will show the Colleners for looking after their own self-interests."

"We've been over this. We had a plan all set. One that didn't involve subjugating multiple Alebolgian cities."

"Yeah, just overthrowing their governments."

"*One* government," Dante said. "And more like one wealthy house within that government. One that had been making all the other cities bow down to it."

Blays scoffed. "Don't tell me that had anything to do with you deciding to work with House Osedo."

"No, but executing our plan would have caused incidental good. Collen's solution caused incidental harm."

"Point is, the only thing we had was a plan. The Keeper saw a way to make their goals real then and there. So she seized it."

"Don't tell me that's the same thing we would have done. Or that you agree with her."

"Obviously, only an idiot of the highest order would doubt our ability to do everything we promise to do. Like, say, kill a single priest." Blays took a swig of water from his skin. "I don't think the Keeper was wrong to do what she thought needed doing. But I do think that in making that decision, she also decided to end our alliance. Meaning you are free to do whatever you want here—whether that's to rush off to Collen's defense, or to ask Mallon to tell you where they make the Basin's grave so you'll know where to piss."

Dante rubbed gunk from the corner of his eye. The Colleners' abandonment of their agreement was, in a sense, a claim that they no longer needed Narashtovik's help. There would be grim justice in doing nothing at all with his spies' information. To let the Mallish fleet arrive without warning and put the Colleners' claim to the test. After everything he'd done for the place, that choice would best satisfy his anger.

For grim justice *was* satisfying. It had a cold symmetry with the original offense. But the thing about ripping everything out by the roots was that it left you with nothing but a bunch of dirt.

Or perhaps it was more like having a childhood friend who won't share his toy with you, so in a fit of pique, you smash it. You'll feel quite pleased with your power in the moment, but when you wake up the next day, *nobody* will have a toy to play with.

"We'll have Jona tell the Colleners about the fleet," he said. "That should keep things reasonably friendly between us. Besides, there's no need to make it easy for Mallon."

Blays chuckled. "I suppose it's one of those 'incidental goods' that keeping Collen strong means Mallon will have a tougher time turning its eye toward Narashtovik."

"The thought had crossed my mind."

Commander Barain had them on their way as soon as it was light enough to see the ruins sticking from the water. It was still raining, the swamps popping with droplets.

"Do you hear that?" Blays said.

Dante cocked his hear. "I don't hear anything."

"Exactly. No birds. No bugs. Nothing but rain."

Now that Blays pointed it out, the lack was unsettling. He searched for hints of fish in the orange waters, or birds nesting in the trees, but saw nothing. Just as he was about to ask Volo what this meant, the morning grew lighter. At first he thought the clouds were breaking up, but the sky looked as gloomy as ever. Rather, the trees were going pale. Abruptly, the small islands of trees and muck were replaced by bare white knobs.

Dante thought they were limestone. But as they floated past one, he saw the island was a heaped mound of bones.

Blays blinked. "We didn't just sail into one of your dreams, did we?"

"Volo," Dante said. "*What?*"

She seemed to have some trouble getting her mouth to open. "The Remains. Only been here once. I didn't stay."

Nearer the center of the fleet, Riza looked mildly unsettled, but the commander's face was as stony as ever. Neither looked especially surprised by the shift in terrain. Around them, the trees grew whiter and whiter. Aside from the trees and a few patches of thorns, weeds, and pale flowers, Dante saw no signs of life. Yet the nether—the sign of life that had been—was thick in the air.

The slow build of pressure in his forehead sped up rapidly. After a few miles, he directed Volo to rendezvous with Riza's boat.

"We're gaining fast," Dante told the nobleman. "If this keeps up, we'll be on them within hours."

Riza's smile lacked all humor. "I had assumed as much. Make your preparations."

Dante motioned to one of the ghastly bone islands. "Were you intending to tell me what we're getting into? Or is it common in Tanar Atain to sail past mass graves?"

"This is the Wound of the World. The place where your enemy — and those who came before him — first learned to create the shadowmen."

"The Andrac? That knowledge came from your people?"

"They aren't *my* people." Riza spat over the side of the boat. "When the Odo Sein cast down the rebellion of sorcerers, they didn't slay all of the magicians. Instead, they turned a few into slaves. These they bent to the task of creating something that could patrol the borders of the Deep Swamp. In time, the slaves produced the shadowmen. At first, the Odo Sein used the abominations as intended, serving the land. Yet as soon as the first rebellion arose, they turned the shadowmen against their own people. This only engorged the demons' bloodlust. As the Odo Sein began to lose their grip on the shadowmen, they had no choice but to destroy them."

"How long ago was this? The Andrac have been used in other lands as well. Nearly four hundred years ago, they appeared in the Collen Basin."

"Learned by dark pilgrims to Tanar Atain, no doubt. As for the when, I can't say with any certainty. The Drakebane's ancestors have altered our history so often we're lucky to have preserved any truths at all. That, among other reasons, is why we fight him: for he destroys our history, and what is a people without their past?"

Dante wanted to learn more — for all the time he'd spent in Tanar Atain, it still felt like he barely knew anything about the place — but Riza left to talk strategy with Commander Barain. As the flotilla carried on, the ocher water turned rusty, streaked with crimson. It smelled like old iron. If not for the thinness of it, Dante would have thought it was blood. Some of the trees were now no more than bent white trunks.

By the afternoon, the force in Dante's brow had become so intense it nearly hurt. Gladdic was within a mile. Hearing this, Barain dispatched small scout canoes ahead. Dante would have sent undead creatures ahead as well, but there was nothing to use—there were no flies or fish, no rats or lizards. He would have tried raising some of the bones, but they were so scattered it would have been impossible to gather up a single body.

The scouts returned within minutes. Barain called for a stop to discuss the situation with his advisors. Awakened by the lack of motion, Naran stirred from one of his lengthy naps. The rain was still coming down, striking the trees and bones with hollow tocks.

The war council seemed to reach a decision. Riza summoned Dante's canoe to him. The nobleman pointed north into the white forest. "Ahead lies the Wound itself. This must be where Gladdic and his aides have decided to craft his new breed of shadowmen."

Dante peered through the trees. "Why here?"

"Besides the fact it looks like a demon's garden," Blays said.

"It is a site of ancient power that will make their task simpler," Riza said. "They might also have believed that we wouldn't follow them into the Go Kaza, considering that they would either starve here, or be forced in time to return to where the animals dwell and the fruit grows—and be slaughtered by the beasts there. Whatever their motives, they've already been here for hours. We must stop them before they create their demons."

"Have you formed a plan?" Dante said.

"Our scouts could only advance so far without risking discovery. They know the Odo Sein have formed a wide perimeter around the grounds, meaning to stifle any outside sorcery. For Gladdic to wield light and shadow, he'll have to be somewhere near the center of the circle inscribed by the Odo Sein, where their powers can't impact him.

"We will attack the perimeter from the south. This should

draw down most of the Odo Sein, as well as the bulk of their soldiers. This will render it exceedingly easy for you to slip past the pickets, locate Gladdic, and assassinate him."

"What about the Drakebane? Isn't killing him the entire reason your troops came all this way?"

"Your elimination of the sorcerer and his demons will make it much easier for us to reach the Drakebane. Additionally, he might confront us with the Odo Sein, expecting for Gladdic to reinforce him soon after—only for no such reinforcements to arrive."

Blays rubbed his knuckles into his forehead. "You're sure you can put up a fight against the Odo Sein? I've seen swords of every size and shape you can imagine, and theirs are the second-most I'd hate to be stabbed by."

"We have developed weapons to use against them." Riza glanced past Blays. "This reminds me. If Volo and your captain wish to accompany you, we can provide them with a small number of flaming stars."

"Flaming stars? It sounds like *I* want one."

"The bursting arrows. You may have seen them in use against the boko mai. They are also quite useful against the armor of the Odo Sein."

"I will take them," Naran said. "Better to fight beside my friends than to sit in safety while they risk their lives for my honor."

Volo tilted back her head. "Wouldn't it be even better to renounce your honor, paddle away, and go live a peaceful life as a farmer?"

"That might be the logical path. If so, then count being illogical as one of my many flaws."

"Me too, I guess, because I don't want to stay with the boat either."

Riza snapped his fingers at one of his servants, who delivered them each two arrows. The heads were plum-sized black bags packed tight with something that smelled smoky and metallic.

"Handle with care," Riza advised. "They explode on impact. 'Impact,' in this case, could include falling on them."

"Fair warning," Dante said. "Gladdic is an extremely skilled sorcerer. Fighting him will probably exhaust me. I doubt I'll be much use after that."

"You've made it very clear your only interest is in your foe. We have formulated our plans to account for this."

Blays loosened his sword in its scabbard. "Ready when you are. The sooner we get this over with, the sooner we can drink ourselves into forgetting we're wandering around in a place that would make Arawn himself wet his divine pants."

After a few more instructions, Riza left, saluting with his forearm lifted high, his fingers held together and pointed skyward like the head of a spear. One of the scout canoes joined them. It led them away from the main force and across a route that would approach the Wound from the west. The trees grew taller, spreading pale leaves that looked like the flensed skin of Gaskans.

Within a mile, a white hill loomed ahead. It didn't look much more than a hundred feet high, but after so long in such a flat and watery land, it loomed like the peaks of the Woduns. The trees closed in again, blocking it from sight.

The next time it emerged, Dante's breath caught in his throat. It was indeed a hill, or at least something like one, but the sides of it were largely open to the air. Long strands of rock or bone stretched between the floor and ceiling, looking like disheveled harp strings or the fibrous mouths of great whales. The floor of the cavern was elevated above the red water. It looked phantasmagoric, the dream of a sleeping god who, lost in his slumber, had accidentally made his nightmares real.

In the canoe beside them, the scout motioned to a shelf of dry land running along the base of the white hill. Dante nodded to the scout, tapped Volo's shoulder, and pointed to the shelf. She brought the canoe up to it and got out. There was nothing to tie up to, but the boat had a thin rope tied through a hole carved into a flat stone. In the slack water, it would be a fine anchor.

Dante got out, the boat swaying beneath him. Once the others were on the ledge, he moved forward to where the wall opened into the vast cavern beyond. Light filtered in from all sides, illuminating a yawning chamber dotted with reddish puddles. The pulse of Gladdic's presence was distractingly strong. The priest was to the east. And he was very close.

Riza had told them to wait on the outskirts of the Wound until they heard the cries of battle, so they stopped a short ways into the cavern, hunkering down behind a boulder the shape and color of a molar. The surface felt almost like sandstone, but Dante couldn't shake the impression of boneness. Water dripped from the high ceiling. The room smelled like rust and wet rock.

Voices rose somewhere to the southeast. As soon as Dante heard the first scream, he rose from behind the boulder, jogging across the cavernous space. As he weaved through the sheets and pillars of rock, he got out his antler-handled knife, opening a short cut on the back of his left arm. He reached for the shadows. They answered.

Near the far end of the cavern, the walls narrowed. A pool of red water filled the way forward. Eighty feet ahead, the rock climbed back out of the water and opened toward the right, where the spike in Dante's skull insisted Gladdic awaited.

Dante glanced at Volo and gestured at the water. She shrugged. He dipped a toe in, discovering it was only a few inches deep. As he advanced, the water rose to his shins, then his knees. The others were strung along beside him. He and Blays kept their nethereal blades sheathed, not wanting to drain themselves, but Naran and Volo carried bows with nocked arrows.

Dante was two-thirds of the way across the pool when its surface rippled on all sides. At first he thought it must be rain blowing in from the cave's edge, but no water was hitting him.

Around him, scores of stark white faces arose from the water, eyes burning with malice.

26

A hundred Tanarians surrounded them in the water. The men and women looked as though they'd been drowned, but there was still some form of life in their eyes. Some were dressed in rags while others were completely nude, red water sliding down their concave stomachs. Black hair hung over their faces in clumps. Most carried jagged shards of bone.

Blays whipped his Odo Sein blade from its sheath, purple and black crackling down its length. "Now listen here—"

Without so much as a word, the mob surged forward. Dante drew his sword in his right hand and the nether in his left. Naran and Volo let loose their arrows and two of the people dropped, trampled by those behind them. Dante slung a hailstorm of black bolts into the front ranks, felling half a dozen in one swoop.

As he reached for another handful of shadows, the nether froze in place. "Odo Sein!"

Blays darted forward, slashing his sword at the closest figure. He struck the man at a downward angle, cleaving through the enemy's collarbone and into his upper chest. Blays pulled the blade free without a hitch, striking at the next man. While the weapon encountered some resistance as it churned through flesh and bone, with deft tweaks of his wrist, Blays was able to keep it moving with little loss of momentum, allowing him to swing his blade about himself like a bolo. As the bodies fell away from him, the wounds seemed slow to bleed. Threads of nether streamed from the navels of the dead and into Blays' weapon.

"Tighten up!" Blays called. "Back to back! Push toward the water's edge!"

Dante shuffled closer to him. A woman stabbed at him with a length of bone. He cut through its shaft, then through her arm. She dropped back two steps, then leaned forward and charged him with both arms extended for his face, one no more than a bleeding stump. He cut her down.

Behind him, Naran and Volo had had no choice but to toss their bows over their left shoulders and draw their weapons. Naran had his saber back—after the Righteous Monsoon had taken the Bastion, they'd found it in the palace's collection of artifacts taken from foreign intruders and criminals—and Volo bore a stout, curved blade with a heavy guard over the knuckles and a metal spike sticking from the pommel. It looked like, and was, a cruel, close-quarters weapon.

Which was very good news, because the enemy was throwing themselves at the four of them with inhuman recklessness. Within moments, the only thing keeping them from being completely overwhelmed was the corpses floating in the water and impeding the advance of those still living. As Dante chopped down a one-eyed man, a woman stabbed past his guard with a bone spear, goring him in the ribs.

Dante stumbled into Blays' back. As the woman moved to finish the job, Naran thrust forward, his saber spearing through her throat. Dante reached for the nether, meaning to heal himself, but it remained as locked up as the realm's crown jewels.

Next to him, Volo stabbed a sunken-eyed man through the chest. He took the blade willingly, sliding closer to her and stabbing down at her neck with a broken thigh bone. She turned her head, grunting as the weapon scraped down her collarbone and shoulder. Dante leaned in and cut off the man's sword arm at the elbow. Volo withdrew her weapon and bashed the man in the ear in with the heavy guard of her weapon.

Blays was the only one of them holding his own against the crush of bodies. For all of the ones they'd already killed, even more pressed in on them.

"No good," Dante said.

"No good about to die," Blays agreed, shearing through a woman's jaw. He gestured his mundane sword behind him toward the eastern face of the canyon-like space. "Cut a lane toward the wall! Volo, behind us with a flaming star!"

Dante and Naran cleaved their way eastward while Blays held off a throng of attackers at the point of their retreat. Volo paired with Naran, whose saber couldn't quite keep up with the frenzied men and women coming at them. Dante's side felt hot, the wound tearing at him with every thrust and hack. As they cut down the last of the enemy between them and the wall, Volo sheathed her blade with a clack, unshouldered her bow, and nocked one of the bag-tipped arrows.

"Ready!" A note of shrillness pierced her voice.

"Chevron," Blays said. He held the middle, Dante and Naran at his flanks. "Push!"

Dante surged forward, swinging his nethereal blade like a machete through the jungles of the Plagued Islands. Blays bellowed in echoing defiance, cleaving a grisly path forward. To that point, their foe had fought with a feral madness, all but oblivious to the wounds they suffered for it, but for the first time, they hesitated. Some even dropped back a step.

"Fall back!" Blays disengaged, splashing across the space they'd opened between themselves and Volo. The girl sighted down the shaft of her arrow, arm quivering. Blays flung himself forward. "*Loose!*"

Volo released her hold. Dante jumped headfirst toward the wall. As he splashed down, reddish light speared through the blood-colored water. A great fist slammed upon him, the impact judding up his spine. The thunder of the explosion followed an instant later. Half dazed, he found his feet, reeling to the side.

Limbs and torsos rocked on the unsettled surface. Pink foam sizzled and popped. Most of the enemy that hadn't been destroyed in the blast had been knocked from their feet. Blays was already wading into them, severing anything he could reach. Dante followed suit.

A man stood from the water, half his face hanging in shreds, teeth and jaw and throat exposed. Unarmed, he threw himself at

Dante. Dante flicked out his sword and cut him down the middle. The man didn't stop reaching for Dante's face until his entire body went slack.

Dante threw the corpse aside, chest heaving. They'd nearly cleared out the right flank of the opposition, but the people to their left were regrouping, gathering to mount another attack.

"Get down!" Naran's clear voice carried over the thresh of legs through water. He had his bow out, body tensed to the draw of the string.

Dante dropped back into the water. An arm bobbed against his head, fingers brushing his cheek. He closed his eyes, but he could still see the flash of light through his eyelids, feel the bang of sound in his chest.

He stood. The pool was slopping around like a storm-tossed sea. The air stank of sulfur and an acrid, insidious tang that made him want to turn away. Or maybe his nausea was the product of the slew of scorched torsos, floating limbs, and exposed organs. A handful of survivors were regaining their feet and moving together. They still didn't look scared. Just hateful and pained.

Blays moved across from them, angling both swords down from his sides. "Now would be a good time to surrender."

The people arrayed themselves in a line. There were only nine left, and of those who were still on their feet, most were bleeding, burned, or both. Despite this, they lurched forward. Blays' face tightened and twitched at the eyes and mouth. It was a fleeting expression, and so subtle that only Dante and possibly Minn would have caught the anguish in it.

He lifted his swords and cut down two men with three swings. Dante ran to join him, but by the time he got there, only a single man was still on his feet. With mild disgust, he put the man to rest.

Their breathing echoed through the cavern. Water dripped from the ceiling. Other than the ripples of the bobbing bodies, the pool was still.

Blays turned, teeth parted. "Is everyone all right?"

"Stabbed." Dante hovered his hand over his ribs. "I've had worse."

Volo was bleeding down her collar, but it didn't look serious. Naran had deep fingernail gouges across his forearm and a gash to the thigh. Painful, but not crippling.

"What *were* those things?" Volo's voice sounded half an octave higher. "They looked like people, but they didn't act like people. So were they people?"

"I've fought a lot of people," Blays said. "And I've never seen them come at you to the last man. They should have been shitting their rags after the first flaming star."

Naran nodded. "There is also the matter that they were lurking beneath the water. Not breathing is not a very peoplish thing to do."

"Either that, or you need to hire some of them as sailors."

"Watch the water," Dante said. "And everything else, too. We have to get moving. If the Monsoon breaks through the Drakebane's lines, Gladdic might decide to run away."

"He tends to do that, doesn't he?" Blays slogged along beside him. "Ought to write his superiors a letter of condemnation. We can send it inside the box we deliver his head in."

The stone sloped up beneath Dante's feet. He left the pool, dripping red everywhere. With a start, he realized he still had his sword out, but he didn't feel enervated in the slightest. If anything, he felt energized, and so did the sword: the nether flowing along its blade was rushing like floodwaters. Yet the nether around him was still frozen in place.

The shelf of rock bent to the right. Ahead, thin white lengths of matter rose in a blade-like forest, obscuring the view of what lay ahead. The roar and batter of combat sounded to the south. The pressure in Dante's head had grown so strong it felt like a spike was ready to press through the middle of his brow.

"We're close." He glanced at Naran and Volo. "If you have a shot at Gladdic, take it."

They made noises of agreement. Naran's gaze was distant but steady, as if his time in captivity had taught him that slaughtering a hundred hostile insane people was just one of those things you did in life. Volo's face looked haunted. On the brink of a breakdown. A stark contrast to the aftermath of the massacre they'd seen on their way to Dara Bode, when her response had been red-hot anger. Then again, that time, she hadn't had to kill anyone herself.

They entered the forest of pale blades. These were smooth, with the occasional knob or curve. It made the formations look organic, like trunks or bones.

Blays let his fingers trail along a flat, rib-like projection. "Know what this reminds me of?"

Dante nodded. "Barden."

"Is that because it *is* like Barden?"

"It has to be. This place is wronger than Lyle's prophecies." A sharp tingle poked into Dante's palm. He jerked back his hand, nearly dropping his sword. Blays twitched, too. Dante looked up. "You felt that?"

"You mean the invisible bees attempting to make a home in the center of my hand?"

"Any idea what it was?"

"Let me ask." He held the hilt up to his ear, glancing up and to the right. "Hello, sword? My friend thinks I am a soothsayer. Any suggestions as to how I should best insult his intelligence?"

Dante turned the sword in his hand, eyeing the handle. There were no obvious signs of trouble, but it was still emitting a tingle that verged on unpleasant.

Something drove into his side. The thing was Blays, tackling him to the hard ground. As the air left Dante's lungs in a rude whoosh, he heard the twang of bows. Arrows swept overhead and rapped into the white trunks behind them. Chunks of chalky matter spat down on their heads.

"Archers," Blays said.

"You don't say?!" Dante wheezed, catching his breath. "Were they the kind with bows *and* arrows?"

Beside him, Volo leaned around a bony trunk and let loose an arrow. She swung back behind cover. "I count about eight."

"Then I hope the last battle gave you double vision." Dante reached for the nether, but it was still trapped fast, as if caught beneath a rock. "Drakebane's men?"

"Either that or the Odo Sein they're with enslaved them from somewhere."

"*Odo Sein?*"

He peeked his head up from cover. The trunks of matter were rarely taller than a man's gut, and while they sometimes grew in small clusters, there was usually several feet of space between them. This meant both cover and visibility were decent. The archers were hunkered down in a line about eighty feet away. One snapped off a shot at him; he ducked, then reappeared on the other side of the trunk he was using for cover. A pair of Odo Sein advanced from hiding, ducking to the next row of bone-trees. As soon as they were in place, a second pair got up to follow them onward.

Two incoming arrows forced Dante back into place. "Four knights." With no nether to draw on, his options felt comically limited. "Advancing in pairs. Naran and Volo, time their advance, then see if you can shoot them down. If you can take them out, that might free me up to use the nether against the archers."

Volo and Naran nocked arrows, sticking an eye from behind cover. The Odo Sein were moving fast, already within sixty feet. When the next pair moved, Volo and Naran both fired at the lead knight. The first arrow struck it square in the helmet, glancing off the tough scales of the swamp dragon's hide. The knight jerked up his shield and caught the second arrow squarely.

A barrage of arrows forced everyone back into cover. When Dante looked out again, the archers were slowly fanning to left and right, searching for an angle of attack through the field of thin white pillars. Volo hit another knight in the breastplate, but the arrow broke with a metal clink.

Dante gritted his teeth. "Hold, and the archers get behind us. Retreat?"

Blays shook his head. "Charge."

"Ha! You first."

Blays rolled from behind cover, crouched too low to see or be seen. Dante ran at his heels. Ahead, he caught a glimpse of black scaled armor. Boots clapped against the smooth ground. A knight spotted them, calling to the others in unworried words. Dante's heart sank. He'd been hoping to take at least one of them out before the enemy knew they were coming. He trusted himself to be able to hold off a single knight while Blays dispatched the two others. But if he had to go two on one…then he'd hope Arawn was watching. Or not, considering how embarrassingly he was likely to lose.

The knights jogged toward them, blades in hand, purple sparks popping from the edges like damp sticks of wood thrown in a fire. They were now too close to the Odo Sein for the enemy archers to fire on them. Dante stood and lifted his sword high, then brought it down to a guard. Blays put his nethereal blade forward, his plain steel weapon held back in reserve.

A pair of knights converged on Blays. The other two circled toward Dante. Dante stopped in place, ready to dance back behind a trunk to try to keep himself from being engaged by both at once.

An arrow zipped past his shoulder. The Odo Sein it was racing toward lifted his shield, ready to knock it aside. The bag-headed arrow thumped into the shield. Dante closed his eyes and dropped his legs out from beneath himself.

The explosion ripped the knight's body into quadrants. Flame spurted between the white trunks. They cracked and toppled, landing with a sound that was heavier than wood but more hollow than stone. Heat breathed over Dante's right arm. He yanked it into the cover of the trunk in front of him.

Blays jumped to his feet and sprinted toward the blast. The dismembered knight's partner was down on one knee, sword on the ground. Blays took off his head with a looping swipe.

The two surviving knights exchanged a wordless look, then turned and retreated through the white pillars.

An enemy arrow whipped over Dante's head. He got down. The air smelled like acrid smoke and an inside-out stomach. The archers covered the Odo Sein's withdrawal, then fell back with them, continuing to pepper Dante and Blays' position with shots.

Crouching low, Blays unbuckled the dead knights' belts. He crossed one belt over his hip, grabbed up a fallen sword, and sheathed it. Naran and Volo joined them.

Blays handed the other belt to Naran. "Leave the sword put away until it's time to use it. That is, unless you enjoy feeling like this guy over here." He pointed to a gobbet of former knight, then to another. "And over here. And here. And—"

"I believe I get the picture." Naran sheathed his sword with a click.

Volo looked up at Dante. "Is your face always that red? You look like a walking tomato."

He scowled at her. "Was that you who shot them? Next time you're going to explode something, try not to do it directly in my face."

"Then keep your face out of my explosions."

Dante put away his sword. "That tingling. It started when the enemy got near us. I think it might have been a warning."

Blays glanced down at his blades in disdain. "And they couldn't be bothered to warn us about the half-zombies in the pool?"

"Then maybe it alerts you when you're in the presence of another sword-bearer."

"Or maybe you don't know what you're talking about."

"In these circumstances, that remains a strong possibility. Everyone fit to go on?"

It turned out he was the only one who'd taken so much as a scratch. The retreating soldiers had gone in the same direction as the spike in Dante's head was pointing. As they moved through the trunks, the ground sloping gently uphill beneath them, he reached again and again for the nether. For years, he'd drawn on it reflexively, often for no purpose but to work his skills near the end of the day. Its lack made him more anxious by the second. A physical repulsion was growing in his gut, telling him to get out.

But there was a second option to get back to the shadows: to destroy everyone who was keeping them away from him.

The rain had stopped while they were inside the cavern, but as they hurried onward, it broke open again, drumming against the stony landscape. At the ridge, they got down on their bellies and crawled over the rim, continuing forward for fifteen feet before Dante was confident their silhouettes wouldn't show against the line of the hill.

Ahead, more white trunks poked from the ground, but there were fewer of them, offering little cover. The land below them was a bowl-shaped valley hundreds of yards across. The white surface was spattered with deposits of iron gray rock which, judging from the shine and the smell, probably were in fact iron ore. Where their edges touched the white matter, the ore had turned not the rusty orange of iron-bearing rock exposed to the weather, but bright crimson. Shallow pools of blood-red water collected in the depressions in the terrain.

A hillock rose in the center of the valley. At the center of the hillock stood a dark cylinder. The two knights and their complement of archers were running toward the cylinder, where a group of thirty people stood in the rain. Multiple Odo Sein held watch on the perimeter of the hillock, obvious in their heavy armor.

Most of the others held position between the knight sentries and the center. But next to the cylinder itself, a figure in gray robes gestured his hands to the sky.

"That's Gladdic," Dante said.

"And there's a small legion with him," Blays said. "Under normal circumstances, I'd tell them to go get some more friends to make it a fair fight, and then kill Gladdic when they fell for my ruse and left. But I'm guessing by the constipated look on your face that you still can't use the nether."

"But again, if we kill all the Odo Sein there—"

"Then we still won't know if there are others lurking around until it's too late."

"Then what do you want to do? Sneak across this almost completely open field and try to surprise the people who are about to be warned by the other people whose asses we just kicked that we're about to sneak up on them?"

"I don't know if you're aware of this, but there's typically a reason that people don't launch attacks on people who outnumber them ten times over."

"Because it's stupid?" Volo said.

"We could return to the Monsoon," Naran said. "Beseech them for assistance."

Dante pinched his temples. "We don't even know if they've won their battle with the Drakebane. Or if they'd help us. Besides, whatever Gladdic's working on, he's doing it right now. If we run off to find Riza, by the time we get back, Gladdic could have one of his new demons ready."

The group they'd skirmished with reached the hillock and ran up it. Blays swept his rain-dampened blond hair back from his brow. "Whatever we're going to do, we better do it before they come hunting for us."

The knights ascended the mound and kneeled before a man in a green and white tunic that hung to his knees. They spoke, the knights gesturing in the general direction where Dante and the others lay in hiding.

"Huh," Blays said. "Suppose that's the ol' Drakebane?"

"Or one of his relatives." Dante wished he'd had a rat on hand to send to listen to the conversation. Then again, in this lifeless land, the appearance of a rat wouldn't draw any less attention than if he were to walk up to the hillock himself.

The two knights stood, backing off. The man in the long green jabat called out an order; Dante couldn't hear a word of it, but there was no missing the way the exercise of command straightened the man's body. Eight Odo Sein and another eight people in less distinguishable dress gathered around the man giving the orders.

The group moved out from the mound. Dante had assumed they were mustering to deal with the threat reported by the two knights, but rather than striking west toward Dante and the others, the royal contingent headed northeast.

Gladdic turned away from his work, watching the contingent depart. They were much too far away for Dante to read his face.

"Well that makes things a little easier," Blays said. "Now we're only outnumbered six times over."

"Still too many knights."

"We don't have to fight all of them. We could walk up to arrow range, lob some insults at Gladdic to distract him, then have Naran hit him with the last flaming star."

"And then run like hell?"

"Unless you've decided to start a vendetta against all of his friends, too."

Dante turned to Naran. "How close will we have to be? How's your bow string feeling in this rain?"

"It's well-waxed," Naran said. "I don't think this is the first time Tanarian archers have had to deal with a little moisture."

They spent the next few minutes sketching out their approach, including ways to try to force Gladdic from cover. As they finalized their plans, Dante glanced over at the cylinder, where Gladdic had been motionless for some time. Two Odo Sein ordered six people in plain white jabats to stand shoulder to shoulder. The knights moved down the line and the people dropped, bleeding. Gladdic knelt over the bodies, arms extended to his sides.

As Dante watched, a looming black figure unfurled from nowhere to stand beside the priest. It spread its clawed hands wide and tipped back its head, rain falling into its star-bright mouth.

"Bastard sons of bastard gods," Dante said. "He's got an Andrac."

The others all looked over. Naran's face hardened in its newly distant way. Volo looked uncertain but defiant, as if her turning back of the Odo Sein had rebuilt the resolve she'd lost after the battle in the pool.

"Right," Blays said. "Shit."

Dante smacked his fist against the ground. "We can't go at them now. The ether's locked down, too—there's no way to hurt the demon."

"That's not the only way to hurt them, is it? I can cut them from within the shadows."

"Which we can't get to, either. We'll have to wait until they make camp. Or see if we can draw Gladdic away somehow."

"Why would we do that? He's just made our job easier."

"Is it our job to die as fast as we can? Because that's the only thing that's going to happen if we go up against the Odo Sein, an Andrac, Gladdic, and whatever else they have over there."

"Think, no-brains. What are the Andrac made out of?"

"Nether," Dante said. "Traces."

"And what are our blades powered by?"

"Also traces." Dante could feel his mind struggling to raise and hold on to the implications of what Blays was saying. Before the logic could slip away, he retreated to the same quiet, impersonal distance he used when working with the ether. A state where things seemed to unfold on their own. He looked up. "It *should* work. But we'd be banking our lives on a theory."

"Yes, but at least if I'm wrong, then you'll get the chance to tell me all about it in the Mists."

"If we wind up in the Mists' version of Tanar Atain, I think I'll skip straight to the Worldsea."

"This idea," Naran said. "It necessitates being engaged by the Andrac before any of their other fighters? Is it safe to assume that will happen? If I have learned anything, it is that the captain who thinks he can predict a battle had better tell his first mate where he'd like to be buried."

"Gladdic will send the Andrac," Dante said. "They're his life's work. An extension of himself. There will be nothing more satisfying to him than to use them to destroy us."

Blays wiped rain from his eyebrows. "Anyway, this is our backup plan. Our main plan is for you to use the last flaming star to blast Gladdic into pious stew."

Plan in hand, Dante remained kneeling behind the screen of bone-like limbs, trying to pick out their best approach to the center of the valley. A minute later, after some fussing about by Gladdic, a second Star-Eater unfolded from nowhere, stretching its broad arms like a man readying to split wood.

Dante swore. Most times, waiting and watching made you better prepared for what was to come. Sometimes, though, it merely allowed you to believe you were preparing when in fact all you were doing was delaying. And a situation that could have been solved slipped beyond your control.

In a low crouch, Dante moved to the next grove of waist-high growths. The others followed behind him, their sandals barely making a sound on the wet rock. For all their stealth, they weren't a third of the way toward the hillock before one of the Odo Sein pointed at them, his voice booming over the hiss of the rain.

Most of the remaining knights gathered to watch them, with a few remaining on the periphery to ward against a sneak attack from another direction. Gladdic turned from his work and stared across the bowl. There was no sense trying to hide; it was only slowing them down. Dante stood and walked toward the raised lump of land, keeping his hand close to his sword. Rain pattered on the flat pockets of iron with a metallic beat.

The walk felt much longer than it was. They started up the hillock. Its sides were half covered in irregular flows of iron, as if the metal had been heated to a liquid and then poured down the slopes to harden.

Dante came to a stop halfway up the incline. Now that they were closer to the cylinder, he could see that the iron monument at the middle of the land wasn't round, but a hexagon, its sides inscribed with foreign runes. It stood fifteen feet high and twenty across, but its solidity was marred by river-like cracks in its surface, their depths weeping bloody rust.

Gladdic stood above them, flanked by his two Andrac, whose wide alien mouths were drawn back in hideous grins. A pair of knights were with him as well, seemingly untroubled by the demons mere feet away. The other knights waited on the flanks, mailed fists resting on the horn-pommeled handles of their swords. A few archers stood twenty feet back from the front line, leaning over their nocked arrows to shield their fletching from the rain.

"Dante Galand." Gladdic's voice was a melodious mix of amusement and scorn. "Do you find your own land so unbearable that you would rather abandon it to follow me into the depths of this one?"

"I'd like nothing more to be home," Dante answered. "But you keep trying to destroy the homelands of others—first in the Plagued Islands, then in Collen, now here."

As he spoke, Naran and Volo spread to either side of him, kneeling down behind small outcroppings of white rock. It wasn't perfect cover, but it was better than nothing. Blays remained two steps behind him and to his right.

Gladdic sneered down at them, his wet gray hair plastered to his head. "Your righteousness sickens me."

Dante laughed. "*My* righteousness? You use the nether—a substance you kill others for touching—to make abominations I would never dream of! And then you claim to be the holiest man in Bressel!"

"I use tools the gods forbid in order to achieve things men can't dream. When at last all heresy is quenched, I will quench it from myself as well."

"That's a very convenient excuse. It would justify you to do anything you want."

"You mean like murder thousands of innocent people?" Blays said.

"You mean in Collen?" Dante said. "Or Tanar Atain? You'll have to forgive me, he's racked up so many massacres that—"

Gladdic took two strides forward. "My purpose here is not to *destroy*. As that is all you do, that is all you can see in others. *I* am here for salvation."

Blays motioned to the demons. "And what are they here for? The free lunch?"

"They are here to undo a threat that could undo us all. So I beg you, slander me with your petty notions of hypocrisy. How much will you care for following your own rules when everything stands at its end?"

"Has it ever occurred to you that you're a raving lunatic?"

"Look around you!" Gladdic thrust his arms apart to take in the twisted landscape of red, white, and black. He laughed, a dry and raven-like caw. "Does this look like a land fit for humans? Here, you face total enslavement. One that will come at the hands of the same darkness you worship."

Dante had meant to engage Gladdic in order to buy plenty of time for Naran to position and ready himself to take his shot—the only one he'd get—but instead, Dante's anger had sucked him into an argument with a madman.

"I know who you are," he said. "And you are a liar."

Gladdic waved a long-fingered hand at the air. "Your words sicken my ears. You must have noticed your nether is powerless here. You will surrender. Or my servants will devour you."

"You're right," Dante said. "I can't reach the nether. But do you really think I'd be here if I didn't know exactly how to kill you?"

He lifted his arm and swung it down. To his left, Naran's bow twanged. The arrow sped uphill. Gladdic's eyes widened. Despite his age, he was nimble, his long thin legs coiling to dodge the attack.

But it would be too late to escape the weapon's blast.

Beside him, an Odo Sein launched himself forward. The arrow struck him in the chest. For the blink of an eye, nothing happened—had the arrow gotten too sodden to work?—and then came the lightning and the thunder.

Dante whirled, shielding his face. Heat whooshed past him. The shock of the explosion rattled his guts. He turned, squinting through the smoke. The knight lay in pieces. Gladdic had been knocked backward onto the rocky surface. Steam whorled from his soaked robes, but he was already stirring, swaying to his hands and knees.

Half his face was pinkened. He twisted his features into a snarl, shouting words Dante didn't recognize, and thrust his finger downhill. The two Andrac spread their jaws wide, throats glowing, and loped toward Dante. The Knights of Odo Sein advanced behind the demons in two loose groups, spreading themselves out to avoid losing more than one at a time to any more flaming stars. One group looked to be headed toward Naran, the other veering toward Volo.

Blays drew his twin blades, making them dance. The rain seemed to sizzle in the purple-black light. Dante drew his weapon, angling the blade toward the nearer Andrac. The handle tingled in his palm. Uphill, Gladdic faltered a step, a line of confusion crossing his face to see them standing their ground.

"So," Blays said. "Plan?"

"Cut it open." Dante dropped back, standing shoulder to shoulder with Blays. "And hope you're right."

The first Star-Eater bunched its legs and flung itself at them, crossing twenty feet in a single bound. It slammed down and raked at Dante with its long black claws. The monster was much smaller than the swamp dragon had been, but the fact it stood upright—twelve feet if it was an inch—made it feel horrifically large. And while he'd fought a far bigger one at the Reborn Shrine, he hadn't *dueled* it. The urge to break and run was almost overpowering.

Dante skipped back, the claws flashing past him and gouging into the rock in front of him. His sandal came down on a patch of iron slick with rain. His foot flew out from beneath him, dumping him onto the metal.

His shoulders hit first, his head snapping back. Light flashed across his eyes. A shadow hung over him, filling the sky; a white sun blared within it. The darkness reached for him. Purple lightning lashed out, cutting across the shadows.

The demon's scream jarred Dante's mind back into action. He was lying on his back and Blays had just struck the demon—and saved Dante's life. Wisps of shadow fizzled away from the Star-Eater's finger, which was now just a stump.

Dante grinned. Blays' sword had actually hurt it. Presumably, as Blays had deduced, because it was churning with trace-nether, the same raw substance the Andrac was made from. While it existed in the real world as a kind of ghostly projection, impervious to steel, attacking it with a trace was in effect attacking it with something from its own realm. Or like when Blays fought them within the shadows, where they *could* be hurt.

To left and right, Naran and Volo were in full retreat. The Odo Sein followed, but gave the two Andrac a wide berth. Volo was somehow firing her bow on the run, searching for a weak point in the knights' armor, keeping control of her footing even as her sandals skidded over rock and iron. There were a few archers on top of the hillock trying to take shots at Naran and Volo, but they were overcompensating in their efforts to avoid hitting the knights, their arrows arcing past.

The demon's hand had already stopped leaking shadows. Unbound by whatever ability the Odo Sein were using to lock the nether in place, the demon's traces reformed its severed finger and claw. Blays rushed the creature. It clawed at him and he spun to the side, raking both swords down its arm. Nether gouted from the wounds like inky blood.

Dante reached for it, but before he could try to take hold, the second demon lunged at Blays from the side. Dante charged and slashed into the second Andrac's leg. It spun on him and swung its claws down at his head. Dante thrust up his nethereal blade, holding it at a 45-degree angle to intercept across as wide a space as possible.

The claws came down on the sword with a sound like a hammer smacking an ingot. The blade held, but something snapped in Dante's wrist. Pain shot up to his elbow. His sword fell from his grasp and landed with a clang. He bent to pick it up, but the Andrac was slashing at him with its other hand. Dante twisted himself under its claws and backpedaled three steps. The Andrac crouched over the sword as if claiming it, then grinned at him and whirled on Blays.

"Behind you!" Dante yelled.

At that moment, Blays was jabbing and slashing at the other Star-Eater with both swords, whipping them around so fast the demon was actually falling back a step, its mouth closed in a glowing white line. Now, Blays spun about, flicking his wrist to send his sword skidding into the other Andrac's claws.

Parrying the blow, he sidestepped to avoid the first demon's attack at his turned back. It was almost as if he could feel the demons' every move. And maybe he could—maybe there was a ripple in the nether, some subtle hint—but watching him parry and counter the attacks of two demons at once, Dante thought he had simply been born to fight.

"Take cold comfort!" Gladdic called from above. "When you die, your souls will mingle to form a new Andrac to fight for me."

The archers had quit firing. A glance their way showed the cause: Gladdic and a pair of soldiers had murdered them with a long lance and a stout blade. Standing over their corpses, as well as those of the servants the knights had killed earlier, he turned away from the battle and swung his hands together. Gathering the traces. A third demon unfurled, shrieking in joy.

Dante's wrist throbbed. Possibly broken. He watched helplessly, casting about for nether that wouldn't budge from its crevices in the earth. The Star-Eaters were attacking Blays more cautiously now, exposing no more than their claws. Blays was too busy keeping himself alive to risk a sustained attack that might wound one of them again.

All the demons had to do was bide their time and wait for him to make a mistake.

Blays retreated a step, then a second. As the demon who'd disarmed Dante followed Blays, it left Dante's sword alone on the rock. Dante rushed up to grab it. The demon who'd disarmed him spun about, backhanding its claws at his head and forcing him back.

"Now!" Dante screamed. "Draw its blood!"

Blays, momentarily alone with the other Star-Eater, pressed hard, blades pinging against its blocking claws. He jerked forward, pressing toward its center. It deflected him, then fell back a step to give its partner the opportunity to rejoin it. As it moved its weight back, it left its left leg extended forward for balance.

Blays collapsed as if struck. He whipped his right wrist downward, slamming his blade into the top of the demon's exposed foot. Shadows spurted to either side.

Dante snapped at them like a striking snake. Unlike every drop of nether in the valley, the shadows bleeding from the Andrac responded to his call—because they were traces, immune to the Odo Sein's oppression.

Great coils of darkness wrapped around his forearms. He hurled some of the nether downhill, into the backs of the knights who were still chasing Volo and Naran across the hellish terrain. Others he pressed to his ribs and wrist. His pain numbed, then vanished altogether.

The demon guarding his sword hissed like crackling fire and charged at him. Still pulling nether from the wounded Andrac, Dante thrust up the rock beneath his lost blade, popping it into the air and spinning toward him. Blays might have caught it out of midair, but Dante let it fall beside him.

The wounded demon was staggering, falling in on itself. Blays hacked at its body with both blades. Dante wrenched out another handful of shadows and plunged them into the ground beneath the Star-Eater charging him, yanking the rock away. The demon tripped into the hole. Dante lunged forward, skewering its arm as it grasped for a hold.

Its nether coursed from the wound. Dante took it and shaped it into black bolts, slinging a salvo uphill toward Gladdic. There, the priest had already crafted another demon from the dead archers. He gestured frantically, calling a third from the traces left by the murdered servants. The three Andrac crossed their arms over their faces and waded into the incoming shadows. Dark tufts sprayed from their bodies. They swatted at any bolt that tried to slip past them, hands fraying into dark clouds that were already starting to reform.

A single bolt made it through, speeding toward Gladdic. The priest threw his right hand in front of his face. The nether sliced through his wrist, his tan hand bouncing once against the iron ground.

Gladdic lifted his stump to his eyes. His mouth fell open. As Dante reached for another round of nether, the demon in the pit hauled its way out, swinging its weakened arm at him. Dante batted the claws aside with his sword and swept away the stone and iron beneath the demon a second time. As it fell, unbalanced, he brought his sword down on its head.

At the top of the hillock, Gladdic was dashing toward the massive iron hexagon, his sodden robes flapping around him. He touched it with a rod-like object in his left hand. A blue flash seared through the air, far brighter than any flaming star.

"You wouldn't let me stop it?" Gladdic's voice shook with hysteria. "Then you can be the first to die!"

Cracks shot across the hexagon. The iron groaned and scraped. Gladdic ran behind the monument. Dante fired a dozen bolts after him, but unable to see his target or sense him in the nether, there was almost no chance of hitting Gladdic.

The demon Blays had wounded collapsed into vapor beneath his swords. Blays ran toward Dante, cleaving into the trapped Andrac's back as Dante chopped at its arms and head. It dimmed, the wall of the pit visible behind its translucent body, then broke apart in a spray of shadows. Whatever was left of the traces absorbed into the white rock.

At the top of the rise, the three Star-Eaters turned away from Dante and toward the collapsing iron hexagon. Great slabs of metal fell from its sides, banging down like the pots and pans of a giant too drunk to cook. Below, the five surviving Odo Sein had quit chasing after Naran and Volo and were now staring uphill in perfect stillness.

"What are we all looking at?" Blays said.

"Clearly, everyone's disturbed by Gladdic's senseless act of petty vandalism." Dante flinched as an entire side of the hexagon fell outward and hammered to the ground. "I have the bad feeling there's something inside there."

He twisted and made a broad "come here" gesture to Naran and Volo. Eyeing the motionless and possibly stunned Odo Sein, the two of them moved laterally across the hillside, further separating themselves from the knights, then trekked uphill. This, at last, spurred the Odo Sein into action. But rather than chasing the man and the girl, they appeared to be jogging to join the Andrac.

With a final dying groan, the ceiling of the hexagon collapsed on itself. A white spar of bone thrust into the air. With a bloom of pulverized iron dust, a towering figure stalked from the wreckage of the monument, spear in hand.

A prickling sensation shot through Dante's sword hand so hard he had to glance at it to make sure it hadn't turned into a writhing mass of ants. In the metal rubble, a gauzy nimbus of light obscured anything more than the man's outline. Though he didn't quite rival the Andrac, he stood taller than any norren, with the build of an axeman or a blacksmith. Long strips of pale cloth fluttered from his forearms.

The light sank into his body, revealing the details of his being. His skin was blue-white and semi-translucent, glowing like sunlight through ice. His face was beardless and weathered in the way of snow that had melted, refrozen, and been scoured by winds. He looked incredibly old—really, he looked *dead*—but at the same time he seemed vibrant, ageless, less of a mortal being and more of a natural force.

His eyes were an unsteady state of blue, shifting from light powder to steel blue and then to something as dark as the ocean under full sunlight. His hair was white, curling around his face. His expression was blank like a lion's. Dante could feel great surges of sorcery within him, barely tamped down by the power of the Odo Sein.

The being glanced at the demons, then downhill. Coming under his gaze was like being struck by a thrown brick.

"Er," Blays said. "Who the fuck is *that*?"

27

The man from the hexagon swiveled his head to face the closest Andrac. He spoke in a voice that sounded like it was coming from inside a copper still. The language was nothing that Dante had ever heard. Other than his mouth, the man's face didn't move at all.

The Andrac twisted its mouth into a sneer, flexed its claws, and charged. The man lowered his weapon and dropped into a fighting stance. Rather than a traditional spear, he bore something like a glaive, with a sword-like blade fixed to the end of a straight pole. Rather than metal, it seemed to be carved from the same stone they were standing on—or, perhaps, from bone.

The blade collided with the demon's claws in a storm of black and white sparks. The blue-white giant twirled his wrists, snapping the blade clear and driving it forward. It dug deep into the Andrac's shoulder, sending the demon back with a squealing hiss.

The other two Star-Eaters planted their feet and sprung toward their foe.

Blays let his swords droop until their tips were nearly scraping the ground. "If the tremendously frightening looking fellow is fighting our enemies, then surely that makes him our friend, right?"

Dante's mouth had gone completely dry. "Not sure we can count on that."

Sandals scuffed up the slope. Naran and Volo ran up to join them. Both showed a few scrapes, but no major wounds.

Naran's face was beaded with sweat and rain. "Should I bother to ask what is happening?"

Blays frowned at him. "Never seen a trapped giant maniac do battle with three nether-demons before?"

Atop the mound, the man twirled and jabbed, the strips of cloth on his arms snapping with each block and strike. On the hillside, the five Odo Sein broke into a dirge-like chant. It felt like a song of their own deaths, but their voices were composed and determined, even joyous or perhaps spiritual, as if they were finally being put to the use they had dedicated their lives to.

The pressure in Dante's head was slightly weaker, but still very much present. "Gladdic's not far. This would seem like a very good time to pursue him."

"Right," Blays said. "And then might I suggest running away? Ideally somewhere very far from here?"

Dante sheathed his sword and ran along the circumference of the hillock. Above them, the titans tore at each other. One of the Andrac was already leaking shadows from several deep wounds. The man had suffered a single claw-rake. His skin seemed to be seeping a glowing white fluid. The Odo Sein joined the battle, but beneath the towering demons and the statue-like man in white, their hulking armor looked as puny as children using sticks to play-fight in the yard.

Dante swung around the back side of the hill. Gladdic was already halfway across the bowl, stumbling along on the wet rock. After they'd gotten a hundred yards toward the far rim, the priest turned around, spotted them, and pushed his pace faster.

Even so, they were gaining. They'd catch him soon after cresting the ridge. And with the sign of his blood pulsing in Dante's brow, he'd have nowhere to hide.

Dante glanced over his shoulder. One of the Star-Eaters and at least one of the Odo Sein were nowhere to be seen. Despite being heavily outnumbered, the blue-white man looked to be fine. His glaive now showed pale blue markings along the shaft that glowed with inner light. They might have been runes, probably the same ones that had been on the hexagon, but Dante was too far away to be sure.

They neared a fold filled with red water. As Dante splashed through, the surface surged to his left and right. Half a dozen of the ghostly white people emerged, their eyes filled with a sick and angry yearning. They jumped to their feet and sprinted after Dante and the others, obliging them to draw their weapons and turn around. The enemy fought ferociously, but with no coordination. The nethereal blades put them down in moments.

The four of them ran on after Gladdic. More of the water-people were arising from pockets of water from around the entire valley. Most were streaming toward the center, faces pulled tight with a focus that looked almost religious in power. They hurtled forward with heedless disregard for their own bodies, slipping on the wet rock and metal, leaving bloody footprints that were soon washed away by the rain.

Others diverted course to come at Dante and the others, forcing them to stop again, find favorable footing, and defend themselves. None of the people said a single word. As the nether-wrapped blades cut through them, rather than pain or terror, their faces warped in anguished frustration.

Few of the pale beings were arising near the fringes of the circular valley and Gladdic appeared untroubled by them. Dante wasn't certain, but they seemed to be losing ground on the priest. Swearing under his breath, he glanced back at the small hill where the hexagon had stood. His eyes bulged.

Blays twisted around for a look. "Tell me the Andrac are charging off to fight an invisible foe. Because if they're actually running away, then I am officially terrified."

The demons' backs were turned to the ice-like man as they fled from the mound, trails of shadows streaming behind them. There was no sign of the Odo Sein except perhaps for some of the red splashed around on the rock. The man planted his long glaive and watched the demons retreat. The next time Dante glanced back, the man had turned to stare at them.

"We should run faster," Dante said. "If you can't run faster, start thinking of ways to beg for your life."

Five more of the water-people plunged through the bony posts, stopping them in their tracks. Faced with the Odo Sein blades, the attackers weren't much of a threat, but by the time Blays sent the last of them thudding to the ground, Gladdic had slipped over the ridge.

The man from the hexagon was on the move, too. He didn't look to be hurrying, yet he sped over the ground as if it were being pulled along beneath him.

"He's coming for us," Dante said. "We have about a minute to find good ground and make the most of it."

Blays pointed to a long platform of rock elevated from the earth around it by a few inches on one side and two feet on the other. It looked to be the best they'd find. They jumped up on it, Blays heading straight for the puddle of blood-red water near its center and swishing his sword around in it to make sure it wasn't harboring any of the undrowned people.

The blue-white man had reached the bottom of the hillock and was now bounding up the slope with a wolfish combination of speed and tirelessness. Streams of water-people were dashing after him with looks of yearning chiseled into their faces, but despite their haste, the giant quickly left them behind.

Dante called out to the nether. With the death of the Odo Sein, he'd thought it would be released, but it remained stuck fast. Was the Odo Sein's power something they carried passively in their flesh, with no need to actively exert it? Were there others lurking out of sight nearby? Or was the whole Wound somehow cut off from the flow of shadow and glow of light that existed in every other corner of the world?

He looked to the ether, but it too was held in place. He moved beside Blays and drew his sword.

The giant man slowed to his equivalent of a jog. He stopped thirty feet away from their shelf of rock. It didn't feel nearly far enough; with one leap and a thrust of his glaive, he could be among them.

The man gazed at Dante, eyes shifting between every shade of blue. His features didn't look Tanarian. In fact, they didn't look like any people Dante had yet seen: the eyes seemed to be too long at the corners, the mouth stretching too wide below his thick nose.

Dante held his sword at his side. "Who are you?"

He'd spoken in Mallish. When the man replied, his voice reverberating through the open air, it was in a flowing language that didn't remind Dante of anything he'd ever heard.

The man lifted his left hand, pointing at Dante's chest. He spoke again, voice rising.

"Whatever it is, it was that guy's fault." Blays pointed in the direction Gladdic had fled. "Unless you're asking who to thank for letting you out. In that case, it was all us."

"He won't stop." Volo's voice was little more than a whisper. "Not unless we swear to serve him. Even then, he might take our souls instead."

The man positioned the glaive horizontal to the ground, held lengthwise in front of his hips. His next words rang with a formal cadence. He stopped, the only sounds the steady bash of the rain and the frenzied beating of the water-people's bare feet as they ran toward the man in white. Though the air was warm, it suddenly smelled like a northern wind.

"Don't make any moves," Dante murmured to the others. "We're not here to—"

Without the slightest hint of anger or enmity, the man bent his knees, swung his glaive forward, and charged.

He mounted the shelf of rock. Blays stepped forward, flicking his left-hand sword into the path of the glaive. The blades met with a wrenching screech. The purplish shadows on the Odo Sein weapon flickered wildly as it bent its nethereal strength to countering the physical power of the blow. The man pivoted to his right, meaning to turn the glaive into a lever to unbalance Blays or even toss him from his feet. Rather than resisting, Blays let his sword fall downward. He ducked under the whooshing polearm and spun inside the giant's range.

He struck at the man's extended left arm. The blade stalled in the man's snapping arm raps, yet fought through to cut into his forearm. Fluid spattered from the wound, a ghostly blue that shimmered despite the lack of sunlight. Blays swung his right-hand sword in a backhand aimed at the giant's ribs.

The man tucked back his hips and swung the glaive across his body. The angle was awkward and one-handed, yet his sheer strength propelled the weapon's shaft into Blays with enough force to send Blays tumbling to the earth.

Volo let loose an arrow. It struck the man dead center in the chest. He pulled it free and flung it aside. Dante and Naran pincered him, drawing his attention away from Blays, who was still pulling himself to his feet. The pale man jabbed at Dante with the glaive's blade. As Dante intercepted its tip with his sword, the man rammed it backwards, thrusting the butt at Naran's head. Naran gave way, cutting at the end of the haft. The nethereal swords had shown the ability to slice through just about anything short of a block of solid rock, but it hit the haft with a hard click and bounced away.

The giant jerked his wrists, whipping the glaive's butt back at Naran's head. Naran just had time to raise his shoulder and tuck his chin to his chest. The impact sent him skidding over the rock. As soon as he was down, the man bullrushed Dante.

Another arrow hit the man in the thigh. He brushed it away. The wounds to his left arm and chest were shining with white light, sealing up before Dante's eyes. Seeing the ether at work, Dante pulled at the nether. It was still no use.

Narrowing his eyes, he focused on the ether spilling from the giant's body, purging his mind of all thoughts. Nothing came.

The glaive's bone point was thrusting for his throat. He swung at it in a broad arc, scuttling to the side. When his blade hit the enemy's, his arm jarred so hard he nearly dropped his sword.

"He's like an Andrac," Dante yelled, backpedaling from another attack. "Healing himself. But I can't pull the ether from him!"

Blays rushed the man from behind. As the man spun about, Blays trapped his glaive with one sword and hurled himself inside the man's guard, poised to strike at his head or chest. Instead, the giant snap-kicked Blays in the gut, sending him flying.

Blays landed and didn't get up. Volo fired another arrow, but it flew past the man's head. Dante tried to rush him, but the man was already spinning about. Dante ducked. The glaive's shaft whooshed over his head. Dante popped to his feet and ran back five full steps.

Blays was still down. Volo's quiver was down to its last two or three arrows. Naran wasn't hurt too badly yet, but he was no better a swordsman than Dante.

Far worse than that, the first of the water-people would be on them in less than a minute. As soon as they arrived to harry Dante from all sides, he and the others would have the choice of being torn apart by the furious minions, or impaled by the impassive giant.

His heart felt like it was being squeezed through a straw. He didn't even know who the giant was. Couldn't even talk to him. He had no desire to fight the man—had, in fact, been trying to avoid that—but whatever Gladdic had released from the hexagon, it seemed bent on destroying everything in sight. Worse, it seemed capable of doing so. It had slaughtered the Odo Sein, killed an Andrac, sent the others scurrying away. Without the nether, what hope did he and Naran have?

There was only one way out. They had to kill the giant with a single stroke. Before he could heal. He was too strong and too fast for Dante or Naran to pull that off—even Blays hadn't been able to do more than scratch him—but Volo's bow didn't have to worry about the man's reach nor the strength of his arms. Dante suspected the enemy's skull was thick enough to protect him from most shots, but he also suspected an arrow in his eye or mouth would do the trick.

Dante turned to yell an order at Volo. As he watched, she nocked and loosed her last arrow. It hit the giant in the shoulder. He pulled it loose, snapped it into fragments, and cast it aside.

Dante bit his teeth together. The water-people were closing in. The giant was undaunted. Dante lifted his sword, reminded himself not to get stuck in the Pastlands, and prepared to die.

He stumbled and slid up the white grimrock, his legs aching, tears flowing down his face to be drowned in the rain. His right arm was numb. It felt twice the size it should. Ironic, considering it was now smaller than it had ever been. He was afraid he might bleed to death—he'd had to apply a tourniquet torn from his robes on the run, and it wasn't a good one—but maybe that would be a blessing.

As Gladdic neared the ridge, he didn't bother to glance back at the fight near the ruins of the Riya Lase. He hadn't had nearly enough time to forge a force capable of destroying the White Lich. The entire attempt had been yet another failure. Yet again, that failure had been precipitated by the nethermancer from the north. He could only pray that by his unleashing of the Eiden Rane unexpectedly early, Galand would finally be destroyed.

The ground leveled beneath his battered feet. He hobbled along, surveying the hellscape ahead for the Drakebane. Blighted loped uphill to make for the Riya Lase, pathetically eager to serve the one who had reduced them to their graceless state, but Gladdic saw no hint of the emperor nor of his retinue.

This attempt had failed. But if he could find the Drakebane, they could withdraw. They could regroup. And they could strike at the White Lich again.

His ether remained locked in the grasp of the Odo Sein, but that which had been disturbed would still show itself when looked at with purity of vision. Tuning his sight to the light, he took another look at the ground. The Blighted had left many tracks of their own, yet there it was: a cluster of dimly glowing white footprints carrying north across the jagged, alien landscape.

Gladdic drew himself up and moved on.

As he walked, he tore another piece from his robe to bind around his stump. The sight of the sliced meat and bone made him breathless. It wasn't the wound itself that disturbed him—flesh had never concerned him; it was a vessel, nothing more; when it was broken, it was no more gruesome than the breaking of a clay pot—but where it had come from.

Galand, again. Was there a symbolism to the taking of Gladdic's right hand? The hand that served the gods? A shudder racked his body, one that had nothing to do with the rain. After the fall of Collen to the barbarous rebels, certain rumors had spread forth. Gladdic had dismissed them as transparent propaganda—or, if that was giving too much credit to the crudely warlike leadership, as the superstitious whisperings of heretics and near-pagans—but what if they were correct? What if Galand truly *was* an avatar of Arawn?

One sent to whisper lies far and wide. To bedevil Gladdic

wherever he went. And, at last, to spread the ultimate darkness across not only Tanar Atain, but the entire world.

The thought frightened him. But fear put a spring in his step. He tottered over the rolling, unholy white rock of the Wound, occasionally spitting on it, and only altering course to avoid an upthrust stone or a passing Blight. He was afraid the Drakebane would make haste for the boats and depart before Gladdic caught up, but within minutes, he gazed across the unclean vista and spied the emperor and his retinue holding a conversation beneath a stand of especially tall bone-growths.

The Odo Sein were the first to notice him. He could feel the judgment behind their masks. Though he begrudgingly admired their dedication, he didn't care for the knights' stoic scorn. Ignoring their gazes, he presented himself to the Drakebane and bowed his head.

"Gladdic." The man's voice was as heavy as his features, which were unusually thick for a Tanarian. The mark of the well-guarded Drakebane line. His black hair was streaked with orange—a sign of general nobility, one significant enough that dyeing one's own hair orange had been illegal for centuries. The emperor stood on that brink of male age when youth was almost all but spent, and in the blink of an eye, a man could collapse from the haleness of a warrior into the doddering of an old fool. "You live?"

"The White Lich is freed." His news caused even the Odo Sein to declare oaths. Used to being at the center of such shock and dismay, Gladdic waited for the hubbub to pass. "Neither the Andrac nor the Odo Sein could stop him. When I saw that this was so, I retreated. For I believe we may yet destroy him."

The Drakebane shook his head slowly. "It is too late, priest. Your promise is broken. You have failed."

"I do not understand, Emperor."

"And you don't need to." The lord nodded to his retinue and turned as if to go.

"Emperor!" Gladdic fought to keep the plea from his voice. "Will you not fight? You've already lost your throne." This caused three of the Odo Sein to turn; even with their helmets in place, he could feel the murder within their eyes. "If you let the foe take free rein, you'll lose your country as well."

"No, priest. I have the feeling Mallon will prove quite welcoming to as many of my people as I care to save."

"While I am sure they will provide accommodations for displaced royalty, I know King Charles well, Your Majesty. I am afraid he will turn away all of your...refugees."

"My line has fought the liches for centuries. We know their power. Do you think we were so arrogant that we never considered a day like today might befall us? We knew our home could be destroyed at any time—you believe we never thought to secure another?"

"Please, Majesty. I do not know what King Charles has told you, but I do know his mind. He will make you promises, if that suits him. And then he will break them, because that also suits him."

The emperor broke into laughter. "We have no need for his promises! We have been preparing since before Charles' time, priest. Why do you think my people have all been made to speak Mallish? Our spies are in your palace. Our priests are in your temples. *Your* priests have been taught to fear the return of the Dragon; they chafe at your faith's denial, champing at the bit for reform. Your military has built boats to carry us from here to Bressel—and to make it our new home. And if your king denies us, then he will soon be king of nothing."

Gladdic's mind felt as though it was tumbling into an abyss. "But I pledged myself to cleanse your land. For this, you betray me?"

"You betrayed yourself when you failed. I do what I must to keep my people alive. I've fought this evil for too long—let it take this land, and the rebels with it."

"No." Gladdic reached for the Drakebane's raincloak. An Odo Sein interposed himself between them, pressing a gauntleted hand against Gladdic's breastbone. "Your Majesty! You can't do this!"

"Oh, priest." Pity and contempt entered the Drakebane's piercing eyes. He lifted a silver charm from his neck showing a snake wrapped around the eyes of a proud man. "I already have."

He turned and walked away. Gladdic's throat closed on itself, his chest tightening. His legs weakened beneath him. Was his aging body about to give out on him at last? He smiled at the thought. Everything he'd worked to build had been ruined; everything he'd tried to make pure had been defiled; where he'd placed trust, it had been betrayed. Worst of all, he had abetted the very man who would now try to take Gladdic's cherished home—Bressel, civilization's north star in a black void of brutality, ugliness, and heresy—and cast it down from the sky.

But at least death, at last, would spare him the fate of watching the shadow he'd helped give birth to as it devoured the world's last lights.

He sank to the horrid grimstone, the rain beating against his gaunt, wrinkled face, and waited for Arawn to claim him. He was an old man and everything he had ever done had only made the mortal realm a more wretched place.

His breathing slowed. The pain in his chest eased. Did he cry then? Perhaps he did. Because he wasn't going to die, and that, finally, taught him the only lesson worth knowing.

There are gods, and they are not merciful.

Dante stood against the wrath of the giant and searched for any meaning to be found in his last moments. He found them as empty as an old skull. He was going to die, and so were his friends, and their deaths would mean nothing. Lost to a fight where victory, even if it were possible, would gain him nothing.

The giant charged and he scampered to the side, feinting an attack to engage the towering man while Naran came at him from the rear. As before, the man was wise to their tricks, batting Naran away with the blade of his glaive.

Dante rushed the giant, sandals splashing through the rain gathering on the solid ground. Before he'd come within range of the nethereal sword, the blue-white man pivoted about, slamming the butt of his polearm into Dante's side. The blow sent him flying. He landed on a span of iron, his forehead cracking into the metal.

Blood dribbled from his eyebrow. It and the ground beneath him smelled the same. Out of hopeless habit, he reached out for the nether, meaning to feed his blood to it. The shadows kept their peace.

He wondered if he should bother to get up. The thought of accepting his fate was so tempting he closed his eyes. An end, at last, to all the struggles he never seemed to be able to escape. Yet this thought troubled him—he'd had it not long ago, when the swamp dragon had nearly drowned him. And he'd discovered he had more backbone than he knew.

He cocked his head. Heart pounding in his ears, he reached into himself, seeking out the nether entwined in his spine. It was there, but his whole body was alive with shadows. Just like when he'd been constructing his sword, he couldn't tell what part might be the trace.

Another drop of blood fell from his forehead. He ordered the nether to it. Nearly all of the shadows within him stayed put, locked in place by the aura of the Odo Sein. Yet some of those braided inside his spine began to stir.

He drew his trace from himself. The act felt startling, a combination of pain and relief, like diving into icy water or removing a long thorn from your flesh. He held the shadows in one hand and made a fist with the other. His face hurt—he was grinning.

He rose to his feet and faced the giant, who'd been distracted by Naran slashing at his ankles as he advanced on Dante. Shaping the nether into a killing bolt, Dante finally understood *why* they went through such strife. Why they fought all the smaller fights even when it was for the good of someone else rather than themselves.

Because when they fought the little fights, they grew strong enough to be able to fight back when it truly mattered.

The giant drove Naran into a full retreat. The enemy glanced at Volo, who was tending to Blays, or possibly trying to take one of his swords, then turned back to Dante. He tilted his head, color-shifting eyes locking onto the shadows in Dante's hand. As Dante hurled them at the man's face, the giant bared his teeth, the muscles of his cheeks striated like granite cliffs.

It took Dante a second to understand the twisted look on the man's face was a grin. At the last instant, the giant turned his head and ducked his chin. The nether gouged across his forehead and into his hairline, sending ether swirling around his head like powdery snowflakes. Faint blue fluid seeped down his face.

"Sorcerer." The man spoke Mallish with a thick accent that made the word sound like "zor-zor-or," uptilted slightly at the end. He laughed like a tin sheet being shaken back and forth. "You have skill. Skill earns choice. I will offer it to you one time."

Dante backed across the iron ground and the giant followed. "Let me guess. Join you or die?"

The blue-white man shook his head in four slow sweeps. "Join me—or join them."

He gestured to the pool-dwellers who had come to a stop to watch them from a hundred yards away. Their faces were sick with anxiety.

"If I join you," Dante said. "What then?"

"You will be made as me. My servant. But to the others, a god."

"And my friends?"

"Keep them. All gods need slaves."

Dante retreated another few steps and the giant strolled after him. The wound on the man's face was already closing. The bolt of shadows hadn't caused more than a groove in his skin. It was like his body was so infused with ether that it had a natural armor against sorcerous attacks. The nether in Dante's trace was limited. Even if he depleted it entirely, he doubted it would be enough. And he did *not* want to see what happened if he used it all.

"And once I serve you." Dante felt for the iron beneath his feet. "What will we do together? Conquer?"

The giant shook his head again. "We will consume."

"Sounds like a generous offer. But I've got one for you: die."

Dante jerked his hand upward. A spike of iron ore shot from the ground, aimed at the giant's guts. With a grunt—it might have been a chuckle—the man stepped to the side. As he put down his foot, Dante sent a second spike jutting beneath it. Yet the enemy seemed to be able to feel the shifts in the nether and was already sliding his foot away. The impromptu blade nicked the side of his foot, drawing blood but causing no major damage.

Looking amused, the giant jogged toward the side of the uneven spread of iron. Dante considered trying to gore him with one last spike, but if the man dodged again, that would be the end.

But just as Dante didn't stand to gain anything from winning the fight aside from his own life, he didn't have to kill the man to survive.

He reached into himself and the metal-rich rock. Drawing deeply on the trace, he heaved a wave of iron over the giant like pulling a quilt over an unruly dog. With the last drop of trace he dared to spend, he shaped the iron to allow the end of the glaive through, then slammed the metallic ore closed around the shaft, trapping the weapon in place.

His makeshift chamber was a poor match for the rune-inscribed hexagon. But inside its walls, the giant bellowed with rage.

Naran gawked. "Will that imprison him?"

"I have no fucking idea," Dante said, feeling lightheaded and ready to vomit. "Get Blays on his feet!"

Volo slapped Blays in the face. He opened one eye. From the slackness of his face, it was exceedingly obvious that he didn't know what was happening, and possibly even where he was, but Blays had always been possessed with a supernatural ability to understand when it was time to move his legs until the landscape changed enough to escape whatever was threatening to kill him. Volo propped him up on her slim shoulders.

Naran moved to join them. The water-people each shrieked once and burst forward, faces drawn back so tightly by their anger that their noses looked ready to slice through their skin. Dante sprinted to join Naran, who jogged to engage the closest people before they could get to Volo and Blays. Naran's crackling sword deposited their foes to the ground in several large chunks.

Naran jogged uphill, Volo and Blays trudging along behind him. Dante took up the rear, decapitating one of the pale people and sticking his sword through the ribs of another. Flickers of shadows stole from the corpses and into his sword.

Behind them, the giant pounded on the inside of his prison,

fists booming like thunder. For the moment, the walls seemed to be holding. The pounding stopped. Dante suspected he was pulling on the glaive—if he could get it free, he could probably carve through the iron in seconds—but it didn't appear to be budging.

The people from the pools were threatening to overwhelm them, but Blays was starting to get a feel for his legs again, running hard. Dante was so dizzy he felt himself reeling side to side. He focused on his friends' backs. A half dozen of the strange people awaited them at the top of the ridge. They carried shards of bone, but apparently the wits had returned to Blays' arms, too. He drew his weapons and sheared through the welcoming party.

Ahead, the land sloped down gently, littered with bony growths and the odd chunk of iron. Dante's first priority was getting the hell away from the giant, but the pressure in his head told him that Gladdic was practically straight ahead of them. Gladdic seemed to know this area. Including, presumably, the ways out of it.

"Volo," Dante said. "You knew what that thing was."

She glanced over her shoulder. "If you've heard of a mountain but never seen one, do you really *know* it?"

"Much better than someone who doesn't even know mountains exist!"

"Okay, but what if you've heard about mountains, but you think the whole idea of a big pile of rock that's miles high is so crazy it can't possibly be true?"

"Quit trying to argue your way out of this. Who was that man?"

Still running, she gazed down at the ground. "They call him Eiden Rane. The White Lich."

"Finally, some progress! And who is this White Lich?"

"He was one of the sorcerers. One that's so old he probably did exist before the mountains were around. But that's all I know."

"You know more than that. You said he might take our souls. What does that mean?"

Volo watched a pair of water-people running toward the valley at full speed. "It means he turns you into them."

Dante blinked. "Was Gladdic trying to keep him sealed up? Or to kill him? Why would he do that?"

"I dunno," she said. "To save the world?"

"Are you being serious?"

"They told us he would help us. But I don't think they were telling the whole truth."

She wouldn't say more, even who "they" was. The ground began to rise again. The white fields and mounds looked like they could be endless. To get some idea of the path ahead, Dante diverted to a small, steep hill. From its top, the western edge of the Wound looked to end in a steep drop that might have been cliffs. The eastern fields were pocked with rifts in the surface. The north, where Gladdic had gone, looked the same as the ground they'd already crossed.

He could also see behind them into the round valley of the White Lich. There, a small army had entered the bowl, flying the colors of the Monsoon. Scouts ran ahead, approaching the iron prison Dante had sealed the White Lich inside. As they neared, a hole opened in the side of the prison, disgorging a massive glowing figure.

Across from the Lich, the members of the Monsoon bent their knees and bowed their heads.

The boy was late. And getting later by the minute. When Raxa couldn't stand it anymore, she scaled the side of the warehouse and crawled across the roof, getting down beside the chimney. Out in the darkness, the fleet awaited at the docks. A small legion of soldiers milled around the grounds. Word around the palace was that they'd be leaving that night.

After ensuring nothing interesting was happening, Raxa backed off to the edge of the roof, but there was still no sign of Sorrowen. She wasn't sure why that irritated her so much. She was better off on her own. Less chance of getting spotted. And if they did see her, she had a much better chance of rabbiting.

An unusual amount of hollering was going on in the neighborhoods around them. Raxa hadn't thought it was a holiday, but maybe it was one of those that the nobles were too good to celebrate with the peons.

Lanterns pricked up along the docks. Sailors detached from the crowd of troops and embarked. As they made what looked like their final preparations, the soldiers began to move. A few hundred men walked onto the piers and divided themselves up between the forty-odd boats. Most of the soldiers remained on dry land. And now that Raxa really looked at it, there weren't *all* that many of them. Not nearly enough to fill the boats. Barely enough to row them.

They settled in at the benches. Sailors cast off their ropes and the oarsmen rowed downstream. Should she climb down and chase after them? See if they pulled in anywhere to pick up more troops? Then again, if they had more soldiers that close, why in the spinning shits wouldn't they have just brought them to Keller's Pier to embark?

More annoyed than ever, she watched the ships' lanterns drift down the river. Rather than coming in at another pier, they were moving toward the center of the Chanset. Another couple of miles, and they'd be out to sea.

She supposed she might as well confirm that. She shimmied down the warehouse. She'd taken three whole steps south when a robed figure swung from behind the building across the alley. Sorrowen jerked when he saw her. His southerner's face had tanned well in the few weeks they'd been in Bressel, but that night, it was as blanched as a Yallener's. The collar of his robe was stained red, but his face and neck looked all right.

"You heal yourself?" Raxa motioned to the blood. "Or is that not yours?"

"There was..." The kid swallowed, eyebrows flexing inward. "I don't know what it was. There was fighting. In the *temples.*"

Raxa glanced over her shoulder. There was a warehouse between them and Keller's Pier, but there had been an awful lot of soldiers thataway. She tugged his sleeve and walked him south.

"Let me guess." Raxa stepped around a fishy-smelling puddle. "Brother Farwin stole Brother Alrod's pudding again?"

"A squad of soldiers came up to the door after we'd closed for the night. Master Gocran told them to go away and come back tomorrow, but Master Waymore let them inside. It seemed like half the monastery was waiting for them. They rousted the rest of us. Master Waymore proclaimed that Daris had returned to the east. That it was our sworn duty to resist him. That we would need the help of a great prophet to slay Daris again. But not to worry, because the Prophet Drakebane was already on his way from the east, and that he would deliver us from the dragon's wrath.

"Master Gocran's face was so red I thought he'd spew wine from his ears. He told Waymore that that was outright heresy. And that if Gocran renounced it then and there, that nobody would have to know about it. Before Master Waymore could say anything one way or another, one of the soldiers..." Sorrowen dropped his gaze. "He stabbed Master Gocran. In the gut. Like he was no more than a pig."

He looked on the brink of tears. Raxa suddenly felt intensely uncomfortable. "Then what?"

"The temple went mad. They were throwing ether around like boys throwing stones. Brothers killing brothers. By the end, Gocran's supporters were all murdered or taken captive. When they told me to fetch water to mop up the blood, I just...started running."

"Smart move. Any idea what this is about?"

"Madness? Stark, raving madness? Something's wrong, Raxa. I don't think it's safe to stay here."

"We haven't been safe since we walked into the city." Thinking she'd heard the march of soldiers, she glanced behind them, but the alley was empty. "If it's too dangerous here, we could always head to Collen. The fleet just left. But they didn't look like they had enough men to conquer a farmhouse."

Sorrowen beetled his brow. "Then why would they even try to invade Collen?"

"Don't ask me. Could be a training exercise."

The alley fed them out into a main road. A patrol of twenty soldiers tromped down the street, boots clopping in time. A block away, two men shouted at each other in anger. Glass shattered. The soldiers broke into a trot. Raxa peered into the darkness. The soldiers' torches spilled light over the front of a temple. Outside, men in robes cursed at each other.

"This is getting weird." Raxa headed south, away from the brewing skirmish. "I want to see if the fleet heads out to sea. But if there's a riot going on, we might have to get off the streets."

They walked briskly. Shouts sounded from all sides, carrying far on the damp seaside air. Small groups of people ran down the street with hoods pulled over their faces. Some carried torches, the smell of pitch unfurling behind them. A few carried swords. In Bressel, that was illegal unless you were a soldier.

Raxa could read cities, and she could read nights. This one felt wrong. Like a lot of people were about to get hurt. On a main thoroughfare, people stood in tight knots, talking in worried tones. Raxa broke into a jog, hoping she and Sorrowen looked like a young couple that had stayed out too late and was hurrying home.

They were still a mile from the mouth of the river when the bells tolled from the spire of the Odeleon. The noise was foreboding. Pendulous. Like the city had opened a door that should have stayed shut.

Around them, everyone went as silent as a mountaintop. They turned as one toward the center of the city. Toward the palace. A few of them broke from their friends and ran like spooked deer. Most drew tighter yet, babbling like a pub on the eve of a tournament.

She raised an eyebrow at Sorrowen. "Any idea what the bells mean?"

Sorrowen swung his head back and forth. "I've never heard them before."

She was about to let it be, but upheaval in the capital was the kind of thing that could stop a war in its tracks. She slowed, approaching a cluster of people. They stared her down. She smiled at a bald man on the outskirts of the group.

"I'm sorry," she said, laying her northern accent on thick. "I am not from here. These bells, they are what?"

The man drew back his head like she'd spit at his feet. "Don't you know anything? That's the toll of the Banished Lord's Bells. King Charles—he's dead."

~

They were nearly to the next major ridge when the shadows tore loose from the power of the Odo Sein.

Freed, they seemed to dance on the wind, darting between the raindrops. Dante slowed, spreading his hands and gathering them up. They had all suffered cuts and bruises and Blays had been running with a tightness of his upper body that suggested he might have cracked some ribs. Dante stopped to heal them all. It was necessary, but after going so long without being able to call to the nether, he would have jumped at the excuse to cure a hangnail.

Blays took a deep breath, spreading his arms wide. "That's better. Spent the last twenty minutes about to scream in your ear until you got annoyed enough to knock me back out."

Naran surveyed the hellscape around them. They hadn't seen one of the water-people in several minutes. "Does the return of your abilities mean that the Odo Sein are vanquished?"

Dante sighed. "I look forward to when I can someday know the answer to a question. Until that time, I once again have no gods damn clue."

"How close are we?" Blays said.

"Close."

"Excellent. By the way, we probably shouldn't kill him right away."

Dante met his eyes. "No?"

"Not until we've beaten the location of his boat out of him. He wouldn't be heading this way if he didn't have a way off this rock."

Dante murmured his assent. As they crested the ridge, the pressure in his head grew unbearable. They found Gladdic huddled under a stand of blade-like white growths. The priest's eyes were closed. He clutched the stump of his arm to his chest. Though the ether now shined on the air, ready to be put to use, his wound was unhealed. His slack face was at peace.

Blays lifted his eyebrows at Dante. "So much for getting him to tell us where his boat is."

Dante leaned closer, reaching out for the nether in the old

man's body.

Gladdic's eyes snapped open. Dante jerked back, calling forth a swarm of shadows.

"You have nothing to fear." Gladdic's chuckle was as dry as the dusts of Collen. "At least, not from me." He glanced between them with no apparent concern. "I surmise you are here for your vengeance."

"You surmise right," Blays said. "It's time to answer for the murder of the Colleners."

Naran tipped back his chin. "And that of my captain, Mariola Twill."

"And everyone else we've left out. I'd list them, but I'd like to be out of here before next week."

Gladdic nodded to himself, then stared up at Dante. "Kill me, then. I beg you."

"Hey now," Blays said. "You're not supposed to *want* it. That spoils the fun."

Dante met the old priest's gaze. "Why?"

Gladdic rolled his eyes. "You cannot pour any more guilt in my cup when it already overflows. If there is any mercy in your soul, you will kill me. If not, you'll make me commit one last sin: my suicide."

"Not until you tell me what's happened here."

The old man sighed, squeezing his eyes shut. "You are the most tediously dogged person that I have ever known. Very well, here is the list of calamities. The Drakebane is taking Mallon. The White Lich will take the world. And it is all my fault."

Dante was so taken aback that he couldn't narrow himself to a single question.

Blays rested his hand on the hilt of his sword. "Did we finally drive you insane? The Drakebane was just kicked out of his own keep. How in the world would he dash off and conquer *Mallon*? By dumping a school of ziki oko into the Chanset?"

"It won't require even that much," Gladdic said mildly. "Not when he's spent decades setting his plans in place. He has infiltrated the priesthood. Inserted spies into the palace. Right now, he summons Mallon's own fleet to bring his people to Bressel."

"That's..." Blays swung his head to bug his eyes at Dante.

"Shit."

"Raxa's fleet," Dante said. "It isn't to invade Collen. It's to move the Drakebane's loyalists out of Tanar Atain. To make a new home in Mallon."

"Yes. But. That's insane."

"You are a man who lacks vision," Gladdic scoffed. "Hence you mistake fanatical devotion for common insanity. In controlling the priests, the Drakebane has command of the ether, along with most of the peasantry, who will do whatever the clergy commands. It seems he has also bent the military to his will. The only thing that stands between him and complete control is the king and his loyalists—and he has assured me that Lord Charles is not long for this world."

Dante narrowed his eyes. "Yet you sound skeptical."

"That he can take Mallon? Not a whit. But even the Drakebane's vision is hampered. For all their complexity, none of his schemes matter. The White Lich is free. No matter how far the Emperor runs from this place, it's only a matter of time until we are all the lich's slaves."

"He's right," Volo blurted. "The Monsoon didn't think we could hold onto the capital. So we thought we could use the lich to destroy the Drakebane's dynasty. And he will—but then he'll kill us, too. Except the ones he enslaves. And then he'll come for the rest of you."

"Indeed." Gladdic bowed his head and shut his eyes again. "So kill me. Take your vengeance while there is still any meaning to be had in this world."

"I can't." Dante's head rang with the beat of his heart. "You say this is your fault. Then will you help me undo it?"

He held out his hand. Gladdic's mouth fell open. Tears welled in the hollows of his eyes. He reached out with his left arm and clasped Dante's hand in his own.

THE WOUND OF THE WORLD

AUTHOR'S NOTE

If you're getting a kick out of these characters, you can read about their younger exploits in *The Cycle of Arawn* trilogy.

ABOUT THE AUTHOR

Along with *The Cycle of Arawn*, Ed is the author of the post-apocalyptic *Breakers* series. Born in the deserts of Eastern Washington, he's since lived in New York, Idaho, L.A., and Maui, all of which have been thoroughly destroyed in *Breakers*.

He lives with his fiancée and spends most of his time writing on the couch and overseeing the uneasy truce between two dogs and two cats.

He blogs at http://www.edwardwrobertson.com

Made in United States
Troutdale, OR
06/11/2024

20485529R00315